# THE SAPPHIRE PORTAL

## IAN IRVINE

SANTHENAR PRESS

THE GATES OF GOOD & EVIL QUARTET
Book 4 – The Sapphire Portal

Ian Irvine

PART OF THE SOUTHERN HEMISPHERE
OF SANTHENAR

LEGEND

Mountains
Hills
Desert
Salt Lake
Marsh, Swamp
Conifer Forest
Broadleaf Forest
Tropical Forest
Grassland
Reef
Main Road

Banthey
Fankster
Gendrigore
Nys
FARANDA
Huccadory
Bel Torance
Tarantia
Strinklet
Roros
Tar Gaarn &
Havissard
Twissel
SEA OF
PERION
Mistmurk Mountain
Jepperand
Guffeons
Katazza
Gosport
Flüde
Maksmord
Nithmak
Ashmode
CARENDOR
KALAR
STASSOR
Tifferfyte
Zile
MELDORIN
Morrelune
Fadd
Thurkad
Great Mountains
Nennifer
Burning
Mountain
Tirthrax
Fiz Gorgo
LAURALIN
MIRRILLADELL
Tiksi
KARAMA MALAMA
(Sea of Mists)
OOLO
HA-DROW
Ogur
LUUMA NARTA
SHAZABBA
Steppe
Noom
KARA AGEL
(Frozen Sea)
Grinding

Maps by the author

SCALE

KILOMETRES

0 100 200 300 400 500 600 700 800 900 1000

0 40 80 120 160 200

LEAGUES

# CONTENTS

PART II
## RESOLUTION FROM DESPAIR

# PART I

# RESURRECTION

# 1

## I ACCEPT YOUR TERMS

Proud of yourself, Chronicler?' said Rulke.

After half a day as prisoners in the Merdrun's camp, and lengthy secret talks between Rulke and their captors, he and Llian had been returned to the construct. Its power controller crystal had already been removed to ensure that it could not be operated, and the construct searched to make sure there were no spares.

Llian flushed. His earlier, daring rescue of Rulke had been utterly negated by last night's failure.

'How does it feel to singlehandedly turn victory into defeat?' Rulke said disgustedly. 'To give my construct to the enemy – and lose the war we stood to win?'

'You know I'm not a man of action, yet –'

'You can say that again! But Skald was on the verge of collapse. You only had to whack him.'

'I hit him twice while you were wrestling him. But –'

'And then you knocked *me* unconscious.'

Even in Skald's gravely weakened state he had been more than a match for Llian. There was no point saying that, either.

'I'm sorry,' said Llian. 'I failed you.'

'Again!' Rulke said relentlessly.

'What are you –?'

Rulke put a finger to his lips. 'Someone's coming.'

The construct quivered as a group of Merdrun climbed the ladder, led by a senior sus-magiz and a group of artisans, and entered the cabin. The sus-magiz, a pipe-thin, flat-headed fellow who looked as though he were half human and half snake, examined the controls, while the artisans opened every door and compartment and noted what was inside.

Two hours later, after they were gone, High Commander Durthix entered, along with the magiz, Dagog, a repulsive little man who stank of rotten meat.

'Well?' Durthix said to Rulke.

'You need my cooperation,' said Rulke, folding his arms. He was a half-head taller than Durthix, and broader across the shoulders, and Durthix did not like it. In the Merdrun army, size mattered.

Durthix gave a derisive snort.

'You have no pilot capable of flying this craft,' Rulke added, 'and you can't complete your True Purpose without it.'

Durthix started. 'Why do you say that?'

'Tiaan is gravely ill, burned inside, and will never fly again. M'Lainte does not have the strength to fly a construct and neither does any other pilot on Santhenar, save myself. You need my aid and you need it now.'

The magiz whispered, 'High Commander, don't let him speak –'

Durthix waved Dagog to silence. 'Lirriam is imprisoned in a fortress without doors or windows. She will be hostage for your good behaviour, Rulke.'

Rulke stepped forwards and stood chest to chest with Durthix. 'And who will be hostage for *your* good behaviour?'

'How dare you!' the magiz exploded. 'High Commander –'

Llian gagged. The stink of rotten meat was overpowering in the closed cabin, and it issued from every part of Dagog.

'Not now, Magiz!' snapped Durthix.

He stared into Rulke's eyes but could not break his gaze. Llian sat in the background, recording everything in his perfect Teller's memory. The contest, deadly though it might become, was fascinating.

Rulke smiled grimly. 'Your people and mine have been enemies for aeons, Durthix, and there can never be trust between us. Unless I can monitor Lirriam's health and safety, I *will not* cooperate.'

'Then she dies!' the magiz blustered, 'and you will feel such tortures –'

Rulke picked Dagog up in one hand, spun him around and booted him across the cabin. Dagog scrambled to his feet, his face purple in outrage, and thrust out his bony right hand.

'Try it and you're dead,' snapped Rulke.

Dagog's eyes went entirely white. Rulke had made a dire enemy. Durthix, scowling, signed to Dagog to stay back.

'If Lirriam dies,' said Rulke, 'I have nothing to lose ... and I can extinguish myself in a moment.'

'You wouldn't,' said Durthix.

'I'm the last of my kind. I was preparing to go back to the void to die when I sensed her out there, and my beacon led her to Santhenar. If I lose her, I'll have nothing left.'

'If she died, you'd want revenge.'

Rulke's smile flashed again. 'My best revenge would be thwarting you – and blowing your stinking magiz to shreds.'

'High Commander,' said the magiz, and now there was a whine in his voice, 'call his bluff.'

'Why don't I call yours?' said Rulke. 'You have one chance to complete the True Purpose, Durthix. The time window is but weeks away, it's only eight hours long ... and after it closes it won't reopen for 287 years.'

With an effort, Durthix controlled himself, but Llian was a master at reading faces. Durthix was shocked at how much Rulke knew, and must be wondering what other dangerous secrets he was privy to.

Rulke squared his shoulders. 'There's only one way to complete Skyrock in time – if I fly the construct for you.'

'High Commander, that would be madness!' said the magiz.

'I will permit you to *see* Lirriam once a day, remotely,' Durthix said to Rulke, 'to reassure yourself that she hasn't been harmed, but you will not be able to communicate with her. In return you will fly the construct strictly according to the requirements of my Superintendent of Works. To ensure that you do, the controller crystal will be removed at the end of each day.'

'I accept your terms,' said Rulke. 'Though I have one additional requirement.'

'What's that?'

'Llian.'

This, Llian had not expected.

Durthix turned and looked down at him with curled lip. 'What about him?'

'He remains in the construct,' said Rulke.

'To what purpose?'

'His incompetence keeps me sane.'

The magiz giggled, a sound both incongruous and alarming, and another blast of rotten meat assailed Llian's nostrils.

After the Merdrun had gone and Rulke had checked everywhere for spying devices, and destroyed several, he began to prepare dinner, whistling a merry tune. It was not the first time he had been unexpectedly cheerful in the last half day.

Llian sat down and thought through the incidents. 'Aha!' he said.

Rulke quirked an eyebrow at him.

'How dare you blame me!' said Llian. 'It was *you*, all along.'

'Your ramblings are more opaque than usual, Chronicler.'

'When you and Skald were wrestling last night, and I was dancing around with the table leg, trying to get a clear go at him, you *deliberately* stumbled into the path of my club.'

'Why would I do such a thing?'

Why indeed? It was the one question to which Llian had no answer. Then inspiration struck.

'You wanted Skald to defeat you and take the construct to Skyrock because Lirriam means everything to you. It was your one chance of getting her back.'

'That would be desperately reckless,' said Rulke. 'And I'm not a reck–'

'Cobblers! You're famous for reckless daring – like the time you led the Hundred out of the void to Aachan and almost single-handedly took the Aachim's world from them.'

'I was young and impetuous back then.'

'You were also recklessly bold after you freed yourself from the Nightland. And you still are – you thrive on impossible conflicts. What if Tiaan had been unable to control the construct, and it had crashed?'

Rulke shrugged. 'There was no other way to save Lirriam.'

'We could all have been killed.'

'It was a strong possibility, even though I was subtly channelling power to the controls. If I hadn't, Tiaan would have been dead before the construct reached the other side of the Sea of Thurkad. No old human could channel that much power, and live.'

'A wonder Skald didn't realise what you were doing.'

'He has an overly high opinion of himself. And I was banking on the Merdrun's lack of experience with our mech-magical devices. Even so, it was a dangerous night; it could easily have gone wrong.'

'It still can. You've made it possible for them to realise their age-old goal, whatever it is. What are they going to do to us then?'

'I don't know, Chronicler, but I had to risk all to gain all.'

'Or lose all.'

'Or lose all,' Rulke repeated soberly. 'Everything – the fate of the Three Worlds and four human species, and you and I – rests on my gamble.'

Another question occurred to Llian. 'Your original construct could make gates and jump from one place to another. Can this one?'

'I wish it could, but there isn't a field on Santhenar that can deliver enough power, these days. Get to bed. You had a hard night.'

'I'm afraid to go to bed,' said Llian.

Rulke looked around sharply. 'Because Skald began to drink your life?'

'Yes. And he started on you first. Are you –?'

'You may want to relive it, Chronicler, but I do not.'

Llian did not want to relive it either, but when he lay on his hard bunk in the dark he was hurled back to that ghastly moment – the worst of his life.

The blind terror of seeing and feeling his life force being drawn out of him and into Skald. The unnatural cold that had crept through Llian's body, the deathly weakness and unbearable pain, and his utter inability to do anything to save himself.

The revulsion that had come from experiencing the emotions and the foulness of a mind that could do such things to another human, and enjoy it. A mind that revelled in the power while he fed on his victim's helpless terror.

It was sickening to experience, second-hand, the ecstasy that Llian's precious life was giving to Skald. And he had been shaken by the realisation that Skald might use up, or even waste, the power gained from drinking his entire life, in a few moments of sorcery.

Worse still was the emptiness of the soul that had followed. People were monsters and life was futile.

Worst of all, Llian could not stop imagining it happening again, his terror conflicting with an inexplicable desire for Skald to begin drinking his life anew, and for the sick union with another human that could be gained in no other way – even if the life drinking went all the way to completion.

## 2

# WHAT ARE YOU LOOKING SO GUILTY ABOUT?

In a dark part of her fierce heart, Aviel hoped Maigraith would sicken and die.

After her disastrous loss at Alcifer, Maigraith had taken to her bed and remained there for more than a week. Her death was the best way out – and if she did sicken, no way would Aviel sit at her bedside again, attending to her bodily needs like a compliant little mouse.

You've lived way too long, Aviel thought, and much of your life has been tormented. The only thing propping you up is your rage against the innocent woman who now has your man, and the burning desire to see her dead. So die, damn you, and make the world a better place!

Unfortunately, Maigraith did not look like dying. Aviel checked on her several times a day, taking food that was never touched, and water which, when Aviel held a cup to her mouth, Maigraith sipped at sparingly. Sometimes she was comatose, though more often she was, by turns, hysterical, vengeful, insanely jealous, and murderous in her rage. Lirriam, who apparently had been captured in Alcifer and gated to Skyrock, had to be eradicated in the most gruesome way possible, and Rulke punished for breaking his promise.

Aviel went about her work absently, struggling to focus. Had she, by knocking Maigraith out on the stair in Alcifer, made a disastrous mistake? It had allowed Skald to take the construct, and Rulke and Llian, and Aviel had a feeling that was going to be very bad. If she hadn't interfered, Maigraith might have beaten Skald, or Flydd might have. She knew a lot about Flydd now, from a copy of the last book of his *Histories* that Maigraith had given her. Had she destroyed the allies' last chance to win the war?

On the eighth afternoon after returning from Alcifer, Aviel went in with a plate of bread and cheese and an apple as wrinkled as the right side of Maigraith's face, and was surprised to find her sitting up.

'What news from Skyrock?' she said, taking a small piece of cheese and nibbling it.

'How would I get any news in this miserable hole?' said Aviel.

The two guards Flydd had hired to protect her had taken the money and run long ago, and the only news Aviel ever heard came from Maigraith's rants and ravings. Presumably she was still making her little spy portals.

Maigraith hurled the plate at her. 'Go and finish my scent potion! It's the only thing you're good for.'

Aviel ducked and the plate smashed against the wall. 'It's one more thing than you're good for, then! You're the foulest old hag in the world, and it's no wonder Rulke has found someone better.'

'You little bitch!' Maigraith, slid out of bed and stood up, too quickly. She swayed, looking as if she might faint, and hastily sat down. 'Your life hangs by a thread.'

Aviel was about to retort, *So does yours, you evil old cow*, but prudence won over passion. 'I know! You're going to kill me as soon as I've made your rejuvenation potion.'

Maigraith went very still. 'Why do you say that?'

'Because you've never done a good deed in your miserable life. Bitterness, malice and destruction are the only things you know.'

'That's not true,' Maigraith said quietly. 'That's not true at all.'

'Well, at least when I'm dying, I'll be able to look back and know that most of my life *I've* done the right thing.'

Maigraith's moment of introspection vanished. 'All you'll see when you look back is how pathetic your life has been, how small your deeds. I've changed the world.'

'Not for good! And at least I've been happy.'

It was true. Even as an oppressed and unlucky seventh sister, Aviel had loved working in her garden, feeding her useless family and making pressed flowers and little scents to give pleasure to herself and others.

And after Shand had taken her in, cancelled her indenture to the disgusting tannery and given the little workshop in his back garden over to her, Aviel had thought she would die from bliss. Sometimes, even here, she was happy working away upstairs. Surprising how much pleasure she'd been able to find in small things, now she thought about it.

Maigraith sat on the bed, rubbing her stringy arms and staring back across the years. 'I *have* known happiness: when I lay with Rulke and we made Julken together; when he and I fought together in Shazmak at the end of the Time of the Mirror. You could never understand ...'

There was no point arguing with someone so self-obsessed, or pointing out that it was impossible to measure happiness, or say that one person's was greater than another's. Maigraith had no empathy for anyone save Rulke, who was so manifestly her superior that it was astounding they had ever got together at all.

'What happened to Julken, anyway?' said Aviel.

'He – *died*.' Maigraith sounded evasive.

'I'm sorry,' Aviel said automatically, though judging by what Karan had said about him, he had been a bully and a brute. 'Did he get sick?'

Maigraith's thin face twisted in grief. 'He was beaten to death by a vicious mob.'

'What! In a riot?'

'It was over a girl,' Maigraith said in a remote voice. 'Julken was a lusty young man with a young man's needs. He was big and handsome and rich, and girls were drawn to him ... and sometimes they got hurt ... but it wasn't his fault. He didn't know his own strength.'

A chilly drop of sweat oozed down Aviel's spine and she remembered something Karan had said about him. Maigraith had taken Julken to Gothryme and it had gone badly. Julken and Sulien had both turned nine, but she was small for her age, while he had been almost as big as a man.

Julken had been offensive from the moment he entered the front door, but he had failed in a little demonstration of magic at the dinner table, and Sulien, who had done brilliantly, had laughed. In the morning her puppy, Piffle, was dead, its neck broken. If Julken could do such a thing at nine, how much worse must he have been as a young man, a giant compared to most other people?

'How did it happen?' Aviel tried to keep her voice neutral.

'The girls' fathers ganged up on him, the cowards. Twenty-three of them! They took him by surprise, otherwise he would have beaten them all.'

Twenty-three girls outraged by this brutal monster? It was a mercy the fathers got him when he was still young. But if Aviel even hinted at that thought, Maigraith would kill her where she stood.

'Um, didn't you have twin boys?' she said.

'Julken came first,' said Maigraith. 'A terrible birth; his head was massive. I was badly torn ... but it was worth it. Even newborn, he looked like his father. Three hours later, Illiel slipped out with barely a contraction; I didn't know he was coming. He was small and slender and pale, almost insignificant ...'

'How could the two be so different?' said Aviel, fascinated.

'I am *triune*,' Maigraith said absently. 'In Julken, Rulke's Charon blood was dominant. But Illiel took after my despised Faellem ancestors, so I sent him south to his people in the bleak forests of Mirrilladell.'

'That must have been hard,' Aviel said automatically. 'Did you see him often?'

'Why would I want to see *him*?'

'He was still your son, and Rulke's.'

'I went looking for him after Julken was murdered,' Maigraith said in a colourless voice, 'but the Faellem kept me away. They said it was better that way. A soft, bookish boy he was, and a shy, scholarly man, no use to anyone. He did not inherit my longevity and he's long dead. Julken's only child, Gilhaelith, is also gone. He died at the end of the war.'

It illuminated Maigraith's nature clearly. She would make any excuse for the child who had inherited Rulke's looks, though not his noble nature, and excuse any depravity. But the other child she had cast aside. Aviel's soft heart rose up in outrage on behalf of all the small, quiet, shy people who were bullied, put down, ignored and forgotten. One day they would rise!

Well, it's good to daydream about it, she thought wryly.

The following morning, she had not yet begun her work when Maigraith stalked in and began to search the workshop bench by bench, shelf by shelf and cupboard by cupboard. Again, Aviel felt that chill. Had she given herself away? How?

'Looking for something?' she said quietly.

Maigraith quivered with barely suppressed rage. 'You're conspiring against me and I'm going to find out what it is.'

Aviel's bad ankle throbbed. 'How could I hope to get away with anything, with you constantly watching me?'

'You've been spying on me for weeks.'

'Lucky I did when you went to Alcifer, or you would have died there.'

Maigraith stared at her. 'Or did you *want* me to die there? I think you struck me down before the roof collapsed.'

'I wasn't anywhere near you,' Aviel lied.

'Something hit me and I fell down the stairs. If I hadn't, Skald would never have got away with Rulke and his man-stealing bitch.'

'What's happening in Skyrock, anyway?'

'How would I know?'

'I'm sure you've been making spy portals there.'

'It's much harder to do now ...'

'But?'

'Skald is recovering. Tiaan is still ill, but their very best healers are working on her.'

'Why do the Merdrun care?'

'She's a brilliant geomancer, and second only to M'Lainte in mech-magic. They need her skills.'

'What for?'

Maigraith shrugged. She probably knew but wasn't going to say.

'How is Rulke?'

'He's safe. He's the only one who can fly the construct, and they need it to build their tower, so he's been able to bargain for some freedoms. But they're holding his doxy hostage. And as soon as I discover where …'

You'll find her and kill her, Aviel thought. Not if I can help it.

'Why did you save me,' said Maigraith, returning to her previous theme, 'when clearly you hate me?'

'I can't say. I do hate you!' Aviel burst out. 'But I would have done the same for anyone in danger.'

'You're incomprehensible,' said Maigraith after a long pause.

Aviel turned back to her bench.

'No one risks their life for nothing,' Maigraith persisted. 'What do you want from me?'

'Nothing – save to be left alone to make perfumes.'

Maigraith looked enlightened, and sourly cynical. 'You want my gratitude, because you need gold and I've got cart-loads of it.'

'I couldn't give a fig for your gold,' Aviel said truthfully.

'I expect others to pay their debts, and I pay mine. If the rejuvenation potion works, when the war is over I'll set you up in the workshop of your dreams.'

'No, thanks! Whatever I get, I'll earn it myself.'

'Saving my life isn't earning it?'

'I didn't save you for what I might get out of it.'

'What an odd little thing you are. What other reason is there for doing anything?'

Another revealing moment. 'Can I get on with my work?' Aviel said irritably.

Maigraith took out every scent phial in Aviel's storage boxes, read the labels and put them back again. Fortunately, Aviel had got rid of the gift-blocking potion before going to Alcifer – though, she remembered with a shock of horror, the method was still written in invisible ink in the back of the grimoire. She should have cut the leaf out and burned it. If Maigraith found it, she would know instantly what Aviel had done to her.

'What's this?' said Maigraith, holding up a phial containing a small quantity of a viscous white fluid.

'The volatile pungency of horseradish. It's an ingredient in a number of scent potions, and when I had some free time I made some in case I ever needed it. I often do that.'

Maigraith put it back and turned the pages of the book Lilis had given her. Most were still blank and it would last for a couple of years. Assuming Aviel lived that long.

'Surely not all scents can be preserved?' said Maigraith.

'Some have to be prepared fresh just before use. Like the smell of a really old book, for instance.'

Maigraith picked up Radizer's grimoire and Aviel caught her breath. Maigraith shot her a suspicious glance. Aviel's heart was pounding; had she left a marker, or some other sign that Maigraith might detect?

Maigraith held the grimoire out in her hands and allowed the pages to fan. If it stopped at the gift-blocking potion, Aviel was dead.

Slowly the pages turned. Stopped. Turned again. Aviel was watching them, but Maigraith was not. She was watching Aviel, who now felt heat rising up her face.

'What are you looking so guilty about?' said Maigraith.

'When people stare at me, I flush. My big sisters used to do it deliberately, then run to Father and tell lies about me ... and because I always went red, I was proven guilty, and punished.'

'No wonder you're such a little mouse.'

'And you're a predatory cat!'

Maigraith smiled. 'So I am.' She looked down at the grimoire. The pages had stopped turning three-quarters of the way through, where Aviel had left the two rose-coloured leaves Maigraith had given her weeks ago. 'My rejuvenation potion. How long?'

Aviel almost fainted with relief. *Don't show it! She'll read something into that, too.* 'When the moon is in its first quarter. Seven days.'

'Not a minute more.'

Maigraith closed the grimoire and put it on the bench, then headed for the door, but stopped and came back again. 'How long does it last?'

'The rejuvenation scent potion?'

'What else would I be talking about?'

'The grimoire doesn't say.'

'Can't you tell from the recipe?'

'As you say, I'm *a stupid little mouse*. I have an instinct for making scent potions, but I've never had a teacher to tell me how they work, or why.'

'Of course,' said Maigraith to herself. 'Why would you know?'

'Can you find out?' Aviel said eagerly.

'*How* a particular piece of magic works, and *why* it works, is seldom written down. Practitioners of the Secret Arts guard their secrets jealously and reveal them to none who do not need to know.'

'But you were the Numinator! If anyone can find out, you can.'

'A baker doesn't need to know how the dough changes on the kneading board, or in the oven, to make good bread. All she has to do is follow the recipe.'

How would you know? Aviel thought. I'm sure you haven't made a loaf of bread in your life.

'Baking doesn't involve the Secret Art,' she said. 'Scent potions do. And whenever the Art is involved, whether it works or not depends on the gift and knowledge and

intentions of the maker. And sometimes, even on the maker's mood or state of mind
...'

Maigraith smiled thinly. Was she testing her? Probably.

'Besides,' Aviel went on, 'scent potions don't work the same on everyone. Some
people can't smell vanilla, or coffee, or even onions. To others the most beautiful
perfumes smell foul – or are overpowering. I want to make sure the potion is right for
you.'

'But is it permanent?' said Maigraith.

'The method doesn't say. The effects of some potions are permanent.' *Like the one
you used on Calluly on her wedding day!* Aviel thought with a flash of rage. 'But it may
be that you have to keep using it, to stay young.'

'Perhaps I should test it on you.'

'If the rejuvenation scent potion can take *you* back to a woman in her thirties,'
said Aviel, meaning, *an old hag like you*, 'it'd take me back to the egg.'

# 3

## NO MORE LIES, MOUSE!

Aviel did not finish work until midnight. She hauled up a bucket of water from the basement well, carried it up to her room and stripped off, washed her hair then stood in the bucket and scrubbed herself all over.

She tipped the water out the window to nourish a little weed that was struggling to grow in the dust, and was towelling her hair dry when she was caught from behind. She tried to pull free but her attacker was too strong.

'Let me go!'

Maigraith released her and Aviel hastily covered herself with the threadbare towel. 'What do you want?'

'You lied.' Maigraith held out Aviel's metal pannikin, squashed out of shape. 'I went back to Alcifer and found this under the rubble, next to the fallen stair.'

'Must've dropped it when I dragged you to safety,' said Aviel.

'Liar! You knocked me out with it.'

'No, I didn't,' Aviel lied.

'Do you really think you can deceive *me*?' hissed Maigraith. 'From the day you started in your workshop I knew you were up to something.'

She struck Aviel across the mouth, tore the towel from her hands and tossed it away. Maigraith wanted her at a disadvantage, and there was no bigger disadvantage than being naked.

'Why did you attack me?' said Maigraith. 'Then save me?'

Aviel licked blood off her upper lip. 'Don't know what you're talking about.'

Maigraith struck her again. 'It was because of Calluly, wasn't it?'

'What?'

'The young woman disfigured by my potion on her wedding day. It was just an accident –'

'You were trying to turn Lirriam into a monster,' Aviel yelled. 'It was manslaughter, at the very least.'

'It was an accident,' Maigraith repeated, 'but you blamed yourself as well as me.'

'I should have resisted you.'

'As if you could break one of *my* compulsions, mouse! But you attempted to. You secretly made a memory-restoring scent potion and used it on yourself.'

'No, I didn't!'

'Liar!' Maigraith held up a little scent potion bottle. 'This was hidden in your mattress. And that's not all you're up to, is it?'

Aviel shook her head, numbly. Did Maigraith *know*? 'I haven't done anything.'

'But you're planning to.'

'I'm not!' Aviel reached out. 'Give me my towel.'

Maigraith threw it out the window, then went to the small table beside Aviel's bed and picked up Radizer's grimoire.

'No more lies, mouse. I always know.'

Aviel crossed her arms over her chest. She had a sick feeling that Maigraith was right, that she had known all along. Again, she held the grimoire out on her open palms and fanned the pages. Aviel watched them slowly turning.

'I lulled you into a false sense of security last time,' said Maigraith. 'I stopped the pages at the rejuvenation potion so you'd think you got away with it. Where do you think they would have turned to if I hadn't stopped them, mouse?'

'I don't know,' whispered Aviel.

Maigraith wasn't looking at the slowly riffling pages, she was transfixing Aviel with those unnerving indigo and carmine eyes. The pages came to rest and Maigraith held the book out. Aviel's eyes were drawn to the open pages. Murderer's Mephitis.

'You're planning to kill me, aren't you?' said Maigraith in an expressionless voice that was far scarier than her fury.

'No,' Aviel squeaked. 'I – I admit I thought about it ... but I would never have done it.'

'You did more than think about it. You made every one of the scents it would take.'

'Some scents are used in dozens of potions.'

'But not this one!' snapped Maigraith, holding up a phial that had the number 177. 'Nor this one, 202, nor this one, 233. These three odours are only used in one scent potion in the entire grimoire and they identify it uniquely. You're done, mouse!'

They were also used in the gift-blocking potion, though Aviel dared not say so. Maigraith might consider the loss of her gift worse than being murdered. 'Doesn't prove anything.'

'What do I care for proof, mouse? I'm your judge and jury. And when you're no more use to me, *your executioner.*'

Maigraith picked up Aviel's nightgown from her bed, plus the clothes she had removed, and her boots, and stuffed them in the pack with Aviel's clean clothes. Maigraith gestured and a set of manacles locked around Aviel's shins.

'Go to bed. You're going to need all the sleep you can get.'

'I need my nightgown.'

'It's a warm night.'

Maigraith gestured at the window, which closed, took the pack and went out. Aviel heard the door lock behind her. She hobbled to the window, but it would not open, and even if she broke the thick yellowed glass the panes were too small to squeeze out. She was trapped.

She got into bed and pulled the covers up around her neck. Having no clothes made her even more vulnerable.

It was not a cold night, as nights went in Thurkad at this time of year, but it was the coldest she had felt since coming to the future, and it was almost impossible to sleep in chains. Tomorrow Maigraith would stand over her until the rejuvenation potion was ready for blending. And as soon as it worked, assuming it did, Maigraith would kill her.

No appeal would move her, for she had no conscience.

# 4

## HE'S GOT YOUR FATHER!

To Skald's bewilderment, he was in a wooden bed in a closed-off section of the healing tent, and he had not slept in a proper bed in his life. Why was he here?

He tried to lift his right hand but did not have the strength. His arms, formerly strong and dark and hairy, were withered, unnaturally pale, and every hair had fallen out. He looked, he thought, like a week-old corpse. Almost as repulsive as the magiz himself. Days must have passed since his desperate return with Rulke and the construct.

Uletta came in, carrying a sheaf of papers and a roll of plans. Uletta with the long nose and nut-cracking jaw, the broad shoulders and massive thighs and big feet. To Skald's eyes, she was more beautiful than ever now.

'What – you – doing here?' he said. Even speaking was an effort.

'I had to see you.' She held up the plans as if they were her excuse.

'Thought – I was dead.'

'You should be. You lost more than half your blood, and the best Merdrun and slave healers couldn't stop the flow.'

'How I alive?'

'The prisoner, Lirriam, knows ways of healing no one has ever heard of. As part of the High Commander's bargain with Rulke, she was compelled to save you. It took her a week, though.'

Why would Durthix bargain with an enemy? He should have commanded. 'What bargain?'

'It's secret.'

'And Tiaan? Worried about her.'

Uletta scowled. Surely she wasn't jealous? 'Recovering. Lirriam worked on her, too.'

Uletta stroked Skald's repulsive, hairless arm. He had lost so much weight that the skin was baggy. 'I'm glad you lived.'

To his horror, tears flooded his eyes and he could not raise a hand to wipe them away.

'Let it out,' she said lovingly.

'Wipe – tears! Please.'

'They're good for you, Skald.'

'No!' he gasped, panicking. 'Merdrun must be strong. Must not give way – to *emotion*.'

'I like you all the more because you have. It makes you seem human.'

'You don't understand. Forbidden! Magiz sees, magiz *kills*.'

'He kills people who show emotion?'

'Human emotions, *weak*. Merdrun must – always strong. Always!'

'Well, I think it's disgusting,' said Uletta. Then, to his astonishment she leaned forward and kissed him on the mouth. 'I'm feeling strong emotions for you right now.' She stroked his hand again. 'I really like you, Skald.'

She was looking at him expectantly but, though he liked her very much, he could not say it. The prohibition, beaten into him from the moment he could walk, was too strong.

'Wipe – tears,' he repeated.

'Wipe them yourself!' She stalked out.

Skald lay there, the tears puddling in his eyes, stricken by the terror that someone would come in and see him weeping. He rocked from side to side, a little more each time, and after several exhausting minutes he managed to roll over and bury his head in the pillow.

Safe from Merdrun eyes, he wept silently for himself, and Uletta too, and for the astonishing revelation that she seemed to really care about him, until the pillow was sodden.

One day the old woman woke Sulien at sunrise, led her outside and handed her a bent iron pick and a shovel with a broken handle. She drew a rectangle at the side of the cabin, roughly the same size, and said, 'Dig!'

'Dig what?' said Sulien.

The old woman clouted her over the ear. 'Insolent little wretch! A cellar, of course. Work harder. You've got to do the other girl's work too, since you drove her away.'

Sulien did not move. '*I* drove her away?'

'I hear everything. I see everything. Dig!'

Sulien dug, resentfully. The ground was hard and stony and, even after she had hammered the pick straight and whittled a new handle for the shovel, it was a labour that would have tested a strong man. How had Flydd come to know the old couple, anyway? After a month, the loneliest of her life, she did not even know their names.

The old man who painted grains of sand was a bit creepy, but he avoided her and never spoke. The cranky old woman was everywhere, watching what Sulien did and giving her a new job the moment the old one was completed. But as long as she worked all day long, and learned the hand-written pamphlets on matters such as pickling disgusting fish organs, composting human waste and making twine from reeds, the old woman left her alone.

If there was news about the war, she did not share it. But Sulien did not think the old woman had any way of getting news, since theirs was the only cabin here and no one ever visited.

Jassika had returned a few days ago, but only to call Sulien a 'selfish little bitch who thinks she's better than everyone else,' and stalk back into the forest.

At the end of the day Sulien had blisters under her calluses, yet she had only lowered the ground level eight inches, and every inch was harder than the one before. Utterly discouraged, she went down to the stream to bathe. The cabin did not have a bathroom and, if the old woman and old man washed at all, it could only have been in a bucket.

Sulien was used to higher standards and, over the past few weeks, she had dug a small pool beside the stream, lined it with flat rocks and cut a foot-deep channel for the water to flow in and out. There was a layer of sand on the bottom and the water was clear and pleasantly cool.

She was washing her hair with a paste made from the pounded leaves of the saponin tree – from another of the old woman's pamphlets – when Jassika materialised, as stealthily as ever.

Sulien started, swallowed a mouthful of water, and spat it out again. 'You scared me.'

Jassika sat on her favourite rock, took off her battered sandals and dangled her long feet in the water. Her clothes were torn and stained, and she was filthy.

'Have you bathed, or even changed your clothes since we came here?' said Sulien.

'Why should I?'

'Because you stink.'

'Can't smell a thing.' Jassika scratched her armpit, her back and her other armpit with grimy fingernails. She kicked her feet, splashing Sulien in the face. 'The war's going really badly, and the enemy are building a tall tower at a place called Skyrock.'

'You told me that last time. How do you know, anyway? Have you got a farspeaker?'

Jassika just smiled. She must be in contact with Klarm, and Sulien thought she had his gift for the Secret Art. Sulien wished she could talk to Llian.

'You're not as skinny as you used to be,' said Sulien.

'I've had a lot of practice.'

'At what?'

'Chucking stones at birds and lizards and other small creatures. I can bring down a meal from thirty feet away, two times out of three.'

'Have you heard any news about Flydd and the others?' said Sulien.

'Only bad news.'

The water suddenly seemed colder than before. What wasn't Jass telling her?

'You've got to do something, Sools,' said Jassika. 'Get into that enemy's mind.'

'Don't start that again!'

'What was his name, anyway?'

As if she didn't remember! 'Skald Hulni.'

'He's an important man now. He's done great things.'

'All the more reason to keep away from him. Besides, I promised Mummy.' The lie was in a good cause. If Jass knew Sulien had refused to promise, she would never stop pestering her.

Jassika scratched her backside. 'We've got to find out the Merdrun's fatal weakness.'

Rulke had extracted part of Sulien's nightmare about that. *A child of a lesser race can defeat us if her mighty gift is allowed to develop* – But what was the rest?

Sulien started to climb out of the pool. '*We* don't have to do anything except stay hidden.'

'Did I tell you the enemy's got your father,' Jassika said casually.

Sulien's heart gave a painful thump. 'Where did you hear that?' Her voice went squeaky.

Jassika examined her broken fingernails. 'Why would I tell you when you're always so unfriendly?'

'Jass, please. I've got to know where he is.'

'He was at Alcifer the whole time. It was Rulke dragged him through that gate in Thurkad.'

'Why would Rulke take Daddy?' Sulien had liked Rulke from the moment he had emerged from that huge statue of himself. Why would he want her father?

Jassika shrugged. 'But Skald got into Alcifer, and there was a big fight, and he caught Llian and Rulke, and found his great flying construct. Skald nearly died, but he got them all to Skyrock – and you know what the enemy do to prisoners.'

Sulien did. Jassika had told her many awful tales on the way to Stibbnibb. She seemed to revel in stories of other people's suffering.

'When was this?'

Jassika shrugged, then looked Sulien in the eye, challenging her. 'You're the only one who can save your father – *but you'd better hurry.*'

Sulien sank to the bottom and washed the soapy paste out of her long hair. When she rose again, Jassika was gone. But Sulien felt sure she was telling the truth this time. They were going to torture Llian, and then they were going to kill him. And she was the only one who could help him.

The thought of reaching out to the enemy, of mind-linking to a sus-magiz, of all people, was terrifying. But she had to disobey Karan.

# 5

# SHE'S IN A VALLEY CALLED STIBBNIBB

A few days after Uletta's visit to Skald, in the middle of the night he felt a little, questing touch in his mind again. He had first sensed it on Mistmurk Mountain just before finding Flydd's *Histories of the Lyrinx War*, and a couple of times since.

Previously, he had not been able to tell anything about the mind-touch, save that it had seemed rather child-like. But partly drinking his own life and Rulke's, and the powerful connection Skald had forged with Tiaan to support her on the eight-hour flight to Skyrock, had enhanced his ability to sense the emotions of others.

He focused on the mind-touch and carefully drew it out. It *was* a child, a girl with a powerful gift. He sensed loneliness and anxiety, and great fear. Of him?

*Who are you?* he sent.

She gave a little start, a tiny squeak. *I'm not allowed to talk to strangers.* She started to withdraw.

*But I'm not a stranger. You've touched my mind before, haven't you?*

She did not reply.

*What's your name?*

Nothing.

*Do you know who I am?*

*You're an enemy ... and a very evil man!*

*I'm a good, obedient Merdrun, doing my duty for my people.* She did not respond, though he sensed that her fear had diminished a little. *And you're afraid of me. So why do you keep coming back?*

After a long pause, she sent, *You're in pain.*

She sounded as though she felt for him, and that was a wonder. Why would a child care about an enemy she had never met? Was she an empath? Probably, but he sensed a greater gift. What could it be?

*You're worried about something – no,* someone, Skald sent.

The pause was so long that he thought he had lost her. No, she was still there; she wanted the connection but was afraid to talk to him. How had she detected him, anyway? Through his own, treacherous emotions? Perhaps if he confided in her.

*My father was executed for cowardice,* he sent. *And all my life –*

'Sulien?' It was another girl, calling her.

*Is your name Sulien?* said Skald.

She was gone.

He thought through the enemy names he had committed to memory, and there was only one Sulien. Sulien Fyrn, and she was also on the Most Wanted list, though she was wanted alive. He did not know why.

Skald was tempted to keep the contact to himself. She actually cared about him, and that was no small thing. Before Uletta, no one had ever cared. But what if Dagog had also picked up the mind-touch? He was the greatest magiz in more than a hundred years and his talents ran in all directions, some known only to him. Skald could not risk it.

His miraculous return with the construct, and Rulke and the other prisoners, had gained him no favour with the magiz. Dagog loathed Skald all the more and had refused to honour his promise to send Tiaan home.

'You had no power to make such an agreement,' he had hissed. 'It is void! And if you're not very careful, junior sus-magiz, you too will be void.'

Skald often dreamed about killing Dagog and leaving his flayed and quartered corpse for the wildcats, but in his heart he knew it would never happen. Dagog was too powerful, too cunning and saw too far. And Skald needed to please him.

Skald rose and pulled on his sus-magiz robes. He was still weak, but fine hair was starting to reappear on his chest and arms, and it gave him hope that he might make a good recovery. He was not looking forward to waking the magiz in the middle of the night, but it had to be done.

'I don't see who the girl can be but Sulien Fyrn,' Skald said after relating what had happened.

The last time Skald had seen Dagog, his lips had been thin and wrinkled and grey. Now they were blood red and swollen, and his eyes had a fiery glow. He had been drinking lives again and the addiction was raging in him.

'She's the only child of Karan and Llian,' Dagog said thickly, 'who found a way to jump two centuries into the future. The child who detected us months before our first attack on Santhenar, and overheard our one fatal weakness.'

'What *is* our one fatal weakness?' said Skald.

'How dare you question me about state secrets?' snarled Dagog, raising his bony, brown-stained hands as if to cast the life-drinking spell.

His stench was more offensive than usual but Skald dared not back away, or show disgust or any other emotion. He met the magiz's gaze and held it, and after a heart-stopping pause when it looked as though Dagog would not be able to rein in his addiction, he turned away, thrusting his hands into his robes.

'So ...' said Skald, unsteadily. 'Sulien is the gifted child that two of our previous magizes could not kill.' He had learned the details of the Merdrun's failed invasion in their long preparation for this one. 'She must have a mighty talent.'

Dagog stiffened, as if Skald had impugned all magizes. Why hadn't he kept his mouth shut?

'And *you* failed to kill Karan when you had the chance. If it were up to me –' The magiz's black eyes glittered. '*Where is the girl?*'

'I couldn't tell,' Skald said truthfully.

'On your knees, dog!'

Was Dagog going to drink his life? If he was, there was nothing Skald could do. He fell to his knees, outwardly calm, inwardly shuddering with terror.

'Rue-har!' said Dagog.

Skald handed his shard to Dagog, who took it between brown-stained thumb and fingers and jammed it into Skald's forehead, into the bone, as he had done when he had made Skald a sus-magiz five weeks ago. It hurt far more this time, though the pain was nothing compared to what he had suffered coming home from Alcifer, and he endured it without a sign.

Taking the sides of Skald's head between his icy palms, Dagog jerked his head left, right, left, right, left. The magiz's eyes closed and his blood-coloured lips moved. Was he intoning the life-drinking spell? Every organ within Skald's body was shuddering now, so vigorously that it the muscles of his torso and back were rippling, but the magiz had taken control of Skald's rue-har and he was helpless.

Dagog's eyes sprang open. 'She's in a valley called Stibbnibb, in the mountain range north of the Desolation Sink.'

He flung a challenging look at Skald, who felt a pang in the pit of his stomach. Sulien had felt for him, in some tiny way, and he had doomed her. It took iron self-control, but he remained expressionless. There was nothing he could do, and besides, she was an enemy. He had done his duty.

But he had done his duty drinking Tataste's life too, and she and her dead children haunted his dreams every night. He could not have another child's death on his conscience.

'Are you going to kill her?' he said in a flat voice.

'To bring the True Purpose to completion, rare talents such as hers, which appears to be a form of far-seeing or far-sensing, are invaluable. But these talents are rare among us – apart from myself and a couple of my senior sus-magizes – and we need slaves who have it. She may be one of the strongest.' The magiz wrenched the bloody rue-har out and handed it back. 'I'll take it from here, Sus-magiz. Dismiss her from your mind.'

*To bring the True Purpose to completion* meant Sulien, an innocent child, only had a few weeks to live. Tataste's infants had also been innocent, and Skald saw their faces again, and her agony. He lurched back to his tent, knowing the fatal emotions were leaking out in all directions and unable to do a thing about them.

And what if Uletta found out that he had betrayed a little girl to her death?

'Last chance,' said Flydd as the sky galleon descended into the secret valley of Nixzy, Faranda. 'Though I don't hold out much hope.'

Karan did not feel any hope. How had Skald, a wreck of a man, pulled off the impossible again and again? A dozen times he had been beaten; a dozen times he should have been taken. If the allies had Rulke and the construct, everything would have been different; she could have hoped again. But how could anyone prevail against an enemy whose will was so indomitable?

In the ten days since Skald's unbelievable escape from Alcifer, Flydd had flown to the Aachim's three main cities, seeking their aid, but had not met any of them. Shazmak and Tirthrax had been abandoned some time ago, judging by the open doorways and dust and decay. He was sure some Aachim still dwelt in the great frozen cube city high in the mountains at Stassor, but no one answered his calls and the vast door was sealed.

Going to Nixzy was pointless. These Aachim, remnants of the ones who had come to Santhenar towards the end of the war, were said to be the most embittered of all. Why would they help Flydd when he had nothing to offer them? Karan had tried to talk him into picking Sulien and Jassika up from Stibbnibb and taking them to Gothryme, but he just reminded her of her promise. Not that he showed any signs of fulfilling his.

The very sight of Nixzy told Karan that outsiders were not welcome. The city consisted of a series of stone domes, not unlike sea urchins, each topped by dozens of spiky towers ending in needle-sharp points, encircled by a series of stone doughnuts, also spiky.

A seven-sided square occupied the centre of the city, though it could not be reached from outside or from the air because the spike towers formed a network across it. It must look even more menacing from below, especially on a cold night at the full moon, where the spikes and their shadows would appear to be moving, alive.

Flydd put the battered, creaking sky galleon down a mile away. 'Don't want to come across as arrogant,' he said. 'We'll walk the rest of the way.'

The ground for several miles surrounding Nixzy was paved in enormous slabs of a coarse-grained yellow and grey stone. The land around was arid, the hills almost bare. It was hot and the air was still.

'Are these the Aachim who came in a great construct fleet from Aachim?' said Karan, as she, Flydd and Nish paced towards Nixzy.

'The last of them,' said Nish. 'They arrived seventeen years ago. Refugees led by Vithis, a cold, angry man. Aachan had been devastated by volcanic eruptions, though it's quietened down since and most of them have gone home.'

'Were the constructs –?'

'Modelled on Rulke's original, though the Aachim's were just ground transports until Tiaan and Malien worked out how to make one fly. Malien went home to Aachan two years ago.'

'She was the leader of Clan Elienor, the clan my half-Aachim father belonged to,' said Karan. 'It's where our red hair comes from.' She ruffled it. 'The red's faded somewhat.'

'We've all faded,' said Flydd cheerlessly.

Before they were halfway, a deputation of nine Aachim appeared from a concealed entrance between two of the spiky buildings, and Karan tensed. Why had Flydd brought her? Her quarter-Aachim blood was irrelevant to them, and most of her dealings with them had been fraught.

Their leader was a muscular woman, shorter than the other men and women, and with a more prominent crest running from her forehead over her skull and down again. In most Aachim it was barely noticeable, and Karan did not have it at all.

'Issilis,' said Flydd. 'From Clan Cloyne. I've not found her unfriendly in the past, though distant.'

'They're a proud, backward looking people,' said Karan. 'Preoccupied by their own culture and their own grievances, and seldom interested in outsiders.'

The Aachim stopped when Flydd's group was ten yards away. He stopped as well.

'Not a good sign,' Flydd said out of the corner of his mouth. He bowed. 'My compliments to yourself and your clan, Issilis, and to your people wherever they dwell.'

'We know why you've come, Flydd,' said Issilis curtly, 'and the answer is no. We will not join you in this war against the Merdrun. We will not give you aid. We wish you gone from our lands with the utmost despatch.'

Karan was shocked at her bluntness. The Aachim she had known had been a deliberative people, long to think and debate and often painfully slow to act. Indecision had been one of their great failings, yet reckless folly had characterised several of their leaders, and it had been extravagantly demonstrated in Tensor, who had been both their greatest and their most disastrous leader. She had scars to prove it, inner and outer.

'May I ask why, Issilis?' said Flydd. 'Your people and mine have been allies in the past.'

'Not often, and whenever we aided you it cost us dear.' She frowned. 'We have no quarrel with the Merdrun; why would we make enemies of them?'

'Because they want Santhenar for themselves.'

'It's not our world.'

'Yet many of your people have lived here for aeons.'

'For four thousand, two hundred and twenty-two *bitter* years,' said Issilis, empha-sising each word. 'Since your thrice-cursed ally, Rulke, brought a host of my people here as serfs, and their descendants remained trapped here until the Way Between the Worlds was broken.'

'I acknowledge your pain –' said Flydd.

Issilis raised her voice. 'But now Rulke has come back from the dead to ruin more lives, not a one of us will stay a moment longer than it takes to prepare the Way. We're going home, Flydd, and you and he and the Merdrun can fight over the bloody entrails of Santhenar to your heart's content. Begone!'

Flydd bowed again, and so did Nish. Karan did not. Her blood was boiling, and she was on the point of calling them out for cowards when Flydd caught her forearm and squeezed hard. She glared at him. He shook his head.

'We wish you well, Issilis,' he said. 'We thank you for your assistance in many difficult times, and may you have joy of Aachan when you go home.'

Issilis nodded stiffly and turned away. The other eight followed.

'No point, Karan,' said Flydd. 'Come on.'

They made their way back to the sky galleon.

'Not a hint of hospitality!' raged Karan. 'Not even a flask of water on a sweltering day. Aachim are cowards to the core. That's how the Charon took their world from them and reduced them to serfs.'

'But surely you appreciate the problem?'

'Rulke?'

'They'll never help anyone who allied with him. I should have realised.'

'But they've long been free on Santhenar ...'

'They are what they are. And I'd have thought you, of all people, would have learned the lesson by now.'

'What lesson?'

'Don't make unnecessary enemies. You've got more than enough necessary ones.'

Karan scowled, thought about it and managed a smile. 'Necessary enemies! Yes, I've always been well equipped with them.'

'What are we going to do, Xervish?' Nish said dully.

'Council of war, but not here. Faranda was a miserable place long before Pitlis's Aachim were allowed to take half of it. We're going where we'll be among friends, to plan our last throw of the dice.'

'Where's that?'

'After Yulla gates Clech, Persia, a pilot and a squad to us, we're making a little diversion to Nennifer. Then we'll collect Aviel and Maigraith, and head to Fiz Gorgo. Yggur, at least, will welcome us.'

'And he has a magnificent cellar,' Nish said dreamily.

'What's Nennifer?' said Karan.

'It was the Council of Scrutators' secret headquarters, in the Great Mountains. Destroyed in the war.'

'Then why are we wasting time going there?'

'It wasn't *completely* destroyed. There's a few things I want to pick up.'

'Can we visit Sulien and Jassika on the way?'

'I'm in a hurry,' said Flydd. 'And taking the sky galleon there may attract the enemy's attention.'

'Please. I have to know she's all right.'

'All right,' he said. 'After Nennifer.'

## 6

# ARE YOU GOING TO KILL ME?

S kald saw me,' said Sulien, trembling. 'The moment I touched his mind.'
'Did you learn anything about Klarm?' said Jassika. She must have been
spying through one of the cracks in the wall. 'Or your father?'

Sulien shook her head. 'Skald closed his mind to me, real quick.'

'Why did you break the link?'

'You called my name! And I'm sure he heard it.'

'So what? There must be hundreds of girls called Sulien.'

'There aren't. Mummy made the name up, just for me – and now Skald knows
who I am.'

'He was bound to find out, sooner or later. Give him an hour to get back to sleep,
then try again.'

Sulien's heart lurched painfully. 'He'll be waiting for me. I never should have
listened to you.'

'Don't be such a scaredy-cat, Sools. You'll never save your father that way.'

She was right, but Sulien wasn't going to be pushed into doing something even
more dangerous. 'I don't have to prove anything to you. When we fought the
Merdrun before, back in the past, I saw things that would give you nightmares until
the day you die.'

'What things?' Jassika said eagerly.

'I'm not going to relive them for your amusement.' Jassika still had not bathed or
changed her clothes, and her smell was overpowering in the small room. 'Go away!'

But when Sulien crept under her thin covers, fully dressed, she was too worried
to sleep. Skald was a clever and dangerous man, and he had been the one to find

Flydd's Histories on Mistmurk Mountain. He would soon know who she was. Why had she done such a stupid thing?

She tossed for ages and was only half asleep when a rushing sigh roused her. Sulien sat up in bed, preparing to tell Jass to go away, but the room was empty. It stank, though it wasn't Jassika's grubby odour. It was disgusting, like something that had been dead for ages.

An icy wind stirred her hair, though the window and door were closed. Sulien was sitting up, goose pimples rising on her arms, when something materialised at the foot of her bed.

No, *someone*. A small, scrawny man in robes, faintly surrounded by a yellow, rising and falling nimbus of light. Lurid eyes that reminded her of Aviel's story about the ghost vampire. Clawed fingers, stained brown on the tips. Plump purple lips like blood-bloated leeches. And his breath glowed blue in the dark and had a revolting, carrion smell, as if that's what he ate. *Or was!*

Sulien knew who he was, because she had previously mind-touched two people with similar, skin-creeping auras. The unnamed magiz whom Karan had killed on Cinnabar months ago, and the mad triplets-magiz, Unbuly, Empuly and Jaguly.

This man had to be the enemy's current magiz. No one else could have induced such flesh-creeping terror in her. And he was between her and the door. What was she supposed to do? It was an effort to think.

The window was tricky to open; she'd never get through it before he caught her. And if she screamed for help, he would kill the old woman and the old man.

'Who are you?' she whispered.

'You know who I am.' His voice was oily. No, slimy and oozy. 'Don't you?'

'The – the magiz. Are you going to kill me?'

'Not for a while. Where's the other girl?'

'What other girl?'

The magiz's lip twitched and something struck Sulien so hard across the face that it knocked her out of bed. *'Where is the other girl?'*

She got up, rubbing her throbbing cheek. Dagog looked absolutely malevolent, and she knew there was nothing he would not do to her to get what he wanted. 'She sleeps in the forest. I don't know where.'

The magiz took an oily green shard from a pouch. Was he going to kill her?

*Mummy, Mummy, the magiz is here, and –*

He jammed the point into her forehead. The worst pain Sulien had ever felt tore through her skull, and she was paralysed.

He held the shard there for a minute or two, his swollen lips moving, then pulled it out. 'I've taken back all knowledge of our secret weakness, but that doesn't mean you're safe. You'll only be safe if you do exactly as I say.' He dematerialised.

Sulien toppled onto her side, her forehead and cheek throbbing. Why had she listened to Jassika? How could she have imagined she would be able to learn anything about Llian? She was a stupid little girl, and she and Jassika were going to pay for it.

But what did the magiz want? He wasn't going to kill her *for a while*.

She tried to mind-call Jassika, to warn her, but did not know how to reach her. Sulien's whole brain felt numb.

She had no idea how long it took for Dagog to find Jassika, or how he had found her in the dark forest, but eventually he reappeared, dragging her by the arm. Her cheeks were red, as if he had used the slapping spell on her too, though Sulien was pleased to see that his thin nose was bent to one side and blood was oozing from his disgusting, greenish nostrils. Jassika had put up a fight.

'Thanks for betraying me,' she muttered.

'I only said you were in the forest. Where else could you have been?'

'And he's going to torture us for the fun of it, then kill us. I hate you!'

'If you hadn't called my name –'

'That's right, blame me. Everyone else does.'

The magiz opened the door, directed a blast of fire towards the front of the log cabin, then took Sulien and Jassika by the arms. The paralysis faded but, before Sulien could move, a gate formed silently and, with a wrench that brought last night's dinner – gruel with fried grubs – up into the back of her throat, the magiz carried them away as the cabin exploded into flames.

'Fire, fire! *Get out!*' Sulien yelled, though she did not think the old woman and man would have heard.

'What did you do that for, you disgusting old creep?' cried Jassika.

The magiz struck her so hard that his hand left thin white finger marks on her cheek.

'Keep your mouth shut, vermin, or you'll soon be begging for death.'

Jassika opened her mouth. She wasn't going to stop. Sulien kicked her in the shins, which hurt her bare toes, and shook her head.

'Very wise,' said the magiz.

The gate opened in a dark space that smelled of freshly cut stone. He dragged them down a tunnel-like hall and thrust them into a small cell whose floor, walls and ceiling were pale, curving stone, evidently carved out of solid rock. A circular hole in the wall, far too small to squeeze through, provided ventilation and a small amount of reflected light. Distantly, from outside, Sulien heard metallic hammering, scraping sounds, the thump of falling rock and the shouts of overseers.

A shelf on one side of the cell held two pairs of coarse, folded blankets. There was a hole in the floor for a toilet, and a bucket of water in the far corner. Apart from that, the cell was empty.

The magiz did not enter. The door, made of wrought iron in jagged curves like the Merdrun glyph, closed and locked. The light outside was extinguished.

Jassika laid one of the blankets on a rock shelf, climbed onto it and lay down and pulled the other blanket over her. ''Night, Sools.'

'That's it?' cried Sulien. 'We aren't going to talk about being abducted by a murderous –'

'What's there to talk about? It's done.'

'Where are we?'

'Skyrock, of course.'

'What are we going to do?'

'You're the *little hero* who got away from the last two magizes. You tell me.'

Soon Sulien could tell from Jassika's breathing that she was asleep. What a strange kid she was. How could she accept this disaster so calmly?

And what about the old woman and the old man? Sulien did not like them, but they had taken her in. She prayed that they had escaped.

It was all her fault. Why had she listened to Jassika? No, don't blame her – Sulien would have tried to contact Skald sooner or later. And if Karan had heard her cry for help, she would come after them and the magiz would catch her too, and kill the lot of them. Despair swamped Sulien and she lay in the dark, cursing herself for being a little fool.

It reminded her of Idlis the Whelm, who had never broken *his* promises. Dear, strange, tormented Idlis. He had sworn to protect her, and he had been true to his word. He given everything for her; given up his own people and, in the end, his life. His faithfulness and his iron resolution were a lesson to her. She could not allow his sacrifice to be in vain.

She would keep fighting. She had to find a way to beat the enemy. Their lives depended on it.

∼

The sky galleon reached Nennifer the following evening, but Karan saw little of it. It was the time of the new moon, overcast and dark. All she could make out was an enormous cliff-line, plunging down into the utter aridity of the Desolation Sink, and a jumble of walls and cavities, as if a city hollowed out of the rock had been destroyed by being cut into slices, some of which had moved up and some down. Now, Flydd said, it was home only to bats and other hole-dwelling creatures.

Karan had heard more than enough about the place from Nish and Maelys and, thankfully, Flydd was going in alone. He landed the sky galleon on the plateau above the cliffs, on a flat expanse that had once been a landing ground for fleets of air-dreadnoughts, and disappeared into the night.

'Do you know what he's looking for?' Karan said to Nish.

'Flydd's never talked much about Nennifer, save that he hated the place. The scrutators tortured him here. But apparently there's all manner of secret stuff hidden in the old catacombs.'

Karan yawned and went to her bunk. She could never get enough sleep these days.

A rumble like distant thunder woke her, after midnight. Clech, the beautiful Persia bel Soon, a pilot and a squad of ten soldiers were coming aboard, gated from Roros.

Flydd was back as well, and the sky galleon lifted and headed for Stibbnibb. He said nothing about what he had brought out of Nennifer.

*Mummy, Mummy, the magiz is here.*

Karan tried to call out, but her legs collapsed under her and she fell hard to her knees on the deck. 'Xervish, he's got Sulien!'

Persia lifted Karan to her feet. 'Who has?' she rapped.

'The magiz.'

The hours it took to fly there, high above the Desolation Sink, were interminable. Karan knew it was pointless but she had to see the place; she had no other clues.

It was a dewy dawn when the sky galleon landed beside the smoking ashes of the cabin. Nothing remained but the chimney, the iron stove, and the charred remains of the old man's easel, which had fallen off the porch before it burned. And two bodies, one long and thin, the other short and fat.

Flydd and Persia went back and forth through the hot ashes, reading the scene. Karan stood there, numb. The enemy had Llian and Sulien and they would never let them go.

Why hadn't she convinced Flydd to go to Stibbnibb first?

# 7

# GET UNDRESSED

The node had been tapped, the massive tunnel carved through the base of Skyrock, and the Merdrun's greatest enemy, Rulke, was in their thrall, compelled to use the construct to complete the tower with impossible speed. Skyrock was almost complete and the rubble and mess were being cleared away. All was going well.

And Skald was the hero who had made it possible. There was even talk, if the True Purpose succeeded, of him leading his people through on the Day of All Days. An unimaginable honour for the son of a coward.

He had recovered sufficiently to resume his position as Superintendent of Works, and he met with Uletta every day to review progress on the tower. It soon became clear that she expected him to reciprocate her feelings, and that there would be trouble if he did not, though he had no idea what to do about it. Such matters were beyond his experience and there was no one he could ask.

Every day, in subtle ways, she made her feelings for him more obvious, and it felt wonderful. She liked him! She cared for him! He wasn't alone, as he had always been. It almost cancelled out his mother's voice in his head. Almost.

Skald was coming to the realisation that he might be in love with Uletta, but after a lifetime of denying his feelings, and living in terror of the penalty for revealing them, it was impossible to respond to her. Any kind of friendship between a Merdrun and a slave was forbidden, but a physical, or worse yet, a *romantic* relationship was both a pollution and an abomination.

Such things were known to occur but they were almost impossible to keep secret, because some slaves would do anything to curry favour with their supervisors and gain extra benefits. When the culprits were exposed the Merdrun was publicly shamed, flogged and reduced to the ranks – or in the worst cases, put to death. The slave, unless he or she was irreplaceable, was killed in a gruesome public spectacle.

And Dagog was ever watchful. He loved catching malefactors in physical congress, often spying on them for days before he denounced them, and he was always looking for ways to attack the offspring of traitors and cowards. Nothing would give him greater pleasure than exposing Skald and publicly destroying him.

When it happened, Skald and Uletta were working late in one of the many rooms and storerooms that had been carved out of the pinnacle. This one was on the topmost level of Skyrock. A plain, bare room, cubic in shape, with curving corners, a wide doorway and a single oval window, open to the air.

The foundations of the iron tower, which was soon to be erected on the cut-off top of Skyrock, had just been completed. Skald was not permitted to know what it was for, though he knew it was one of the critical elements of their True Purpose. It had to be strong and stable, able to withstand the gales that seldom stopped blowing at that height, and every detail of Uletta's drawings, laid out on the floor of the cubic chamber for protection against the wind, had to be checked against the specifications.

It was well after midnight when they finished and, though Skald's insides were healed now, he was still weak. They were seven hundred feet up and he faced a long climb down the inner stairs of Skyrock, then a mile-long walk back to his tent in the officer's compound. The thought was exhausting.

'That's all I can do today,' he said.

'We still have to recheck that the south-western foundation bolts reach full-depth in their sockets,' said Uletta, 'If they pass, we'll be on schedule, and you can start later tomorrow.'

Being on schedule was a miracle in itself, and largely due to having the use of the construct to lift great slabs of polished stone cladding into place on Skyrock, and the power of its Source to cut the tunnel. The work had been behind schedule since it began, and he ached to tell Durthix that they had caught up.

He laboured up the stairs after Uletta, his eyes fixed on her muscular buttocks and strong thighs. There was no moon, and the stars made ten thousand brilliant points of light in the clear air, though it was bitingly cold, and he felt it far more these days. Tapping and clattering came from far below as the last of the rings of scaffolding were removed.

Skald and Uletta checked the massive foundation bolts with a pair of glow-lamps, agreed that they had reached the required depth in solid rock, and he plodded down to the cubic room to sign the plans and complete the records.

'Don't go yet,' she said softly, when all was done. 'This deserves a celebration.'

Merdrun did not celebrate achievements, only great military victories, but Skald was too tired to deny her this little request. 'All right.'

'Not here. It's too cold.' She went down a couple of levels to a storeroom, one of many on the upper levels. 'In here.'

He followed her in, uncomprehending. The walls, floor and ceiling were bare rock, though it was pleasantly warm here. Lengths of timber were stacked on the left, head-high bundles of bamboo scaffolding poles towards the back, and coils of rope and tall stacks of folded canvas on the right. She pushed the door closed, went behind the bamboo poles and spread a canvas on the floor, and began to take off her clothes.

'What are you doing?' Skald said hoarsely, unable to take his eyes off her big, strong body.

Uletta's laughter was low and rich. 'You know exactly what we're going to do. Get undressed.'

Terror struck him. He was about to commit a forbidden act. Common sense told him to walk out and denounce her, or at least make sure he was never alone with her again, but Skald could not resist her. She must really love him, to take such a risk.

And he wanted her love. All his life, Skald had yearned for it – ever since the day he had asked his mother if she loved him, and she had beaten him so badly that his back still bore the scars. At the time, just after his father had been executed, Skald had thought the beating was because she hated him.

Had she done it out of love? Perhaps his poor mother had been so terrified for Skald that she'd tried to beat the unmanning emotions out of him, the ones that had caused his father to break and run from the battlefield. If she had been trying to save Skald, she had done so. She had made him what he was today.

Uletta was naked now, holding her arms out and smiling. She completed his damaged self and he had to have more of her. The urge was a bit like drinking a life – once started, there was no way back.

But all the while they were fondling and caressing one another, and while they engaged in the carnal act, he imagined the magiz spying on them, leering at their beautiful, private moment, and gloating over their coming ruin. Skald knew ecstasy, and then he knew terror.

Afterwards, as they lay together, she said softly, 'You do realise what I've done for you?'

'Um?' he said sleepily.

'I've just betrayed my people and put my life on the line – and now I want you to do something for me.'

Skald thought he had; she had certainly enjoyed it.

'You won't ever drink a human life again, will you, Skald?' said Uletta. 'I could not be with a man who did that.'

How could he make such a promise – he was a sus-magiz! But because he wanted more of what she offered, and because, at that moment, he thought he was experiencing the delightful but utterly forbidden emotion, *love*, he took her hands in his and said, 'Uletta, I swear that I will not drink a human life again.'

He meant it, too.

But as soon as she had dressed and left, while he waited so they would not be seen coming down together, Skald's terror rose to the surface. What if the magiz was setting a trap for them, even now? What if the schedule slipped again, or the power they drew from the node and the Source wasn't enough? If Dagog ordered Skald to drink a life, how could he refuse?

The addiction had faded after he'd partly drunk his own life a month ago. The experience had been so traumatic, and it had brought home to him so clearly what a monstrous thing he'd done to other innocent people, that his craving had died.

But attempting to drink Rulke's mighty life in the construct, and Llian's, and taking the sus-magiz's instead, had rewoken Skald's addiction. He fought it every day, and it felt good to keep it at bay. He prayed that his oath to Uletta would give him the strength to continue.

For she had woken another craving in him. He had to have more of her, too.

Occasionally, as the work on the pinnacle and the tower continued at breakneck pace, there was more to do than they had power available, and the only source was to drink a slave's life. Each time, Skald ordered a more junior sus-magiz to do it, saying it was part of their training. Afterwards he was terrified that Uletta would find out. She was the best thing in his life now.

*Hypocrite!* he thought.

But the magiz burned to drink Skald's life, and if he got the chance he would. And over the following days, whenever Dagog looked at him oddly, Skald felt a terrifying foreboding that the magiz was just waiting for him to slip up.

'Skald!'

Skald turned and Dagog was on the steps above him. 'Yes, Magiz?'

'The girl I captured has a quite remarkable gift. Study it and train it.'

'Immediately, Magiz. May I ask to what purpose?'

Dagog scowled and Skald braced himself for more threats, but instead Dagog said, 'You will reveal what I am about to say to no one.'

'No one, Magiz.'

'After the True Purpose has been achieved, we will need to create many gates in a very short time. The girl's gift for far-seeing may come in handy. Get going!'

Skald puzzled about Dagog's words as he made various arrangements, then hurried up to Sulien's cell. What came after the True Purpose was known only to Dagog and Durthix.

He took Sulien to a small, plain room shaped like an octagon. It had no furniture or window, just three small triangular ventilation holes set at the corners of an upside-down triangle. He pointed to the floor and she sat.

He studied her, reviewing what he knew. Nine years old but small for her age. Heart-shaped face, green eyes, red hair in a plait running halfway down her back. A quiet, anxious, clever girl. Sulien had once overheard the Merdrun's secret weakness – a secret Skald was not privy too – and two previous magizes had failed to kill her to protect it. It wasn't a problem now, though. Dagog had erased the memory.

'Are you going to kill me?' Her voice was high, quavering. She was terrified and trying desperately not to show it.

'I'm going to test your gift for far-seeing. Tell me, Sulien, how do you far-see?'

'I – I just think about what I want to see, or who, and concentrate hard. Sometimes it works. Though, mostly, nothing comes. Um, why do you want to know?'

'I'm going to help you develop the gift.'

Her small jaw tilted up. 'You're our enemy, and I'll never help you.'

'You have a friend here,' said Skald mildly.

'No,' she said, shivering. 'I don't have any friends.'

'Don't lie! You mind-called me, and fell into the magiz's trap, and if you don't cooperate, Jassika will be punished.'

'You're an evil, nasty man. Do you kick puppies, too? I'll bet you do.'

Oddly, her judgement stung, but this was war. 'Do you really want to know the things I've done?' he said direly.

'No,' she squeaked.

'Then we'll begin. The room next to us contains but one object. What is it?'

'I don't know.'

'You're not trying. Close your eyes.'

Goose pimples rose on her bare arms. 'What are you going to do to me?'

This wasn't going to work. She was too anxious. 'Nothing,' he said, trying to sound calm.

'I can't think with you standing over me,' she whispered.

'The gift of far-seeing works better if you don't think.'

'How would you know?'

'I have it too.'

She looked down at her lap, shaking her head. He was intimidating her, and in her short life she had seen horrors no child should have to experience. Skald, who knew all about childhood horrors, felt for her. He backed away to the door.

Sulien crossed her legs and put her hands on her knees. 'Further,' she whispered.

Feeling that he was getting somewhere, he went out, waited a couple of minutes and returned. She had not moved. Her eyes were closed.

'It's a bowl,' she said. 'Carved from orange rock. It's half full of water with ... something floating in it.' She wrinkled her nose as she strained to discover more. 'Little white squares, slightly pink. Petals. Rose petals?'

The hairs stood up on the back of his neck; she had far-seen almost perfectly. 'The petals are from apple blossoms,' said Skald. 'They're similar to rose petals.'

He replaced the bowl with another object and repeated the exercise, but this time she could not see it at all, even after half an hour of encouragement, followed by threats.

'What is it?' she said at the end.

'My officer's sword,' said Skald.

'I suppose you've killed hundreds of people with it.' Sulien shuddered. 'I wouldn't be able to see that.'

'It's new. I haven't killed anyone with it.'

'What happened to your old sword?'

'It was taken from me when I was pretending to be dead.'

He could see that she was intrigued, but she did not ask for the details.

'Well, I can't see your sword. I won't!'

'If you don't try, I'll punish Jassika.'

'Won't make any difference. I can't far-see stuff like that.'

Skald retrieved his blade, simmering. How dare a slave girl defy *him*! But he had to put the anger aside, explore the limits of her gift and find a way to heighten it.

'At the very top of the tower there's a room the same size and shape as this one,' he said. 'It's also empty, apart from one object. Tell me what it is.'

This was a far harder challenge, since Sulien had to locate the one identical room, among hundreds of rooms, before she could far-see what was inside it. He wasn't sure whether he wanted her to succeed or fail, though. If she succeeded, as he suspected she would, it would demonstrate an astonishing gift for far-seeing, but what did the magiz want her for?

And if she failed, what then?

He was waiting outside when Uletta came by. He loved everything about her, even the way she walked, but dared not show his feelings in public. The magiz was bound to be watching him and he must not do a single thing to arouse suspicion.

He nodded as she went by but did not speak. She looked hurt, but continued.

Skald went in. 'Did you find the room at the very top, shaped like this room.'

'Of course,' Sulien said scornfully. 'It was easy.'

He sighed. She was *highly* gifted. 'What do you see inside it?'

'A gigantic crystal, shaped like the letter V, set on a circular platform.'

He took a step backwards. 'What are you talking about?'

'The crystal was as clear as anything. It's bigger than I am and it's got patterns inside it, like a spider's web.'

'That's not it at all. I left a braided leather belt with a silver buckle in the top room.'

She closed her eyes and tilted her head back. 'I can see your belt, in the topmost room of Skyrock. But you said *at the very top of the tower*. The iron tower stands above Skyrock, and at its top there's a room with eight sides, with walls made of canvas. That's where I looked, and that's what I saw.'

Disturbed and wondering, Skald led Sulien back to the cell she shared with Jassika, who had no gift for far-seeing, and locked her in. He took many sets of stairs to the top of the twisted blue and white spirals of Skyrock, then climbed the rungs to the tip of the iron tower.

He had not been up here before, because the topmost element of the iron tower was not part of his duties. It had been designed and built by M'Lainte to meet the magiz's requirements, then assembled in a walled-off section of the compound. Yesterday, after it had been inspected and tested by the magiz, Rulke had lifted it lifted to the top of the iron tower with the construct and it had been bolted into place.

The plan Skald had seen weeks ago had shown the iron tower ending in a point with a white ball fixed to it. But the top, when he reached it, terminated in a platform twelve feet across, surrounded by an eight-sided, canvas-walled enclosure, the same size as the room he had told Sulien about.

Skald froze. Clearly, what lay inside was a secret. But he had to know if Sulien had seen true.

He unlaced a flap of the tent and climbed up onto the platform. A huge twinned crystal sat in a heavy brass mounting, akin to the mountings used for star sightings. It would allow the crystal to be rotated both horizontally and vertically, and be fixed at any desired position. And the crystal had silvery inclusions inside it, like hexagonal spiderwebs.

What was it for? He had no idea, and neither, he was sure, had Sulien. But clearly she had a formidable gift and it could turn out to be vital, for the Merdrun – and for himself.

# 8

## TAKE A DEEP SNIFF

Y ou look like you died in the night, and were buried and dug up again,' said
Maigraith, shaking Aviel awake at dawn.

'Ugh!' She felt like it, and her flyaway hair was a mess of tangles. 'You took my hairbrush.'

'You trying to look beautiful for someone?'

Not you, you hag!

Maigraith dumped a blouse, knickers and pants on the end of the bed and stood back, arms folded.

'How am I supposed to dress when I'm manacled?' snapped Aviel. It had been a bad night and the day promised to be worse.

'Get out of bed.'

Aviel did so, shivering, though it was not cold. It felt no better having Maigraith staring at her than it had last night. She removed the ankle chains.

Aviel dressed, awkwardly. Maigraith reapplied the chains.

'Where are my socks and boots?'

'You're not going outside.'

'You're determined to make this as hard for me as possible.'

'Adversity is character-building. And you have so much to build.'

'At least it's *good* character,' Aviel said feebly.

'Your moral compass must be pointing the wrong way.'

So the day went, and the next, as she extracted and prepared the remaining three scents for the rejuvenation potion. Maigraith did not leave Aviel's side whilever she was in her workshop, and she questioned everything Aviel did, and double-checked each step.

There was no possibility of changing the method to undermine the scent potion or make it go wrong. But finally, late on the second day, the last two scents, the evanescent smell of green, smouldering grass, herbaceous and smoky, and the odour of fresh phoenix droppings, sharp and pungent as hot mustard, had been extracted.

Only the final step remained – blending all the scents to make the rejuvenation potion.

'You're shaking,' said Maigraith. 'What's the matter with you?'

'You're going to kill me the moment you get what you want.'

'You should have thought of that before you plotted to betray me.'

'*You* plotted to betray Skald.'

'It's not betrayal when you do it to an enemy.'

'Exactly what I was thinking.'

Maigraith smiled thinly. 'But *you* didn't provide yourself with a way out.'

'Actually, I did,' Aviel snapped. 'My conscience got the better of me.'

'More fool you.'

'Better a fool than a knave!'

'You're too tired and emotional. You'll do the blending in the morning. Bed!'

'I can't sleep with chains on. And if I'm too tired I'll make a mistake.'

Maigraith thought about that, head to one side, then removed the ankle chains and went out.

The manacles had chafed Aviel's twisted ankle, making walking more painful than usual. She heaved herself onto her stool to think things through. Blending a double batch of the rejuvenation potion would only take a couple of hours. Then Maigraith would test it and, assuming she was satisfied that it was working and Aviel was no longer needed, she would put her to death.

Aviel's heart was trying to thump itself to pieces. She opened her box of scent phials, lifted the racks out and saw that a lot of phials were missing. Seventeen, to be precise, and they were only used in one potion she knew of. Murderer's Mephitis.

Was Maigraith planning on killing her with a scent potion Aviel had considered making to rid herself of Maigraith? The irony might please her.

No! Maigraith could simply point a finger at Aviel and stop her heart. She must be planning to gate into Skyrock and use Murderer's Mephitis on Lirriam, and it was a very unpleasant way to die.

Aviel could not think of any way to stop her.

It started to rain in the night and Aviel, who had slept little better than the previous two nights, was listening to water running off the roof when Maigraith entered. It was still dark.

'Judgement day,' she said breezily, and laid a set of clean clothes on the end of the bed.

Aviel did not bother to answer. There was no reason to engage with her. She dressed and followed Maigraith to the workshop without a word.

'What's the matter with you today?' said Maigraith, redoing the ankle manacles.

Could it be that she actually craved human company, that even Aviel's presence was better than being alone? Well, damn her to hell! Aviel wasn't giving her anything.

She did not respond to anything Maigraith said. Acting as if she had been stricken dumb in the night, Aviel took out each of the twenty-one scents required for the rejuvenation potion and set them in order in a small rack, then smiled and bowed and stood back, making a sweeping gesture to Maigraith to check her work.

She frowned and did so. Aviel began the blending in a larger tube, three drops of aloes and five of the ginseng, swirling it anticlockwise then adding a further drop. Then she put it in the rack, pointed to it and said, 'Check it!'

Maigraith scowled and did so. Aviel blended the third scent and then, with a deliberately fawning bow, called Maigraith forward.

She looked irritated. Too damned bad! Aviel continued, in turn peremptory, casual, obsequious and in yawning indifference, but never replying to any of Maigraith's questions or saying a word save for, 'Check it!'

Maigraith was starting to get rattled. Perhaps she could not comprehend how someone under sentence of death could seem so unfazed. Aviel could never be indifferent, but defiance had given her a tiny element of control, and it was as good as an extra two hours' sleep.

Or was Maigraith fretting that Aviel had found a way to change the scent potion after all? Could she foster that fear?

She was down to three tubes now – the first a viscous yellow blending of seven scents, the second, diamond clear, a blend of eleven scents, and the third, which contained the essences of phoenix ordure, smoky green grass and horseradish, had the consistency and colour of cream. Once she blended them in the correct proportions the rejuvenation potion would be made. And she knew it would work because she had done everything perfectly.

But Maigraith did not know that.

She watched, unblinking, while Aviel mixed the first blend with half of the second, exactly as the method specified, added five drops of the third blend and watched as the mixture changed from pale green to white with little scintillating specks suspended in it, then foamed up and filled the top of the corked tube with vapour which slowly condensed and ran back. The foam subsided, the bubbles popped and the scent potion went clear.

Aviel held it up, and smiled to herself. She always felt a surge of exhilaration after completing a difficult scent potion. She made sure the tube was tightly stoppered, bowed insultingly low and handed it to Maigraith.

She looked really anxious now, as well she might. Had Aviel, burning for revenge, managed to make it with a flaw after all? How could she have, when Maigraith had checked on her so carefully? But Maigraith had a very poor nose and had to take Aviel's word that the scent phials contained what the labels said, since she could not check them for herself.

Her greater worry must be whether the scent potion would work at all. If it did not, she had lost. Even if she succeeded in using the Murderer's Mephitis to rid herself of her rival, Maigraith would never replace Lirriam in Rulke's affections.

Maigraith had to be young, attractive and fertile. Her true, aged self could never get Rulke back because she had undermined her own self-belief in this desperate quest over the last month and a half. She could never go back to being old.

For a moment, Aviel pitied her. Wilm liked Aviel for what she was, and he would not like her one bit more if, through some great magic, her bad ankle could be made like the good one.

'What if I can't smell it?' whispered Maigraith.

The hand holding the tube was shaking so violently that Aviel feared it would fall and smash. 'Sit down. Don't squeeze the tube; you might break it.'

Maigraith sat on the only soft chair in the workshop, holding the tube in both hands. 'I'm – afraid.'

So would I be, Aviel thought, if my future happiness rested on the rejuvenation potion, and on becoming someone I had no right to be. Fearing Maigraith would break the tube, she took it from her and tipped the scent potion into a little, pale green cut glass bottle, which she stoppered and handed back.

She wanted to hate Maigraith, wanted her to fail and be crushed, yet her soft heart was touched. 'Don't expect too much, too soon. Some scent potions can take days, even weeks, to work completely.'

Maigraith removed the stopper, allowed the vapour to rise and wafted it towards her nose. 'I can't smell anything.'

'You're not getting enough. Put your nose to the opening and take a deep sniff.'

Maigraith eyed her suspiciously. 'You're trying to overdose me. There are scent potions that only require a tiny sniff.'

'Yes, the disgusting Eureka Graveolence, for instance.'

'What was that for?'

'I used it to locate the summon stone.' Aviel clamped down tight on those memories. 'But its effects were subtle. The rejuvenation potion is entirely different.'

'I don't understand.'

Aviel was willing to bet Maigraith had not made such an admission in the last couple of centuries.

'The stronger the effect of the potion, the more is required and the longer it takes. Rejuvenation of an adult human – *a really old one*,' Aviel could not resist saying, 'is one of the greatest transformations of all. I read that it's almost as difficult as the renewal spell, or the change from a normal human to a were-beast.'

Maigraith considered that, seemed to find it logical, put her nose to the mouth of the bottle and took a deep sniff.

'And another two.' Aviel held her breath; she wanted to see it work. It was one of the Great Potions, it had taken nearly six weeks of her life, and it was by far the most difficult scent potion she had ever attempted.

Maigraith sniffed twice, carefully stoppered the bottle and slipped it into her pocket. 'Where's my mirror?'

She had obtained a round one to replace the one she had smashed. Aviel pointed to her ankle manacles. Maigraith gestured absently and they fell away.

'I assume it's in your salon,' said Aviel.

Maigraith ran out. Aviel packed her gear away. Her heart was racing again. She rubbed her chafed ankle and followed. Maigraith was sitting at the long table with the mirror propped up in front of her, staring at her face as if she could make herself younger by will alone.

As Aviel entered, Maigraith said dully, 'It's not working.'

'Do you really expect such a mighty transformation to occur that quickly?'

'The other scent potion started working on Calluly in a single minute.'

'Is that really the change you want to dwell on, right now?'

'Look at me!' Maigraith cried, distraught. 'What do you see? Tell me the hard truth.'

Aviel went around the table and sat down on the far side. The light shone on Maigraith's face and it was not kind, though neither was it cruel.

'You look like a woman of seventy years,' said Aviel. 'One whose life is etched into her face, the good and the bad. It's not a bad face. I've seen worse.'

'*I've seen worse!*' Maigraith wailed. 'It's not the face of the woman he swore to, 224 years ago. Is it?'

'I didn't know you then. And if I had, I'd only have been six.'

'Rub it in, why don't you?'

'You've had hundreds of years to enjoy life. I've only had sixteen.'

'You're not helping.'

'You asked me to tell you the hard truth.'

'Then tell it! Has the rejuvenation potion done anything?'

Aviel leaned closer. 'The lines around your eyes don't seem quite as deep as they were.'

'That's all?' Maigraith said shrilly.

'Now you're being pathetic! And stupid.'

'What – are – you – talking – about?' Maigraith grated.

'Rejuvenation has to change every bone and cell, organ and sinew and hair in your body, and only a fool would expect all that to happen in an instant. I told you it could take days, even weeks – and the greatest changes happen when you're asleep. It's also very painful.'

'I don't care about pain.'

'I've heard that the renewal spell is more agonising than anything in human experience,' said Aviel. 'And rejuvenation has a lot in common with renewal.'

'How dare you lecture me?' said Maigraith, her mood changing in an instant. 'This scent potion better be working by dawn, or tomorrow will be your last day.'

Chills shivered through Aviel. How had she forgotten? 'If it isn't,' she said carefully, 'you'll need me to find out what's gone wrong, and fix it.'

Maigraith pointed and the manacles were back. She favoured Aviel with a nasty smile. 'I've located another scent potion-maker, thousands of miles away. He's got forty years' experience, and if I need to I can gate him here within days. I don't need you anymore, Aviel the mouse. You might have considered that possibility before you betrayed me.'

Surprisingly, considering that she expected to be put to death in the morning, Aviel fell asleep as soon as she got into bed and did not wake until an hour before dawn. What was that strange, rising and falling noise?

Well, Thurkad was full of strange noises, and she thought no more about it until she heard it again, at dawn. It was louder this time and seemed to be coming from inside the building.

Her door handle turned; the door was unlocked. The noise was louder outside and it was coming from Maigraith's room. It sounded as if she were crying!

Aviel's scalp prickled. The potion must have failed. But the notion that Maigraith was capable of tears was so astounding that Aviel had to know what the matter was. She opened the door of the salon and looked in.

Maigraith, barefoot and in a nightgown, was seated at a small table, the mirror propped against the wall, mechanically brushing her brown hair, and sobbing.

Brown hair?

'Maigraith?' Aviel whispered.

She rose and turned in one lithe movement. Maigraith looked wan, as if she had spent the night in great pain – but her face was a young face, the skin smooth, the age spots, wrinkles and sagging gone, and the droop at the end of her nose. Her arms were slender, the muscles smooth and sleek. Her bosom was fuller, her teeth whiter, and with her back straight and her shoulders squared she was a couple of inches taller.

She wiped her eyes. Some people look wretched when they cry but Maigraith was not one of them; it only enhanced her austere beauty.

'It's working,' she said.

'Was it very painful?'

'And still is.' Maigraith pressed her hands to her belly. 'And,' her face lit up, 'I think I'm getting my period! I haven't had one for a hundred and eighty years.'

'I wish you joy of it.' Aviel's periods were painful and messy and lasted a long time, and she rather thought hers was coming too. 'Are – are you going to kill me now?'

'When you've just given me the greatest gift of my existence? Of course not.'

Had she changed her mind, or had she been toying with Aviel all along? Perhaps Maigraith did not know herself.

Aviel's knees went weak; she could not take it in. 'Then ... I'm going back to bed.'

# 9

# NONE OF THEM WILL COME BACK

W e have to deal with Xervish Flydd,' said Durthix.

'He hasn't had a victory since he took the thapter a month ago,' said the magiz. 'And we turned it back on him in minutes.'

'After which he escaped assassination, then went within a minute of snatching Rulke, Tiaan and the construct. If he had –'

Durthix frowned at Skald, who did not need reminding. He ached to remedy the blemish on his reputation.

'Flydd's been all over the place lately, trying to rally his allies,' said Durthix, 'and he recently visited Nennifer. I think he's got a new plan, and he's heading to Thurkad now.'

'What for?' said Dagog.

'We don't know, but he'll arrive in four or five hours. It's our chance to take him, his key allies and the sky galleon, and eliminate the threat for good.'

'You'll need someone reliable; someone who can react instantly to neutralise whatever cunning trick Flydd pulls next.'

'I have just the man,' said Durthix, looking at Skald.

Dagog choked. 'He doesn't have the strength. He nearly destroyed his inner organs last time.'

'Lirriam healed him – enough to lead, if not to personally engage in combat.'

'You're planning to let a man lead who can't actually fight?' Dagog said incredulously.

'He's not going up against an army.' Durthix turned around. 'Skald, state what you need and it will be supplied –'

'Within reason,' said Dagog.

'Flydd and his allies must be taken or killed. What do you need to make absolutely sure of them, and capture the sky galleon, Skald? There cannot be the tiniest chance of anyone escaping.'

Skald thought for a moment. 'I want three gates, opening in a triangle around the sky galleon the moment it lands in Thurkad, as close as is consistent with safety.'

'*Three* gates?' cried the magiz. 'Durthix, his hunger for power knows no bounds. How can I get my urgent work done if he's draining half of what I have?'

Durthix held up a hand. 'Skald delivered us power undreamed of, and once Flydd is gone you can have it all.'

Skald took a deep breath and continued. 'Three squads, each of twenty soldiers, plus ten of the new air-scooters, a flight tracker, three farspeakers, a field blocker – and two sus-magizes.'

'How can you possibly need all that?' said Dagog.

'Justify the request,' said Durthix.

'The three squads –' began Skald.

'I understand the need for soldiers.'

'None of them will come back,' gritted the magiz. 'Skald always survives – and I acknowledge his courage and determination – but none of his troops have returned from his previous missions.'

'The prize outweighs the cost.'

'It takes seventeen years to replace a soldier and we've already suffered twice the anticipated casualties. How many more will you let him lose?'

'I count the loss of every man and woman,' said Durthix, 'but even if we lose all sixty troops, it'll be worth it to eliminate Flydd.'

'I need ten of the new air-scooters,' said Skald, 'because there's nothing like them in the world, and Flydd can't have seen them before.'

'We only have twelve and I need them here,' said Dagog.

'They're faster than a galloping horse, almost as manoeuvrable as a warrior on foot, and at need they can rise above arrow or javelard height, then attack with impunity.'

'I know their capabilities!' snapped Durthix. 'But there's considerable danger sending field-powered devices through a gate.'

'I believe it's been solved, High Commander.'

Durthix turned to Dagog.

'It's not completely safe,' Dagog said. 'We might lose one in ten.'

'I can let you have five air-scooters, Captain,' said Durthix. 'What else? Farspeakers? You may have two. No flight tracker – we need it here. And a field blocker, you said?'

'A last resort in case Flydd makes a run for it, High Commander.'

'It's *our* secret weapon,' said Dagog. 'And we only have the one.'

Durthix frowned. 'I don't want to risk it.'

'I'll make sure it comes back,' said Skald. 'I'll put it before my own life.'

'No, you won't. You will *direct* the attack but you won't put yourself in danger – I can't lose my Superintendent of Works at this late stage.'

'You're forbidding me to lead my troops in the attack?' cried Skald.

'I am.'

Skald crushed down the shame. The order had been given and he must obey. 'I'll get ready, High Commander.'

'Make damned sure you replay my trust, Captain.'

Skald was going to. Flydd would be outnumbered and outclassed. No heroics would be needed this time, just good, risk-free captaincy.

Flydd and his allies were as good as dead.

# 10

# THE ROOF'S GOING TO FALL IN

W hen Aviel roused in the mid-morning the manacles were gone, her pack sat beside the bed and yesterday's clothes had been washed and folded. Did this mean all was forgiven?

Only a fool would think so. Maigraith never had a generous impulse, nor a kind one. Everything she did was calculated.

But there was no sign of her, and for the moment all Aviel's work was done. She dressed, ate a leisurely breakfast and went out onto the dusty avenue. The sun was shining and a warm wind blew from the north. It was going to be a hot day. A good day to have nothing to do, and she was going to make the most of it – in case it was her last.

She strolled down the empty avenue to a bridge over the river. Built long before the sea level fell and left the great port city stranded miles inland, it was a huge affair with seven arches of dark brown stone. The river, a muddy stream she could have tossed a pebble across, meandered under the central arch.

Aviel was looking down at the water when she heard a familiar humming sound, growing to a howl, and the sky galleon came hurtling across the sky. It was scratched and battered and crumpled at the bow, and twisted strips of brass were hanging off. Someone must have recognised her, because it banked sharply and set down so hard in the centre of the bridge that sparks flew out to either side from the keel.

'What are you doing out here, you little idiot?' bellowed Flydd.

Aviel's good mood vanished. She was so sick of people ordering her about. 'Why shouldn't I be out here?'

'There's a war on. Get in! Come on, come on!'

She hobbled to the sky galleon and began to climb the ladder. It was hard on her ankle and she was struggling up the rungs when a short, stocky man she had not seen before caught her under the arms and heaved her in.

The moment she was aboard, the sky galleon lifted and raced away. Flydd was up the back, talking to a beautiful, dark-skinned young woman. The pilot was also dark, but small. A squad of soldiers stood at the stern, looking out.

'I'm Nish,' said the stocky man. 'You Aviel?'

'Yes.' She ducked her head, always shy with strangers.

'The old bastard's in a particularly bad mood today.'

'I heard that!' Flydd yelled.

'Nothing's gone right this morning – and precious little in the last month.' Nish grinned. 'But from now on it's going to be better.'

She smiled back.

The sky galleon crash-landed on the roof above Aviel's workshop, shaking the building and knocking a section of wall over the side.

'Get packed!' yelled Flydd.

'My pack is packed,' said Aviel.

He picked up a cubic box with green crystals set in its four corners and a glass lens in the middle, peered into the lens, started, and put the box down. 'Hurry, damn you!'

'What do you want me to do?'

'Pack your most important scent potion gear!' he said as though she was an idiot. 'Five minutes! Nish, help her! Where the blazes is Maigraith?'

'I haven't seen her in hours,' said Aviel.

'Go, go!'

She scrambled down to her room, grabbed her pack and the last book of Flydd's *Histories* from her bedside, then raced up to her workshop. She pointed to items on the bench: brazier, mortar and pestle, a selection of flasks, the small glass still, retorts and crucibles and various other items. 'Pack those.'

Nish began to pack them. Apart from her own three books, which were in her pack, her most vital resource was her library of scent phials, in their little wooden racks. There were no gaps now – Maigraith had put back the phials she had previously taken. Why would she do that? Because she'd deduced that Aviel was incapable of harming her?

Aviel buckled on the belt containing her most important scents in individual loops, slipped the six racks into their little padded box and fastened the catch. Nish was putting her equipment in a crate and a large box. She packed her spoons and spatulas, spare tubes and phials and little bottles, her waxes and oils, into another box.

'What's happening?' she said to Nish.

He laid the glass still in the crate without any padding. 'No, not like that!' She wrapped a blanket around it, protectively, and packed the sides and top so it would not move in transit.

'Flydd thinks we're about to be attacked,' said Nish.

'To take Maigraith?'

Nish shrugged. 'Go, I'll bring these.' He put the lid on the crate and began to fasten a strap around it.

Aviel scrambled up to the roof and was passing her scent phial box up to Karan, who was further up the ladder and looked like death, when, with a ground-shaking peal of thunder, a gate opened on a flat roof a couple of hundred yards away and a squad of twenty Merdrun troops stormed through.

*Boom!* Another gate opened on the street to their left, a quarter of a mile off. Then *boom*, a third gate on another rooftop to the west.

'Why three gates?' said Aviel.

A shadow passed across Karan's face. 'They nearly assassinated Flydd a while back. They're making sure this time.'

'Are you all right?'

'The magiz caught Sulien and Jassika the day before yesterday. Took them to Skyrock. I'm terrified.'

Arrows hissed overhead but Karan did not move. She did not seem to have noticed the danger. Aviel ducked instinctively and Karan lost her grip on the box. Aviel made a desperate grab for it, missed, it landed on a corner on the roof, the catch burst open and scent phials went everywhere.

'Leave them!' roared Flydd, ducking out of sight as a flight of arrows slammed into the side of the sky galleon. 'Get to cover.'

It would take the best part of a year to replace all those scents and some could never be replaced, the raw ingredients being so rare. Aviel hunched over and jammed the phials into their racks.

Nish appeared at the top of the roof stair, carrying the crate. He slid it across the flat roof and ran down for the boxes. Aviel stuffed the last phial into her little box – five had broken – and made sure the catch was secure this time.

She was about to carry it up when Flydd bellowed, 'Get clear!'

Karan raced up the ladder. Aviel backed out of the way. The sky galleon took off with a lurch that shook down more of the broken side wall, and turned towards the westerly gate.

The third squad had come through on the roof to the west, and the sky galleon was heading right towards them. Was Flydd mad? Arrows arced towards it, most glancing off the metal hull.

He swerved at the last minute and headed for a rusty iron staircase running down the outside of the building. Aviel scurried to the wall, bent low, and looked over.

Seven Merdrun were halfway down the staircase. The side of the sky galleon struck it hard, squashing it against the wall and hurling soldiers off.

'He was hoping to tear it right away,' said Nish, 'to keep them on the roof. But they can still get down.'

Three soldiers got up. Two ran towards Aviel's building and the third hobbled after them. The sky galleon curved around, heading towards the second gate. It was gone now but another squad of twenty was coming down the middle of the street, led by a tall, muscular officer she recognised at once, because he greatly resembled Rulke. Chills ran down Aviel's back. Rumour said that Skald was unstoppable.

A huge, sad-eyed man heaved a small barrel over the side of the sky galleon from eighty feet up. It smashed on the cobblestoned avenue, liquid went everywhere, then dark red flames exploded from one side of the avenue to the other.

Skald's squad raced down an alley and disappeared.

'That'll only gain us a minute,' said Nish, coming up with the boxes. 'Stay back, Flydd's coming in.'

The sky galleon hit the roof hard and the huge man leapt over the side, carrying another barrel. He smashed the bung in and ran around the perimeter of the roof, running out a thick, tarry oil. Flydd leaned over the rail and set it alight with a blast from his staff. Thick black smoke belched up, concealing the roof and the sky galleon.

'They can still shoot through it,' said Nish, coughing.

'Firing blind,' said Flydd, coming down onto the roof.

'If I'm hit, I die just as hard.'

'But not as often,' Flydd retorted. 'Finished down there?'

'Yes. I didn't see any trace of Maigraith.'

Flydd cursed. 'She'll have to fend for herself.' He poured the last of the oil down the stairs, tossed the barrel down as well, and fire-blasted the black oil, which caught alight.

'Thurkad's dry as tinder,' said Nish. 'You could burn the whole place down.'

'No bloody loss. Get the gear in. That won't hold them long.'

Arrows were still hissing through the black smoke and clanging off the sides of the sky galleon, but they had to risk it. The huge man carried Aviel's boxes up and Nish heaved the crate aboard, *crash*.

'Sorry,' he said.

Aviel prayed it wasn't her irreplaceable still.

Skald appeared on a nearby rooftop, his arms extended. The closed western gate exploded open again and a long, canoe-shaped object shot from it.

'What the blazes is that?' said Nish.

'Air-scooter!' said Flydd. 'Spies said they've been making them at one of our old manufactories.'

A pair of Merdrun sat astride, the female pilot holding a cross-tipped control lever and the rear man a small globular device with spines sticking out of it.

As Aviel hauled herself up the ladder into the sky galleon the smoke barrier along the walls was thinning, though flames from below came part-way up the stairs. The mechanism of the sky galleon was making a low, whining sound and it was shuddering fitfully, but it would only lift an inch. Flydd was swearing.

'What is it *now*?' said Karan.

'That spiny object must be a field-blocker – I can't draw enough power to lift us.'

'What about the storage crystals?'

'Drained on the way here.'

'What are you going to do?' said Aviel.

'How the hell would I know?' he snarled.

She looked over the side. Flames and smoke were gushing from the windows of the building.

Nish ran from the bow to the stern, looked down, and answered her unasked question. 'Reckon we've only got minutes before the roof collapses.'

Considering that would plunge them into an inferno from which there could be no escape, he was unnaturally calm. They all were, even Karan.

Aviel went to her. 'I was really worried about you. There's been no news for weeks and weeks.'

'But Flydd's spoken to Maigraith regularly,' said Karan.

'She never tells me anything.'

The flat roof shuddered and cracked from one side to the other. Skald roared orders; another flight of arrows crashed against the sides and superstructure of the sky galleon.

Aviel was bracing herself for the worst when the second gate reopened away to their left, followed by the third behind them, and two air-scooters hurtled from one gate and one from the other. The second rider of each air-scooter was armed with a crossbow.

'Merdrun learn fast,' said Flydd. 'They haven't used archers much before.'

'Doesn't take much skill to use a crossbow,' said Nish.

'Do something about that field blocker, or we're all dead.'

Nish ran to the loaded javelard at the bow, swung it around towards the first of the air-scooters, aimed and fired. The heavy javelard spear, eight feet long and an inch through its metal shaft, hissed through the air into the pilot's middle, lifting her off her seat and carrying her through the air on a gentle arc for many yards.

The pilotless air-scooter kept flying towards a grey, stone building. Nish reloaded the javelard and was aiming at the pilot of the second air-scooter when something collapsed below them. The roof shook and flames roared up out of the stairwell, twenty feet high.

Nish, who had a better view than anyone else, bellowed at Flydd who, clearly, could not hear him.

'Nish said *Go!*' shrilled Aviel. 'Roof's going to fall in.'

Flydd working the controls furiously but the sky galleon wasn't lifting. Flying embers were now raining down on the half-ruined buildings all around, starting new fires.

Aviel crouched at the side, peering over. The soldier with the spiny field blocker was still using it as the pilotless air-scooter arced towards one of the massive columns at the front of the building. A second before impact he tried to jump off, but his left boot caught in the saddle. He was dangling upside-down, trying to free himself, when the air-scooter smashed into the column, thirty feet up, crumpled at the front and fell, crushing him beneath it. He jerked for a few seconds and went still.

The roof cracked under the sky galleon and the quarter that included the stairs fell in. The flames belched higher; they were coming up on all sides now. The mechanism of the sky galleon moaned. The roof shuddered, cracked across and across, and walls of flames belched up all around them, the heat scorching Aviel's face and frizzing her fine hair. She ducked under the bow, unable to breathe. They were going to be burned to death.

'Fly, damn you!' said Flydd.

As the roof collapsed, the mechanisms howled and the sky galleon hurtled upwards. The pilot headed down the main avenue but the mechanism died again and they hit so hard that cobblestones were hurled like cannonballs against the buildings to either side.

'Nish, that blocker's still working,' Flydd yelled.

They were in desperate straits now. Skald appeared on a different roof, directing his squads, which were coming from three directions. They were advancing through the ever-thickening smoke and the sky galleon did not have enough power to lift.

Flydd ran to the bow, spoke urgently to Nish and raced back to Aviel. 'They'll storm the sides once they wear us down a bit. Any scent potion you can blend to stop a soldier or two?'

'You're joking.'

'Does this look like a joking situation?'

'Um ... let me think.'

'Be quick.'

Aviel ran desperately through the possibilities. Scent potions were seldom used for self-defence, since few acted quickly enough, and the smallest breeze could render them useless or, worse, turn them back on the user. To be useful, such a scent potion had to be incapacitating within seconds in small dosages, which also meant it had to be used with exquisite care. But how would that be possible in the chaos of an attack from all sides, by a superior force?

Radizer's *Grimoire* listed several that might work. Aviel mentally ran through the fast-acting, debilitating potions, rejecting the ones that took a long time to blend or required scents she did not have.

'The Paralysis Stench might do it,' she said. 'It's quick-acting, and –'

'Can you blend it in a couple of minutes?' said Flydd.

'It'll take at least five.'

'In five minutes we'll all be dead. Make it three.'

No, pressure, then! 'If I get it wrong,' she said, 'the only person it'll stop is me – or everyone on the sky galleon.'

But Flydd had turned away. In hope, or disgust? She could not tell.

She ran under the javelard platform at the bow, hardly limping at all. It felt good to be part of a team, fighting for their lives, and on the side of light rather than darkness. But how could she possibly do it in time? The Paralysis Stench wasn't a difficult potion, though in normal circumstances it would take her fifteen minutes to blend it, double-checking as she went.

Aviel opened her box of phials and swore an oath she'd learned from her reprobate father, Gybb. After the phials had spilled, there had not been time to repack them in order. She tipped them into a small depression under the bow, where they wouldn't roll away, and sorted through them frantically, putting the ones she needed to one side.

Arrows whistled overhead and clanged off the flaring bow shields and the sides of the cabin. Flydd was rifling through a crate. He collected a dozen little round black objects, handling them gingerly, put them in a scarf which he whirled around in the air like a sling, and let them fly. They soared high in the air, landed in front of the leading squad and bounced into their ranks. There were a series of small explosions – no, they burst *inwards*, not out – and everything for a couple of feet around each one was sucked into nothingness.

He hurled an object like a fat yellow cigar at Skald. It ignited in the air, gushing bright yellow flame for a couple of yards out of each end. Skald blasted it aside and it fell into an alley, which was soon full of choking white fumes.

Flydd's troops were firing at Skald but none of their bolts hit him; he must be shielded in some way. Flydd ran across the deck on tiptoes, a small device hanging from a chain around his neck bouncing against his chest.

He raised his arms, his staff upthrust in his left hand, and let out a great cry. The sky went dark; cables of light writhed and crackled across it, then an almost transparent dome formed around the sky galleon.

'Shield device,' said Nish. 'He picked it up in Nennifer. Among other things.'

Aviel came to her feet for a few seconds to check on the enemy. The walls of the burning building, her home and workshop for more than six weeks, were collapsing in on the fire, sending torrents of sparks coiling upwards like miniature whirlwinds.

The line of burning oil across the street was dying down, no barrier anymore, but behind the sky galleon more buildings were ablaze, and a breeze was driving sparks and embers onto the adjacent blocks of the empty city. Nish's prediction was coming true.

He swung his javelard around, aimed at Skald, and fired. At the same instant, Skald seemed to blur, then reappeared three feet away as the javelard spear howled through the spot where his chest had been. It would have spitted him.

'Bastard!' muttered Nish. 'No point wasting them on him.' He aimed at another target, the javelard snapped again and, distantly, someone screamed.

The enemy squads were slowly advancing, still directed by Skald. They would reach Flydd's shield in a few minutes, and once the sus-magiz broke it they would swarm over the sides and it would be over. Flydd's small squad of guards could not possibly hold them out.

Aviel had all but one of the scents and reeks she needed. Where was 74, the earthy smell from the bottom of a compost heap? Damn – it was one of the five phials that had broken, and she could not make the Paralysis Stench without it. What else could she blend from those listed in Radizer's *Grimoire*? Think, think!

The only one she could remember was the Mustard Miasma. It required fourteen different scents and reeks, some of them nose-burningly pungent, one being hot mustard and another the acrid emissions from a wagon load of horse dung. Did she have them all? Yes, she did.

Outside her tiny shelter the world had gone mad. Air-scooters raced overhead, shooting with crossbows and swerving violently to avoid return fire. The sky, which kept turning dark and light, was split by writhing, incandescent bolts, so bright that it was painful to look at them. Flydd's shield deflected most of the attacks but an occasional spear or arrow came through.

Maelys stumbled in next to Aviel, coughing. She wiped her watering eyes on her forearm, aimed a crossbow at the pilot of an approaching air-scooter, and fired. He swerved as if he had known she was aiming at him and disappeared below the level of the gunwale. Evidently Flydd's shield allowed the defenders to fire out. Aviel could not imagine how that worked.

Maelys wound the crank, loaded another bolt and grinned at Aviel, her teeth startlingly white in her smoke-grimed face. Aviel smiled back. She supposed she must look the same.

'How's it going?' Maelys squeezed a round, shiny metal object that hung on a chain around her neck.

'A few phials broke. Making do.'

'Me too.' Maelys fired again.

Aviel set out the fourteen phials she needed, in order, and began to blend the scents from memory.

Maelys wrinkled her nose. 'How can you do that?'

Aviel shrugged. 'It's … just what I do. Though I'd rather be a perfumer.'

'You'll be a great one – when the war's over.'

Nothing to say to that.

The air-scooter reappeared, and its archer was aiming at Maelys from point-blank range. Aviel let out a little cry – Maelys was going to be shot. But she snatched at the metal object around her neck and he missed by a couple of feet, the bolt embedding itself in the side.

'What just happened?' said Aviel.

'My taphloid protects me. To a point,' said Maelys, which explained nothing.

Flydd came racing up. 'Ready, Aviel?'

'Two minutes more. But … they'll have to be close.'

He laughed hollowly. 'They'll be close all right.'

# 11

## AND IT'LL INCAPACITATE A GROWN MAN?

Flydd ran to the side, where Karan was crouched, and whispered in her ear.

'A psychic sending?' she said. 'On *Skald*?'

'You're good at that kind of thing, I hear.'

'Not good enough to take on a sus-magiz. What if he uses it to drink my life?'

'He couldn't ... at least, not from so far away.'

'How do you know?'

Aviel, listening while she worked furiously, did not think Flydd did know. But she could tell he was desperate.

'Skald's tightening the noose, Karan,' he said. 'If you can't take him out of the attack for a few minutes, we're beaten.'

Karan was trembling. 'I can't.'

'You killed their magiz on Cinnabar,' said Flydd. 'And you took on the triplets, too.'

'And they nearly killed me.'

'They died, you lived, and it made you stronger. You can do this. You've got to.'

'What kind of a sending?'

'Attack the Merdrun's greatest fear. They have to be in control – something you know plenty about,' he added pointedly.

She thought for a few seconds. 'I'll try.'

Flydd ran back to the controls, bent low. Karan pressed her hands to the sides of her head, her face twisted as if concentrating hard. She stood upright, pointed at Skald and crouched again.

Silence fell. No fiery bolts crackled across the sky. Behind them, the fire had died down and there was a temporary respite from the swarms of arrows and bolts.

Then Aviel felt a hot pressure in her head and an awful, shuddering fear, worse than death itself – of helpless, grinding enslavement. It was a fear she had once known well, after her father had indentured her as a child worker at that disgusting tannery in Casyme. She would have been worked to death there within years.

Some distance away a man screamed, a horrible sound that went on and on.

'What was that?' she whispered.

'It's working,' said Maelys, her dark eyes huge and round.

Aviel peeped over the bow and Skald was on his knees on the rooftop, his arms wrapped around his head. 'How did Flydd know how to attack him?'

'The Merdrun *know* they're the superior race, and the thought of having no say over their lives or deaths terrifies them. Maybe Skald is more susceptible than most.'

Aviel knew about having no say about her life. She blended the fourth last, third last and then the second last scent, the acrid fumes from ripe horse dung, into her mixing bottle, shook it and took a careful sniff. The mixture had no smell at all. She put all but the last phial back in the box, closed the lid and latched it.

'Isn't that dangerous?' said Maelys. She was working her crossbow mechanically, as if she'd had years of practice. Cranking the wire bowstring back, setting a bolt in the groove, aiming and firing, again and again.

'What?'

'Sniffing the scent potion.'

Maelys' last bolt found its target, the archer on the rear of an air-scooter racing towards them. As it passed overhead he went off backwards and landed draped over the gunwale, blood pouring from his mouth. Nish scurried forwards, crouched low, and shoved him out. His blood continued to run down the side.

Aviel looked away. A living soldier, possibly a good man for all that he was an enemy, had been robbed of life in a moment. She had seen people killed before, all too many of them, but each death came as a shock. And a reminder that her own life might be taken any minute.

'In most cases the scent potion only comes together when the final scent is blended in. Right now it smells of nothing much at all.'

'What if the first lot of scents make a different potion?'

It was a risk that had never occurred to Aviel. 'I suppose ... the method would warn about it ...'

She hadn't seen any such warnings in the grimoire, though Radizer might not have written down dangers obvious to himself. Aviel hesitated, then tried to dismiss it. She did not have time for doubt.

She put five drops of the final ingredient, the eye-wateringly pungent odour of the scorpion radish, into her mixing bottle, capped it carefully, whirled it one way and then the other and then, holding the cap on, inverted it three times.

'Any way to test that you've got it right?' said Maelys.

'Only on the enemy.'

Aviel put the bottle in her pocket, stood up and had a hasty look around. The street was littered with the bodies of enemy soldiers and thick with drifting smoke. None of the gates were visible. It must cost too much power to keep them open. But the field blocker was still working because the sky galleon could not move.

Behind them the flames roared ever higher. Fortunately, the wind was driving the fire away. How quickly Thurkad was burning. Nothing could stop it now.

One sus-magiz lay dead in the middle of the street. She could not see the other one. Only two air-scooters were still flying. The other two were down, though one lay on its side in the middle of the street and did not appear to be badly damaged.

The beautiful young woman Flydd had been talking to earlier crept out of a narrow alley, ran to the air-scooter, heaved it upright and took off. She flew after the other air-scooter and came at it from behind. In the smoky gloom its riders must have thought she was one of them, for they did not look around as she approached. The tip of her air-scooter nudged past the rear rider, she came level with him, caught his right leg and tipped him off.

The pilot drew a sword and hacked at her so violently that he nearly went off the saddle. She ducked, then slammed the nose of her air-scooter into his leg, crushing it. He hacked again. She spun her air-scooter in its own length and the rear of it swept him off. His air-scooter continued down the street and slammed into a building at the end.

Skald was still on his knees, but his squads were just outside Flydd's protective shield now, and it was wavering. Aviel did not think it was going to last much longer. Maybe the field blocker was affecting it too.

She scurried to Flydd, who was in the cabin, working on some complicated device. 'It's ready,' she said, holding up the small bottle.

It only contained a couple of teaspoons of scent potion. He looked at it, then at her, and nodded. *He trusts me to get it right*, she thought. A warming moment in a dark day.

'What is it?'

'Mustard Oil Miasma.'

'And it'll incapacitate a grown man?'

'Yes.'

'How long does it take to work?'

'Grimoire says a couple of seconds.'

'A soldier can do a lot in two seconds. Run twenty yards. Kill a couple of people.'

'I don't know any potion that's quicker,' she said in a small voice.

'It wasn't a criticism.'

'How am I supposed to use it? If I fling the scent potion at them, the drops might only hit one ... or none ... And I'd have to be really close ...'

And a second later the closest soldier would hack her in half. No escaping it. Even if the Mustard Oil Miasma worked perfectly, it wouldn't act quickly enough to save her.

'I brought this from Nennifer. Just in case.'

Flydd handed her a short, fat tube, bulging in the middle, with a nozzle at one end and an orange handle at the other.

'What is it?'

'A magical blaster – ' fire, water, ice, grit – depending what you put in it. Lift the cap on the tube, like this, and put the scent potion in the hole. Make damned sure you close the cap, otherwise it'll blast up into your face.'

Aviel used an eyedropper so none of the Mustard Oil Miasma spilled, and pushed the cap down until it clicked.

'When the enemy start coming over the side – they'll attack together – point the blaster at them and pull this little black lever. Let it go as soon as you've blasted all the soldiers, otherwise you'll have none for the other two squads.'

'All ... right,' said Aviel.

She did not have to worry about the other two squads. Within seconds of spraying scent potion on the first squad, she would be dead. She wanted to run and hide like the little mouse Maigraith had made her out to be, but Flydd was relying on her. Everyone's lives relied on her incapacitating the first squad.

He looked up, and blanched. 'Persia, look out!' He ran towards the bow, waving his arms.

The beautiful woman, who must be Persia bel Soon, was flying her captured craft back, but a fifth air-scooter had inched up from behind a ruined building and was coming after her. She did not realise it was there.

'Persia, behind you!' Aviel screamed, but the din had resumed and Persia did not hear.

Karan was also yelling. Persia was gliding down towards the front deck of the sky galleon. The other air-scooter was only fifty feet behind her, point-blank range to any competent archer. The pilot leaned to the right to give his archer a clear shot and, as Persia slowed to set the air-scooter down on the deck, he shot her in the back.

Blood blossomed in the middle of her chest and she toppled and fell. She must have been struck through the heart but could not have known anything about it – she was dead before she hit the deck. Nish, who was back at the javelard, let out a cry of anguish and stumbled down to her.

He knelt beside her for a moment, kissed her forehead, then stalked back to the javelard, loaded a spear and heaved the arming lever until the metal cable was drum-taut. He swung the javelard around towards the last air-scooter.

The cable made a snapping noise and the heavy spear, moving too fast to see, struck the air-scooter amidships and passed straight through it. Fire formed inside it and became a conflagration that erupted out in all directions, consuming the two riders and the broken flier as they fell.

Nish lowered his head onto the javelard, and wept.

Flydd bent over Persia, brushed the hair back from her forehead, then picked her up in his arms. She was bigger than he was and it must have been an effort, though he showed no sign of it. His face racked with grief, he carried her inside and laid her down next to four other bodies, three men and another woman.

Aviel looked down at the device he had given her, trying to remember what it was for. Her mind felt as though it had been wiped clean. There had not been time to introduce her to Persia or anyone else on the sky galleon, and already four of Flydd's guards were dead. The deck was red with their blood.

Everyone on the sky galleon was exhausted, and the three squads of Merdrun were slowly advancing. They were in no hurry.

Flydd reappeared, his gaunt face racked, and called Maelys and Nish down. 'I don't have the strength to hold the shield much longer. It's already letting too many missiles through.' He glanced at the bodies. 'The moment it goes down the Merdrun will storm us and I've only got one hope left – but for it to work I need time.'

'What do you want us to do?' said Nish.

'Everyone who can use a crossbow, keep firing as long as your bolts last. Nish, do the same with the javelard. How many spears have you got?'

'Only five.'

'Use four of them, then keep going with your crossbow. I need another five minutes, at least.' He waved a crossbow at Aviel. 'Ever used one of these?'

'No.' And she never wanted to.

He frowned. 'All right. The moment they come over the side, blast them with your scent potion and run down to me. I may need an extra pair of hands. Keep your heads down, everyone. And keep a few missiles for the end ... whatever that may be.'

They ran back to their positions. Aviel crouched behind the bow shields, knowing nowhere was safe from a stray spear or arrow or bolt, but when they attacked she had to be ready. She thought there was enough scent potion for three or four sprays with the blaster, though unless she was within spitting distance of the enemy the potion would be wasted.

Spitting distance is right, she thought grimly. As soon as I blast them, they'll spit me.

The largest force was creeping down the street towards the bow of the sky galleon. The attack would probably be concentrated near the front, where the scalloped shields were lowest. They were highest at the stern, around the catapult; it was the least likely place to attack.

Karan ran down the left side of the sky galleon, pouring oil onto the brass gunwale, and back up the other side. As she went past Aviel she said, 'Every little helps.'

Not enough!

Aviel planned to wait in the shelter of the bow until the first squad was scrambling over the side, then run past, blasting the scent potion into their faces. If she survived – no, there was no point thinking further ahead.

*Boom!*

Further up the street a gate had reopened. It was a brilliant white with jags of yellow lightning radiating out from it, and it was surrounded by a swarm of ball lightnings, the glowing spheres whirling and dancing and crackling, colliding with one another and combining and breaking apart again. Shadows waited within the gate. Were they reinforcements?

The shield went down. 'Go!' Skald roared. He had recovered from Karan's psychic sending.

The leading squad of Merdrun stormed the sky galleon on the left side as if it was a race they were determined to win, the archers firing and reloading as they ran. The other two squads were not far away. There was little answering fire from the sky galleon now; they were saving their bolts. Nish still had his crossbow, and one javelard spear left. What, or who, was Flydd keeping it for?

Aviel rose, trembling all over, and raised the blaster. Twenty seconds. The shadows inside the gate had not moved. What were they waiting for? She glanced at Flydd, who gave her an anxious thumb up. Was he afraid she would let him down? Would she?

She felt an overwhelming urge to run and hide. She was not designed for this, and even if the scent potion worked, she would be slow at running along in front of the attackers. Why hadn't he given the job to someone who could do it properly?

Aviel's heart was beating so fast that it was painful. She could not do this. But she had to. It was impossible to overcome her terror. She tried to console herself with the thought that this would make up for her other failures and she would die without a stain on her conscience.

The consolation failed. She was choking with terror. Shaking wildly. Almost wetting herself.

Ten seconds. Five. The first squad, twelve soldiers, closed in on the left front side of the sky galleon and each attacker held a rope with a grappling hook. It was fifteen feet from the ground to the lowest point of the gunwales and they would swarm up so as to reach the top at the same time.

As each soldier let go of his or her rope to clamber over, there would be a second when both hands would be occupied. And if she timed her attack perfectly ...

No, it would not disable them quickly enough, and the moment the first soldier's feet hit the deck he or she would cut Aviel down. This was the bravest thing she had ever been asked to do, and she knew, at the moment she stepped forwards, that she was going to be killed.

'The shield's down; we've got them,' said Skald, wiping the sweat off his face. 'It'll be over within the minute.'

The attack should have been easy. With the blocker preventing the sky galleon from moving, and Flydd from drawing much power from the field, Skald's troops should have overwhelmed their outnumbered enemy in minutes.

But Flydd kept pulling off one trick after another – the dome shield that had allowed his people to fire out but had blocked almost all incoming missiles, the little black imploding devices that had drawn half a dozen of his troops into nothingness, then the overwhelming psychic sending that could only have come from Karan. But it had not been the Merdrun's greatest fear that had done for Skald, bad though the terror of perpetual imprisonment had been.

It had been the small, personal attack she had slipped into her sending at the end. The message that, deep down, he was a coward, and one day he was going to break and run just as his father had. It had paralysed Skald and, despite all his heroics in the past, it was still undermining his confidence and making him question his judgement.

But they had nothing left now. Flydd was down to half a dozen guards and, judging by how seldom they returned fire, they must be almost out of bolts and spears.

How Skald was going to enjoy taking Flydd, Karan, Nish and Maelys back to Skyrock.

The grappling hooks came over the side, were heaved back and latched on. A second later, even quicker than Aviel had expected, helmeted heads appeared. Should she blast them? No, not yet!

Fire roared past Aviel, setting the oil alight. Flydd pointed his staff to a dozen places until fire burned the length of the gunwale, but there wasn't enough oil, or enough fire, to deter the attackers.

It had slowed them a little, though. One soldier had fallen backwards, flames licking around his fingers. Another was trying to beat the flames out, and two more were heaving their hooks sideways to reach a point where there was no fire. The attacking line was ragged now.

Terror overwhelmed her – they were far bigger and faster. They were scrambling up. Two held blades in their teeth and they were preparing to spring.

'Now, Aviel!' Flydd bellowed.

She aimed her weapon at the closest soldier's face, pulled the lever, ran and swept the mouth of the blaster along the line of attackers, spraying a fine mist of Mustard Oil Miasma at them. She scrambled backwards.

The three lowest soldiers disappeared below the side but the other eight hit the deck together, raising their blades. A shift in the breeze carried a trace of scent potion back at Aviel and it went up her nose, a thousand times worse than hot mustard. She gasped, struggling to breathe, her eyes stinging, stumbled backwards and fell. She braced herself for a sideways hack that would cut her in two. She would not see it coming.

'Clech!' yelled Flydd.

The huge man with the lantern jaw heaved her effortlessly out of the way. Aviel wiped her eyes with her sleeve. The leading soldier stopped dead, six feet from her. He was choking, his eyes flooding, his nose flowing yellow muck so copiously that he could not breathe. Most of the others were the same.

Clech waded into them like a berserker, swinging a gigantic sword. He beheaded the leading soldier, hacked another two Merdrun down with a single blow, skewered a fourth, then cut two more down where they stood.

He had just struck down the next man when the soldier at the end of the line rose from a crouch and thrust his blade in between Clech's ribs. He stiffened, turned and tried to reach him but was already dying, the blood flooding out of him.

'Aimee!' Clech whispered. He hit the deck and did not move again.

The soldier who had killed him had been a couple of feet behind the others and must have been shielded from the scent potion by the soldiers next to him. His eyes were watering and his nose was running, but he wasn't incapacitated, and he was looking right at Aviel.

He sprang. She screamed; there was nothing else she could do. He was within a backhanded swing of her when his head jerked sideways and he fell, a bolt through his skull. Nish had saved her with his last missile.

Aviel was too numbed by the violence, and the incomprehensibility of her survival, to move.

Nish leapt down and dragged her away. 'The next squad's coming. This time, blast them as soon as their heads appear over the side – and then, *don't just stand there.*'

As she reached the other side, grappling hooks latched on. The Merdrun were too close to see in, and she hoped they were ignorant of what had happened to the first squad. When their heads appeared, she stepped forwards and blasted the scent potion into their faces.

Most fell off, and Maelys and Nish heaved their ropes in. Three reached the deck, half blind and choking, and were dispatched.

Aviel hobbled to the bow, which the remainder of the Merdrun were climbing, and blasted the last of the scent potion at them from close range. A breeze drifted some towards her and her eyes flooded so copiously that she could barely see. None of them made it over the side.

But Flydd had said he needed a spare pair of hands. She tottered down through the litter of bodies to him, her nose streaming. Her knees were weak from shock and trauma, and the relief of still being alive.

'Good work,' he said absently. 'Hold this.'

It was a small round box with loops of cord and cloth-wound wires hanging out of the bottom, and a series of slots and crescent-shaped holes in the sides. He was prodding something inside one of the slots with the point of a knife.

She held the box in her left hand. She had to keep wiping her eyes with the sleeve.

'How long does your miasma last?' he said absently.

'Grimoire doesn't say.'

'Have a guess.'

'Five minutes.'

'Then I've only got another couple to get this contraption working.'

'What is it?' Aviel knew nothing about such things.

'An experimental device two scrutators put together in Nennifer decades ago, though at the time they didn't have the power to make it work. I'm hoping I can – assuming I can draw enough power past the blocker to use it. Or –'

Flydd looked at her, assessingly, but did not go on. Aviel did not ask; she did not want to know.

Up the front, Nish and one of Flydd's hired guards were going from one helpless enemy soldier to another, putting them down and heaving their bodies out. She turned away. It was necessary work, because once the scent potion wore off they would attack again, but she did not need to see it.

They finished and climbed down to the avenue, where, she assumed, they were dispatching the rest of the soldiers disabled by her Mustard Oil Miasma. She also had a role in their deaths. Thirty-two of them. The stain on her soul was spreading.

The distant gate with the shadowy watchers inside it faded, then reappeared, closer.

'What's it doing?' said Aviel. 'Why don't they come to their troops' rescue?'

'Observers.' Flydd did not look up. 'Probably waiting for reinforcements.'

'Then we're doomed.'

He glanced at her. 'I had faith in *you*, Aviel.'

She flushed. 'But you don't know anything about me.'

'What do you think we talk about in the evenings? Karan and Wilm told me all about you.'

Aviel felt that she ought to reciprocate. 'I – I've read bits of your story.'

'Really?'

'Maigraith gave me one of the enemy's copies of your *Histories*. The final book. I used to read a chapter each night before bed, when I wasn't too tired. For inspiration.'

'I wonder where she got it,' said Flydd.

'She said she could get anything she wanted, in Thurkad.'

'I dare say she could.'

'Except get Rulke back from Lirriam. Maigraith hates her; she tried to kill her –'

'And?' said Flydd. He looked up at her, his fingers still working.

Aviel wished she had not said anything. But Flydd had trusted her, and he probably needed to know. 'I ... um, used one of the forbidden scent potions on her to stop her. It robbed her of her gift for a week.'

'Really?'

'I'm too soft,' cried Aviel. 'I only used half the dose, otherwise her gift would have been gone forever. I wish it was.'

'Why so?'

'She betrayed us. She let Skald into Alcifer; that's how he got the construct, and Rulke and Llian. I followed her and I saved her life when the roof fell in.'

'Did you indeed? And Maigraith's dramatic younging – were you involved in that too?'

'How did you know that? Have you seen her today?'

'Not in the flesh, but we spoke via one of her spy portals, and I saw her new face and figure.'

'I made her a rejuvenation scent potion,' Aviel said unhappily. 'To my shame.'

'Extraordinary! Well, it's a good thing you didn't destroy her gift. If we're to have a hope of beating the Merdrun, we're going to need it.' He looked up. 'And now they come. This had better work.'

## 12

## FINISH HIM!

Y ou need *more* troops?' roared Durthix, speaking via his leader's cube. 'Are you utterly incompetent, Skald?'

'I warned you,' Skald heard Dagog say, in the background.

Skald still did not understand how Flydd had beaten him. One minute, three squads totalling thirty-two soldiers had been storming the sky galleon to capture or kill everyone inside, and he had been sure their great enemy was about to die.

And the next minute Skald's troops were falling, some inside the sky galleon and the rest from their scaling ropes. From his vantage point he could not tell how they had been incapacitated, and as they lay there, helpless, the enemy had put every one of them to the sword.

Shameful deaths, and an even greater shame to their leader. Skald should have led them into battle, to victory or to death, but Durthix had forbidden it.

Skald pressed the speaking device to his lips. 'Flydd's down to half a dozen people, High Commander. They're almost out of missiles and I have the sky galleon trapped with the field blocker.'

'Then storm it and finish the job.'

'I – I'm the only one left.'

'Out of *sixty*?' said Durthix. 'Plus the air-scooters and sus-magizes?'

'Flydd had secret weapons, ones we hadn't seen before. But all I need is a dozen troops –'

'If we don't know what his secret weapons are, there's no way to defend against them. All right, Skald. I'll send a stronger force – and this time *you* will personally lead it in the attack. But if you fail me, I'm handing you over to the magiz.'

Skald's skin was crawling. How could he have fallen so far, so quickly, yet not understand how it had come about? 'I – I won't fail you, High Commander.'

Behind the sky galleon, driven by the hot northerly wind, smoke from the fires consuming the eastern half of Thurkad had risen thousands of feet high. The gate, barely visible now, was disgorging soldiers by the score. Two ranks each of forty stood to its right and another two to the left, and still they came. And everyone in the sky galleon was dead except Flydd, Nish, Maelys, Karan and Aviel, and the pilot.

'Why aren't they attacking?' said Aviel, still holding Flydd's experimental device while he adjusted a knurled wheel.

'Skald doesn't know how we defeated his last attack,' said Flydd. 'The Merdrun have suffered an important defeat, their first in over a month, and they've got to turn it around. Skald will take his time – he's got plenty.'

'How can you stay so calm?'

'I'm not calm on the inside. If my mad idea fails, we die.'

Aviel had nothing to say. Earlier, he had asked her to have faith, but faith required an underpinning of hope and, no matter where she looked, there was none. They had almost no power, few weapons, even fewer people – and no hope that anyone would come to their rescue, unless ...

'What about Maigraith? She must be able to do something.'

'Her strength isn't the kind that can take on an army. Besides, she's not here.'

'Where is she?'

'You made her young again. Where do you think she is?'

'Spying on Rulke while she waits for the potion to finish younging her,' Aviel said dully. 'And making plans to kill Lirriam.'

He checked the gate again. 'Two hundred soldiers, no doubt Durthix's very best. And without power, I'm stuck.'

'I wish I could help.'

'You've done all anyone could ask of you ...' He stood up, frowning at her as if weighing her up, but shook his head. 'No, it's out of the question.'

'If there's any little thing I can do, say so.' Why had she said that? Never volunteer!

He tapped crooked fingers on his knee. 'How's your ankle?'

'It's not too bad today. Why?'

'And your courage?'

Ulp! 'What for?'

'I can't spare anyone who can use weapons. I need them to defend the sky galleon.' He looked up the avenue, and back down at her. 'Remember that spiny metal ball the first air-scooter was carrying?'

'The field blocker?'

'It's still operating, keeping us here. Reckon you can sneak up there and find it?'

'Up towards the enemy?' she croaked.

'You're good at not being seen, and the smoke is getting thicker. If you creep along in the shadows on the eastern side of the avenue there won't be much risk.'

Where the Merdrun was concerned, any risk was too much. If they saw her, they would kill her. 'Um ... maybe. If I knew where to look.'

Flydd indicated the wreckage of the first air-scooter, perhaps a hundred and fifty yards away, where the avenue opened out at a five-way intersection with an ancient stone-lined well at the centre. 'Can't be far from there.'

'What do you want me to do with the field blocker? Break it?'

'No – it's liable to burn you to a cinder.'

'I could drop it down the well.'

'Might not stop it. Bring it here, if you can.' He scratched his scarred chin. 'I might find a use for it.'

'Is it dangerous to carry?'

'Depends how sensitive you are.'

'I was sensitive to the summon stone.'

'Don't touch it with your bare hands. Pick it up in this,' he took a grey canvas bag out of a compartment, 'and hold it away from you.' He turned back towards the gate, counted the enemy numbers again and grimaced. 'If you find it, run back here.'

'I can't really run.'

'Fast as you can, then. If you can't get back without being seen, hide. And if they attack the sky galleon, get into shelter. *Solid* shelter, with a strong roof over you.'

'What's going to happen?'

'I don't know. What I'm attempting hasn't been done before. Maybe ... maybe nothing. Go! No, wait!'

Relief flooded her. He did not want her to go after all. But he passed her a dark, baggy hat. 'Your hair's too obvious, even in all this smoke. Tuck it under this.'

Aviel did so. She climbed down the side of the sky galleon facing away from the coruscating gate and, keeping to the deepest shadows on the eastern side, crept past the heaps of bodies, soldiers she had helped to kill, and up towards the five-way intersection.

There were more enemy dead up here; they were everywhere.

It was clear to her that Flydd's plan, whatever it was, was hopeless. The enemy's numbers were too great and, once the attack began, the defenders on the sky galleon would run out of crossbow bolts in the first minute. Then, if they were lucky, they would be slaughtered. If unlucky, they would be taken alive.

Aviel was tempted to turn left at the first intersection, head away from the fires and try to lose herself in the mazy ruins of old Thurkad. But that was no choice either. The city was home to hundreds of renegades and predators, vicious brutes who might treat her even worse than the Merdrun would.

Besides, she had given her word and she had to go through with it. She crept on, grimly.

The wind had died down, but the smoke was thickening and now coming from the north as well. Some embers must have drifted that way and started more fires. If the wind increased again, they would be trapped between two walls of flame.

But at least it meant she was less likely to be seen. Aviel reached the intersection. The broad avenue continued ahead. The small army that had come from the gate was only two hundred yards away now, barely visible though the smoke. A dark alley ran off one of the intersecting roads, her best chance of a hiding place if she needed one.

The air-scooter she was looking for had slammed into one of the massive portico columns of Thurkad's former courthouse and broken in half, and a dark, oily fluid was oozing out of the rear section. The soldier who had operated the field blocker lay in the puddle. The pilot Nish had shot was thirty yards away.

The field blocker, she recalled, was roughly the size of a grapefruit and had many thick black spines protruding from it. If it was out in the open, she would have seen it. She checked under the wreckage, and, gingerly, under the oily corpse. Nothing. Aviel looked around. It might have rolled a distance on those spines.

She searched the gutters along this side of the avenue, but it wasn't there either. She wasn't game to creep across the empty avenue; that would be asking to be caught. She looked up and down. It would not have rolled far up the slope. Aviel went the other way and spotted a single spine in the gutter. The field blocker had gone partway down a stormwater drain and jammed there.

She was lifting it out when her fingers began to sting. She scooped it out with the canvas bag, slid into the shadows and was about to head back to the sky galleon when Skald shouted orders and the column of soldiers marched forwards. They would be level with her within the minute and she dared not scurry across the avenue to the alley. Even through the smoke they would see her before she got halfway.

Aviel slipped back to the broken air-scooter and hunched behind the widest part, next to the body, praying they did not see her as they charged past.

'Hold!' Skald bellowed. 'What's he up to?'

The Merdrun stopped as one, their nailed boots skidding on the worn paving stones. They were only thirty yards away, and if she even breathed too vigorously they were likely to notice her.

She flicked her eyes the other way. Flydd was standing on the cabin roof of the sky galleon, holding up something dark and lumpy that emitted gleams of red and black light.

'Go back, Merdrun!' he shouted. 'Or I put an end to the lot of you.'

Skald laughed. 'You've got nothing, you old fool, and soon you'll be screaming in our torture chambers.' The soldiers roared. 'Finish him and we put an end to the resistance.'

Skald went ahead and they continued down the avenue. They would reach the sky galleon in under a minute.

Then, back at the gate, a high, fearful voice rose above the dull roar of the fires. It came from someone standing inside the gate, and the gate was creeping down the avenue, a couple of feet above the cobblestones. It was an eerie sight, the yellow lightning radiating out in all directions from it, the sparks, the air rushing in and forming a mist that concealed whatever lay on the other side. The ominous crackling.

Flydd raised his right hand, pulled it back towards him and the gate moved a little faster. Was he controlling it? He had to be. It was gaining on the soldiers now. Skald had stopped them a hundred yards from the sky galleon and they were looking back at the gate, uneasily. It moved past Aviel's hiding place. Under her hat, she could feel her fine hair crackling and sparking. She held her breath.

Flydd lowered his fist and the gate stopped twenty yards from the soldiers. Someone stepped out of it, a meagre little man, robed, twisted, but clearly powerful. Shivers crept down Aviel's backbone and across her shoulders.

'Skald?' he said in a harsh voice that crackled with anger. 'Why are you moving the gate?'

Skald paced around the side of the soldiers and faced him. 'I haven't touched it, Magiz.'

An elderly woman, wearing the robes of a senior sus-magiz, stepped from the gate, pointed a spy glass at Flydd and studied him for some time. 'He's up to something. Call them back, Magiz.'

'This is Skald's mission,' said the magiz, 'and he's under direct orders from the High Commander. I can't interfere.' He stepped into the gate and disappeared.

Skald returned to the front and led his troops on. Flydd raised his arm again, and the red and black rays issuing from the device in his hand were brighter now. A pang struck Aviel and she remembered his order to get into shelter if Skald attacked. *Solid shelter.*

Flydd swung his arm sideways and the gate drifted across the street. The woman followed the magiz.

No one was looking in Aviel's direction. She ducked through the broad open doorway of the old courthouse and around to the left, into a large, empty chamber. All the furniture had been looted long ago but at least the roof above her looked sound.

She peered out through an empty window hole. The gate was still drifting, approaching the wall of a massive building built of dark red stone, the former Governor's Red Palace. It was so solid that it might have stood for another thousand years, even if everything around it fell into ruin.

Skald took several steps towards the gate and froze, gaping at it. It was growing ever brighter and swelling mightily, and a roaring sound now issued from it.

One edge of the gate touched the granite wall of the Red Palace and was squashed flat. The gate shuddered, radiating white lightning from its semi-circular side. The wall quivered.

Something dreadful was about to happen. The gate shuddered, squashing into an ever-narrowing oval against the wall, and the wall was rocking ever more violently.

# 13

## ANNIHILATED BY THE GATE

S kald had never been afraid to die in battle. It was the honourable way, the way
most Merdrun warriors, male and female, expected to go. But as the gate flat-
tened itself against the granite wall of the Red Palace, and he had an inkling about
what was going to happen, he was stricken by such a terror of annihilation that he
was momentarily paralysed.

Except for his racing thoughts. He had been a sus-magiz for seven weeks and had
made a number of gates, though he had not yet learned how they worked. Brilliant
though his successes had been in the field, in knowledge and understanding of the
Secret Art he was still a very junior sus-magiz.

Had Dagog not fled, he might have elaborated on the danger of a captured gate
being forced against such a solid wall. Skald could only guess, and his guess was
horrifying.

How had Flydd taken control of the gate, anyway? Something he'd brought from
Nennifer? Skald had spent too long trying to puzzle it out, and fruitlessly trying to
work out how he could take the gate back, and not long enough considering the
nature and perils of gates.

Now he did. A gate, or a portal, was a dimensional pathway. It could be opened in
air because air was a tenuous fluid that could easily flow from one opening of the
gate to the other. A gate might also, with difficulty and only by a master, be opened in
water, though the current dragged through the gate would sweep away everything in
its path.

But not even the tiniest gate could be opened in a solid object – such as rock or
wood or earth or metal – without tearing it down to its component elements and

releasing forces that would destroy everything nearby. And probably all evidence of how it had occurred.

Skald had this realisation at the moment the round gate was squashed flat against the wall. He reached out, thinking to close it, but knew instantly that it was beyond him. This mighty gate had been crafted by the magiz using magic Skald had no knowledge of, and perhaps no one save the magiz *could* close it.

'Archers, shoot Flydd down!' Skald roared.

He only had ten archers this time. They obeyed instantly, firing arrow after arrow and bolt after bolt, and at that range they should have spitted him, but not a single missile met its target. Flydd was shielded again.

Was there anything he could do to save his troops? Another gate was their only hope, and a slim hope at that, because he had only made small ones by himself – the bigger gates he had made to the Sink of Despair had been assisted by a primed focus. But he had to try. And Durthix had to be told precisely what Flydd had done.

Skald hesitated. On the battlefield, Merdrun either advanced to victory or died where they stood. Only cowards retreated from the enemy. He would make a gate to carry his troops down past the sky galleon. Then, the moment Flydd's manipulation of the greater gate was done, Skald would storm the defenceless sky galleon from the other side. He could do that even if he only had a handful of troops.

In desperate haste, he began to create the gate. It was a dangerous business, because gates opened too close together could interfere in disastrous ways. To save two hundred troops in a few seconds he needed a gate broad enough for a dozen to sprint through, abreast, though that was way beyond his abilities.

Better he save half his troops than none, but first he had to far-see the destination. Skald tried to focus on the smoke-wreathed avenue a hundred yards past the sky galleon but kept seeing Skyrock. The magiz's mighty gate was overwhelming Skald's ability to far-see the destination.

He drew more power, blocked Skyrock, refocused and attempted the biggest gate he could hope to control. But the one that formed was no wider than his shoulders, and unstable – the rim was fluttering and folding back on itself, and emitting wild, blood-red discharges. The magiz's gate, now under Flydd's control, was interfering.

And Skald's gate was creeping away from him; the device Flydd had used to take control of the other gate must be affecting this one as well.

'Merdrun!' he bellowed, over the crackle of his gate, the pounding of the larger gate against the Red Palace, and the roar of the fires consuming the southern part of the city. 'We're attacking from the other side. To my gate! Now!'

Two hundred troops turned as one, but they had only taken a couple of steps when a cataclysmic blast propelled Skald backwards through his gate. For a fleeting instant he saw the magiz's grim smile, then the destination was torn from his mind.

The irresistible force of the gate, which had been squashed almost to a pair of parallel lines by the immovable granite wall, snapped back to its original shape and passed through the wall.

The gate flared until it outshone the sun. Aviel, momentarily dazzled, scrunched up, put her head between her knees and covered her ears with her hands. Even so, the noise was so loud that she feared it had shattered her eardrums.

Rubble slammed against the outside walls of the courthouse and blasted through the window hole. Chunks of broken stone and plaster fell from the high ceiling and one landed only feet away, spraying her with stinging bits of sand and gravel. The room was a maelstrom of dust and smoke and violent gusts tearing one way and then the other. Outside she heard collapsing walls, possibly whole buildings, and screaming people.

Silence fell, apart from the distant roar of the fire consuming the southern half of Thurkad. No one was screaming now. Aviel slowly raised her head. Her ears throbbed from the blast, her eyes were painfully gritty, her nose and mouth and hair and even her ears full of grit and dust.

She crept to the window hole, her boot soles rasping on grit and gravel. The dust was slowly settling, revealing the outlines of buildings across the street, though they were battered and broken. A long way down the street the sky galleon lay on its side. There was no trace of the two hundred soldiers, or Skald.

Or the front of the Governor's Red Palace. It had been annihilated by the gate. Or had it and the gate annihilated each other? There was no sign of the gate, either.

Had Flydd known what he was doing? Was that what he'd expected when he'd used his device to take control of the enemy's gate and force it into a solid wall? Had he survived the cataclysm? Had anyone in the sky galleon – or was she lost in a shattered, burning city?

Aviel picked up the canvas bag and headed down the middle of the street. The catastrophe had drained her; she could not think of a time when she had been wearier. Even on the terrifying climb up to Carcharon, with that murderous brute Unick closing in on her and nowhere to go, she had not felt this exhausted.

She passed the point where the two hundred soldiers had stood. The paving stones and the battered sections of wall that still remained upright were stained red and flecked with shards of grey. She did not care to think about that. The air had a pungent smell, like the aftermath of a thunderstorm. There was no smell of blood, though, and even the smoke had cleared for a few hundred yards in all directions.

Further on, deep gouges had dislodged the cobblestones in parallel lines that ran all the way down the street to the sky galleon. The blast had sent it skidding for hundreds of yards before it came to rest and toppled over, the deck facing away from her.

Aviel's ankle was killing her. She hobbled around the stern. On this side the gunwale was so low that she could step aboard. She scanned the deck. People were strewn everywhere: Nish, Flydd, Maelys, Karan and the small, dark-haired pilot. Persia and Clech, and all the guards who had been killed earlier, and had been neatly laid out on the right side of the deck, were jammed together under the bow in a tangle of limbs.

She hauled herself in. Maelys was closest. Aviel felt her neck. Still warm, and there was a pulse. She checked the others. The little pilot was dead of a broken neck but Nish, Maelys and Karan were still alive. And Flydd.

None had escaped injury, though. Flydd had lost two front teeth, Nish had a huge gash across his forehead and another down his left thigh, and Maelys had a black eye. Karan did not appear to be injured but was comatose.

Aviel shook Flydd until he roused. He groaned, rubbed red, swollen eyes, felt in his mouth and grimaced. He went down on hands and knees, probed in a side gutter, picked up two crooked teeth and forced them back into their sockets.

'Merdrun?' he said in a croak.

'Gone.'

'Gate?'

'Gone. And Skald. And the Red Palace. If that's what you expected, you might have warned me.'

He hauled himself up the sloping deck and peered up the street. 'I expected a fair bit of damage, if it worked, though nothing like that.' He slid down again, shaking his head. 'To my knowledge, what I just did has never been done before.' He rubbed his eyes and peered at her again. 'How'd you get on?'

Aviel passed him the bag containing the field blocker.

'You're a marvel,' he said.

# 14

## RAN LIKE THE SON OF A COWARD YOU ARE

S kald whirled and tumbled, was stretched as if on a torture rack, then squashed flat. He lost sight and hearing, was blasted through blackness for an indeterminate time, bright lights appeared in front of him and he hurtled out the exit.

But he was not further down the avenue. He was nowhere near Thurkad. Incredibly, the gate had ignored the destination he had far-seen and had brought him back to Skyrock. He was hurtling through the provisioner's tent, toppling tall tables and crates of ledgers, until he came to rest at the feet of Provisioner Tiligg.

A gale of gravel and grit sandblasted the writing off open ledgers and hurled them at the far wall of the tent, then the gate closed. None of his troops had come through.

Skald tried to sit up but could not. The brutal gate had taken too much out of him.

The other workers, thinking they were under attack, stampeded for the open southern end of the tent and were only stopped by the magiz, who was walking by.

Dagog put himself in their path, his stained hands upraised. 'What is the meaning of this?' he snarled. 'Get back to your tables, or ...'

He did not need to complete the threat. Everyone knew how he loved to drink lives.

'A gate, Magiz!' quavered Tiligg. 'It opened in the tent and a man was hurled through, all bloody and battered, in a fearful gale.'

'What man?'

'The Superintendent of Works.'

Dagog stepped into the tent. 'Oh, happiest of days!' he crowed. 'You,' he said, handing a metal triangle to the nearest clerk. 'Take this token to the command tent and give it to the High Commander. Tell him the magiz bids him to come at once.'

Dagog came up and stood over Skald.

Skald forced himself to his knees but could rise no further. He was shattered. 'Magiz,' he croaked. 'It's not what – it's not –'

'Save it for the High Commander.' Dagog turned to Tiligg. 'Clear the tent!'

Tiligg started to protest, saw the look on Dagog's face and ordered everyone out. They were glad to go, and so was Tiligg.

Shortly Durthix entered. Dagog met him halfway. 'Skald fled from the attack in Thurkad and ended up here.'

Durthix's dark face went almost purple. 'What do you mean, *fled*?'

'Ran like a coward; like his gutless father.'

'Is he badly injured? Dying?'

'Skald doesn't appear to have suffered any worthwhile injuries. He came back alone, through a little gate. I fear for the worst in Thurkad, High Commander. I can't sense his two hundred at all.'

'It's a long way from here, and the lifelines of common soldiers are thin.'

'I can't sense the sus-magizes either,' said the magiz. 'And they carried crystals that link back to me.'

'Let's see what Skald has to say,' said Durthix.

Skald was still on his knees. The magiz prodded Skald's forehead with his staff, strength trickled into his limbs and he heaved himself to his feet. Every nerve in his body burned.

'Report!' said the magiz.

'I fear it – it's gone badly, High Commander,' said Skald. His teeth chattered; he could not prevent it.

'What do you mean, *badly*! Before I sent your reinforcements, you informed me that most of Flydd's people were dead, the sky galleon was trapped by the field blocker, and the survivors had shot their last bolts.'

'We were advancing on the sky galleon, and we would have taken them within minutes ... but then –' Skald shuddered.

'What could Flydd do to stop such a mighty force?' said Durthix. 'Your *relief* force,' he added, to drive the message home. 'After you lost the first force.'

'The magiz's great gate was still open. And ... and ... somehow Flydd seized control of it. I can't imagine how.'

Durthix glanced at Dagog, questioningly.

'Such a device was mentioned in top secret papers we captured. Though not how it could be made.'

'Was Flydd using a device? Did you see?'

'Yes,' said Skald. 'Though I have no idea what it was.'

'Why didn't you close the gate?'

Skald looked to the magiz as if hoping he would say something to help. The magiz looked back at him stonily.

'I tried, but it was a mighty gate and it wouldn't close. I haven't learned how to close someone else's gate. And perhaps its maker –'

'That would be me,' Dagog said coldly.

'Perhaps its maker was holding it open. Flydd turned the gate off the avenue towards the former Red Palace, the most massive building in Thurkad. I ordered every archer to fire at him, but nothing got through his shields.'

'You could have taken the sky galleon in minutes,' said Durthix. 'They could not have resisted you.'

'When I realised what Flydd was planning to do with the gate, it was too late. I had less than thirty seconds to act.'

'What I don't understand, Captain Skald, is how you ended up here. In battle a captain's place is with his troops, to the bitter end. I ordered you to personally lead them until the sky galleon was taken.'

'Flydd drove the gate at the Red Palace ... he kept forcing the gate until it squashed flat against the front wall. And I feared what was going to happen.'

'Oh yes, you *feared*,' said the magiz. 'And then you ran like the son of a coward you are.'

'I – did – not – run!' choked Skald.

Durthix gestured the magiz to silence. 'What was your fear, Captain Skald?'

'That the gate would rebound and pass through the solid wall ... and annihilate the wall *and* the gate – and everything nearby.'

'You feared that would happen,' grated the magiz. 'But did it?'

Skald was trapped and he knew it. 'I assume so.'

'*You assume so?*' said Durthix in a voice he normally only used with hardened criminals. 'Why weren't you with your troops?'

'I tried to create a second gate, one large enough for two hundred to race through –'

'Are you saying,' said Durthix in a low but deadly voice, 'that you wanted them to run like cowards from a battlefield?'

An officer of the High Command could and should save himself if needed, for without experienced leadership the Merdrun army was nothing. But an officer leading his soldiers in battle never had that option. He was expected to fight to the death to win the battle, and if his force was overrun and all hope of victory was gone it was his duty to die with them.

'No, High Commander! We weren't running from the enemy – *it was our own gate.*'

'If an enemy takes your sword and uses it against you, and you run, you're running from the enemy.'

Skald choked. 'Never! When I realised what was going to happen I far-saw a destination further down the avenue, so we could attack the sky galleon from the other side. I only had a few seconds to –'

'Save yourself.' The magiz's voice tolled like an executioner's bell.

# 15

## LET HIS DEATH DO SOMETHING USEFUL

Skald forced himself to meet Durthix's eyes. 'I ordered my force to my gate, and they were coming. *I far-saw our destination!*' he cried. 'I saw the sky galleon from further down the avenue, and I knew we could take it.'

'But?' said Durthix.

'The magiz's great gate rebounded through the wall of the Red Palace and the whole world went mad. Everything turned red and white; the noise was deafening; walls collapsing; rubble and bodies hurled in all directions. I was flying through the air, blasted into the mouth of my gate ... I saw the magiz's face, and he was smiling, and the destination was torn from my mind. I ended up here ... and ... no one else came through.'

'You're blaming me?' cried Dagog. 'You're actually trying to shift the blame for your cowardly failure *to me?*'

'I didn't say that,' said Skald. 'But I've never lost the destination before.'

The magiz could scarcely contain himself. 'High Commander, this is a tissue of lies. Skald ran from the battlefield. He abandoned his troops and the punishment must be carried out, in public. Let me do it –'

His eyes burned; he was desperate to drink Skald's life, and this time Durthix would let him.

'Enough, Magiz!' snapped Durthix. 'Take us to Thurkad.'

The magiz looked like a man who had found a dog turd in his dinner. 'High Commander, I've warned you about Skald. Over and again I've warned you.'

'And he's made a liar out of you, over and again. A hero who has proven his courage many times doesn't suddenly become a coward, Magiz.'

'Skald cares for no one but Skald. No *One for All* for him.'

'I must see the scene of battle. If any of our troops survived, even leaderless they will have captured the enemy or killed them. Take us there, immediately.'

The magiz cleared a space and effortlessly created a gate that hovered silently a couple of feet above the floor of the provisioner's tent.

'Go through!' said Durthix.

Skald stepped through, then Durthix, and the magiz came last. The gate opened at the five-way intersection and they walked down. The devastation was staggering; the front half of the Red Palace had been erased, and part of the foundations, down to a yard below ground level. Parts of the rear half still stood, though it looked in imminent danger of collapse.

'This is unprecedented, unimaginable,' said Durthix, shaking his head. 'No one could have survived such a cataclysm.'

He inspected the red stains and grey flakes on the surrounding buildings and his grim face hardened. 'Blood and bone. All that's left of two hundred of my best and most loyal troops.'

Even the magiz looked shocked.

'How did Flydd do this, Magiz?' said Durthix.

'I don't know.'

'The devastation is worse than anything we've ever done in war. When I was young, a whole magazine of blasting powder exploded – twenty wagon loads. Yet the ruin wasn't a tenth of this.'

The magiz was silent, his mouth open, his eyes staring. He looked afraid.

'Find out, Magiz. If they can do this in defence, they might learn to do it in attack.'

'At once, High Commander.'

'Where was the sky galleon? Could it have been destroyed as well?'

'It was down there.' Skald pointed down the street.

'I didn't ask you,' Durthix said coldly.

This was a very bad sign. Did Durthix believe Skald was a coward?

'Magiz?' said Durthix.

Dagog walked past the ruins and on down the avenue, to a point where a set of parallel gouges began. 'The sky galleon was here. Trapped by the field blocker.'

'But was it destroyed? Is Flydd dead?'

'I don't think so. The damage is much less here; most of the buildings still have their roofs.' Dagog crouched and felt one of the gouges. Dislodged cobblestones lay to either side. 'See the scrape marks from its keel. The blast drove it this way –' He walked on for a couple of hundred yards. 'To here.'

'And now it's gone,' Durthix said, so quietly that Skald could barely hear him from four feet away. 'Flydd killed 270 soldiers and the two sus-magizes, and then he escaped, *in triumph!*'

He turned, and Skald had never seen such molten rage. 'You begged for this mission, Captain Skald. You specified what you needed to make victory certain, to allow Flydd not the slightest chance of escape, and I gave it to you.'

'Yes,' said Skald, 'but –'

'Do – not – interrupt! Flydd had less than twenty people, yet they annihilated every one of your sixty troops and destroyed five precious air-scooters and their crews. I should have relieved you of your command, but the sky galleon was immobilised and vulnerable, so I sent you a relief force to finish the job – two hundred of my finest warriors – *and you lost them as well.*'

'And two of my remaining sus-magiz,' said the magiz, 'out of thirty. This is a very bad day, High Commander.'

Merdrun did not make excuses. It was Skald's failure, but he had to make Durthix understand that he had been fighting to the end. He would never run because, for the son of a coward, death was infinitely preferable.

'I failed you, High Commander, and I await your punishment. But I did not run from the battlefield. To the last second, I was trying to save as many of my troops as possible, and gate them down the avenue so we could take the sky galleon and destroy our enemies.'

'Can this be proved?' said Durthix to the magiz. 'Or disproved?'

'It is sometimes possible to recover the path of a gate from origin to destination,' said the magiz, sucking on one of his brown-stained fingernails. 'But not here.'

'Why not?'

'The annihilation of my great gate has twisted the fabric of space so badly that every trace of Skald's little gate would have been erased.' Dagog cast a soul-shivering smile at Skald.

Skald thought Dagog was lying but had no way of proving it. It was over for him and he prayed that Durthix would kill him out of hand, though that did not seem likely. So disastrous a failure required a suitably horrific punishment, in front of the assembled Merdrun nation.

'What happened to our only field blocker?' said Durthix.

'I – I don't know, Commander.' Skald's head was splitting apart; it was an effort to think at all. 'The first of the air-scooters used it to immobilise the sky galleon ... and after the pilot and operator were killed I sent another air-scooter to retrieve it, but it was shot down.'

'Did the enemy get it?'

'I believe they did,' said Dagog. 'But I'll institute a complete search, to be sure.'

Skald had nothing more to say. How had the day – no, the hour, for that was all it had taken – gone so disastrously wrong? When the attack began he had been everywhere, directing his forces against first one enemy weakness and then another. He'd expected casualties, for Flydd was a mighty foe, but he had not considered that they could fail.

Then, halfway through the battle, Karan had attacked him with the sending that had heightened his most terrible fear – that he was going to turn into a coward like his father. He had fought to overcome those fears but after that it had been a struggle to focus. Flydd had seized the advantage and Skald never got it back.

'When we return,' said Durthix, 'I'm calling a strategy meeting. We've got to think everything through again.'

'The Skyrock compound is guarded by fifteen thousand,' said Dagog, 'and our other compounds there are also ringed with steel. Besides, the Day of All Days is close now. Even if Flydd should decide to mount an attack, how is he going to do it?'

'He's the wiliest opponent we've ever faced,' said Durthix.

'But what can he actually do? The Skyrock compound is impenetrable to enemy gates, and his sky galleon can carry no more than fifty troops. Even if he raised an army tomorrow, it'd take months to march it to Skyrock.'

'He destroyed the gate, and our two hundred, in a way no one thought possible. What other tricks has he got up his sleeve?'

'We'll go through all the captured secret papers and enemy devices, identify every conceivable way of attack and create a defence for each.'

'You've lost half your sus-magizes since the invasion began. How can you do all that, and your other work?'

'I've confirmed ten new sus-magizes and I'll soon have more.'

'But they lack experience.'

'High Commander, we can do it. I can go without sleep for a week if I have to, and make it up later. Ten thousand years we've waited. Longer!' The magiz's face lit. 'Oh, to be finally going home. It almost makes me weep.' He shot a sideways glance at Durthix.

Skald felt the same emotions but suppressed them. Hope was not part of his future, nor joy. He had no future. His failure was too monumental.

'It's permissible to display emotion at so glorious a thought,' said Durthix, his own face glowing. 'Even for magizes.' Then the passion and the expectation vanished. 'What are we to do about him?'

They were talking about Skald as though he was not there. As though he did not exist. He soon would not.

'Deserting one's troops on the battlefield is the foulest of all failures,' said Dagog. 'He must suffer the prescribed death, as a lesson to all.'

'There's no proof that he deserted his troops, and I'm not convinced he did. This is a man, a hero, who has previously overcome his deepest and darkest fears to do his duty. A hero who saved the True Purpose, Magiz – and his peculiar return to Skyrock troubles me. How could a gate go so wrong – unless ...'

'It might have been caught up in the path of my far larger gate,' Dagog said hastily. 'Such things are not well understood.'

'Perhaps you're right.' Durthix did not sound convinced.

'But his failure has cost us dear in troops, and devices, and power,' said the magiz.

'Though not a tenth of the power he brought us. The construct is worth more than all the magical devices in your armoury, Magiz, and Rulke alone is worth thousands of lives.'

'I've acknowledged Skald's contributions, but he's lost his nerve. Let his death do something useful.'

'You want to drink his life.' Durthix looked disgusted.

'By his many deeds and mighty magecraft Skald has accumulated great power, and it can be recovered from him. We need it, High Commander.'

'I'm mindful that you've always hated Skald and you've done your best to frustrate him.'

'From the first I saw something weak in him. Something carefully hidden that's always troubled me. He's his father's son, no question. A coward engendered by a coward.'

'No!' said Durthix. 'I forbid it.'

'What are you saying, High Commander?'

'You will not drink Skald's life. In fact ... I wonder if I should allow him to live.'

Skald's head jerked up. He deserved to die. He had to pay for this failure.

'High Commander?' said the magiz.

'You're desperately short of sus-magizes and you now have far more work for them. Can you afford to lose another one?'

'Skald is poison!'

'He's also our greatest living hero, and an inspiration to all ...'

'Are you suggesting we *cover up* this disaster?' Dagog grated.

'Time is short. We need absolute focus to get everything done in time, and every sus-magiz we have. We can't afford to waste him.'

'He abandoned his troops and ran, High Commander!'

'I dispute that, Magiz! If you could have proved it, you would have done so at once.'

'But –'

'I'll never give him military command again. But time is short, and Skald has done well as Superintendent of Works. If I put him to death, I'll have no one to get the last of the work finished, and everything powered, in time.'

'So, you're planning on rewarding a *coward*?'

'I'm getting the job done, Magiz,' Durthix snapped. 'Make sure you do the same.'

'All right,' said the magiz, softly, silkily. 'But the moment we no longer need him, I want his life.'

'Agreed. When that day comes, I'll find a pretext for his trial and execution.'
'No – *I* want his life.'

## 16

## THE BODY MAY BE WITHERED

The bitter victory in Thurkad had done nothing for Karan. Had the magiz abducted Sulien to torture her for her part in past defeats? Or to kill her because she had once seen the Merdrun's secret weakness? Or to lure Karan in with false hope of a rescue?

The sky galleon wheeled over river and swamp forest and estuary, then dropped towards Fiz Gorgo. This was where the affair of the Mirror had begun, two hundred and twenty-six years ago as time ran in this world. Thirteen years ago, in her life. And it had utterly changed her. Changed everything.

Maigraith had compelled Karan to accompany her to Fiz Gorgo, to do what she could not – break into Yggur's supposedly impregnable fortress and steal the Mirror of Aachan. Yggur had been Karan's enemy for years afterwards, yet they had ended up friends.

The sky galleon landed in a walled courtyard lined with wet grey flagstones. The day was damp and chilly, as it often was here, even in summer. A reluctant sun occasionally popped through low, rushing clouds, and the keen southerly wind was uncomfortably cold after the dry heat of Thurkad.

But what aid would they find here? Yggur had been gravely injured in the final battle against the God-Emperor two years ago and was not well. And for much of his exceptionally long life he had suffered from fits of black depression where he hid from the world.

No one came to greet them. 'I don't like this,' said Maelys. 'Has the enemy been here too?'

'The enemy hasn't been here,' said Flydd, and led the way inside.

The deaths of Persia and Clech had left him lower than ever, and Nish and Maelys had been at each other's throats ever since they left Thurkad. Everything was falling apart.

When Yggur caught Maigraith back then, she had ordered Karan to flee with the stolen Mirror of Aachan, and Karan had eventually escaped into the leech-infested swamp-forests. She rubbed her calves, as if leeches were still clustered there in their hundreds. She shuddered, wrenched her thoughts back to the present and followed the others in.

The hallway was wide enough for ten people to walk abreast, and lit by sunshine filtering in through thick, yellow glass skylights that appeared to have been installed recently.

Up a wide, shallow set of steps, then a steeper set that curved to the right. The bannister rail was carved from dark green jade with swirling patterns through it. Flydd pushed open a pair of doors and stepped out into a tropical garden. An enormous conservatory with glass walls and roof, and louvred windows to let the breeze in and, when needed, the excess heat out.

'This is new,' said Nish, sniffing the scented air. 'And not before time.'

Small trees of all kinds were in blossom, and some in fruit. Birds chittered and swooped, picking up snails and grubs. Flydd wove across to a wall of creamy yellow stone hung with small plants in mossy baskets, around a corner, and the conservatory opened out. A number of well-worn chairs stood there, and in them sat two old people.

The woman, tall and slender, Karan did not know. She might once have been beautiful but only ghostly remnants remained. The man was even taller, but had a rug over his knees, and was so aged that at first she did not recognise him. Then he turned those frost-coloured eyes to her and gave her such a smile that it warmed her heart.

'Karan,' he said in a faded voice.

Time was when his voice had been so powerful that he could control people with it, but here, she saw, was a man who no longer felt the need to command anyone.

Yggur started to push himself up with his arms, grimaced and waited while the old woman took his hands and helped him to his feet.

'It's not been long for you,' he said, 'but my centuries have been long and hard, and you find me sadly reduced. Though not unhappy; the inner scars hardly trouble me at all these days, thanks to time and Tulitine. Tulitine, my dear friend Karan has come all the way from the past just to be with me.'

For long seconds Karan wondered if his mind had given way, then he laughed and took her hands in his own.

'No need to worry,' said Yggur. 'The body may be withered but the mind still ticks over.'

'I don't remember you making jokes before.'

'If we don't change, we decay.' He shook hands with Nish, Maelys and Flydd. They were old friends. 'Is this all of you?'

'Just about,' said Flydd grimly. 'Aimee was killed at Nifferlin, Flangers and Chissmoul fell a month ago and we lost Persia and Clech yesterday, in Thurkad. And many, many more over the course of the invasion. But Klarm is still at large, somewhere ... and Maigraith.'

'Ah, Maigraith,' said Yggur.

'And Wilm!' said Aviel, stepping out from behind Nish.

'What a treat you are, my dear. I could gaze at your lovely face all day.'

Tulitine subtly cleared her throat.

'But that would be most ill-mannered. Sit, friends, and take refreshment – *I* won't turn you away without so much as a mug of water. There are platters, there.' Yggur pointed to a table under a tree laden with creamy blossoms. Swarms of bees hummed from one to another. 'And on the far side, my best goblets and your choice of wine and ales and waters.'

They sat. Karan filled a plate with morsels that might have come from a palace kitchen, and took a glass of water. She had not had any kind of drink since the traumatic night when she had told Flydd about her mother's death. But this was a time for celebrating with old friends and new, or at least toasting them. She put the glass aside and took a quarter goblet of a green-gold wine that sparkled in the glass and smelled like watermelon.

Yggur looked approving. Flydd took a small glass of a translucent red wine, and Nish a brimming goblet of something dark purple. Maelys scowled at him. She took neither food nor wine, but surreptitiously got out the Mirror of Aachan and gazed at whatever it showed her.

'You knew we were coming,' said Flydd. 'And you know where we've been.'

'I may be not long for the world,' said Yggur, 'but I'm passionately interested in what's going on – and I still have my contacts. You're in a bad way, otherwise you wouldn't have come to this tired old backwater, but I have no aid to give.'

'What I really need is your perspective.'

'The Merdrun have cut off the top of the pinnacle of Skyrock and reshaped the rest – rather elegantly. I would not have expected it of them.'

'They enslaved hundreds of our best architects and artists and put them to work adapting an age-old design. And very beautiful it's going to be when it's done, any day now.'

'It's reminiscent of Katazza,' said Yggur. 'The big difference is that they've carved a prodigious tunnel through the base and they're cladding it with sapphires. Countless millions of them.'

'Sapphires? What for?'

Yggur shrugged. 'The Merdrun have raised secrecy to a higher plane. They've also used Rulke's construct to lift sections of a tall iron tower up there, with a shrouded crystal at the very top. I can't guess how they plan to use it, but it disturbs me.'

'They took Sulien,' Karan said quietly. 'Along with Klarm's daughter, Jassika.'

Yggur leaned forwards and clasped her hands again. 'I'm sorry. Can you guess what they want from Sulien?'

Karan hesitated, for she had not told this to anyone. 'I've picked up a few things. They're training her in far-seeing. Sulien has a gift for it.'

'But the magiz has a mighty gift for far-seeing,' said Yggur. 'Why does he want her?' He leaned back, folded his long fingers and gazed at her, thoughtfully.

'And they also have Llian.'

'But he's not the Merdrun's prisoner,' said Yggur. 'Llian remains in Rulke's custody.'

Flydd, who had been sipping his wine with his eyes closed, sat up abruptly. 'Why?'

Yggur gave a small, fleeting smile. 'I can still surprise you. That's good. The condition was set by Rulke when he reached Alcifer.'

'How was he in a position to set conditions?'

'They have Lirriam.' Yggur turned to Flydd. 'You had a victory yesterday. In Thurkad, of all places.'

'Of sorts,' Flydd said grimly.

'Well, the telling will be good for all of us.' Yggur rose, unaided this time, and took a goblet of the dark purple wine. 'Don't spare any humiliation you inflicted on the Merdrun, or any triumph of yours, however small.'

Flydd gestured to Maelys. 'You love the tales most, and you're the best at telling.'

Maelys, who had seldom looked happy in the time Karan had known her, put the Mirror away. She began with their arrival in Thurkad and the realisation that the enemy knew they were coming and had set a mighty trap.

'How did they know?' said Tulitine curiously. 'Were you betrayed?'

'I don't know,' said Flydd. 'Though it's clear the enemy can track flying craft by the way they draw power from the field.'

'Then they could know you're here.'

'I took precautions. But it's possible.'

Maelys continued, and as she told the tale of that impossible battle, her sad face glowed. Nish was gazing at her, perhaps seeing the Maelys he'd known and loved of old, before she lost her baby, her sister and her aunt. Was it too late for them? And is it too late for Llian and me? Karan thought.

'You fought well together,' said Yggur.

'Everyone did their job. But it came at a cost.'

'Every year we lose old friends ...'

'And it's harder than ever to make new ones.'

No one spoke for a minute or two. 'A bold endeavour,' said Yggur, 'seizing their gate and forcing it into a solid wall. How did you know it would work?'

'By bold you mean unbelievably reckless,' said Flydd. 'I didn't – for all I knew, the gate might just have closed. Or alternatively, annihilated us and half of Thurkad. But since the alternative was capture and torture and certain death ...'

'Quite.'

'But *how* did you do it?'

'An experimental device the scrutators made long ago, but never used because it was deemed too dangerous. Speaking of devices, Aviel snatched this from under the enemy's nose.'

Flydd passed over the canvas bag, holding it open so the spiky metal ball showed.

'And it is?' said Yggur, taking the bag in one hand and turning the ball over.

'A field blocker. They used it to stop the sky galleon.'

'I'll take a closer look later, if I may. What are your plans?'

'Resting for a few days and making plans. We have intelligence that the enemy's True Purpose, whatever it is, will be put into effect on the sixty-fifth day after the invasion began,' said Flydd. 'Nineteen days from now.'

'And?' said Yggur.

'There's a monster node under Skyrock. I saw it, first-hand, long ago.'

'How come?'

'We had an important mine there, during the war. A tin mine. The veins radiated out from below the Skyrock node, and there were some problems, so I went there to investigate.'

'I hope you're not considering what you and Irisis did at Snizort,' said Nish.

'What was that?' said Karan.

'The lyrinx were stealing power with a node-drainer, underground at the Snizort node. Flydd and Irisis went down and blocked it, but it began to feed all that power back where it had come from, and it destroyed the node.'

'A plume of fire and molten rock blasted half a mile into the air,' said Flydd, blank-eyed. 'Leaving our army of sixty thousand, and hundreds of clankers, trapped without power on the battlefield. And the Aachim and thousands of their land constructs. Then the lyrinx swarmed out of their underground city and cut us to pieces.'

'And to this day the Aachim haven't trusted us,' said Nish.

'Surely you're not considering destroying the Skyrock node?' said Yggur. 'The cost in lives would be monumental – and many of them slaves.'

'Including Sulien and Llian,' said Karan.

'I wasn't thinking of *exploding* it,' said Flydd. 'Just cutting off their power.'

'How would you get into such a heavily guarded place?' said Yggur.

'I don't know,' said Flydd. 'But if we could free Lirriam, I'm sure Rulke will come back to our side.'

'We don't know where she's held,' said Nish.

'I'll bet Maigraith does,' said Aviel, speaking up for the first time. 'If anyone knows where she is.'

'She's here,' said Yggur.

'What's she doing here?' said Karan.

'We occasionally come together, to talk. Do you want her?'

'After she discovered Rulke was alive, she offered reparation for the harm she done to my family. I refused – I wasn't going to be bought to alleviate her conscience. But ...'

'You need all the help you can get.'

Yggur rolled a glassy sphere between his palms, it lit momentarily, and a few minutes later Maigraith appeared. She did not look surprised to see them.

Karan goggled at her; Aviel's rejuvenation potion had transformed Maigraith. 'You look younger than when we first met. Younger than I am now.'

It was *so* wrong. And yet, Karan wondered if a slight younging would help her with Llian.

'What do you want?' said Maigraith.

'You offered me reparation.'

'And you refused.'

'I've changed my mind.'

'How much do you want?'

'I don't want coin! I want a talent.'

Maigraith stroked the heavy golden ring Rulke had given her long ago, the sign of their eternal bond. 'Very well. In full reparation, I will transfer one magical talent to you – if you swear to help free Rulke.'

'No gift without an obligation,' said Karan. 'You haven't changed.'

'You're the one begging for favours.'

'It's reparation!'

'State what you want, then.'

'The gift of mind-speaking.'

'That's all?' said Maigraith. 'You can already make sendings and mind-links.'

'Only to a few people, and mostly it doesn't work. I want to be able to mind-speak at will, to whoever I choose, even if they have no talent for the Art.'

'Even to dunderheads like Llian? It's a mighty gift you're asking for,' said Maigraith.

'Yours is a mighty debt.'

'It comes at a big cost.'

'I'm sure you can pay it.'

'A big cost to *you*, Karan. The pain will be tremendous, and the aftersickness worse.'

'I'll pay the price,' said Karan, with some trepidation.

# 17

# THE LAW OF RESTRICTIONS

Late that night, after they buried Clech, Persia, the pilot and the guards who had died in Thurkad, Karan just wanted to go to bed. Only sleep could release her, briefly, from the horrors of the past days.

But there was work to do. She returned to the conservatory, reeking of oil of citronella to keep the incessant night midges and mosquitoes at bay. Already, her head was throbbing.

Maigraith had passed the mind-speaking gift to her with a single touch, but it had been exceedingly painful, and the pain would recur whenever Karan mind-spoke. It was always that way, Maigraith had said, when an adult was gifted a magical ability that would normally have developed slowly, from childhood.

Karan sat in the dark, surrounded by the scent of many unusual kinds of citrus blossoms. She turned her chair east, in the direction of Skyrock, and prepared to reach out to Llian.

Since he lacked any gift for the Art, first she had to picture him as clearly as possible. She thought about their first meeting at the Graduation Telling, when he had told his new version of the Tale of the Forbidding so sensationally – and the cruel way she had treated him the last time they had been together, before he was taken through Rulke's gate, leaving his little finger behind.

She began to form a picture of him in her mind's eye. Not just his face and form and dress. The good, proud father, the insatiably curious Chronicler, prone to prying into things that were none of his business, the incomparable Teller of tales great and small, the impractical man, unskilled at arms, who nonetheless could be brave and daring ... and the depressed, apathetic man he had often been under the ban from the college.

*Llian?* she called. Then aloud, in case it helped, 'Llian?'

She did not expect to reach him first time. Mind-speaking was an Art that required much practice and extreme concentration.

*Llian, are you all right, with Rulke?*

Rulke had always been ambivalent towards him. Rulke had admired Llian's dedication to his profession, his vast knowledge of the Histories and the Great Tales, and his ability to move people by the sheer magic of his words.

Yet Rulke had been contemptuous of Llian's physical awkwardness and his malleable sense of right and wrong – he often overstepped the boundaries in pursuit of a story. One time, he had found the way into Gothryme's concealed archives and read the secret parts of Karan's family Histories. He noticed everything and, she thought guiltily, it was almost impossible to keep things from him. Soon, if they survived, all her secrets would have to come out.

*Karan, is that you? Where are you?*

She dared not say. *The magiz took Sulien and Jassika.*

She felt his shock across the mind-link. His anguish. But if he replied, she did not hear it, because the pain Maigraith had warned her about struck like frozen needles being forced through her head from front to back. It was a struggle to think but she had to get through to him; they might not have long.

*What does he want with her?* said Llian.

*I don't know. But their True Purpose has to be ready in nineteen days' time.*

*He drinks lives for the fun of it. I'm only alive because Rulke protected –*

The pain swelled until it was like glass being smashed inside her head. Was it an assault? Had she been detected?

Llian was gone and she could not get him back. And she'd gleaned nothing about his situation or his state of mind. Was he in danger? Terrified? Close to a breakdown?

Aftersickness came in pulses of nausea so strong that she had to lie down, knees drawn up and arms wrapped around them, rocking gently until it began to fade. That might have been an hour later. She could not tell.

Karan tried again but, the moment she attempted to visualise him, more glass was smashed inside her skull. Was it the enemy's psychic defence? Or just the aftereffects of a gift she had no right to have?

But she had to reach Sulien. Karan should have mind-spoken to her first. It would have been easier and far less painful. She conjured up her daughter's image, and her face was so clear that it brought tears to Karan's eyes but, though she tried until her head throbbed and boiled and burned, she could not get even the tiniest sense of Sulien. The magiz must be blocking her.

Aftersickness hammered Karan down, worse than before. She lay doubled up, rocking and shivering, while the stars wheeled above her.

'Karan?' Yggur touched her on the shoulder.

She sat up. 'Maigraith didn't exaggerate about the pain.'

'Mind-speech might seem simple, but it's powerful mancery. Pain is part of the natural order.'

'How do you mean?'

'The Law of Restrictions says that the greater the spell, the greater the restrictions on its use. And rightly so. If people could use powerful magic easily and at little cost, it would change the world for the worse. Nature is always working to restore the balance. How did you go?'

She told him. 'It felt like I was blocked.' She felt the panic rising. 'Why did I leave her at Stibbnibb?'

'If you'd taken her with you, she might have been killed on many occasions. You did the best you could.'

And it wasn't good enough. 'Tell me what to do – you've seen everything in your long life.'

He gave a small smile. 'I no longer offer advice; it usually goes wrong. I only have this: trust that the Merdrun badly need Sulien's gift and will look after her ... until they get what they want.'

Karan wasn't sure whether to laugh or scream. 'If she can't do what they want, they'll put her down without a thought.'

Yggur sat and put an arm around her. 'Let it all out, Karan. Then let it go and focus, as you've never focused before, on saving the people you love. No one knows, better than I do, what you can do when you have to.'

He was so changed from the cold, repressed Yggur she had first met. She gave him a watery smile. 'But none of us have faced odds like this before.'

'Talk to Nish about beating impossible odds,' said Yggur.

'What for?' she said dully.

'Inspiration. Sixteen years ago, Chief Scrutator Ghoor took this place and caught the lot of us, then built an aerial amphitheatre above where we sit now.'

'What for?'

'To try, torture and publicly execute Flydd and all his allies, including me. Ghoor had hundreds of crack guards and many mighty mancers, and we were bound and helpless.'

Karan did not speak, but she could not help wondering.

'Ghoor's torturers had just begun to flay Flydd's skin off him when someone realised that they had not caught every single one of us. Nish was still free, somewhere ...'

Yggur stared into the night, and shivered.

A mosquito whined by and she felt a sting on her neck. She slapped, flicked the dead mosquito off her palm and wiped the blood on her pants. 'What happened?'

'He had no hope of saving us, but he refused to give up, even though his former lover, Ullii, was hunting him and planning to cut out his heart.'

'Why? What had he done?'

'He'd accidentally killed her long-lost twin brother, Myllii. Ghoor's guards were hunting Nish too, yet he kept going. It was the greatest feat of courage and sheer, bloody determination I've ever seen.'

It hadn't helped. It made her feel worse. 'But we're not facing *hundreds*. We're up against 150,000 and we can't even get near Skyrock. We flew over it weeks ago, and even then the defences were impregnable.'

'If we stop hoping, it means accepting that everyone we care about is lost. That the world we love is doomed and nothing can be done about it. *Do you accept that, Karan?*'

'No,' she said quietly.

'If I've learned one lesson in life it's that there's always a way.' He rose. 'Bed for my old bones.'

But Karan had nothing and could come up with nothing. She had already spent hundreds of hours going through the possibilities. She had thought of little else since Skald got away with the construct from Alcifer.

Yggur stopped, looking up at the leafy canopy and the moths flitting between night-scented blossoms. 'This mind-speech business – I don't think it's as restricted as other means of farspeaking.'

'How do you mean?'

'By distance.'

Her head was full of shards again. 'Haven't got the faintest idea what you're talking about.'

'On a clear, still night, you might even reach your kinswoman.'

'But Malien went home to Aachan.'

'Doesn't mean her advice wouldn't be valuable.'

He closed the door quietly behind him. Karan closed her eyes and lay back. She'd felt alone from the moment she'd come to the future. Even now, among friends old and new, she was alone. But blood kin were different and, apart from Sulien, Karan only had one living relative. She pictured her in her mind's eye. The way she looked and spoke and thought.

*Malien?*

Karan did not call with any expectation of a response, since Aachan was very far away.

*Malien?*

She realised that she did not have the faintest idea where Aachan was, in relation to Santhenar. The Three Worlds weren't linked by proximity, but by *accessibility*. Since the Way Between the Worlds had been reopened, they could sometimes be reached from one another when the conditions were right, if one had the knowledge and the power, though few did. But how did the link actually work? She did not know; the topic had never come up.

*Malien?* It wasn't a call, just a thought.

*Yes, Karan?*

Karan fell off her chair, hitting her left elbow on the funny bone. She scrambled to her feet and peered up through the leaves at the sky, which was, considering her recent deliberations, ridiculous. Since Aachan could be in any direction, she might as well have looked down at the floor.

*I'm in Fiz Gorgo. With Yggur and Flydd, Aviel and Maelys and Nish.*

*It's lovely to hear from you after a couple of centuries – though I appreciate why you've been so tardy.* Malien laughed softly. *You reached the future safely, then?*

Jagged pains struck through Karan' head, though not as badly as when she'd spoken to Llian. *A month and a half ago. Unfortunately, the Merdrun turned up a few days later.*

Karan filled Malien in as briefly as possible. Her head was throbbing unbearably by the time she reached the present day.

*Keep searching for a way,* said Malien. *I have faith in you.*

*How much?*

*Just enough.*

*Is Aachan very bad?*

*It's getting better. It's been hard, Karan. Very hard for an old woman.*

*You're not old!* Karan said stoutly. But how would she know, after all this time?

*Clan Elienor was never one of the longest-lived clans and I was past my prime when you last saw me. But I can't tell you how wonderful it is to come home at last ...*

*You're fading,* said Karan.

*Call again. I may think of some useful thing.*

Karan sat there for another hour or two, until the aftersickness was gone. The despair was gone as well; Yggur and Malien had helped her more than they could have imagined. She was going to save Sulien, and that ridiculous man of hers. There had to be a way!

They spent a number of days in Skyrock. Flydd and Nish were closeted with Yggur much of the time, making plans and preparations, though no details were revealed. Karan ate and walked and read and swam, glad of the chance to get her strength back. Her physical strength, at least. Inwardly, she was struggling again. There seemed no way to get into Skyrock, secretly or openly. The enemy were too strong and they had thought of everything.

When she rose on the final morning, having slept unusually late, the sky galleon had been scrubbed out by servants hired in the nearby village, the mechanism that drove it had been taken apart and put back together again, the water tanks cleaned and filled with fresh water, and the pantry restocked with food and wine, and some sealed crates from Yggur's stores.

After lunch he locked the main door of Fiz Gorgo and pocketed the key, then took it out and, with a rueful smile, handed it to Tulitine.

She raised an eyebrow.

'I've a feeling I won't be back,' said Yggur.

'Then why give it to me?' said Tulitine. 'I'm not staying in this grim old place by myself.'

He laughed and put it under the doormat. 'Finders keepers, then.'

Only when they had taken to the air and were well away did Flydd tell them his plans. 'We're heading east, a way past Skyrock, to rendezvous with Wilm and Ilisial.'

'What about Klarm?'

'He's ... elsewhere.'

'And when we get to the rendezvous?' said Nish. 'Are you planning a suicidal attack on Skyrock?'

'We'll talk about that when we get there.'

# 18

# NATURE ABHORS IMPOSSIBILITIES

F lydd's desperate stratagem to defeat Skald in Thurkad had come as a great blow to both Durthix and the magiz. If Flydd thought Santhenar had nothing to lose, who knew what reckless attack he might try next.

'Double the patrols on the walls of the Skyrock compound,' Durthix ordered. 'And henceforth, everyone will strip naked before passing in through the gates, and they and their clothes and gear will be checked for magical devices, even the smallest.'

'Everyone?' scowled Dagog.

'Everyone up to and including the highest general, and you and I, Magiz. No exceptions will be made.'

'That's going to take a lot of precious time.'

'Any sus-magizes and artisans who need to go in frequently can move into Skyrock. There are empty rooms and cells enough. How good are the protections against gating into the compound?'

'I designed them myself.'

'That's not an answer.'

'No one can gate into the compound. Or into Skyrock itself, or its tunnel.'

'What about to the top of Skyrock? Or the top of the iron tower?'

'I have gate-blockers there too.'

'Have they been tested?'

'No, but I'm sure –'

'Test them. Have you considered someone gating *under* Skyrock?'

Dagog rolled his eyes. 'Into the tunnels leading down to the node?'

'Yes.'

'They're so narrow and winding, High Commander, that no one could *far-see* their destination accurately enough. If a gate went just a foot astray – and no gate is *that* accurate – and opened in solid rock, they would be annihilated. And everything for many yards around them. Only a fool would do anything that risky.'

'Or a man with nothing to lose and an implacable determination to stop us – by destroying the foundations of Skyrock.'

'I don't think it could be done.'

'Why not?'

'Nature abhors impossibilities. It's almost certain that the gate would fail to open.'

'*Almost certain* isn't good enough, Dagog. Flydd did a similar thing in Thurkad and he might do it here.'

'I'm stretched to breaking point, and so are my sus-magizes.'

'Do I need to repeat myself?' said Durthix.

'All right!' Dagog snapped. 'I'll have another gate-blocker made and installed in the tunnels.'

'Is there any other way the enemy could get into the compound?'

'Only by flying over the walls in their sky galleon, or some other craft.'

'I have a ring of platform-mounted javelards, and any one of them can knock the sky galleon out of the air a mile before it reaches the compound. Plus power-trackers that can pick up any flying craft day or night, from miles away.'

'And these have been tested?'

'On secret night flights of the construct.'

They looked at one another, then Durthix smiled. 'There's no way in. No way they can touch us now.'

Why did Dagog want Sulien's gift trained when he had such a brilliant gift himself? It made no sense, but it had to be important, and Skald needed to know why. He had been trying to find out for days, without success.

He had moved into one of the empty rooms in Skyrock and he was pacing up and down the long stairs from the control chamber to the sapphire-crusted tunnel; it helped him concentrate and he needed focus more than ever. His life hung by a fraying thread and, if he did not prove himself extraordinarily useful, the magiz would snap it.

After his failure in Thurkad, Skald was only alive because they were desperately short of sus-magizes. The others were all working twenty hours a day and not even sus-magiz magic would allow them to keep it up much longer.

Skyrock, the iron tower and the great tunnel were almost complete now, and the moment the finishing touches were done he would become a lowly junior sus-magiz again. Someone who could be disposed of at Dagog's whim.

By the following morning the node was finally supplying enough magical power. The tower was finished, inside and out, the huge control chamber had been fitted out and Dagog had personally tested all the devices needed for the Day of All Days. The last decorations and furnishings were being installed, and anyone competent could supervise these works. Skald expected every new hour to be his last.

Part of him wanted it to be.

*I did* not *abandon my troops; I did* not *run like a coward. I was trying to take the battle to the enemy when I was blasted through the gate.*

Though no matter how often he recited these words, they could not heal him. One of the two men who held power over his life had always tarred Skald with the same cowardly brush as his father, and the other, Durthix, doubted him. But Skald's father had been a common soldier and his cowardice under fire would soon have been forgotten by all save his family, had it not been for the magiz.

An officer accused of abandoning his troops in the heat of battle was a very different affair, and so were the consequences – torture and execution in front of the assembled Merdrun nation, a prominent entry on the Tablet of Infamy read to both soldiers and civilians every twelve-day, and a cautionary tale told to children with all the fire and blood and torment the Merdrun's best tale-spinners could devise.

For Skald, who had devoted his life to escaping his father's shame and defeating the doom his mother had predicted for him, to be so wronged was unbearable. There were times when he considered ending it to escape the torment, though that would only cement his name on the Tablet of Infamy.

Only one thing kept him going now – Uletta's faith in him. She had heard him out, then said, 'That's not you. There's not a cowardly bone in your body – *and I love you.*'

The moment was so powerful that he gave way to his emotions for a few seconds. Uletta was pleased, but it terrified Skald.

Her belief in him sustained him, which was why he was working so hard on far-seeing, a gift all sus-magizes used for making gates and other purposes. But as far as Skald knew, only Dagog could far-see strongly enough for what had to be done on the Day of All Days.

The magiz thought, because of Skald's early successes, that he also had the gift strongly, and it was probably the only thing keeping him alive right now. Skald's gift had improved over the past week of training Sulien, but not by much.

'Hoy, Coward?'

Skald started. His nemesis was at the bottom of the steps, scowling up at him. Dagog no longer called Skald by name; he only ever addressed him as *Coward*, and Skald could not acknowledge it. He waited for the magiz to speak.

'How's the far-seeing going?' said Dagog. 'With Sulien, I mean?'

'Very well, Magiz. She has an astounding talent.'

'Work her harder. From now until the great day, it will be your first priority.'

Dagog turned back to his chamber. What was he working on, anyway? Every device had been checked and checked again, and every spell rehearsed until perfect. It should have been the magiz's time to relax but he was more frantic than ever.

Lately, he had got into the habit of drinking the lives of half a dozen slaves at midnight, before snatching a few hours' sleep. If ever he would give anything away, it would be in his post-drinking euphoria.

That night, Skald crept up the dark tower at half past midnight. The door to Dagog's bedchamber was open and he was reeling about like a purple-faced, bloated drunkard; he must have drunk more than the usual number of lives tonight.

Senior Sus-magiz Yallav, a short, thin woman with blotchy skin, pinched features and yellow, watering eyes, hugely magnified by half-inch-thick, square spectacles, lay on his bed. She was reputed to be a spy for the magiz, and also his lover – and clearly, she was, since she was naked. The thought was repulsive.

'Come to bed,' she cooed. 'You've earned it, Dagog.'

Dagog lurched to his table and sat down. 'One more thing to do.'

'Surely it can wait, this once.'

'It can't. I've got to master it before the day.'

'Master what? You're already the greatest magiz in more than a century.'

'I'm going to be the greatest since Merdrax the First,' he said without looking up. 'Perhaps even greater than he was.'

Yallav shivered and sat up, drawing the covers around her. 'I'm not sure that's a good idea, Dagog.'

'Merdrax set us on the true path, but we've slipped off it.'

'And you're going to haul us back?' She did not look pleased.

'Once I master this new Art.'

'What new Art?'

'I've found a way to drink not just lives, but the victim's *gift* as well.'

'I don't understand.'

'When we drink lives, a gifted person's gift dies at the moment they die. I've found a way to take it as well – that's why I've been drinking so many lives these past nights. But I still have a few problems to sort out before I can use those stolen gifts.'

'But ... why now?'

'We'll only get one chance, Yallav.'

'For what?'

'To take power back – and restore the magizship to its rightful supremacy over the military. One chance to restore the Merdrun nation to what Merdrax the First meant us to be. I've got to be ready.'

Skald almost choked. Dagog was planning to overthrow the High Commander and turn the Merdrun back into the honourless brutes they had been in olden times. It would destroy the True Purpose. But what could he, Skald, do? Dagog was his master, and informing on one's master was a capital crime.

After a long silence, Yallav said, 'How are you going to do it?'

'When the slave girl's gift is fully trained I'm going to drink her life *and* her gift, and my far-seeing gift will be enhanced tenfold. I won't just be able to far-see places, I'll be able to far-see into the minds of my enemies. And once I know their weaknesses, *no one* will be able to stand against me.'

## 19

# YOU'RE A PERFECT LITTLE COLLABORATOR

Every lesson Sulien had with Skald made her feel more like a traitor, because she knew what she was learning was really important to the enemy. And more like a bad friend, because on the rare times she failed, or the aftersickness built up and she had to stop far-seeing early, Jassika was punished.

After a few days, the far-seeing of objects had become too easy, and Skald now required Sulien to far-see places she had been, near and sometimes far, and send the image to him via a mind-link, clearly enough for him to go there.

The cave on the Isle of Gwine where the triplets magiz had stabbed Karan and planned to kill Sulien and Llian. Sulien's cosy little corner room at the top of the old keep at Gothryme – she had wept at those memories. The great chamber in Alcifer where she had first sensed life in Rulke's statue, and other places.

Several times, Skald had left as soon as he received the image and was away for some time. Once he had returned wet and smelling of pine resin, and wood rotting in perpetually saturated forests, and it had brought Salliban back to her as if it was just outside the door. He was making gates, at considerable cost in power, and using her image to go to these places and check.

Skald was a hero and an important Merdrun with many duties, so why had the magiz ordered him to spend so much time and power on training her? Whatever the magiz wanted, it must be bad.

Two days later, when Sulien could visualise places she already knew perfectly, Skald changed the lessons again. 'Now I want you to far-see places you've *never* been.'

'Why?' she said.

He did not reply. Slaves had no right to question their masters.

In a twelve-sided room he showed her, one by one, life-like paintings of many places: desert landscapes, ice-sheathed mountains, forests and heathland and scrub, a rocky island with massive waves crashing against it, a coral island in a deep blue sea, the inside of a glow-worm cave, and a city in the tropics, its graceful avenues lined with gigantic rain trees.

Skald did not name any of these places and he only gave her a few minutes to far-see each one before moving to the next painting.

An hour went by, then another, and he did not let up until she cried, 'I can't see anything else! My head's killing me.'

After that he took it more slowly, with frequent rests so her aftersickness did not build up.

'Why do I have to far-see all these places?' she said, not expecting him to answer.

'I'm building your skills.'

'For what?'

He did not reply.

Soon, though, whenever Skald showed her a new painting, most of the time she could far-see the place within minutes, and a couple of times he returned her to her cell while he made a gate there, to check.

'The enemy must think you're really clever,' Jassika said waspishly that night. She had been beaten again for Sulien's failures today. 'How does that make you feel, knowing you're so important to the enemy's plans? It must be *great* being you.'

'I'm really sorry,' said Sulien.

'I don't mind being beaten for your failures. It's the days when I don't get beaten that bother me. What have you've done for the enemy on those days, Sulien? They must really love you; you're a perfect little collaborator.'

Sulien turned her head to the wall and pretended to be asleep. Was Skald training her to see places vital to their True Purpose? She had no clue as to which places mattered and which did not. Every picture was different, and deserts were no more common than forests or swamps or islands, towns and cities, farmland or icy wastes. He was too clever to make any pattern that she could identify.

But she had to find a clue. It was the only way she could ease her conscience.

And the following day an opportunity came. When Skald led her to the twelve-sided chamber, dozens of large pictures were stacked against one wall. The land-scape painters must have worked day and night because she had envisaged more than a hundred of them now. In the night, when she lay on her stone bunk in dark-ness, she could picture one or other of them for hours, and often she dreamed about them.

But today was different. Skald began with a set of three paintings, all of the same grassy hill that came to a rocky point at the top, but painted from different angles. And this time, after she could visualise the first painting, and the second, he required her to bring the two images together in her mind so they converged into a three-dimensional image that she could move around in her mind's eye.

After she could do it with two of the images, she had to use three, and that proved too much.

'Can't do it!' she gasped.

She dozed on a pile of rugs in a corner until she felt better. Skald did not leave the room; he walked in figure-eights the whole time, checking papers and drawings. Then he started again, just with the first two paintings, then went to three again.

After lunch, Sulien was far-seeing the next trio of paintings, depicting a pebbly path through a gloomy, moss-covered wood that reminded her of the old forest in the mountains west of Gothryme, when Uletta came to the door with a roll of drawings.

This had happened twice in the past week and each time Skald had been away for a good while, and returned flushed and looking pleased with himself. Sulien could guess what they were up to, but this time she saw that, in his haste, he had left the door unlocked.

She slipped out and crept through the empty corridors to his chamber, which was up on the next level. This section of Skyrock had been completed more than a week ago and there were no workers here, nor any guards. None were needed in such a secure place.

She went in, her heart thumping and her mouth dry. If she were caught spying, at the very least she would be flogged. At the worst, she might be handed over to the magiz for some unspeakable punishment.

Sulien had no idea what she was looking for. She found plenty of papers, charts and drawings, but all the ones she could read had to do with the design and building and powering of the tower. A few pages were in jagged Merdrun glyphs which meant nothing to her.

It did not take long to search the room; Skald's only possessions were three sets of uniforms and two pairs of boots, all in perfect repair, his sword and knife, a pair of sus-magiz robes and a wooden box containing a copy of Flydd's *Histories of the Lyrinx War*. The fifth volume sat on a small pedestal beside his bed, which was a simple canvas stretcher.

She turned and saw a small, oily green shard, like a piece of a smashed bottle, hanging from a steel chain. The magiz had pricked her forehead with a similar though larger shard, temporarily paralysing her. His brown-stained fingers had stank, and his breath had been even worse, as if the lives he had drunk were rotting inside him.

Sulien touched the shard with a fingertip and sensed a dark and perilous power bonded to Skald, as well as a twinge of emotion – guilt. What did he feel guilty about? She gingerly touched the shard to her forehead.

Pain pierced her head, she heard a boy howling, then she had the clearest far-seeing she had ever experienced. It was as if she were looking through a freshly washed window at a small, black-haired boy. His back was bare and bloody, and a woman was flogging him and screaming at him.

'How dare you say such a wicked thing! You're as bad as your coward of a father and you'll come to the same end. Go away!'

'But ... all I said was, *Do you love me?*'

'A Merdrun does not show emotions. A true Merdrun does not *have* emotions – save after victory in battle.'

It reminded Sulien of something, but she could not recover the memory. She put the shard back and hurried back to the far-seeing chamber.

But the pain in her head grew ever worse. After Skald returned, looking more pleased with himself than usual, she convinced him that she was too ill with after-sickness to continue far-seeing. She was lying on her stone bunk, her head throbbing, when Jassika hobbled in, wincing with every step. She had been punished again.

Sulien dragged herself upright. 'Jass, I'm really sorry. I was too ill –'

'Merdrun lover!' Jassika hissed. She crouched in a corner, trying not to cry. 'You didn't even try this afternoon.'

Sulien felt so guilty that she told Jassika what she had done. Jassika's eyes flashed, but she did not say anything, and Sulien could not tell whether she was proud of her, or furious.

The following morning, she found out. Skald took Sulien to the far-seeing chamber as always, closed the door and put his back to it, and said very quietly, 'You went to my chamber yesterday. You touched my sacred rue-har, that no one but myself and the magiz is permitted to touch.'

Sulien's heart gave a painful lurch. There was no point denying it. 'How did you know?' she whispered.

'The other slave girl informed on you. Why, Sulien?'

'I – I wanted to know why you're training me to far-see.'

Was he going to flog her too? Sulien had been beaten daily while the Whelm were looking after her, but any Merdrun punishment would be far worse.

'Magiz Dagog could drink your life for that. And mine.' Skald paused and, judging by the fear etched into his normally impassive face, he was not exaggerating. He lowered his voice to match hers and crouched down until his face was just inches away. 'And if he should find out, he will. You won't do anything like that again, will you?'

≈

Since returning from the disaster of Thurkad, Skald had only been able to snatch a few minutes with Uletta at a time. But Dagog had left this afternoon on a secret mission, taking three sus-magiz with him, and would not be back until the morning. Skald had given Uletta their secret sign and now, late that night, he was heading to an empty chamber chosen for their tryst. They used a different one each time.

After they were done, and they lay in each other's arms, she said, 'What happens once the tower is finished?'

He swallowed. He had not thought past the Day of All Days, because it was to be his last. Once Durthix no longer needed him, or heroes, he would hand Skald over to the magiz. And then –

A moan escaped him; he could not hold it back. No Merdrun hero had suffered such a crushing fall in more than eleven hundred years, and it would erase the entire purpose of his life since the day he'd been told about his father's cowardice and execution. The day Skald had vowed to become a hero, a man whose courage could not be doubted for an instant. But everything he'd striven for, and every good thing he had done at such cost to himself, would be erased. No, reversed.

He reached out and clung to her, desperately. She was the one good thing left in his life.

'Skald?' she said, turning onto her side to gaze at him. 'Is something the matter?'

'Just thinking about the Day of All Days,' he said. 'And ... afterwards.'

No one knew what was to happen on that day except Durthix and the magiz. Skald's guts knotted and the agony he had suffered bringing the construct here from Alcifer revisited him. What if Dagog suspected Skald was having a forbidden liaison with Uletta?

'Will – will the magiz have us put to death?'

Skald feared that Dagog would drink the lives of all the gifted slaves who had worked on the tower, to make sure its secrets remained his.

'I don't know.' He stroked her thick hair. 'I've got to get you away to somewhere safe. Somewhere he'll never find you.'

'I can't leave without you, Skald.'

*You'll have to. I'm doomed.* But he did not want to ruin what might be their last time together.

'I can't go without you, either,' he said.

And it hit him like a shard thrust into his forehead. This was no casual liaison; this was the real thing. Was there a way to save her, *and himself*?

'Your people would see you as a traitor,' said Uletta, evidently divining part of his thoughts. 'We'd have to go far away and hide.'

But a traitor would be hunted down, no matter how long it took. Besides, the Merdrun's motto was *One for All*; it was how they had survived, alone against the universe, all this time. For a Merdrun, the sole comfort in a perilous world was to be one small part of the whole, and contribute to the whole. Personal freedom was anathema to them and few Merdrun could survive in exile. Could he?

The irony struck him. All his life he had striven to be the perfect Merdrun. The bravest, the most loyal, the hardest working. And now, when he would soon be falsely accused of failing in his duty to his own troops, he was contemplating the greatest dereliction of all – abandoning his people on what was to be the greatest day of their lives.

'I'll think of a way,' he said rashly, trembling at the very idea. But how? As the Day of All Days approached, the magiz would watch him ever more closely. He would not be cheated of the opportunity to destroy a man he had always despised, nor of taking the life he most longed for.

She studied Skald for a moment, then made his impossible dilemma a hundred times worse. 'But how can I abandon my friends, knowing they're all going to killed?'

Uletta drew back a little, and cold air rushed in under the blankets, between them. Skald stared at her, not knowing what to say.

'Skald?'

'I – I can't do anything for them. It'll be hard enough just saving you.'

She hurled the blankets off and sat up, giving him a hard stare.

'Uletta, please,' he said, yearning for the warmth of her skin on his and her strong arms around him.

She stood up and began jerking her clothes on. 'You've got to save all nine of the slaves in my team, Skald – or none. It's your choice. Good, or evil?'

She stalked out. He dressed but remained there, staring at the wall. Uletta had begun to heal his tormented soul. She had brought out emotions he had always been terrified of revealing, and he was a better man for it. He could not lose her now.

But putting the lives of slaves ahead of the True Purpose would definitely be betraying his people. Skald was a condemned man, but he was also a true Merdrun. How could he do it, and on the Day of All Days?

And if he did find a way to escape his fate, and betrayed his oath and his people to save Uletta and the other slaves in her team, how could he live with himself?

She had pointed out the nature of his choice, but could an entire race of people be evil? Had Stermin been right, at the dawn of their existence, when he'd created the Gates of Good and Evil and forced everyone to choose either the Azure Gate or the Crimson Gate? Had he been right when he had called all those people who chose the Crimson Gate irredeemably evil? Or had his condemnation been self-fulfilling?

These were weighty matters. Too weighty for a Merdrun who had been taught, through abuse and beatings and unrelenting discipline, that thinking for oneself was wicked and selfish.

Late that night the magiz returned and Skald was called to his chamber. Skald's heart almost tore in his chest. Had Dagog set someone to watch him, or used a hidden spy portal? If he had spied on Skald lying in Uletta's arms, they were doubly doomed.

Then an even more dreadful thought struck him. What if Dagog knew what Skald and Uletta had talked about? Conspiring to betray the Merdrun meant instant death for any slave involved, no matter the inconvenience, and Skald would suffer the cruellest fate that the past one thousand magizes had been able to devise.

There had not been a traitor's execution in Skald's lifetime, but there were plenty in the cautionary tales that every Merdrun child learned by heart. And even worse than the agony, often prolonged for days, was the knowledge that the traitor was cast out from his people, in life and in death.

Skald knocked on the door of the magiz's chamber.

'Enter, Coward.'

Skald went in, desperately trying to conceal his fears. Dagog was engaged with a stack of papyruses and did not look up. He had not slept in days and looked exhausted. He looked as though he had not drunk a life in days.

'Yes, Magiz?'

'The gifted girl, Sulien. How have you fared?'

Was this a trick question? 'She far-sees further and more clearly than anyone I know ... except yourself.'

Dagog looked up. 'Further than you, Sus-magiz?'

If Skald lied, surely the magiz would know. 'Much further, Magiz. Though ...'

'What?'

'I could train her more effectively if I knew what you need her for.'

Skald knew why Dagog wanted Sulien's gift trained – so he could take it when he drank her life, and become so powerful that he could overthrow the High Commander and make the magiz supreme. It was a monstrous plan. Treasonous, and Dagog would never admit to a word of it. But he might give something away.

'You have no need to know more than I've already told you.' The magiz scanned a papyrus sheet, frowning.

His attention was elsewhere, and Skald thought he could get away with a small lie. He had to make himself more valuable; he needed every small advantage he could get. 'I'm learning a lot from training her, Magiz. My own gift of far-seeing ... it's improved remarkably.'

This wasn't a total lie. His own far-seeing abilities had improved, though not by much.

He held his breath, but Dagog merely grunted, screwed up the papyrus and tossed it on a brazier behind him, and picked up another. 'Good, he said absently. 'Go, Coward.'

# 20

# THE MAGIZ MUST DIE!

Skald slipped out from his latest tryst with Uletta in a state of bliss. She had been more passionate than ever, more loving, and, though beforehand they had talked about how they might save themselves and where they might flee to, she had not repeated her demand for him to save her fellow slaves. She must have realised that it was impossible.

He felt like bursting into song, though that would have been deeply suspicious. His people only had two kinds of joyful songs, one as they went into battle, the other after victory had been won. They also had dirges, sung after defeats and disasters, and one had been sung after the catastrophe in Thurkad. The dire tune ran through his mind. He forced it down; he could not bear to relive that day.

From the corner of an eye he glimpsed Sus-magiz Yallav, hurrying towards him down a side passage.

'Sus-magiz Skald,' she said, falling into step beside him. Her voice was as meagre as the rest of her, hoarse and wispy and flat. 'What are you doing all the way up here?'

Was it a loaded question? 'Inspections.' He did not look at her.

'You inspected up here yesterday, and the day before. The very same level – a level that was completed and signed off last week.'

Skald stiffened, and had to force himself to act as though nothing was amiss. He looked down at her upturned face.

'When changes are made, Yallav, or faults identified and repaired, I have to recheck. Everything must be done perfectly, according to the plans.'

'When faults are identified and repaired, I have to recheck,' she echoed, and turned aside.

Was it a warning? No, the magiz's spy would never give a warning; it could only be a threat. The magiz knew something and wanted Skald to know it. Dagog wanted him to be scared and make another mistake. His last.

There was only one way out now, for Skald and Uletta.

The magiz must die!

Skald froze in mid-step, appalled at the very thought. Dagog was vital to the success of their True Purpose – his gift of far-seeing was almost irreplaceable. To even think of getting rid of him at such a critical time was the most monstrous betrayal that could ever be contemplated. Killing him would betray the Merdrun nation's strivings these past ten thousand years and more.

And yet, Skald thought, Dagog was a selfish and self-indulgent man, drinking ever more lives to feed his sickening addiction. He had consumed six slaves today, and the chief miner, for alleged incompetence. Dagog did not care about *One for All*. Everything he did was for himself, and his treasonous plan to overthrow Durthix was a far bigger threat to the True Purpose.

Yes, if Skald and Uletta were to survive, Dagog had to die. But how could so powerful and cunning an adept be killed in a way that could never come back on Skald? And if he could be killed, how could the True Purpose be saved?

# 21

# I VERY MUCH DOUBT THAT I'LL BE BACK

Ilisial, Wilm and Klarm had been labouring on the air-floater for weeks, and finally everything was complete. Ilisial glowed. The weeks of using her craft had rejuvenated her; she hardly ever reverted to the bitter hostility of a month ago.

In the evenings they sat around the campfire, Klarm drinking vinegary wine from bottles retrieved from the scrutators' private pantry in the buried hull of the air-dreadnought, and telling tales of his adventures as a scrutator, and afterwards. He was a fine tale-spinner, and pleasant company, most of the time.

Klarm broke off from telling a scarcely believable yarn about his time as a young acrobat on a pirate ship. He was staring at Ilisial, who sat on her rock, her eyes fixed, breathing shallowly and shuddering. She was often like that in the evenings, when there was no work to occupy her, but she seemed worse tonight.

Klarm touched her on the shoulder and she roused. 'You're safe now,' he said. 'Get to bed. Nothing's going to happen tonight.'

'I just want to go home.'

'Where do you call home?'

'I've got some cousins in Ossury. That's in Borgistry. We don't get on ... but they'll take me in ... as long as I drudge for them.'

'You can do better than that,' said Klarm. 'You've a great gift.'

'But I have no teacher. I'll never see M'Lainte again.'

'I'll speak to Flydd. After this is over, if we win, he'll find you another teacher. And when you've finished, with skills like yours –'

'It's no use, Klarm,' Ilisial said in a dreary voice. 'I – I don't have the strength.' She stumbled to her tent.

Klarm stared at Wilm as if daring him to ask what was the matter with her.

'I'm worried,' Wilm said softly.

Klarm sighed. 'You saved her life. You've a right to know.'

Wilm waited for him to go on. It was usually the best way.

'Not everyone can come back from a partial life drinking,' said Klarm.

'But Skald had only just started when I got to her.'

'A lot of a life can be drunk in a few seconds. Only Ilisial knows what she's lost, and the true horror of it, and some people don't believe they'll ever escape the nightmare. Or they live in terror that it's going to happen again, and just want it to end.'

'Do you think Ilisial feels that way?'

'I don't know, Laddie. But ... I'm afraid.'

Wilm too. What had it done to an already troubled young woman? He would have had nightmares about it to the end of his days.

In the morning Ilisial was her normal, organised and efficient self as they made the final preparations. They laid out sheets of rubber-impregnated canvas on an area cleared of every stick and sharp stone, checked for cracks and nicks, repaired them with thread and gum where necessary and cut the sheets to shape to form a teardrop-shaped airbag. It was one of the rare, windless days at the Sink of Despair and by the time the sun went down they had cleaned the overlapping seams of every speck of sand and grit, sewn them together and sealed them with gum.

By mid-morning of the following day, every seam had been checked and rechecked, every peg and rope and knot tightened, and their dwindling supplies had been stowed in the canoe-shaped hull, which Ilisial and Wilm had made by binding together bamboo hoops from the wrecked air-dreadnought. Wilm loaded a barrel filled with bitter water from the seep. Klarm tied down everything moveable.

'Ready?' said Ilisial. She and Wilm raised the upper part of the airbag on canvas-wrapped props, so the floater gas could rise to the top.

'Ready,' said Klarm.

He turned the stopcock and, with a tinny hiss, floater gas flowed out of the steel tank, through the hose and into the airbag, though more than ten minutes passed before Wilm saw any perceptible signs of inflation.

But slowly the upper part of the airbag started to rise, and the rest to fill. 'Hold it higher,' said Ilisial. 'We don't want it to fold on itself, or tear.'

Wilm went up on tiptoes, raising his prop another six inches. The strain was immense, but shortly the airbag lifted into the air on its network of ropes and rose until it was directly above the hull.

'Check the pegs!' cried Ilisial.

He ran to the other side, where a couple of the pegs holding the hull down were in danger of pulling out under the strain. He hammered them in.

'All good here,' said Ilisial.

'And here,' yelled Klarm. 'Get aboard.'

Wilm tossed his mallet in and clambered up the side. Ilisial was already in.

'Pull the pegs,' said Klarm.

Wilm took up position opposite Ilisial. 'Now!' she said.

They heaved their pegs out of the ground, ran to the next opposite pair and did the same, then the third pair. Only one pair of pegs was holding the air-floater down now, and the hull was shuddering under the strain.

'Shut off the floater gas!' she yelled, and the hissing flow ceased.

As Wilm reached for his rope, the peg tore free and the hull, which was still held by the last peg, tilted up sharply, throwing him off his feet and slamming Ilisial hard against the side.

'Pull the damned peg!' Klarm roared.

Ilisial was writhing on the deck, holding her right knee. The bamboo hull of the air floater rotated around the last peg. Wilm raced across but could not free it. He drew Akkidul and hacked through the rope.

The air floater righted itself with a jerk, tossing him off his feet, and hurtled upwards. A few hundred feet up it caught a breeze and drifted west.

Wilm looked back at the exposed wreckage of the air-dreadnought's hulls. They had been at the Sink of Despair for the best part of seven weeks.

'Good riddance!' He sheathed the sword and bent over Ilisial.

'Kneecap!' Her face was blanched.

'Is it broken, do you think?'

'Can't tell.'

'Do you want me to take a look?'

'Get Klarm.'

Klarm probed her knee all over and around. 'Just badly bruised,' he said. 'It's going to be painful. Rest it; I don't need anything else from you today.'

As he turned away, the farspeaker made a burping sound and Flydd spoke, his voice distorted.

*Where the hell are you, Klarm?*

'We just took to the air. What do you want?'

*I thought you were leaving a week ago.*

'We were lucky to leave at all.'

*Why didn't you tell me? I've got you in my plans.*

'We tried,' said Klarm. 'Couldn't raise a squeak from you.'

*There have been ... more problems. Which way is the wind blowing?*

'Carrying us east-north-east.'

*Any chance you can go east-south-east?*

'Towards Skyrock?'

*In a general sense. Can't talk over this farspeaker.*

.

'Ilisial has rigged up a crude rotor but it doesn't have a lot of push. But if the wind turns southerly, there's only one way we're going and that's due north.'

*Do your very best. I'll call you tomorrow.*

'Something the matter?'

*Can't talk,* said Flydd, and he was gone.

'Why does he want us to go east-south-east?' said Wilm.

Klarm heaved on the six-foot-long rudder arm and turned a triangular wheel a quarter of a turn. The air-floater turned a little to the left. The rotor drew power from the weak field here and spun a little faster.

'How fast are we going?' Wilm wondered after a while.

'Your guess is as good as mine.'

Wilm looked down, comparing obvious landmarks to his mental map of this part of Santhenar. 'The Sink of Despair is about fifty leagues long, and we started halfway along it, so when we reach the eastern end, we'll have gone about twenty-five leagues. Seventy-five miles.'

He noted the time, and after an interminable couple of hours saw that they were almost opposite the eastern end. 'We've flown about thirty-five miles in the last hour,' he said. 'I thought it'd be more than that.'

'It would be if we went higher,' said Klarm.

'Then why don't we?'

'Wind could be going in a different direction, but without any clouds, I can't tell.'

They continued east-south-east during the night, Klarm sighting on the stars to make sure they were going in the right direction and adjusting the rudder arm as needed.

Wilm slept, and woke to realise that they were on the ground. It was still dark, though firelight showed that the air-floater had been tied to the trunks of a couple of small trees. Ilisial was asleep. He climbed out.

Klarm was sitting by a small, smokeless fire with a mug of black tea, talking quietly into his far-speaker. His pack was beside him. He held up a hand and Wilm stopped.

Shortly Klarm put the far-speaker into a concealed cavity in his wooden foot, and beckoned.

'Wilm my lad, listen carefully because I only have time to say this once.'

'Should I wake Ilisial?'

'She needs her sleep. You can tell her later.'

'You talk as though you're going away.'

'And I very much doubt that I'll be back.'

'Where are you going?'

'I can't talk about it.'

'What's happened? Something's changed, hasn't it?'

'What did I just say?' Klarm paused. 'I'm walking the rest of the way. Take this.'
He handed Wilm a small, round brass object.

'What is it?'

'My knoblaggie; my magical focus. It performs much the same function as Flydd's staff. But it can do other things as well. Give it to Jassika when you next see her.'

'I will,' said Wilm. 'What do you want us to do? Ilisial wants to go home to Ossury, but –'

'The wind's turned westerly and the rotor isn't strong enough to take you there. But it will carry you east to the rendezvous with Flydd, only twenty miles from here.' Klarm showed Wilm a small point on the map. 'There's a massive granite cliff and it runs for miles; you can't miss it. Land along the base, wherever you can, and wait for him to find you.'

'That's all?'

'Yes.' Klarm held out his hand. 'I doubt we'll ever see each other again ... but thanks. You're a good man.'

Now you tell me? Wilm thought. He shook Klarm's hand, wondering what the last month and a half of abuse and mockery had been about, and where Klarm was going. Nothing made sense about him.

Klarm picked up his pack and walked into the darkness.

# 22

# HANDS IN THE AIR, LITTLE MAN

Walking seven miles across rough country on an inflamed stump was not something Klarm would forget in a hurry.

Why was he doing this for an ungrateful world that had never given a damn about him? He could have bought a ship and gone back to sailing the Great Ocean, fishing and drinking, drinking and fishing. He might have taken up watercolours, or wine making, or engraving the Histories on the head of a pin. Or sleeping in with one or two of his favourite lovers – or all of them. Anything would be better than this.

Even teaching Jassika better manners and becoming a proper father to her.

Jassika, his joy and his torment. He had not been able to contact her, but Sulien was a steadying influence. If this went badly – no, *when* this went badly, he prayed that Flydd would keep his promise to take care of Jassika. Assuming he, Klarm, could get her out of Skyrock.

Though Flydd was no more father material than Klarm himself. Flydd would find a good foster home for Jass, faithfully manage the coin and ensure that she had the best of tutors, but he wouldn't have a clue about looking after her emotional needs, or those of the young woman she would all too soon become. Flydd would put her in someone else's care, and Jassika had suffered far too much of that already. She needed stability and discipline. And love.

If Flydd lived, which looked increasingly unlikely. If Klarm's suspicions were right about the Merdrun, and why they had carved out the great spiralling tower and installed that shrouded device at its top, he wasn't sure anyone would survive.

No point thinking about such things. It was why he had lived a life of danger, drink and dissipation – they kept the ever-present dread at bay. But now he had to focus as he had never focused before.

He climbed a wall-like ridge of rock, one of a number of vertical dykes radiating out from the base of the pinnacle for miles, though all had been cut to ground near Skyrock and the rock used to build the compound wall around it. Ahead of him the dyke was fifteen feet high and the top would give him a clear view into the bowl-like depression.

He slowly made his way up, being careful not to create a silhouette. Merdrun guards never rested, and they would be constantly scanning their surroundings with spy glasses.

His practiced eye identified the civilians' compound, a smaller compound further up the slope for the Whelm, and the army camp and officers' and slaves' compounds. A dam on the left provided water, though it wasn't nearly large enough for four hundred thousand people and would be empty within weeks. What then? The thought was chilling.

Inside the Skyrock compound, on the far left near the circular wall, sat the construct. It wasn't being used today; all the lifting and carrying had been done.

On the other side of the compound a large pile of waste rock was oddly blurred. Hiding something? He had no way of knowing. A few hundred yards to the right of the ten-fold compound gates, luminous vapours wisped up from a broken-edged hole or mine pit. Curious.

Klarm activated the farspeaker magically concealed inside his wooden foot and, when Flydd answered, told him what he could see.

*Any way in?* said Flydd.

'Nothing obvious.'

*How are their forces arranged?*

'Ten thousand troops outside the compound gates, five thousand to each side. The gates are closed, but in the event of an attack on Skyrock the troops could be there in minutes. Thousands more guards patrol the top of the wall and outside it, and others man their heavy javelards and other defences against aerial attack.'

*We've got personal experience of those.*

'The rest of their army is only a mile away up from the gates, and everyone who goes in and out of the compound is stripped naked and searched.'

*What about the construct?*

'Three guards outside.'

*Karan mind-called Rulke. There aren't any guards inside.*

'Did he say anything else?' asked Klarm.

*Each night, after he completes whatever flying the Merdrun require, they take the controller crystal. Tell me about that pit.*

Klarm felt a shiver of unease. 'Looks like a pit of impossibilities – a dump for all their magical waste.'

*We called them chaos chasms. I investigated several, in the war. Deadly places.*

After Flydd was gone, Klarm changed his far-speaker to call but not receive and closed it down. He sat there, doing mental exercises learned long ago to calm himself. They weren't entirely successful. This was going to be bad.

It was time. He raised his head for a few seconds, lowered it, waited and raised it again. Then ducked down and began to make labelled sketches in a small notebook. The guards must spot him but there could be no suspicion that he had done it deliberately.

An air-scooter came humming towards him, carrying two heavily armed soldiers. Klarm made a play at scrambling down, then stopped; there was no getting away from such a craft. It settled on top of the dyke, a few yards away, and the soldier at the rear sprang lightly off.

'Name?' said the soldier.

'Klarm.'

'The former scrutator.' The soldier was well-informed. 'We thought as much. Hands in the air, little man.'

Klarm complied, his heart thumping rather harder than usual. Everything depended on what happened now. An ordinary spy would probably be interrogated by an officer, assisted by a sus-magiz. But Klarm was a man of vast experience, particularly with magical devices, and hopefully they would want to learn from him ... before they tortured him to death.

The soldier searched Klarm, put everything in his pockets into his pack, including his notebook and pencil, bound him and tied him to the centre of the air-scooter. It carried him down, looped across a corner of the slaves' compound, then proceeded above the broad, gravelled road to the closed gates of the Skyrock compound.

Klarm was untied, stripped, his clothing searched and his wooden foot checked, then he was ordered through the gate and allowed to dress. *Good*, he thought, shivering in the chilly wind. He needed to be inside Skyrock. And, ideally, interrogated by the magiz himself.

However it was not the magiz who came to take him in – it was the big sus-magiz who had attacked them on the mountainside near the Sink of Despair. Skald had done far greater deeds since; he was a clever, dangerous man.

Though he did not look it now.

Klarm assessed Skald as he approached. He had lost a lot of weight since capturing M'Lainte and taking the spellcaster. His arms were almost hairless and his short, dark hair was thinner. He looked, Klarm thought, like a horse that had been spooked once too often and now jumped at shadows. It might not be obvious to anyone else but Klarm was a superlative reader of people. What was Skald so afraid of?

If Klarm's outlandish plan was to have a hope of succeeding, he had to know what motivated Skald, and what he so feared.

Klarm reviewed what he knew about the man. Skald's father had been executed for cowardice on the battlefield when Skald was a little boy, and that, and the stigma of being a coward's son, would have scarred him. It must be what drove him to succeed, even at the cost of his own health.

Skald had almost killed himself escaping after the failed assassination attempt, Flydd had said a long time ago, and he had done more damage capturing Rulke and bringing the construct here. No wonder he looked wasted.

He had since led his troops to a humiliating defeat in Thurkad, and the Merdrun harshly punished leaders who failed. But Skald was still, apparently, in a high position, which could only mean that his worth to Durthix and the magiz outweighed that failure. Skald's fear, then, came from something else. Something personal?

Skald stopped and looked down – in both senses – at Klarm, who was used to it. Let the swine underestimate him; it would give him an edge.

'This way,' said Skald, turning towards Skyrock.

He did not call for a guard, which was surprising. Nor did he bind Klarm or blindfold him. Skald did not care what Klarm saw inside the compound because he wasn't going to live long enough to tell anyone about it.

It was half a mile from the gates to the pinnacle, which stood at the centre of the compound, and the ground had been stripped bare and levelled. A series of roads and paths were made from crushed rock.

The pinnacle was surrounded by a circular paved area that extended out for a couple of hundred yards, the black and grey flagstones arranged to spell something out in an inwards spiral of the Merdrun glyphs, which Klarm could not read. The writing ended outside the entrance to the tunnel.

The transformation of the pinnacle was complete. The scaffolding Flydd had seen when he'd pursued the construct to Skyrock was gone, revealing how the hard rock had been cut away, shaped and clad to form interwoven blue and white spirals surrounding a central, partly hollowed-out core. The top, seven hundred feet up, had been levelled off, and on it reared the tapering iron tower with the canvas shroud at the top. What did it hide, and what was its purpose?

'It's one of the wonders of the world,' said Klarm, and meant it.

'It had to be beautiful,' said Skald. 'Perfect in every way. Pure. Untainted.'

He led Klarm into the tunnel. The centre of the arch was supported with lines of slender columns, and the walls and top of the tunnel had been clad in sapphires, billions of them.

They went up a series of steep stairs that tested Klarm's endurance to his limits, and Skald directed him into a rectangular room carved out of the living rock. There was a table and four chairs.

Skald went out and closed the door. The room was windowless apart from some inadequate ventilation holes. Warm air issued through slots low in the side walls, and it was stifling. Klarm could feel sweat trickling down his back. He sat on a chair facing the door. It was bliss to take the weight off his bloody stump.

The door sighed open. It wasn't Skald this time. From the meagre body, choleric face and stained, claw-like fingers, and the smell like a predator that fed on carrion, it could only be the magiz.

'Nuceus Klarm,' he said, sitting at the other end of the table. 'Former acrobat, former scrutator, former traitor. Santhenar has no army and no way of forming one, so what did you hope to gain by spying on us?'

'Information is power,' said Klarm.

'Are you after it, or offering it?'

Klarm hesitated, deliberately. He had to play the role of his life here. 'Perhaps both.'

The magiz breathed out noisily, and the carrion smell grew stronger and more sickening. 'For the glory of my people and the furtherance of our True Purpose, I sometimes have dealings with traitors. But I always despise them.'

Klarm lifted his jaw. 'I've been despised by better people than you.'

'But have you been tortured by better torturers, you absurd little dwarf?' Dagog cracked his bony knuckles. 'More cogently, has your daughter? I believe her name is Jassika.'

Dagog had found his weakness, but Klarm dared not show it. 'You wouldn't harm a child,' he said feebly. Why hadn't he anticipated this? Had he failed before he began? No, if he did nothing else, he was going to save her.

The magiz rose, opened the door and gestured, and a soldier entered, holding a struggling girl. Klarm's breath tore strips off his throat. This was unbearable.

'Klarm?' she cried. 'Daddy, I'm so sorry.'

She never called him Daddy. 'Jassika?' he whispered.

'She's a bad influence, your daughter,' Dagog gloated. 'She led Sulien Fyrn to disobey her mother's orders, and I set a trap for them and took them both.'

'What – do you want them for?'

The magiz flicked his fingers at the soldier, who backed to the door. 'Sulien's gift is proving most useful. It's all that's keeping her, and your daughter, alive. For now.'

'Daddy!' screamed Jassika as she was carried out.

It was the worst moment of Klarm's life. The second worse was about to come.

## 23

# THE WITHERED BODIES WERE DRAGGED OUT

The screaming stopped. *My screaming*, Klarm realised. Dagog had not touched him, but he was an expert in magical forms of torture. The pain was so bad, and had gone on so long, that Klarm had lost all sense of his own identity. But he had not given way; he had drawn on all his training as one of the scrutators, and serving the God-Emperor afterwards, and he had kept his secrets.

He opened his eyes. The room was empty apart from Dagog, who was eyeing him hungrily.

He aches to drink my life, Klarm thought. He burns for the power he can get from a mancer as strong as me. If I still had my knoblaggie, I'd smear him on the wall like paste.

'The spellcaster,' said Dagog.

Finally, we get to what he really wants. 'What about it?' said Klarm.

'It's a mighty weapon of war.'

'It can be.'

'Skald saw it annihilate half of his troop, but it no longer does anything. Why not?'

'From the moment it was built,' said Klarm, 'it was dangerously unpredictable. That's why we sent it to the middle of nowhere, to test it.'

'Why was it unpredictable?'

'The original conception was flawed.'

'Did Mechanician M'Lainte have anything to do with it?'

Klarm shook his head, which turned out to be a bad idea. The pain was excruciating.

'She was busy on other projects. The designer, Rilty Smeal, was killed in the air-dreadnought crash at the Sink of Despair, as was the master crafter, Winnula ni Kurst, who built it. That left only one person from the team of three that created the spellcaster.'

'Give that person a name,' said Dagog, surreptitiously consulting an oscillating device in his pocket that Klarm assumed to be a timepiece.

'The spellcaster was my idea,' said Klarm. 'I conceived it and wrote down what it had to do, and supervised while Rilty designed it and Winnula built it.'

'I repeat, why isn't it working now?'

'Its persona is emotionally unstable – it's angry, bitter and resentful. It hates life, basically.'

'Why would you make such a device?'

'We were losing the war against the lyrinx. We had to test every idea we could come up with, no matter how absurd or dangerous. The spellcaster was one of the better ones. Had it worked we would have made thousands of copies and sent them out to hunt the lyrinx down. It would have turned the war in our favour.'

'Can the persona be removed and replaced with a better one?' asked the magiz, unable to conceal his eagerness.

'Clearly, *you* don't have them in your magical devices,' said Klarm, putting on an air of world-weary superiority.

'Why do you say that?' Dagog snarled.

'If you did, you wouldn't have asked the question. A persona isn't *enchanted into* a device or a weapon, such as a magical sword. The persona *forms* in the device as a result of the spell that enchants it. Every persona is different, as every device is different, and the persona reflects both the enchantment and the nature of the device itself. And, it need not be said, how it's been used.'

'I don't understand.' Dagog really hated to admit it.

'The persona is the *spirit* of the device, and if the device is used for dark deeds, the persona will also become dark or twisted. If the persona is abused or mistreated by the user, it may become angry or bitter, or retreat into itself and refuse to come when called. It may even betray the user of the device. In short, personas can be every bit as unreliable as people themselves.'

'Find a way to make it reliable. Your daughter's life depends on it.'

Dagog consulted the timepiece again, and frowned. Clearly, he had other urgent matters to deal with. He went to the door, opened it and said, 'Bring them in.'

Guards escorted three young slaves in, two male and one female, manacled at the wrists. Leg shackles only allowed them short, shuffling steps. The first male and the female were shaking in terror. The second male's face was blank, as if he saw nothing, feared nothing, and knew nothing. The poor wretch had passed beyond despair and was now indifferent to his fate.

'A small demonstration,' said Dagog. 'A spur to encourage you.'

He gestured towards the first male, a stocky lad with curly, dirty-blond hair and a broad, plain face. He screamed and tore at his manacles until they scraped curls of bloody skin off. The magiz chuckled; the more his victims resisted, the more the swine enjoyed it.

Klarm clenched his fists in impotent fury. Impotent for now, but give him the chance and the magiz would know a greater terror than any of his victims. Klarm was a vengeful man.

The youth began to shrivel, and as he did Dagog's thin limbs engorged and his face flushed. It was sickening. It only took a minute, fortunately.

'There's a modicum of power in young slaves,' said the magiz. He prodded the shrunken corpse with a black-nailed big toe, and another carrion waft assailed Klarm's nostrils. The magiz stank as if he were dead inside. 'But little piquancy and no complexity. The lad was a raw red wine, tasted from the vat. Unbalanced, astringent, and unripe.' He licked his lips, which were now red-purple and bloated. 'Let's see if the second is better.'

The second youth was taller, black of hair and eye. He would have been a good-looking young man had his features not been so utterly blank. Terror had broken his mind, and it was a mercy.

Dagog drank his life in a gulp, then spat on the floor. 'Flat and dull and sour – too much acid and too little fruit.'

He was a human being, you bastard!

The magiz turned to Klarm, and for a second Klarm thought that his own life was to be drunk. Try it, he thought, and you'll get the shock of your life. But the magiz was just enjoying Klarm's horror and feasting on his helplessness.

The young woman was slender and pale, and her grey eyes were fixed on Klarm, pleadingly.

'I'm sorry,' he said quietly, holding out his empty hands. 'There's nothing I can do.'

When the magiz finished sucking her life out he was swollen like a human balloon, his fingers fat brown sausages. His lips were almost bursting, and a tickle of blood made its way from his nose.

'Flat champagne,' he sneered. 'An ordinary year. Her life might have been worth drinking with another ten years.'

Since there was nothing Klarm could do, he composed his face and waited. The magiz was baiting him but Klarm was a master at that game. He would never have survived and prospered among the scrutators if he had not been.

Now irritated, the magiz called the guards and the withered bodies were dragged out.

'I trust you see the threat to sweet little Jassika,' said Dagog. He went to the door, spoke to a guard outside and came back.

Dagog was playing with him in this as well. He had no intention of letting Klarm live, or Jassika. Klarm was ready to die, if it came to that, but he wasn't going to have his life drunk by this swine. Or Jassika's either. Though he still did not know how he was going to stop the magiz.

'How I'm going to feast on the Day of All Days,' leered Dagog. 'With the lives of a thousand slaves under my belt, and the spellcaster, I'll be the greatest adept the world has ever seen.'

Why did he want the spellcaster, anyway? Having seen Skyrock's defences from outside and inside, Klarm could not identify any weakness. Besides, their True Purpose would soon be complete and what could they possibly want spellcasters for, afterwards?

Some threat must lie in their future. But what? And where?

Skald entered. 'You called, Magiz?'

Klarm read, from Skald's manner and bearing, that he was terrified of the magiz, though he did a passable job of hiding it.

Dagog repeated what Klarm had told him about the origins of the spellcaster, and the nature of its persona, then said, 'But the dwarf is lying – he knows how to get it working. Extract the secret from him, then double-check every part and every operation. Make sure he hasn't sabotaged it.'

'As if I would,' Klarm said with fake cheer.

Dagog pointed at him and the agony of his previous torture flared again. The magiz hurried out.

'Come with me, Klarm,' said Skald.

He said it politely, as if Klarm were a human being. A most unusual Merdrun.

He led Klarm up three steep flights of steps, waiting at the top while he struggled up them, the treads being higher than Klarm's legs were long. As they passed down a hall hewn from rock, a big, beefy slave artisan came the other way. An important artisan, given her dress and the inner confidence she exuded.

She caught Skald's gaze and held it until they passed, but did not speak. Skald stopped, staring after her, then went on.

Interesting, Klarm thought.

In a pyramid-shaped chamber at the end of the corridor, the partly disassembled spellcaster sat on a long table carved from the pale, hard rock of the pinnacle. A round window looked towards the Great Mountains in the distance. Outside, the wind howled.

'You attacked my troops with it the first time we met,' said Skald. 'But it's been lifeless ever since. Why, Klarm?'

Klarm shrugged. 'Personas! Who can tell what will set them off, or make them withdraw into themselves?'

'You were one of the greatest scrutators. Don't play the idiot with me.'

'Personas are like proud, clever people, trapped in a mechanism and used by others for purposes they may never understand. Or agree with. Is it any wonder that they can grow angry, embittered, even treacherous?'

This was why they were keeping him alive. Their slave artisans could take the spellcaster apart and, in a suitable manufactory, make a thousand like it. Clearly, they needed to, presumably to equip themselves for some future battle. But until they understood how to control the spellcaster it was no use to them.

Klarm knew exactly why the spellcaster wasn't working, and how to fix it. He had spent years thinking about the device after the air-dreadnought crashed and it was lost, and he had finally solved the problem in the triangular cave high up the ridge, in the days he had spent there before Wilm and Ilisial tracked him down. It was why he had escaped on the spellcaster in the first place.

'Get started,' said Skald. 'Explain every step.'

# 24

# A SICKENING BETRAYAL

K larm took the spellcaster apart, crystal by crystal, wheel by wheel and wire by wire. He could have had it working in ten minutes, but he had to look convincing. Skald sat across the table, watching everything he did and sometimes asking questions. It was clear that he had a fine appreciation of magical devices, but also that part of his mind lay elsewhere.

On his fear of the magiz?

The big slave artisan entered, carrying a large roll of paper which she spread out on the floor beside Skald. An architectural drawing; she was a senior architect or designer.

Her demeanour was professional, though when they talked her gaze lingered on Skald in a way that revealed almost everything Klarm needed to know. He watched as they bent over the drawing, a detailed design for the carving at the capitals of the columns supporting the roof of the tunnel.

Skald could not keep his eyes off her, and once, as she turned, his right hand caressed her bottom. She elbowed him in the ribs, looking sideways at Klarm, who pretended not to have noticed. She took the drawing and hurried out.

'The deputy architect,' said Skald, evidently feeling a need to justify the visit. 'Uletta. A detail that needed my approval.'

He was having it off with a slave! A mortal offence for her, and possibly for Skald as well, but he was so hungry for a real, human connection that he could not say no.

Could Klarm make use of this preoccupation? He worked steadily through the day, taking intricate mechanisms apart and reassembling them. Occasionally he issued quiet orders to the spellcaster, and one part or another rotated or oscillated or made reciprocating motions.

'It's controlled by voice?' Skald's brow wrinkled, partly obliterating the black glyph tattooed there.

'*My* voice. Only one person can have control at a time.'

'That can be changed, of course.'

'Of course.'

'Show me how it's changed to my voice.'

Klarm looked up at Skald, assessingly, but said nothing.

'You don't look like a man who would risk his daughter's life,' said Skald.

Klarm allowed his shoulders to slump. He showed Skald how to empty the persona's memory of his voice and replace it with Skald's.

'The persona is called Obberly, and it will now obey you, and only you.'

Uletta came back, ostensibly with more drawings for Skald to check and approve. She kept her distance this time, save for a brief, low-voiced exchange where his answer failed to satisfy her.

She hissed in his ear, 'It's got to be *all* my team,' and went out, stiffly.

Clearly, Skald was in her thrall, and she wanted more than he could give. Escape? Freedom? Was he so in love, or lust, that he would conspire with a slave against his own people? Perhaps he was. Klarm had interrogated many traitors in his time, and their reasons for betraying their kind had been surprisingly mundane.

That afternoon, when the spellcaster was almost completely reassembled, Dagog reappeared. He was less bloated with power than he had been earlier; he must have used much of it already. It was also clear that he loathed Skald, and it was not hard for Klarm to work out why.

The magiz was small, twisted, and ugly, and in a society where size and physical strength was everything, he had probably been mocked and abused from a young age. His way of escape had been the magical arts. He would never be liked or admired, and he had since become so repulsive that he might never attract a partner, but he would be feared.

How galling for him to see big, handsome Skald – the son of a coward, no less – achieve success after success. Did Dagog fear that Skald's ambitions ran to becoming magiz as well? A magiz could never retire, for he or she knew too much. A magiz's tenure was only ended by death, often at the hands of a rival.

'Is it done?' said Dagog.

'Yes,' said Klarm.

'Show me.' Dagog set his rue-har on the table next to the spellcaster and touched the tip of the shard, which lit faintly from within. 'This is a mighty deception-breaker. If you attempt to deceive me, I will know.'

Klarm had expected something of that nature, since the magiz trusted no one. His heartbeat rose a trifle. Who knew what might set the deception-breaker off? On the other hand, the scrutators had been the most accomplished liars of all and Klarm had been better than most. He touched the raised square on top of the spellcaster.

'What do you want, dwarf?' came a querulous voice from inside.

'That's Obberly, the persona that controls the device,' said Skald. 'But it's now controlled by my voice alone. Show him, Klarm.'

'Rise a foot in the air and hover, if you please, Obberly,' said Klarm.

The spellcaster did not react.

'Rise a foot in the air and hover, if you please, Obberly,' said Skald.

The spellcaster's internals hummed, then it rose exactly one foot above the stone table and hovered, slowly revolving.

'Fly around the room and return to the table, and set down.'

The spellcaster did so. Dagog looked grudgingly impressed.

'Are all your mechanisms in working order?' said Skald.

'You know they are, son-of-a-coward,' sneered Obberly.

The magiz chuckled. He picked up the faintly glowing rue-har, touched the side to his head above his right ear for an interval, as if reading what it had to tell him, then rose.

'Skald, recheck everything. Then bring the spellcaster and Klarm to the septagonal meeting chamber in precisely two hours, where you will transfer control of the spellcaster to me.' The magiz went out.

Having watched Klarm take the spellcaster apart and put it back together again, Skald believed he knew the purpose of every part of it, but he went over it minutely, rechecking everything. Had Klarm blocked it from working, in the triangular cave? Why would he?

And why had he allowed himself to be caught spying when he was bound to be tortured and killed? Skald was sure the dwarf had wanted to be discovered; he was far too clever to have made a mistake so close to Skyrock.

Why hadn't the magiz thought of that? Perhaps because, with the Day of All Days drawing nearer, he was utterly overloaded with work that only he could do, and he had barely slept for days. Even with the vast magics at Dagog's command, lack of sleep must be affecting his judgement.

Klarm was a cunning man and a strategic thinker. He had probably allowed himself to be caught in the hope of getting inside Skyrock and rescuing his daughter. In the unlikely event that he succeeded, he would try to escape on the spellcaster. It had easily carried his weight before and it could probably carry hers as well. But was that all he wanted?

Unable to think of anything vulnerable to sabotage by a man unable to roam freely, Skald focused on assassination. Durthix or Dagog? Killing the high commander would be a setback, but the second-, third- and fourth-in-command were always ready assume leadership.

A magiz was far more difficult to replace and there was only ever one at a time. Had there been two, they would have spent the bulk of their time conspiring against one another until one was killed. So Klarm's target was probably Dagog, though how could he kill the magiz when he lacked control of the spellcaster?

Skald inspected it again and his brilliant visual memory picked up an almost insignificant change – a tiny crystal, previously incapable of drawing power from the field, was now doing so. But what function did it perform? He could not tell. Would it allow Klarm to seize control from the magiz? Skald did not see how; it seemed too small and insignificant. But it was possible.

What if Skald pretended he had not noticed the change? Dare he?

His hands shook. He was contemplating betraying the master he had sworn to serve. But the moment the magiz no longer needed Skald he would drink his life, and the lives of Uletta and the other slaves.

The choice seemed a simple one – Dagog's life, or Skald's and Uletta's. But if he chose to betray Dagog, he would be repudiating everything he had believed in and worked towards as a good, loyal Merdrun, all his life.

Yet, how could Skald's act be more monstrous than the things Dagog had been doing for decades? Uletta was right. The Merdrun had become evil. And General Chaxee had also been right, weeks ago, when she had told Skald that the Merdrun must be cleansed of their corruption before they could go home. What better start than to erase this treacherous magiz who was planning to overthrow the high commander *he* had sworn to serve?

Assuming Skald could. More likely than not, the spellcaster would do nothing.

When Klarm finished reassembling the spellcaster, Skald carried it up to the septagonal meeting chamber, which was empty. Two guards escorted Klarm in and brought a chair for him. A seven-sided table occupied the centre of the room but there were no other chairs. Merdrun stood for meetings.

The magiz came in, laid his rue-har on the table again and Skald carried out the steps to transfer control of the spellcaster to him. The magiz made it climb and settle, rotate and fly across the chamber to the irregular, seven-sided window, and back to the table, then dismissed Skald.

He returned to Sulien's far-seeing training, but could not concentrate, so he took her back to the cell she shared with Jassika. Skald returned the darkened far-seeing room, wishing his own gift was strong enough to see what Dagog was doing with the spellcaster. He was bound to discover what Skald had done. And then –

Skald would die the worst death the Merdrun could devise – a traitor's death.

# 25

## FALSE INFORMATION

There they are,' called Maelys from the top of the javelard frame.

Ahead of the sky galleon, a vast dome of granite terminated in a bluff, more than a thousand feet high, that ran north and south for miles. Waterfalls tumbled over it here and there, occasional wind-twisted trees grew out of cracks in the cliff face, and water seeped from shears and fractures at its base, forming pools so clear that, as they passed over, fish could be seen twenty feet down.

Wildflowers and flowering bushes grew out of every crevice. It was a pretty place and, as far as Karan could see, untouched by human or enemy hands. The top of the tower of Skyrock was visible, a good thirty miles to the west, but the Merdrun had no reason to come here.

Not far from the base of the cliff, the deflated airbag of a ramshackle air-floater had been spread out across a jumble of boulders, and Wilm was waving both arms. Flydd landed nearby. Karan climbed down into knee-high grass and Wilm came running. Ilisial, who had been watching them, went into her tent and pulled the flap closed.

'What's the matter with her?' Karan said to Wilm, embracing him.

'Just before Skald took the spellcaster,' he said quietly, 'he started to drink her life. Klarm said some people are never the same again.' He pulled free. 'Where's Aviel? Is she –?'

'Down below. She's good, Wilm.'

He scrambled up the ladder. Karan smiled. It was wonderful to see him. Then the import of his words sank in. 'Xervish?'

He was studying the air-floater. 'Mnn?'

'Rulke said Skald tried to drink Llian's life. I never considered what that would do to him. I'm so stupid!'

'Some people make a good recovery from it,' said Flydd. 'Others are broken. But ... Llian's in good hands with Rulke.'

He bent to study the rotor mechanism. Karan walked away, needing to be by herself. She had seen the white-eyed sus-magiz drink lives on the mountain pass during Nish's rescue, and even from a distance it had been hideous. Would Llian ever be the same again? Or would he just want the nightmare to end?

Aviel and Wilm were walking between the jumbled boulders. She was sniffing the flowers and herbs, running from one to another and calling out to Wilm, and it was as if the traumas of the past month and a half had not happened for her. But Wilm's own smile had faded. He stopped and looked back at Ilisial's closed tent, anxiously.

Karan unpacked some clean clothes and headed for a pool further along the bluff. She had not had a proper bath in weeks. The water would be freezing but the shock might keep her fears at bay ... for a while.

When she came back, half frozen but invigorated, the camp had been set up and the sky galleon was covered in the airbag, to break up its outline from the air. Nish and Yggur had plundered one of the pools and there were fresh fish and greens for dinner. The sun passed westwards, almost touching the top of Skyrock in its descent. Ilisial still had not emerged from her tent.

'What a beautiful place,' sighed Aviel. 'I could live here.'

'The nearest town must be fifty miles away,' said Wilm.

'Suits me. I've had enough of people.' Seeing the hurt on his face she added hastily, 'Most people.'

'But what would you *do* here?'

'Build a workshop and make perfumes. I haven't seen any of these flowers and herbs before. Nature would give me everything I need.'

'I'm glad for you,' he said dully.

Wilm sounded beaten. How fortunate Aviel was, to want so little and have it all within her reach. Karan's very being ached for Gothryme and her lost family. If only she could go back six months in her life, before anyone had heard of the Merdrun, when her only problems had been the unending drought – and Llian's unhappiness.

Though it hadn't really started six months ago, when Sulien dreamed of the enemy's secret weakness. Had it begun when Maigraith and Karan were pregnant, ten years before that, and Maigraith had conceived that mad obsession for their children to be partnered when they grew up?

Or 1,100 years earlier when the young Mendark made that fatal bargain with Magiz Murgilha that had allowed her to send the summon stone to Santhenar, to prepare the way for the Merdrun invasion?

Or when Rulke, thousands of years before that, led the Hundred out of the void, captured Aachan and subsequently commissioned Shuthdar to make the golden flute that had opened the Way between the Worlds and allowed the Merdrun to see the hidden Three Worlds?

Or an aeon before that, when Stermin, that arrogant, obsessed fool, made the Gates of Good and Evil and forced the people who became the Merdrun through the Crimson Gate?

Or had it begun even earlier? Nothing begins from nowhere, she thought. And nothing truly ends. But we probably will, very soon.

Klarm had sat back, his guts aching, as Skald checked and rechecked the spellcaster. If he was absolutely meticulous, he ought to notice the tiny crystal Klarm had linked to the field, and disconnect it. He prayed that Skald, distracted by desire for Uletta and the urgent need to save her and himself, would not check closely enough.

Could he divert Skald's attention? 'Where's my daughter, Skald? Where's Jassika?'

Skald looked up. 'You can't save yourself, Klarm. Nor her.'

'Have you ever loved?'

Skald went very still. 'I – I have.'

Klarm lowered his voice to a whisper. 'The architect.'

The blood drained from Skald's face. 'That's absurd. I've proven my loyalty, and my obedience to our commandments, over and again.'

'Of course you have,' Klarm said blandly. 'I beg your pardon ... but as a man who loves, you'll understand that my daughter is all I have. I have to know she's all right.'

'She's not been greatly harmed. She's in the cells, two levels above the control chamber.'

'With Sulien?'

'All the prisoners who work in Skyrock are held there ... but don't tell anyone I said so.'

Klarm laughed. 'Dagog and I aren't planning afternoon tea together.'

The hour passed. Skald's hands, obscured by his body, might have fixed the spell-caster. Klarm could not tell.

'Time to go,' said Skald.

He picked up the heavy spellcaster and lugged it out. A pair of guards escorted Klarm after Skald. He entered a seven-sided meeting chamber, which had a large, asymmetrical window on the wall opposite the door, and set the spellcaster down in the middle of the table. Dagog entered and Skald made the changes so it could be controlled by Dagog's voice.

One of the guards brought a chair for Klarm, who sat at the end of the table nearest the door, and went out, as did Skald. Shortly, five senior generals filed in, followed by two senior sus-magiz and two of medium rank. They spaced themselves around the table, all standing.

Klarm had no idea what Dagog was planning, though he had a bad feeling about this meeting. On the pretext of easing the pressure of his wooden foot on his stump, he pressed down on the bolt that turned on the farspeaker hidden inside it, which he had previously set to transmit but not receive.

'Generals, sus-magizes, this is the enemy's long lost spellcaster,' said Dagog. 'A fearsome killing machine that seeks out its victims by itself. Since it was captured five weeks ago our most skilled artisans have examined every part of it, and one of the enemy's manufactories was reopened to make copies. A thousand have been built so far, and more will be ready by the Day of All Days ... a little over two days from now.'

*Two days!* Klarm struggled to hide his shock. The Day of All Days was supposed to be twelve days away. They must have fed Flydd's spies false information.

This was a disaster. Flydd could not possibly make any meaningful attack in two days' time; there was far too much to do. Did it also mean the enemy would kill their slaves in two days' time?

Panic flooded Klarm. He needed to think, but fear for his daughter crowded out all other thoughts.

He forced his mind back to the present, and what Dagog was saying.

'... this sad little dwarf,' the magiz concluded, 'is Nuceus Klarm, once one of the most powerful of their former scrutators. He conceived the idea of the spellcaster and oversaw its design and construction, which is why I brought him here today.'

'Has he been neutralised?' said the one-armed general at the far end of the table. She wore a red patch over her right eye.

'I'm about to, General Chaxee. Would you all put on your silver-wire helms?'

The five generals, the four sus-magiz and Dagog donned helms, made from woven silver mesh, that enveloped their heads and faces down to shoulder level. So that was why they had taken all the silver and abducted every silversmith they could identify. But what did *neutralised* mean?

Dagog turned to Klarm, smiling crookedly. 'You're going to be the first old human to test our gift-burner. Once we know it's worked, on the Day of All Days we're going to extend it worldwide.'

Klarm choked. This was bad – no, catastrophic. And as far as he was aware, neither Flydd nor any of his spies had ever gleaned the faintest inkling of this threat.

'What's a gift-burner?' he croaked, desperately trying to gain time – and vital information, if Flydd happened to be listening to his farspeaker.

The magiz did not oblige. He raised a small rectangular box with a lever on one end – then, as Klarm threw vainly himself to his left, the magiz pushed the lever down.

Pain flared behind Klarm's eyes, spread up across his forehead, and reverberated back and forth through his skull, growing worse with every pass. Terrible pain, as if the inside of his head was on fire. Though it could not have been, since he could still think clearly.

Then it vanished, and so did his gift for the Secret Art. It had been burned out of him.

He would never be able to work magic again, not even the tiny spells that gifted toddlers did by instinct. He had lost the Art and would never get it back. He was utterly ordinary now, and the anguish was so awful that he cried out in agony.

The magiz laughed until tears ran from his eyes.

His malice cut through Klarm's pain and he saw the way out – though not for himself. You've just made the biggest mistake of your life, Daggs, he thought. You think you've neutralised the threat, but you've released me from all constraints.

'The spellcaster's persona is called Obberly,' said Dagog, 'and I alone can control it. Obberly, rise from the table and hover.'

The spellcaster rose and hovered, slowly rotating.

Dagog ordered it to fly around the room, to rise and fall, and to train its blasting arms on various things in the chamber, which it did, exactly as ordered.

'All it needs for it to seek out and kill our enemies,' said Dagog, 'is my order. At the Sink of Despair it located Skald's attacking troops one by one ... and blasted each of them dead.'

'Let's see it then,' said General Chaxee.

'Obberly,' said Dagog, 'fireblast Klarm to a cinder.'

Klarm stood up on his chair, and for once he welcomed the pain in his stump, because it cut through his agony and allowed him absolute focus.

'Wake!' he said commandingly. 'Take over from the usurper.'

The spellcaster continued to hover in mid-air.

'You can't do magic,' Dagog said gleefully. 'Your gift is gone.'

'I don't need to,' said Klarm. 'All I have to do is give the order.'

'But Obberly is under my control. Obberly, blast Klarm down!' roared Dagog.

'Can't – move – can't – sp–' said Obberly, each word softer and slower than the one before.

'Magiz,' said the General Chaxee, 'what's going on?'

'Obberly!' cried Dagog, but the Obberly persona made no reply.

'No one alive knows this but me,' said Klarm, grinning.

'Knows *what*?' snarled Dagog.

'The great weakness of the spellcaster, Daggs, old mate,' Klarm said pleasantly, 'was that it had *two* competing personas. Obberly was as normal as any persona could be, and it controlled the spellcaster most of the time. But the second persona was a paranoid and malign intelligence, designed to take over in desperate times, and it was stronger. In a battle of wills it almost always won, and *that's* why the spellcaster was too dangerous for the scrutators to use.'

'Why didn't our artisans find –?'

'A persona isn't a physical thing. You can't *find* it in the spellcaster, any more than you can dissect the head of a human being and identify what allows that person to think and feel. Before Skald captured the spellcaster, I made sure that the little crystal where the second persona resides had no power. It went into a coma until earlier today, when I allowed that crystal to reconnect to the field.'

'I ordered Skald to check every part!' Dagog snarled. He looked around at the staring generals, the bemused sus-magizes. 'The incompetent fool! I'm going to drink –'

'Skald – isn't – incompetent,' said Klarm slowly, as though explaining to an idiot. 'He saw what I'd done ... and ignored it.' Klarm did not actually know this, but Dagog was bound to believe it. It was unlikely that he would appreciate the irony.

'No Merdrun – would ever betray –'

'He outwitted you. He meant for the spellcaster to kill you.' Klarm paused. 'Though I don't think he considered that you'd bring in your five top generals and four key sus-magizes, so you could boast about your cleverness. Big mistake, Daggs.'

'What's he talking about?' rapped a red-faced general. 'Magiz, what's going on?'

'Obberly,' snapped the magiz, 'Kill the dwarf!'

'You don't get it, Daggs,' exulted Klarm. What a way to go out! 'Obberly isn't in charge anymore. Obberly has been overpowered. The malign intelligence has taken over and it's just waiting for my order.' The magiz was afraid, and it did Klarm's vengeful heart good. 'No one in this chamber is going to see the Day of All Days.'

'Malign intelligence, blow Klarm to bloody rags!' shrieked the magiz.

'Alas,' said Klarm, 'Haggergrind only answers to his name.'

'Kill him, Haggergrind!'

The spellcaster continued to hover, rocking in the air with its funnel-tipped arms fixing on one target, then another.

'And only when spoken by me. And he will always protect me.'

Klarm wished he had the time to savour the look on Dagog's face, the sneering malice turned to fear, but the generals and the sus-magiz were armed and Klarm wasn't giving any of them the chance to stop him.

'Haggergrind,' he said, 'this room is full of enemies. Take down the generals first. Then the sus-magizes. Then Daggs.'

'Kill the dwarf!' hissed the magiz.

'Do your worst,' said Klarm. 'Haggergrind has his orders and only I can take them back.'

'Take Klarm, *alive!*'

Boots rasped on stone as the generals drew their useless swords, then hesitated.

Nothing could have induced them to run from any normal enemy, but this incomprehensible terror-weapon was another matter entirely.

The closest two of the generals rushed Klarm but they had to come around the curve of the table to get to him, and they could never be as fast as the spellcaster. Haggergrind's stubby arms rotated until one blue-glowing funnel pointed at the red-faced general and blasted him down. Then rotated, aimed and blasted again and again.

The five generals were hurled backwards, uniforms charred away and flesh torn; they were dead before they hit the floor.

'Kill him!' Dagog hissed to his sus-magizes.

The sus-magizes attacked Klarm but the spellcaster deflected their blasts, targeted them and blasted them, driving them against the wall hard enough to break their bones.

'It protects its true master,' said Klarm.

Dagog was screeching in dumb terror as he scrambled over the bodies of the generals, desperately trying to get away. Gusts of carrion stench issued from his open mouth. His eyes were staring, his mouth a gaping hole. He seemed unable to understand how the catastrophe had come about.

'My spies told me that you've wanted to drink Skald's life since the day you met him,' said Klarm. 'And that you've undermined him every way you could, ever since. But he's a brave man, an enemy I can take my hat off to, and he's beaten you, Magiz. Galling, isn't it?'

'Kill him, Obberly, Haggergrind, whatever you name is! Kill the shitty little dwarf!'

As Dagog stumbled past the oddly shaped window, the spellcaster blasted, slamming him against the pane so hard that he stuck there, bleeding in a dozen places. The fire-blasting arm of the spellcaster rotated in an oval, melting the glass all around him until it folded over to encase him. He quivered there, screaming, his flesh smoking and charring, while the glass set, then another blast tore it free and he plunged out of sight.

Klarm remembered that he'd turned his farspeaker on. He hoped Flydd was listening; the allies desperately needed some good news.

'Dagog's the last of them, and it's four hundred feet to the ground. He'll splat nicely when he hits. Best I can do, old friends.'

They could not reply. The far-speaker was not set to receive.

He turned to the spellcaster. 'Haggergrind, old comrade, can I ride on you to find Jassika?'

'The compound walls are lined with javelards, short-arse,' said Haggergrind in a mechanical rasp. 'There's no way in and there's no way out.'

'What about the chaos chasm?'

'What's that?'

'The sump where they dump all their magical waste.'

'Half the people in Skyrock just saw the magiz splatter on the paving stones, and hundreds of guards are on their way. We'd never get there.'

Klarm glanced at the dead generals and sus-magizes, and the hole in the window. He had devastated the enemy's leadership at the worst possible time, and Durthix would not treat him kindly. 'But – my daughter.'

'Can't be done, short-arse. You have to let everything go.'

Klarm had once helped to rule the world, and it was hard to accept. Even harder to let go of his beautiful, neglected daughter, by far the best part of him.

He wiped his eyes. 'Oh well, I've had a good life. A great life!' He looked down at the far-speaker concealed in his wooden foot. 'So, don't mourn me, Xervish – avenge me! You now know how to get into the compound. Save the girls. The prisoners are held in Skyrock, two levels above the control chamber. Remember your promise to look after Jassika.'

He paused, but of course there was no reply. Had Flydd heard any of this? More than likely, he had not.

Klarm would never know. And now that he had no gift, the torturers might well break him. He could not take the risk; he knew far too much.

'One last thing. May be of some use. Skald, a man who has gone to superhuman lengths to do his duty at all times, has committed one of the greatest crimes of all and taken the deputy architect, Uletta, for his lover.'

Klarm braced himself. This was going to hurt, but at least he had redeemed himself. 'Do your worst, Haggergrind.'

Haggergrind blasted him, though gently. As Klarm fell, the spellcaster whirled out the magiz-shaped hole and into the cool summer evening.

# 26

# BLOW KLARM TO BLOODY RAGS!

*G*enerals, *sus-magizes, this is the enemy's long lost spellcaster. A fearsome killing machine that seeks out its victims by itself. Since it was captured five weeks ago –*

The grating voice issued from Flydd's tent. He ran and came back with his farspeaker.

'Who's speaking?' said Karan.

'Dagog. Via Klarm's farspeaker. And Klarm wouldn't risk contacting me in the magiz's presence unless things were dire.'

'What's he doing at Skyrock?' said Wilm. 'He hasn't –?'

'No!' snapped Flydd.

'How do you know?'

'Say it and you prove yourself a fool,' Flydd snapped. He stroked his fingers down a tiny ball embedded in the side of the farspeaker and the magiz's voice grew louder.

Karan listened with mounting horror as Dagog continued.

*... and the first of our thousand spellcasters will be ready for action by the Day of All Days. A little over two days from now.*

'A thousand of them could wipe out a city,' whispered Nish.

'Two days!' Yggur rose to his feet, staring at Flydd. 'The other day you said they still had weeks to go.'

Flydd put the farspeaker down, wearily. 'They must have fed us false intelligence. We can't do anything in two days.'

Pain ripped through Karan's head, so bad she felt sure she was dying. Sulien lost. Llian damaged by Skald and perhaps losing the will to live. And no possibility of saving them in so short a time.

Aviel reached across and took her hand. It did not help. Nothing could help.

*You're going to be the first old human to test our gift-burner,* gloated Dagog. *Once we know it's worked, on the Day of All Days we're going to extend it worldwide.*

'What's a gift-burner?' said Aviel.

No one replied.

Aviel's fingers clenched around Karan's hand, painfully, then the insides of her skull burned and a scream of anguish rang through her inner ear. A thin cry came through the farspeaker.

'What was *that*?' said Maelys, holding her head.

'The magiz burned Klarm's gift right out of him,' said Yggur. 'Turned him into an ordinary man.'

Fear cleared Karan's numbness. Losing her gift, small though it was, would be like dying inside. There would be nothing left of her.

Flydd's gnarled face was the colour of plaster. 'This is not going to end well.'

*Obberly,* said Dagog, *fireblast Klarm to a cinder.*

Karan scrambled to her feet. She did not want to hear any more.

'Stay!' said Flydd.

After an exchange Karan did not catch, Klarm said, in a conversational voice, *the great weakness of the spellcaster, Daggs old mate, was that it had two* competing *personas. Obberly was as normal as any persona can be, and it controlled the spellcaster most of the time. The other persona was a paranoid and malign intelligence, designed to take over in desperate times, and it was stronger. In a battle of wills it almost always won, and* that's *why the spellcaster was too dangerous for the scrutators to use.*

Dagog was shouting, almost incoherent, but Klarm seemed supernaturally calm, almost as if he were enjoying this.

*Before Skald captured the spellcaster, I made sure that the little crystal where the second persona resides had no power. It went into a coma until earlier today, when I allowed that crystal to reconnect to the field.*

*I ordered Skald to check every part,* the magiz snarled. *The incompetent fool! I'm going to drink –*

*Skald – isn't – incompetent,* said Klarm, as though explaining to an idiot. *He saw what I had done ... and ignored it.*

Choking sounds issued from the farspeaker. *No Merdrun – would ever betray –*

*He outwitted you,* Klarm added. *He meant for the spellcaster to kill you. Though I don't think he considered that you'd bring in your five top generals and four key sus-magizes, so you could boast about your cleverness. Big mistake, Daggs.*

*Obberly, kill the dwarf!*

*You don't get it, Daggs.* Klarm sounded richly amused. *Obberly isn't in charge anymore. Obberly has been overpowered. The malign intelligence has taken over and it's just waiting for my order. No one in this chamber is going to see the Day of All Days.*

*Malign intelligence, blow Klarm to bloody rags!*

*Alas,* said Klarm, *Haggergrind answers only to his name.*

After another exchange, during which it was clear that the occupants of the meeting room were becoming increasingly panicky, Klarm said –

*Haggergrind, this room is full of enemies. Take down the generals first. Then the sus-magizes. Then Daggs.*

Yggur whistled. 'Klarm has exceeded himself.'

'Not yet,' said Flydd. But for the first time in ages, he looked hopeful.

Everyone around the campfire rose, staring at the little farspeaker. Karan could hear the generals knocking over chairs and roaring orders as they tried to get away from this malevolent device, unlike anything they had ever faced. But it was too quick. It finished them with sizzling blasts and their death cries came through the farspeaker.

Now the spellcaster turned on the sus-magizes, who were directing every spell they had at it, judging by the racket. They fell silent, one by one.

'It can deflect most spells,' said Flydd absently. 'And protect its controller.'

*Kill him, Obberly, Haggergrind, whatever your name is!* screeched the magiz. *Kill the shitty little dwarf!*

There came a blast, a thud, the sound of glass smashing, and a whining howl that trailed away to nothing.

'You've done it, you beautiful man,' said Flydd.

'Five top generals and four sus-magizes,' said Nish. 'He's crippled the enemy's military leadership, and their Arts. No one else could have pulled that deception off. Klarm's given us a chance – and I'll bet he's got a way out, too.'

There were tears in Flydd's eyes, but he was shaking his head. 'His gift is gone. There's no way out.'

'I told you he wasn't a traitor.' Ilisial had finally left her tent and was glaring at Wilm. 'But you knew best.'

Wilm, who was standing along with everyone else, sat down, his face brick-red with shame. 'I'm a stupid, judgemental fool,' he said loudly, as if making sure everyone could hear. 'Don't listen to my worthless opinion on anything.' He leapt up and ran into the night.

*Dagog's the last of them,* said Klarm, *and it's four hundred feet down. He'll splat nicely when he hits. Best I can, do, old friends.*

After a pause, he went on, *Haggergrind, old comrade, can I ride on you to find Jassika?*

*The compound walls are lined with javelards, short-arse,* said Haggergrind, *and some of them are aimed at the window. There's no way out.*

*What about the chaos chasm?*

*What's that?*

*The sump where they dump all their magical waste.*

*Half the people in Skyrock just saw the magiz splatter on the paving stones, and hundreds of guards are on their way. We'd never get there.*

*But – my daughter –*

*Can't be done, short-arse. You have to let everything go.*

*Oh well, I've had a good life. So, don't mourn me, Xervish – avenge me! You now know how to get into the compound. Save the girls. The prisoners are held in Skyrock, two levels above the control chamber. Remember your promise to look after Jassika.*

There was a long pause. Flydd, who had set the farspeaker down and was pacing around the fire, ran back.

*One last thing,* said Klarm. *May be of some use. Skald, a man who has gone to superhuman lengths to do his duty at all times, has committed one of the greatest crimes of all and taken the deputy architect, Uletta, for his lover.*

'Klarm?' Flydd yelled. 'How do I get into the compound?'

*Do your worst, Haggergrind.*

Flydd cursed, yanked out a knob and yelled at the farspeaker, 'Klarm?'

There came another blast, the humming whirr of the spellcaster, then silence.

'Farspeaker was set to receive only,' he said in a dead voice. 'He couldn't hear me. He died alone.'

There was a very long silence, then he rose slowly, tears coursing down his raddled cheeks. 'Klarm was a flawed man. A womaniser and a pisspot, and his moral compass sometimes went badly astray. But he was a true friend. The oldest and closest friend I had left. Forty years we went back.'

He was walking into the darkness when Karan called. 'He knew he was sacrificing himself when he allowed them to catch him, didn't he? To give us a chance.'

Flydd came back. 'I think he hoped to rescue Jassika and Sulien with the spellcaster, but once his gift was burned away there was no way out. But he had to make his death mean something.'

'Not even Klarm could have hoped to take out all their top generals bar Durthix, and some of their most senior sus-magizes,' said Yggur.

'He's given us a chance, but are we up to it?'

'What did he mean when he said, *Xervish, you know how to get into the compound,*' said Nish. 'Every conceivable way in is blocked or guarded. How can there be a way in?'

'I don't know,' said Flydd.

It was dark now, and chilly. He sat with Nish, Maelys and Yggur, going over maps and diagrams, proposing one plan after another, listing the few pros and the many cons of each, and dismissing them all.

Karan did not join them; she did not have anything to contribute. Her hair was finally dry, so she gave it five hundred strokes of the hairbrush, which did nothing to tame the untameable. She climbed into a sleeping pouch, pulled it up around her shoulders and rested her back against a boulder.

Why had Klarm said, *I know you'll save the girls*? What had Flydd missed?

She sat there, hour upon hour, gazing across the miles to the great glowing spirals. What would Durthix do about this disaster? It would not be good to be a slave there, right now.

She tried to reach Sulien but got nothing and ended up with a blinding headache. She could not contact Llian, either.

Karan bound up her hair, lay by the fire and dozed, but was tormented by dreams where she and her friends, and Sulien and Llian, were being hunted by a horde of all-seeing, all-powerful spellcasters. They picked her allies off one by one. Then Llian. Then, as Karan scooped her daughter up and ran, they blasted Sulien. Karan kept running, her dead daughter in her arms, running to nowhere.

Then the magiz raised a little box, pulled the lever sticking out of it, and her gift, the only thing she had left, was gone forever.

# 27

## IN SILENT GLEE

Skald must have dozed, for he was woken by a great commotion outside, the sound of running feet, then a bellow from Durthix.

'Where the blazes is Skald? Find him, immediately!'

He had been found out, and now he was going to die a traitor's death. Skald rose and squared his shoulders – at least he could face death and disgrace like an officer.

He strode out into the broad main hall. 'High Commander? What's wrong?'

Durthix ran up to him, his boots hitting the stone floor with small thunderclaps. 'Bloody ruin in the main meeting chamber and the magiz smashed to pulp on the ground below. Come quickly.'

'The magiz is *dead*?' Though Skald had hoped for it a thousand times, it did not seem possible that such a mighty presence could be gone.

'Not just the magiz,' Durthix said grimly.

Skald wasn't listening. His nemesis was dead! This changed everything. He might survive after all – if he was very, very lucky.

But he was not lucky at all. Skald had thought Dagog wanted to show the spellcaster to one or two of his sus-magizes, but the meeting room was splattered with blood and littered with bodies, including Dagog's spy and lover, Yallav. At the end of the table, sitting in his chair without a mark on him and still smiling, was the body of the dwarf. The spellcaster was gone.

'This is a catastrophe,' said Durthix. 'I – I don't see how we can recover from it.'

Skald had never seen him so shaken. 'I'm sure the remaining generals –'

'The loss of my five most senior generals is a grievous one, but it can be filled. Losing my magiz is another matter entirely. What do you know about this, Skald?'

Skald's life hung by a fraying thread. 'The dwarf, Klarm, was caught spying –'

'I know!' Durthix snapped. 'What do you know about *this*?'

Skald had to weave truth and lies as he had never done before. 'It looks to me as though the spellcaster went rogue.'

'How could it?'

'The magiz was desperate to understand the heart of the device – the inner spirit or persona that allows it to think for itself and choose its targets. He ordered the dwarf to get it working again, and told me to watch everything he did. I did so, though I didn't see Klarm do anything suspicious. I also checked the spellcaster afterwards but ... I don't know anything about personas.' The last part was true enough.

Durthix met Skald's eyes. Did he believe him? 'No, how could you? But Dagog did. He should have checked it himself.'

'He did, and pronounced it safe.' Skald felt he could get away with the lie since both Dagog and Klarm were dead. 'But the dwarf was known as a very cunning man.'

'I told Dagog the spellcaster was too dangerous to use,' said Durthix. 'But he always knew best.'

Should Skald reveal that Dagog had been conspiring to overthrow him? No, Durthix would want to know why he had not been told. 'The magiz genuinely thought it could help us in future battles,' he said carefully. 'After the Day of All Days.'

'That decision wasn't his to make. Go on.'

'I carried the spellcaster to the meeting chamber, and Klarm was escorted there. The magiz said he was going to test it. He didn't say that the generals and sus-magizes would be there. Then he ordered me out, and that's all I know.'

'He didn't tell me, damn him,' growled Durthix, 'or I would have forbidden it.'

'Do you think the dwarf set the spellcaster off, hoping to get away, but it went rogue and killed him too?'

Durthix shrugged. 'It can't get out of the compound. I'll have it destroyed. Send a detail to take the bodies away, then come to my command tent, down in the tunnel.' Durthix rubbed his bristly jaw. 'How can we get back on track with so little time left?' He frowned at Skald. 'Dagog said you've been making good progress on far-seeing.'

'Yes,' lied Skald, 'though I'm a little short of his skill.'

'Far-seeing is critical. Without it, we can't –' He scowled. 'You've been working with a gifted slave child?'

'The girl, Sulien Fyrn, has a remarkable talent. I've been training her, under the magiz's orders. But I don't know to what end.'

'Keep at it. If I need you to know, I'll tell you. We have two and a quarter days, Skald.'

He trudged out. Skald slumped against the wall, staring at the bodies. He had taken the gamble of his life and it had paid off. The magiz was dead! But he did not feel good about it.

He was now a traitor and an oath-breaker. By betraying Dagog to his death and causing the deaths of nine other leaders, Skald had almost certainly robbed the Merdrun nation of the goal they had striven for, for their entire existence. The magiz's unparalleled ability to far-see, vital on the Day of All Days, might take months to develop in any of the other senior sus-magiz.

There was no rationalising it away – Skald had betrayed the Merdrun nation. He had believed himself a good citizen, and he had portrayed his struggle with Dagog as good versus evil, honourable versus corrupt, but Skald now saw that he was worse than Dagog had ever been.

The old, honourable Skald would have thought, *There has to be a way. I can save the True Purpose. I will do everything conceivable to make it so.*

In the past he had driven himself beyond human limits to rise above the taint of his father's cowardice. Now he had cut the ground from under himself. Nothing could change him from a traitor back to a hero.

He sent for a squad of guards and a dozen labourers and ordered the bodies of the generals and sus-magizes to be collected and carried to the burning grounds, where they would be placed on pyres appropriate to their rank and service.

Skald carried Klarm's corpse down to a chilly basement below the tunnel and left it there with the other old human dead of rank. He had been an honourable man and a hero, and Skald saluted his body before he went up to deal with the last. The one that required an entirely different end.

The mess that had once been the magiz was scraped off the paving stones and searched for dangerous devices and secret objects. None were found, apart from his massive rue-har, which Skald boiled and locked away for whoever became the next magiz.

The magiz had not been honourable. No magiz ever was. His body was burned and the ashes quartered and re-quartered, then the sixteen small piles of ash dumped, widely separated, in the hills surrounding Skyrock. With magizes, you had to be sure.

Finally, around midnight, Skald reported to Durthix in his temporary command tent in the tunnel. Three generals were with him and the two most senior sus-magizes, Filsell and Lurzel. Neither approached Dagog's skill or experience, and in normal circumstances neither would ever have risen any higher.

'I don't know what we're going to do,' Durthix was saying as Skald trudged in, drained in body and soul. He had not had the chance to wash and he reeked of the stinking smoke from Dagog's pyre.

'A new magiz must be raised,' said General Halia, a stolid old plodder, a stickler for the rules and for doing things the old way.

'It can't be done in time. Besides, Dagog, curse his shattered bones and stinking flesh, was negligent in preparing his subordinates for the succession. Not one of the remaining sus-magizes have the necessary experience.'

'What about Widderlin?'

'Lost in the south.'

'Lurzel?'

'I can't far-see well enough,' said Lurzel.

'Then we've failed.' Halia, that grim-faced old soldier, looked beaten. 'It'll all been for nothing.'

'But we'll keep trying,' said Durthix. 'We must begin on our True Purpose at midnight, two days from now, so all is ready when the conjunction begins at sunrise. It only lasts eight hours and if we miss it the chance will not come again in any of our lifetimes.'

'But without a magiz, how can we?'

'I'm thinking to elevate Skald.'

All the blood drained from Skald's face. The room swayed and blurred; he thought he was going to faint. He grabbed the nearest tent pole and clung to it, desperately.

'He doesn't know a tenth as much magic as any of the senior sus-magiz,' sus-magiz Filsell said furiously.

'I'm thinking to elevate Skald to *acting* magiz, just for the next few days,' Durthix continued.

'Why?'

'Dagog ordered him to train Sulien's far-seeing gift, which we're likely to need *after* the Day of All Days. And in doing so, Dagog informed me, Skald's own gift has advanced tremendously. He alone has the one skill vital to our True Purpose – the best developed ability to far-see – and as acting magiz it's the only skill he needs. What do you say, Skald?'

The pit of Skald's stomach, which he had torn so he could take Rulke by surprise in Alcifer, burned as if the scar had opened again. Not only was he a fornicator with the enemy, a traitor, an oath-breaker and a murderer, he was also a liar. He did not have a tenth of Dagog's skill at far-seeing; not a hundredth.

The only honourable course was to confess his crimes and his treachery and take his punishment. Skald was tempted. Durthix's plan was absurd. The True Purpose could not possibly be achieved now, and it was all his fault.

But who was he to be thinking about honourable courses? He had no honour left. And the elevation to acting magiz would free him from scrutiny and give him the chance, once the moment had passed and the True Purpose had failed, to escape with Uletta. She was more precious than ever, now that he had lost everything else.

'Working with the gifted child these past weeks has greatly expanded my understanding of far-seeing,' he said truthfully. Then he lied, '*and* my ability to far-see. Dagog said my ability, though far below his own, was the best among the sus-magizes.'

Skald held his breath in case Dagog had told the sus-magizes differently, but no one spoke.

'Well?' said Durthix.

'I won't lie that I wanted to become magiz one day,' Skald said humbly. 'But not for many years – I don't know nearly enough. In no way am I worthy to assume the magiz's mantle at this stage of my life, not even temporarily.'

But no magiz was ever humble, and no one else could do it. He looked around the open-walled command tent, met the eyes of the people there, one by one, and his voice rang out and echoed back and forth off the crystal-clad walls of the sapphire tunnel.

'I swear to you, on my honour as an officer and a sus-magiz, that I will find a way to achieve our True Purpose on the Day of All Days. We're going home!'

And he was so inspiring that the assembled officers and sus-magizes gave way to an allowable emotion and raised their blades or their rue-hars.

'*We're going home!*' they roared, as one.

Skald, as astounded as anyone at his elevation, wanted to laugh, to cry, to leap in the air and roar in triumph. With the magiz no longer hissing poison in Durthix's ear, he might see the truth about Skald at last. But he concealed his emotions and said, 'Thank you for your trust in me, High Commander.'

Safe at last! He had escaped his father's curse. Surely even his mother, had she still been alive, would have been proud of him now.

But later, alone in his tent, Skald was struck by the terror that he had missed something, and that his role in the magiz's death would be exposed. He slumped on the bed, head in hands, expecting, at any moment, to be taken for public denunciation and execution.

Don't be a fool! No one knows, or can know. But he felt no better. The moment he was called upon to use his far-seeing gift, two nights from now, he would be exposed as a traitor.

Was there any way around it? Could he use the child with the most brilliant seeing gift he had ever heard of, the gift he had been training and exploring for two weeks now, to far-see the destination for him? He had to, for the sake of his people and his own survival. But if he failed, the tales of his fate would strike terror into every Merdrun child for the next thousand years.

∼

Sulien sat by herself in the slave girls' dining room, not knowing what to say to Jassika. Dagog was dead, and that was good, but Klarm had been killed as well and Jassika did not want to talk about it.

'Stinkin' magiz was blasted right through the winder,' a cross-eyed girl whispered. A dozen other slave girls stood around her, licking their gruel bowls. 'And he fell, screamin' in terror and flappin' his arms, a *million* feet onto the pavin' stones. Nillie was workin' only a stone's throw away, weren't ya, Nillie?'

Nillie lowered her voice. 'The slimy old pig splattered like a bag of jelly. Left quivering lumps of his brains all over the paving stones. And,' she said in a whisper, 'they were *black*. Black and foul and festering. The stink was horrible.'

'The funny little dwarf was killed as well,' said the cross-eyed girl. 'Why'd he attack all those generals? He must'a known he'd never get away.'

Jassika, who was by herself in the far corner, stalked across and shook the girl until her teeth clattered together. 'Klarm wasn't a *funny little dwarf*. He was the bravest and cleverest and kindest man in the world, and if you say another word against him I'll heave you out the window and we'll see the colour of your tiny brains!

She looked so fierce and proud that the other girls apologised and said they hadn't meant any harm. Jassika whirled and ran, and hunched up in a corner with her arms over her face, sobbing as though her heart had been torn in two.

She had not said a word since the news spread among the slaves about Klarm's heroic deeds, but the most important slaves, including M'Lainte and Tiaan, who were also imprisoned in the tower, went about their work in silent glee.

Sulien went over and took her hand. 'If we survive, it'll be because of Klarm.'

Jassika shivered and shuddered. 'I'm sorry,' she said softly. 'I'm really, really sorry, Sulien.'

'What for?'

'For telling Skald that you sneaked into his room and used his shard. I'm a rotten, rotten person.'

'No, you're not. It wasn't fair, you being punished when I failed. That was just cruel.'

'It wasn't your fault. Why does Skald need you to far-see, anyway?'

'I don't know,' said Sulien, which wasn't completely true. But if her inkling was correct it was dangerous knowledge.

'What did he say after I told on you?'

'Not much. But I think he was worried about what I'd seen.'

'What did you see?'

'His mother, flogging the skin off his back when he was a little boy – just because he wanted to be loved. Merdrun aren't allowed to have feelings, except after victory. *Feelings are for weaklings*, his mother said. He never did that again.'

'Skald's killed lots of people!' said Jassika. 'He's our enemy and he *drinks lives*.'

'I know. But he's also in terrible pain.'

## 28

## JUST EMPTYING MY TEAPOT

C hronicler?' Rulke yelled. He sounded irritable, and usually was. He did not take well to captivity, being forced to follow orders, or using his precious construct to aid the enemy.

Llian wiped the nib of his quill, blotted his last paragraph and closed the journal. Rulke was seated at the tiny table in the galley, eating a vegetable that resembled a turnip, though it was blue inside and had a strong, smoky odour.

'I've just spoken to Flydd,' said Rulke.

'I didn't know you had a farspeaker.'

'What you don't know, Chronicler, would overflow the miles-deep basin of the Great Ocean.'

Lately, Rulke had punctuated every verbal exchange with insults about Llian's strength, size, manhood, morals and intelligence. He was thick-skinned; a Teller had to be, but it was wearing, nonetheless.

Clearly, Rulke was worried. He had engineered things so that Skald would bring the construct here, knowing it was his only hope of rescuing Lirriam, but the Merdrun had locked Rulke up too tight and time was running out.

'There's only two days!' he added, as if that was supposed to mean something.

'For what?' said Llian.

'Fifty-three hours, to be precise. To free Lirriam ... before they fulfil their True Purpose and kill all the prisoners.' Rulke summarised what Klarm had done and what had been revealed.

Fifty-three hours to save Sulien and Jassika. Fifty-three hours before everything ended.

'You're blocked from leaving the construct,' said Llian, 'but you can get me out.'

'I might be able to, but why would I want to?'

'So I can find Lirriam for you.'

Rulke snorted, though there was pain in it. 'How, Chronicler?'

'We know she's held somewhere in the compound. It's the only secure place here.'

'And she could only be in three places,' Rulke mused, forgetting to insult Llian. 'Though the tower is unlikely – too much going on there. And the tunnels down to the node are too dangerous. Which only leaves the cubic temple ...'

'What cubic temple?'

'It's concealed by powerful Arts, but not from me. They always have one, and it's where they'd keep their most important prisoners.'

'Get me out,' said Llian, 'and I'll check it.'

'You'd be caught the moment you stepped down onto the ground.'

'Not if you give me a talent to help me get around unseen.'

'You keep letting me down, Chronicler. Why would I trust you again?'

'You used to be called the Great Betrayer,' Llian retorted. 'How do I know you don't want to take Santhenar for yourself?'

'If you search your knowledge of me and my people,' Rulke said coldly, 'you'll realise that I never wanted Santhenar. It was just a way station on the road.'

'Well, I'm your only hope. Are you going to let me help, or not?'

'I think I can guess your price.'

'I don't have a *price*. We're all in this together, and it's the only way we can save those we love ...'

'But you want something from me if we prevail. Name it.'

Llian had wanted it for ages, and this was his only chance to get it. 'I've got to make amends for letting you down before, and for Thandiwe's dreadful little *Tale of Rulke*. I want to tell your tale properly, from the beginning. All you can remember.'

'I don't need to *remember*.'

'But Thandiwe took your papers to the college, and most of them were destroyed in the war.'

'Do I look like a man who would entrust my Histories to a single set of documents?'

'There's another set? Where?'

'Hidden.'

'Well?' said Llian.

Rulke stalked out but came back a few minutes later. 'Not even I could give a blockhead like you a talent for the Secret Art; there's not a smidgeon of the gift in you.' He was grinning now. 'Not an iota, a speck, a mote, a –'

'I get the picture!' Llian snapped.

'How to do it?' said Rulke, studying Llian, head to one side. 'I could make you look like a guard, I suppose.'

'The Merdrun guards are all tall and heavily built, and I'm only five-nine ...'

'And on the weedy side.'

'I'm not weedy!' Rulke had said it to get a rise out of him.

'A sus-magiz, then; they come in all shapes and sizes. And their comings and goings aren't questioned.'

Llian squirmed. 'I'm not sure I can pull off a sus-magiz.'

'You're a great Teller,' said Rulke. 'You won't have any trouble imitating the voice of a junior sus-magiz.'

'Not well enough to fool another sus-magiz.'

'They don't have many left. It's not likely you'll encounter one.'

'If I do, I'm dead.'

'I thought you wanted to save your daughter.'

But now it was actually happening, Llian knew what a dumb idea it was. He was not cut out for this kind of thing.

'Ready?' said Rulke.

'You want me to go *now*?'

'I can't help Flydd until I know Lirriam's safe.'

Rulke cast his spell, and it hurt, everywhere. Llian's face stung and his skin and muscles felt as though they were stretching like rubber. Even the bones of his skull and jaw seemed to be moving around.

'Funny kind of illusion,' he muttered, and the voice was deeper and harsher than his own. He was now dressed in a junior sus-magiz's shapeless red and grey robes.

'An illusion wasn't safe enough; I *metamorphed* you, just for an hour. Now listen carefully. Sus-magizes are creepy and scary, and other Merdrun avoid them. No one but a senior army officer, or another sus-magiz, will question you.'

'If either of them questions me, I'm dead.'

'There'd be no fun in it if there weren't a few obstacles.'

'Since when is deadly danger *fun*?'

'You wanted the job. Take this.' Rulke handed Llian a stubby crystalline rod, some four inches long and half an inch through.

'What is it?'

'It temporarily dispels illusions, so you can find the cubic temple. You'll have to be close for it to work.'

'If it dispels the whole illusion, the guards will know there's an intruder.'

'It only dispels the bit you're pointing at – while you're pointing the rod. Get moving.'

'What about the guards outside the construct?'

'Leave them to me. Go.'

Rulke opened the secret door at the rear. Llian waited by it until he heard a clatter at the top of the construct, then slipped out.

The guards ran towards the front and one held up a globe on a pole. 'What's going on up there?'

'Just emptying my teapot,' said Rulke cheerily.

'Inside!' said the guard.

'I don't take orders from you.'

Llian moved away into the fog, orienting himself by the curving line of lanterns on the compound walls nearby, the blurred blue spike of Skyrock in the centre, and an eerie yellow and green miasma arising from the chaos chasm where the toxic magical waste was dumped. If he steered a path between the chaos chasm, which was ahead and to his right, and Skyrock until it was behind his left shoulder, he would be close to the hidden cubic temple.

The compound was eerily quiet. The stone carving had been finished days ago, the bamboo scaffolding removed, and tens of thousands of slaves had carted away the waste rock and laid the last of the interlocking paving stones that encircled Skyrock. Nothing could be allowed to mar the dreadful beauty of the spiral tower.

All he could hear was the distant moaning of the wind through the stone spirals, and the guards tramping along the top of the compound walls, muffled by the fog.

As he approached Skyrock, the windsong swelled. It was a wind trio now, moaning through the tunnel at the base of Skyrock, whistling around and between the outer stone spirals and the inner core, and shrieking through the iron tower at the top.

He diverted around Skyrock to avoid the guards stationed across the tunnel entrance and exit. After a couple of hundred yards his new path took him close to the chaos chasm, and the prickling and itching that grew in his head reminded him of Demondifang, and the corruption that had leaked from the summon stone and corrupted half the mountainside. It had nearly killed him.

He was panting and cold sweat was trickling down his back. He turned away; better the dangers of Skyrock than the toxic magic of the chaos chasm.

Soon Skyrock was behind his left shoulder and the chaos chasm behind his right. He must be close. Ahead, through the fog, was a vast pile of rock left over from cutting the pinnacle to shape. He walked around it but there was nothing on the far side.

He was crouched there, wondering what to do, when a guard appeared out of the fog, carrying a heavy box, followed by a robed female sus-magiz and a pair of guards, each carrying two buckets. Ahead of them the rock pile shifted, settled, and they were gone. It had to be an illusion.

He drew his rod and pointed at the rocks next to him. They remained rocks. He crept across to the point where the Merdrun had disappeared, used the rod again and a small, ragged passage appeared. The rocks here were an illusion, and beyond the far end of the passage he made out a stone wall.

Llian crept down the passage. The rock pile was just a ring of stone with an open area in the middle, and at its centre stood a cubic building some forty feet on a side, with a guard at each corner.

The sus-magiz touched the wall with her staff, made a sign in the air and an arched opening formed there. She went in, the guards with the box and the buckets followed, and the opening turned back to stone behind her.

It had to be Lirriam's prison. Presumably they were bringing food and water for her, and for guards inside.

Five minutes later the opening reappeared. The sus-magiz and guards emerged, she vanished the opening and they went away. Llian headed back to the construct. The cubic temple must be where Lirriam was held, but how was she to be freed when Rulke could not leave the construct, and the temple had no entrance?

# 29

# RULKE CAN ROT IN A DITCH!

N ever thought I'd see you give up so easily,' said Llian, hours later. 'What happened to the Rulke who led the Hundred to take Aachan from the Aachim? I still get shivers when I remember the story you told in our great Telling competition. What a barbaric splendour it was.'

'A competition you 'won' by cheating,' Rulke said sourly.

'Your judges didn't think so.'

'You nobbled them!'

'Surely you're not suggesting that *I* outwitted the great, the incomparable and superlative intellect of Rulke? Where's your plan? You always have one.'

'I can't break the spell that confines me to the construct – and I can't use it without its controller crystal. I'm stuck.'

'You're in sad decline, Rulke.'

'If you're trying to goad me into something reckless, it's not working.'

'I *am* trying to goad you,' said Llian. 'Otherwise, when the Merdrun use their gift-burner, they'll erase everyone gifted on Santhenar.'

'Won't worry you. You've got less of a gift than a tapeworm.'

'It'll destroy a lot of people I care about. Karan and Sulien, Aviel – even you.'

'You care about me? I'm touched, Chronicler.'

How could the greatest warrior, and the greatest mancer, the world had ever seen, be unable to lift a finger? Because he dared not do anything to put Lirriam's life at risk.

'All right,' said Llian. 'I can see it's going to be up to me. I'll have a go at rescuing Lirriam.'

Rulke, who had been sipping from a mug of chard, choked, spraying it halfway across the cabin. 'Even if you could free her, which is so staggeringly unlikely that it's not worth thinking about, it doesn't get us out of here.'

'Tell Flydd to gate in and bring a controller crystal.'

'He can't; the enemy have gate-blockers everywhere. And even if he could, the construct would drain any crystal he could bring within minutes.'

'You can do a lot of damage in a few minutes. The moment I come back with Lirriam, you attack for as long as the power lasts. And we take it from there.'

Rulke looked at Llian pityingly. 'All that would do is get everyone killed.'

'They're going to kill everyone anyway. And Lirriam will be one of the first.'

'Why do you say that, Chronicler?'

'Because you're their greatest enemy, and she's your –' Llian paused. He wasn't sure exactly what Lirriam was to Rulke.

'You can say it. Lover. Paramour. Not that it's true, but I'd like it to be.' Rulke sighed. 'No, I won't allow it.'

'Why not?'

'I've seen your physical ineptitude at close hand, Chronicler.'

'You've also seen me prevail in a crisis.'

'Usually one you created. Go away and leave me to think.'

Karan shivered, pulled her coat around her and moved closer to the fire. It was hours after midnight but no one wanted to go to bed, least of all her. She was afraid of her dreams.

Only forty-five hours until Founder's Day began, the Day of All Days. And by the end of it, after the Merdrun had achieved their True Purpose, they would erase the gift of every gifted person on Santhenar. Then, presumably, kill all the prisoners.

An hour passed, then another. And another. Everyone had gone to bed except herself, Flydd, Yggur, Nish and Maelys, who was dozing, wrapped in her cloak. Yggur had not moved in hours, though his frosty eyes were open, the firelight reflected there. He had retreated into some inner world.

Flydd's maps and plans were spread out on the ground in front of him. Perhaps he thought that, if he stared at them long enough, some means of rescuing the prisoners in Skyrock would come to him.

'Doesn' seem real.' Nish was on his third goblet, or perhaps his fourth, and slurring his words. 'All my life, and my ancestors' lives back for a hundred and sixty years, it was us against the lyrinx. Then we defeated them, but next minute we were fighting the God-Emperor. My lousy father! Then the Merdrun.'

Maelys woke with a start and gave him a disgusted look. 'Your point is?'

'And now we've been defeated in a heartbeat, without a proper fight? I can't come to terms with it.'

Karan picked up a half full wine bottle and took a small swig. It was strong and harsh. She grimaced. 'If they're going to rob me of my family and my gift, I might as well –'

Yggur's big hand slapped across her mouth. 'Don't say it!'

Had anyone else done it, Karan would have thumped them. She shoved his hand away.

'No one knows more about despair than I do,' he said quietly. 'It's been my bane for most of my life.'

And yet, Yggur sounded almost serene. He's accepted things the way they are, she thought. He's ready to die. An end to all suffering, all pain. A part of her wished she could find such acceptance. Another part was determined to fight to the last choking breath.

'If anyone knows about despair, it's Rulke,' Flydd said ruminatively. 'He spent a thousand years imprisoned in the Nightland, never knowing if he would get out. And after he escaped, he saw the last handful of fertile Charon, whom he had protected for aeons, wantonly killed.'

'I know!' Karan snapped. 'I was there. And Rulke can rot in a ditch. If he'd helped after we freed him from stasis, we might have stopped the invasion. I hope the Merdrun drop him down the chaos chasm and it carries him back to the Nightland for another millennium, the bast –'

'What'd you say?' Flydd sat up suddenly, staring at her.

He and Nish had consumed three bottles already and were making steady progress on the fourth. Flydd seemed unaffected, apart from a red flush that highlighted the livid, criss-crossing scars on his face.

'I said Rulke can rot –'

'After that.'

'I hope the enemy drop him down the chaos chasm, and –'

'That's it!' said Flydd.

'Wad aboud id?' said Nish, blinking at him.

'It's the way in, you drunken oaf,' snapped Maelys. 'That's what Klarm was hinting at.'

'The chaos chasm is the one place the Merdrun can't protect with their gate blockers,' said Flydd, 'because the Secret Art doesn't work properly there. The very nature of reality is twisted and perverted.'

'And deadly,' said Karan. 'Llian went through the edge of a patch of magical waste once, on the island of Demondifang, and he was lucky to get away. No one could survive a pit full of the stuff.'

'I did,' said Flydd.

'When?'

'Ages ago, after I convinced the scrutators to fund the first manufactory, to make clankers. I worked there for several years, with M'Lainte.'

Karan sat up, staring at Flydd.

He went on. 'It used so much power that the waste magic built up and began to corrupt everything around it. The foreman ordered it dumped in an old quarry out the back – the first chaos chasm – but waste magic was twisting the artisan's minds and damaging their work, and I was ordered to find a solution.'

'I'm wondering what the point of this story is,' said Karan.

'The only way to get inside a chaos chasm,' said Flydd, 'is to gate in a particular way, to the base where the forces cancel each other out.'

Yggur leaned forwards, the firelight reflecting in his frost-grey eyes. 'That would have been an experience like no other.'

'Not one I'm anxious to repeat. And my companions weren't so lucky.'

'How did you manage it?'

Flydd closed his eyes and leaned back against a rock. A couple of minutes went by. 'We wore protective suits drawn from woven copper and silver threads,' he said in a distant voice, 'studded with buttons made from tin and antimony. And lead boots. Very hard on the ankles.'

'Who came up with that idea?' said Nish.

'Can't remember.'

'We can't make woven metal suits in the next day and a half.'

'There was a whole storeroom full of them at Nennifer.'

'There isn't enough time to fly there and back.'

Flydd went to the sky galleon and came back with the knoblaggie. 'Klarm left this with Wilm, to give to Jassika.'

'Klarm said he could no longer make gates,' said Karan. 'And you said you couldn't, either.'

'But I can,' said Yggur, holding out his hand. 'With that.'

'Are you sure you're up to it? Back in Fiz Gorgo you needed help to stand up.'

'There isn't any choice, is there?' said Yggur. 'And to go adventuring one last time, with a beautiful young woman ... it raises the spirits. Would you take my elbow, Maelys, just in case?'

Maelys rose, smiling up at him.

'What about me?' said Nish.

'You're pissed,' said Flydd. 'The ruins of Nennifer need a clear head.'

'When you get the metal suits, are you going to use the knoblaggie to gate into the chaos chasm?' said Karan.

'I can't go down there,' said Yggur. 'It'd bring back the worst –'

'Don't think about it,' said Flydd hastily. 'I'll ask Maigraith.'

'You'd put your life – our lives – in *her* hands?' cried Karan.

'She can make gates to places no one else can,' said Flydd. 'If you're ready, Yggur?'

Maelys took Yggur's elbow, and Flydd his forearm. Yggur rotated the knoblaggie in his big hands, the firelight reflected brassy red off it, and he, Maelys and Flydd were gone to Nennifer.

# 30

# NOT THE CONSUMMATION I DESIRE

A day and a half went by before Yggur, Flydd and Maelys gated back from Nennifer, Flydd hauling out a trolley loaded with woven metal suits and lead booties. It was after nine in the evening, only hours remained until the Day of All Days began, they still did not have a plan, and Karan was in a state beyond panic.

The dark-faced moon was full and riding high, and the weather was getting wilder by the hour. She had mind-spoken to Rulke and he now knew where Lirriam was held, but he would not help them unless Llian could get into the guarded cubic temple and free her.

'I can't bear to think about it,' Karan whispered. 'The guards will kill him the moment he gets there.'

'Llian's our only hope,' said Flydd. 'Rulke won't move until Lirriam's safe, but we'll have to gate into the chaos chasm well before that, otherwise we'll run out of time.'

'Why can't you and Nish try to free her?'

'We can't get into the cubic temple.'

'And Llian can?'

'Apparently.'

'What if he fails?' said Nish.

'Everything fails,' said Flydd. 'Maigraith will make the gate and I'll –'

'Where is Maigraith?'

'She'll be here.'

Karan did not find this comforting. Maigraith always caused trouble and she always had her own agenda.

'I'll direct her gate to the pit of the chaos chasm,' said Flydd, 'to the point where the flux of waste magic cancels itself out. Then we'll all go through, and underground –'

'How?' said Karan.

'The tin mine we had here during the Lyrinx War. I told you about it.'

'Remind me.'

'The chaos chasm is the old mine pit, but after the ore body was worked out the miners followed the veins underground towards the node. I dug out the old plans in Nennifer. I reckon we can get through to it, to attack the node.'

'What for?'

'Wilm, Ilisial and I will try to cut off the enemy's power so they can't use the gift-burner on everyone, then head back to the gate. Nish and Maelys will climb to the surface, avoiding all perils, and take the controller crystal to the construct so Rulke can make a diversion.'

'Avoiding all perils,' snorted Nish. 'You make it sound so easy.'

'It's a wet, wild night and the Merdrun believe no one can get into the compound, so there shouldn't be many guards inside it,' said Flydd. 'Karan will attempt to sneak into Skyrock, concealed by one of Maigraith's illusions ... for as long as it lasts. The wards in the tower will eventually break any illusion.'

'There's bound to be guards in the tower,' said Karan.

Flydd handed her a baton, a foot and a half long, with a spiny layer on the end. 'Jam it against bare skin and it'll stun a sus-magiz, or anyone else, for at least an hour. You know where the prisoners are. This,' he gave her a small device with seven thin needles sticking out of one end, 'should open the cell doors. When Rulke makes his diversion, at 2.30 a.m., be ready to lead the prisoners down and back to the base of the chaos chasm, and into the gate.'

'The chances of all that going to plan –'

'Don't say it!'

'Llian, wake! It's time.'

Llian roused sluggishly. His sleep had been so deep that, even after his mind roused, his body seemed reluctant to follow. The wind was howling around the construct, the driven rain streamed down the portholes, and the lamps on the compound walls had blurred into yellow streaks.

'I've renewed the temporary sus-magiz metamorphism,' said Rulke. 'You go in five minutes.'

'How do I get into –?'

'Lirriam's space shearer.'

'What's that?'

Rulke laid a metal case on the table. Llian reached for it but Rulke knocked his arm aside. 'Not until I instruct you.'

He drew out a knife with a cream-coloured handle carved from a tusk, or perhaps a fang. The blade was ten inches long, thick in the centre but tapering at the edges, and had a two-pronged tip. And it was ever so slightly blurred, as if vibrating at high speed. One side was pale blue, the other a shimmering white.

'What does it do?' said Llian.

'Mostly, remove a careless user's body parts.'

'I get that it's dangerous.'

'But not *how* dangerous. When the blue side is up, the left-hand edge will cut through rock, metal, crystal or bone – anything, in fact. When the white side's up, the left-hand edge can make a temporary dimensional hole through a solid – such as a stone wall – without affecting the wall itself.'

Llian reached for the space shearer. Again, Rulke blocked him. 'There are other dangers, Chronicler. If you're halfway through the wall when your temporary passage closes, it'll be ugly.'

'How ugly?'

'Are you familiar with the concept of atoms?'

'Of course. Matter is made from them.'

'And in solid matter, each atom has to be in the proper arrangement and bound to its neighbours.'

'If you say so.'

'If the passage closes while you're halfway through it, your body and the stone wall will try to occupy the same space. This, Chronicler, violates the laws of nature, and nature will violently resist it.'

'How violently?'

'Both you and the cubic temple will be rendered into your component atoms. And everyone inside it, or nearby. This is not the consummation I desire.'

'I'll bet it's not,' Llian smirked.

Rulke was not amused. 'That's a dangerous remark, considering our earlier conversation.'

'About what?' said Llian.

'Karan's secrets.'

Rulke thrust the space shearer into its case until it clicked and handed it to Llian. He pocketed it gingerly. It would be just his luck if the blade slipped out and took his leg off.

'How long does a dimensional hole last?'

Rulke shrugged. 'Maybe five minutes. Maybe ten.'

A troublingly short time. Though the longer it lasted, the greater the risk of the hole being discovered. 'What are Flydd and the others planning?'

'None of your business.'

'But surely –'

'You're liable to be caught, Chronicler. What you don't know, not even the enemy's most fiendish tortures can force you to reveal.' Rulke chuckled.

'Your glee isn't helping.'

'I want you to be well prepared.'

'You seem to think I'm still the callow young man I was when we met.'

'Nothing you've done lately has proved otherwise.'

'The ten hard years I've lived since your 'death' have transformed me, and it'd help if you showed a speck of confidence in me.'

'If I didn't have a *speck* of confidence in you, you wouldn't be going. And you certainly wouldn't have the space shearer.'

'Then why the hell don't you say so!'

'You're a needy man, Chronicler. No wonder Karan –' Rulke thought better of it. 'Get moving! I've cast a confusion on the guards outside but it won't last ...' He dragged in several shuddering breaths. He was worried, though not about Llian's safety. 'Don't fail me, Chronicler.'

Llian went out the secret door and into the darkness. It was a miserable night, stormy and with cold, driving rain. Skyrock, half a mile away, was a blurry blue-white spire.

He strode briskly across the compound, as a sus-magiz would. Ten minutes later he reached the rock-pile illusion that concealed the cubic temple and pointed the crystal rod to clear a small passage through it. The cubic temple was only twenty yards away and a guard stood at each of the four corners.

How could he get in unseen?

# 31

## TRAITOR'S CRAG

In an hour the Day of All Days would begin, the day the Merdrun had yearned for and fought towards for more than ten thousand years. The day that, had Skald not made it possible for Klarm to kill the magiz, would have utterly transformed them.

Skald lay beside Uletta, probably for the last time. He had barely slept in days. Dagog's death had left the surviving sus-magizes with many devices to learn and a mountain of procedures to master, and only in the past few hours had it all been done to Skald's satisfaction. But could his mad plan possibly succeed?

If it did, his people would no longer be exiles, and he, more than any other Merdrun, would have made it possible. His heart glowed. How far the son of a traitor had come!

But it would be a bittersweet moment, because he would not be going with them, and ever afterwards, when the tales were told, his name would be cursed and reviled. He would be the Merdrun who had abandoned his people, at the moment of their greatest triumph, for a despicable slave woman. An enemy.

Uletta must have sensed his pain for she rolled over, put her arm around him and pressed her naked body against his back. How he loved her! She had found good things in Skald that had been hidden from him. The bitter, burning knot inside him was smaller now, and less painful, though it never went away.

He had devised a plan to save her and, possibly, the other slaves in her team. At the critical moment he would open a gate to a distant part of Santhenar and take them through. He had far-seen the place several times now and knew he could create a gate there in an instant.

Life would not be easy for the one Merdrun left on Santhenar, but he had the plundered gold Dagog had amassed, more than enough to set them up and buy the protection he would need.

He was in two minds about taking the rest of Uletta's team, though. They would hate him and try to bring him down, and probably despise Uletta for becoming his lover. It might be better to leave them behind, or make the gate go wrong and send them somewhere else. That would mean lying to her, but what was the alternative?

However, he and Uletta would only be safe if the True Purpose succeeded, and he had finally been told what that was. The tunnel through the base of Skyrock was to become the sapphire portal, the greatest ever crafted. It would be wide enough for the Merdrun nation, three hundred thousand strong, to pass through in less than an hour to Traitor's Crag, the place from which they had been exiled an aeon ago.

And as they did, the cunningly crafted portal would undo the curse put on them by Stermin when he'd ordered them through the Crimson Gate and called them irredeemably evil.

The magiz's most important job had been to visualise the destination so that the exit of the portal could be opened safely on Traitor's Crag. But he was dead and, though Skald had told Durthix he could take his place, Skald's far-seeing ability was far too feeble.

However, Sulien could now far-see almost as clearly as Dagog had been able to, and for the past two days Skald had been adapting her training to the purpose. But what if she could not see the true, top secret destination clearly enough, or took too long to see it in three dimensions? He had trained her with many destinations on Santhenar, taking her far-seen image and using it to make a gate there, and it had worked every time.

But he could not rehearse far-seeing the true destination and opening the sapphire portal, because the astronomical conjunction that allowed it to open did not begin until sunrise. It only lasted for eight hours, and in that time the destination had to be far-seen, and the full power of the node drawn upon to open the gigantic sapphire portal, and hold it open long enough for the Merdrun nation to pass through.

If Sulien could not see Traitor's Crag clearly enough, the sapphire portal could not be opened. Durthix would demand to know how the failure had occurred and Skald's lies would be exposed. No safe haven, even at the far end of Santhenar, would avail him then. The sus-magizes would trace the gate, put Uletta and the other slaves to death in the manner prescribed, and bring Skald back for trial and execution as the traitor who had destroyed the Merdrun's dreams.

Then the Merdrun army would go on a rampage across Santhenar. They might slaughter hundreds of thousands of people before their blood lust sated itself.

He had to succeed. Boldness, quick thinking and utter determination had carried him all the way from being the ostracised son of a coward to acting magiz. He could leap this last hurdle. He must.

Skald turned over, and Uletta turned with him, and he embraced her and closed his eyes. A few hours yet before he needed to rise. He sighed and drifted back to sleep.

Ghiar, the second of the two sus-magiz that Dagog had set to spy on Skald, put her eye to the crack in the door and saw him lying there, his arm around the deputy architect. The disgusting worm. How dare he!

But Dagog was dead, so who was she to report to? She could not go to Durthix – reporting on her own master was a capital crime, and she so wanted to go home.

Yet Skald had to pay.

## 32

# HER STONE TONGUE BECAME FLESH

It was after midnight and Aviel still had not finished the scent potion she was blending for Flydd in her tent workshop. If any of the attackers were caught, they would sniff it and their recent memories would be erased, ensuring that they could not reveal Flydd's plan under torture.

Maigraith had agreed to make the gate. No one else could target one so precisely as to open at the one safe point at the bottom of the chaos chasm. The place where the forces of toxic waste magic cancelled each other out.

But to Aviel's mind, Maigraith had agreed too willingly. Now that she had regained her youth and fertility, she would seize the opportunity to get into the compound, hunt Lirriam down and kill her. And Aviel could not tell anyone about it, or write it down, or hint about it in even the subtlest way. Maigraith had renewed the block, and the memory-recovery potion Aviel had used before did not work on this spell.

But where was Maigraith? Aviel had not set eyes on her since their time in Fiz Gorgo.

The memory-wiping scent potion was finicky and had to be blended exactly according to the method. One drop too many, or too few, of any of the scents meant the difference between it not working at all, working perfectly, or erasing a lifetime of memories.

Aviel was also crafting a curse-breaker potion to break the speaking block so she could tell Flydd what Maigraith was up to, but it was taking longer than expected and she did not see how it could be ready in time. It was also dangerous; a couple of drops too much and it could strike her dumb forever, or possibly kill her.

But since she had contemplated taking Maigraith's life, it was only right that Aviel should risk her own. Atonement wasn't just saying *sorry* – she had to prove it by putting something that really mattered to her on the line.

The memory-wipe scent potion was done. Aviel put a small amount into six phials, one for each of the attackers, and took them across to the camp. They were dressed in the shiny suits of woven metal brought from Nennifer, to protect them against the uncanny forces in the chaos chasm, and they looked hot and heavy and uncomfortable.

Aviel taped one of her phials to the inside of Flydd's forearm. She did the same for Karan, who looked ghastly, then Maelys and Nish, who, as usual, were barely speaking to one another. Wilm gave Aviel a gentle, heart-warming smile and held her two hands in his. Ilisial hardly reacted when Aviel taped the phial to her forearm; her eyes were empty.

'If you're caught,' said Aviel, 'break the phial, bring your arm right up to your nose and take a *deep* sniff. Your memories of the last few days will be gone.'

'What if it gets broken in the attack,' said Nish, 'and I sniff it by accident?'

'It has to be a deep sniff. A little whiff will only wipe fragments of recent memory. You may end up confused, though.'

'Just what I need in an attack on the most heavily guarded compound in the world.'

'It can't be otherwise,' Flydd said coldly, 'and Aviel has done her best with what she had.'

'How long until we go?' said Karan.

'Fifteen minutes.'

'Where the blazes is Maigraith?'

'She'll be here.'

Aviel wanted to tell them that Maigraith intended kill Lirriam, which would ruin the plan, but the moment she thought about it the curse locked her tongue. It lay in her mouth like a cold lump of stone and her throat closed over until it was a struggle to breathe. Get the curse-breaker done, now!

She hurried back to her tent. The blending still had to be done and the consequences of getting it wrong were dire. Don't think about that. Just think about making it perfectly.

The seconds ticked down to minutes. The minutes jumped one by one. Five. Ten. Eleven. Twelve. Aviel's racing fingers slipped and five drops fell, rather than three. Instinct kicked in and she knocked the rack holding her blending tube aside. The five drops went down the outside of the tube, not within.

She stopped for a moment, to steady herself. That was too close. Five drops would have ruined the scent potion and there was no time to blend it afresh.

Thirteen minutes. It wasn't going to be ready in time and she was panicking again. She recited a list of scents backwards, which was always calming, wiped the outside of the blending tube with a wet rag, rinsed her fingers and continued.

Fourteen minutes. She gave the tube the prescribed swirls and shakes, stoppered it and shook it. Now it had to settle for a full minute.

Fifteen minutes! Maigraith was nothing if not precise. She would be there by now; she would be opening the gate.

Aviel heard a gentle *pop* and the rush of air. She instinctively turned to look, a pang shot through her ankle and she stumbled and dropped the wet tube. She caught it before it hit the rocky ground and hurried out, pain stabbing all the way up to her right hip.

Sixteen minutes. She was going to be too late.

The gate was hissing and crackling when she got there, and Nish was about to go through. Flydd, Wilm and Ilisial were next, then Maelys and Karan. Maigraith looked even younger now, not yet thirty, and almost beautiful.

Aviel lurched towards them, trying to shout a warning, but her tongue turned to stone in her mouth and all she could do was gasp and flap her arms.

'What's the matter?' Flydd signalled to everyone to wait.

Maigraith was staring at her suspiciously. Aviel yanked the stopper out of her tube and took a deep sniff, then another. Her stone tongue became flesh, her throat opened.

Maigraith blasted the tube from her fingers.

'Stop!' gasped Aviel. 'She's going to betray us.'

'You stinking little liar!' cried Maigraith, and dived for the gate.

Karan hooked an arm around Maigraith's throat, heaving her off her feet and cutting off her air, and Nish held her.

'Make it quick,' said Flydd.

'Maigraith is only helping us so she can get into Skyrock and kill Lirriam.'

Maigraith tore free and pointed her right hand at Aviel. Nish tried to knock her arm aside but there was a blast, a *crack-crack* and he fell, holding his own right arm. The rest of the blast struck Flydd on the left shoulder and drove him backwards. Maigraith tried desperately to get to the gate but he spoke a command and it faded out.

She cursed him and Aviel, touched herself on the breastbone, and vanished.

'You all right?' said Flydd.

Nish was holding his right arm, his face screwed up in pain. 'It's broken. In two places.'

Flydd was supporting his own shoulder, which appeared to be dislocated.

'What do we do now?' Karan said frantically.

'Maelys, have a look at my shoulder,' said Flydd.

Maelys removed the top of his metal suit, and his coat and shirt. The whole of his scrawny upper arm and shoulder, and the left side of his chest, was bruised from the force of Maigraith's blast. His shoulder hung low and he had to support his left arm with his right.

'Dislocated for sure,' said Maelys. 'I can heave it back into its socket but – it's going to be painful for some time. And weak.'

'What about Nish's arm?'

'Tulitine can do a healing, but he won't be using it in the next few days.'

'Then you'll have to go by yourself.' Flydd swore, long and hard.

Aviel felt shaky and had to sit down. Everything was going wrong and they hadn't even left yet. Karan looked as though she was going to scream. Aviel turned away as Maelys heaved Flydd's shoulder back into its socket. It made a horrible noise. She made a sling for his left arm.

'Then Santhenar is lost,' said Wilm.

'Not yet,' said Flydd. 'I didn't close Maigraith's gate, I just hid it. Let's run through things one last time.'

'If Llian succeeds in rescuing Lirriam,' Karan said in a dead voice, 'he'll be leaving about now. What if he fails?'

'I say we follow our plan, without Rulke's diversion,' said Maelys.

'It can't succeed without the diversion.'

'We're going to be killed, or have our gifts burned away, which amounts to the same thing. This way, at least we'll die trying.'

'The Merdrun lost their five top generals and their magiz,' said Flydd. 'Things could go wrong for them too. We've got two farspeakers, and Karan can talk to us via mind-speech. We'll just have to adapt.'

He turned to Maelys. 'Your sole aim is to get the controller crystal to Rulke so he can make a diversion, with the construct, that will give Karan the chance to get Sulien, Jassika, M'Lainte and Tiaan out. Karan, you mind-spoke to M'Lainte?'

'Briefly. I know where her cell is. And the enemy's final preparations are to begin at 4.00 a.m.'

'We've got a few hours. Enough time, even if a few things go wrong.'

'*If* Llian pulls off the impossible,' said Nish.

## 33

# NICE WORK ... FOR A CHRONICLER

Ten deadly yards from Llian's hiding place to the nearest wall of the cubic temple. The guards were a few yards out from each corner; he could see the back of one and the front of another. The darkness, wind-driven rain and a ground mist were his only advantages.

If he timed it right and had a lot of luck, there might come a minute when no guard was looking along his section of wall. Or if one was looking, the mist might conceal Llian long enough to cut through the wall and crawl in. The other difficulty was the dimensional hole. If it lasted too long the guard might glimpse it if he paced by.

He gnawed a knuckle. Every second increased the risk of something going wrong. He had not been told about Flydd's plan but Llian knew everything relied on him – and he wasn't up to it.

Both guards were looking away from this side of the cubic temple. He scurried across, keeping to the ground mist, and gingerly unsheathed the space shears. He pressed the blue blade to the wall, it went *zzzt* and a small piece of stone fell with a little *clack*.

Fool, it's the white blade!

He reversed the space shearer, pressed the pronged tip against the stone and the blade slid into it as if into a tub of grease. He carved around in a circle a couple of feet across and a hole appeared there, though it did not go all the way through the wall. Llian pushed along the circle, his arm went in to the elbow and he cut again, and again, until there was no resistance.

The mist was thicker next to the wall and the guards had not seen him. He wriggled into the hole, and it was a most uncanny feeling. There was far more resistance than there had been to the blade; he had to drag himself through. And if the dimensional hole closed again, with even so much as a length of bootlace inside ... *annihilation.*

He pulled his boots through. He was in! And when the guard went by, hopefully he would be looking away, watching for people approaching, and would not notice the grey hole, low down, in the grey wall.

The cubic temple was dimly lit by silvery grey light coming from the walls and ceiling. It was bitterly cold, and the air was stale and still. He was in an open space that occupied one end of the building, up to the full height of the roof. A corridor ran along the wall through which he had entered, down to the far end. Another corridor ran along the opposite wall. The wall between the two corridors was featureless.

This end of the temple was empty apart from a cylindrical pedestal carved from red stone – the poisonous mineral, cinnabar, he thought – with something mounted on its top.

He went closer. It was a foot-long crystal. A gigantic, perfect zircon a few inches through the middle, with a sentence etched down each of the long sides in an ancient script still used by the Charon. Llian had learned to read it long ago. Could these words be the enemy's reputed Sacred Text?

*The greater good requires the doing of evil to evil.*

His knees went weak. This had to be the very crystal Stermin had cast his enchantment upon, aeons ago, after he created the Gates of Good and Evil. To send half his people through the good, Azure Gate to become Charon, and the other half through the evil Crimson Gate to become the accursed Merdrun.

Was this great zircon the crystal that Merdrax, the first leader and first magiz of the Merdrun, stole after they passed through the Crimson Gate for the first time and used to kill Stermin? Was this the Founder's Stone?

It must be so. It was surely the oldest writing in existence, and a priceless historical document. Llian's insatiable chronicler's curiosity stirred. What did the words mean? Were they a self-justification, an apology, an attempt to explain to posterity, a manifesto – or the ramblings of a deluded old fool?

*You're the fool!* he thought. *You're wasting precious time. Find Lirriam or all fails.*

He crept down the far corridor and at the end saw, in the dim light, a row of six cells guarded by a Merdrun soldier. The nearest two cells had open doors and a sleeping guard lay in each.

The guard on duty must be bored witless; what threat could occur in a prison with no entrance? Beyond him, Lirriam was pacing in her cell and appeared unharmed. The cells beyond were empty. She turned and must have seen him, and perhaps saw through the metamorphosis, though she gave no sign.

Llian could not take on an armed Merdrun face to face. Or an unarmed one, for that matter. He slipped back to the chamber with the Founder's Stone and approached the cells from the other side. The hole he had cut was still open, mist drifting in.

The guard had his back to Llian now and was yawning and rubbing his eyes. Perhaps the stale air had made him drowsy. He walked back and forth, swinging his arms, then leaned against the wall.

Would Llian's Merdrun-like metamorphosis and sus-magiz garb give him a chance? He had to try it. He turned the corner, drew the space shearer and concealed it behind him, then went soft-footed towards the guard.

He was only a lunge away when the man whirled.

'Halt, soldier!' said Llian, using his Teller's voice in an arrogant and commanding Merdrun accent.

The soldier froze, eyeing him warily. He knew something wasn't right but dared not challenge a sus-magiz. Llian took another step, then whipped the space shearer out from behind his back. The guard went for his sword.

Llian hacked desperately and the white blade passed right through the man's fist – he had used the wrong edge again. The soldier gaped at his fist; there was no blood or, evidently, any pain. He wrenched out his sword and Llian knew he was going to die.

He threw himself to the side, the space shearer flailing, and the blue blade took the hand holding the sword off above the wrist. Blood sprayed across his chest and arm and the wall behind him, but the wound did not stop the guard, who bent for his fallen sword. Llian made a wild sideways slash and the blue blade carved through the Merdrun's chest armour and ribcage. He went down, blood flooding the floor.

The other guards were rising. Lirriam was at the door of her cell, pointing to the lock. Llian hacked through it, she heaved the door open and went past him in a blur. She scooped up the dead guard's sword, pried off the amputated hand that still clutched the hilt and ran forwards, barefoot, to attack the guards.

They towered over her, but she moved faster than any human should have been able to. She cut the first guard down with a sideways blow, danced around him and thrust through the defences of the second guard, and into his heart.

'Nice work ... for a chronicler,' she said, panting.

His mouth opened and closed. 'How did you do that?'

'I was one of the Five Heroes.' Lirriam took the space shearer from his hand and sheathed it.

Llian had no idea what she was talking about. But he wanted to know. 'This way,' he said.

He picked up one of the swords. It was too long for him, and very heavy, but he had to be armed. How had she wielded it so effortlessly?

Llian headed back to the dimensional hole, which was still open. He had only been inside a few minutes, and could not help thinking that the rescue had been a little too easy. But they weren't safe yet; it was a long way back to the construct.

He put his head out into the driving rain, shuddering at the feeling of the living rock surrounding him, and saw a guard lying dead on the ground, and another at the next corner. He clawed his way through and felt an overwhelming relief. Flydd must be here.

Lirriam had not followed. He looked through the hole. She was staring at the Founder's Stone, reading the inscription.

'Hurry,' said Llian. 'I don't know how much longer the hole will stay open.'

As he pulled back, he glimpsed a shadow from the corner of an eye, then something came down hard on the back of his head.

# 34

# I CAN CUT TWO THROATS AS EASILY AS ONE

Flydd reopened the gate to the base of the chaos chasm and he and the other four went through. Aviel helped Nish remove his metal suit and lead booties, since he could not do it with a broken arm, and Tulitine splinted it and did a partial healing. Nish, simmering with rage and clearly in a lot of pain, went to his bunk in the sky galleon. Tulitine and Yggur returned to their tent and extinguished the lamp.

It was cold and windy and wet. Aviel pulled her coat around her and sat by the fire. Would she ever see Wilm again? Or the others? Their chances of surviving the chaos chasm, and the Merdrun, were slim.

She felt very low. From the moment they had left Fiz Gorgo, and Flydd said he was going to pick up Wilm, Klarm and Ilisial, she had been looking forward to seeing Wilm and Klarm. She had really liked the dwarf, rogue though he had been. He had overcome far greater obstacles than she had, yet they did not seem to have coloured his life the way her small, painful disability had coloured hers.

But Klarm had not been at the rendezvous. He had gone off on a secret mission to Skyrock, and now he was dead.

A sudden downpour drove her to her tent and she sat there in the dark, looking out. Wilm had been glad to see her but the easy friendship they'd had of old was gone; he was preoccupied with his troubled friend, Ilisial, and kept Aviel at a distance. And why had she expected otherwise? He had made his feelings known on several occasions, and each time she had pushed him away.

Little wonder that, after a month and a half fighting and working with Ilisial, he should have developed feelings for her. She was an attractive woman, tall and slim, quietly spoken and skilled at the work she did as an apprentice to M'Lainte. Perhaps he loved her.

Now they were gone on a suicidal mission, and Aviel felt sure they weren't coming back.

She was sitting at the entrance of her tent, gloomily listening to the rain drumming on the canvas, when Maigraith materialised at the point where she had made the gate to the chaos chasm, and reopened it. Wisps of waste magic drifted out, blue and yellow and green, twisting and twining in the air like transparent snakes.

She wore one of the metal suits, though she had adjusted it so it clung to the curves of her youthful body. She was a striking woman now, bold and determined, and Rulke would be sure to fall for her again. She loosened a knife in a sheath on her right hip and went through the gate.

And Maigraith knew the plan! Knew she had to strike now and kill Lirriam before Llian could free her. Aviel had no choice, since she had made it possible. She had to follow.

There were three metal suits left. The smallest was too big, and rather baggy, but it would have to do. She dragged it on, and the smallest pair of lead booties. What else? A knife and a dark cloak were all she had, to take on the most dangerous woman in the world. And the enemy, if she encountered them, as was all too likely.

The metal suit was hot and heavy and surprisingly noisy, the woven fabric rasping and squeaking with every step, and the lead booties were incredibly heavy. Aviel laboured across to the gate, took a deep breath and stepped in, and was hurled through into the madness of the chaos chasm.

It was dark, though not completely so, and bitingly cold. Coloured vapours swirled through the air, as if stirred by the wind, though there was no wind down here. It was like being at the bottom of a slowly whirling vortex. Maigraith was not in sight.

Aviel was at the bottom of a benched mine pit, a bit like an amphitheatre, where frost needles glittered on every surface and crunched under her lead boots. The rock felt oddly soft, though – it gave under her weight as if she were standing on cheese. Had the waste magic done that? What would it do to her if it got through her suit?

The place smelled like stinking toadstools, and odd-shaped growths sprouted from cracks in the rock here and there, swaying slowly back and forth as if seeking prey. A low, dark opening yawned in the rock behind her, one of the tunnels the miners had used long ago as they'd followed the veins of tin ore towards the node under Skyrock. Flydd, Wilm and Ilisial would have gone that way. And Karan, to try and get into the tower.

But Maelys would have climbed out of the pit, to take the controller crystal to the construct, and Maigraith to get to the cubic temple.

Aviel's head felt hot and fuzzy. Was the waste magic getting to her already? A crumbling cart track, littered with fallen boulders and thick with uncanny growths sprouting from every crack, wound its way up to the top. She was following it up when a glowing black toadstool bent over and lunged at her bad ankle, leaving slimy marks across her lead bootie. Aviel let out a screech. The toadstool pulled away and started to shrivel.

She plodded up the track, stepping over the smaller growths and lurching around the larger ones, and emerged, weak-kneed and exhausted, into pelting, almost horizontal rain. Aviel took off her suit and booties and concealed them a little way down the track. Unlikely she would ever need them again.

It was miserably cold, and the rain had soaked her before she could don the cloak. She oriented herself by the blurry blue and white glow from Skyrock. Maigraith was several minutes ahead and the cubic temple was on the other side of Skyrock. Aviel made sure her silvery hair was tucked well under her hood and headed that way.

Wilm must be approaching the node now, if he, Flydd and Ilisial had found their way safely through the old tunnels. But what would they find there? Having read part of Flydd's *Histories*, Aviel knew about the catastrophe that had ensued years ago when he had tried to block another great node.

What if Flydd knew he could not succeed, and had a secret plan to explode the node and destroy Skyrock? He was a ruthless man, and he might think it was worth the sacrifice of his life, and all the allies' lives, to prevent the enemy from destroying every gifted person on Santhenar.

Aviel could not think about that. She pressed on through the rain and mist as fast as her ankle would allow. The temple was concealed by an illusion, a pile of broken rock, though a track had been dispelled through it. Maigraith was in such a hurry to get rid of her rival that she had not bothered to renew the illusion behind her.

Aviel passed through, looked along the wall, and stopped. Two guards lay on the ground, one at each corner, and Llian, halfway along the wall. His face had a strange, warped look; some kind of magic, she assumed. She ran to him and felt his throat. He was alive, but unconscious. Maigraith still had a tiny bit of conscience left, then.

A circular hole had been cut through the stone wall, low down. It had a most uncanny feel and Aviel was reluctant to go through, but it was that or fail. She dragged herself through the disembodied stone, feeling sure it was going to return to its proper state at any second. It shivered her from scalp to toenails.

Inside it was icy. She was in a large, empty space containing a central red pedestal with a big, silver-grey crystal mounted vertically on it. A line of glyphs, unreadable by her, ran down one crystal face. Aviel was reaching out to touch it when she was stricken by the terror that she had felt near the summon stone. But this was worse; it was overpowering. She backed away. Was this the master device, the one from which all the Merdrun's corruption came?

Where was Maigraith? Aviel turned away and crept down the passage to the left, and with every step she could feel the power of the crystal beating at her, calling her back. Her ankle bones grated together, and she almost screamed.

Before she turned the corner, she could smell the blood. Three soldiers lay on the floor, dead, and the puddles of blood had frozen solid. Maigraith, her back to Aviel, was driving a curvy woman into a cell. She had shining, opal hair. Lirriam.

The cell was empty apart from a stretcher with a couple of blankets, and an iron water bucket, half full, with broken ice on top. A Merdrun sword hung from Lirriam's right hand but she seemed unable to resist Maigraith.

Maigraith shoved her in the chest. Lirriam stumbled backwards, dropping the sword. She thumped into the wall and slid sideways onto the stretcher.

Maigraith had a small bottle in her hand, and Aviel was willing to bet that it contained the scent potion, Murderer's Mephitis. It would be a terrible death.

'You're Maigraith,' said Lirriam in a low, slow voice, as if it took an effort to speak.

'Yes,' said Maigraith.

'You want Rulke.'

'He swore to me, *forever*,' said Maigraith icily. 'And I've seen you flaunting your breasts and buttocks at him, you sneaking little trollop.'

Lirriam's lip curled. 'I never flaunt. I simply *am*. Besides, who says I want him – or any man?'

Aviel crept closer. Maigraith did not appear to realise she was there. Lirriam could see her but her face showed nothing.

'Liar!' cried Maigraith. 'You're not having him. He's mine!'

She drew a knife from a sheath on Lirriam's hip. It had a pronged tip and one scintillating blade was white, the other blue. Lirriam tried to lunge for the dropped sword but could not move.

Maigraith laughed. 'I've mesmerised you like a chicken – so it can no longer run from the axe.' She looked at the potion bottle in her left hand, the knife in her right, then put the bottle away and raised the knife.

Aviel sprang and caught her by the collar, but Maigraith whirled and threw her off. Aviel landed hard on her knees, next to the water bucket.

'What a sad creature you are, mouse,' said Maigraith.

'At least I'm not a killer!'

'Only because you lack the courage.'

Aviel threw her arms around Maigraith's thighs and tried to pull her down. They swayed back and forth, the knife flailing dangerously. But Maigraith was a lot stronger; she brought a knee up under Aviel's chin and her teeth snapped together on her tongue. She stumbled, dazed and tasting blood. Maigraith forced her back against the side of the cell.

'I can cut two throats as easily as one, mouse.'

Lirriam still could not move. Maigraith turned back towards Lirriam. Aviel, with the strength of desperation, grabbled the handle of the bucket and swung it at Maigraith's head.

She looked around instinctively and the iron base slammed into her forehead, cutting a long curving gash there. Icy water drenched her, and she stumbled and fell. Aviel tore the strange knife from her hand and tossed it through the doorway. The blue blade made a sizzling sound as it cut a chunk out of the stone floor.

Maigraith lay still, blood pouring down her face.

Lirriam stood up, shakily, swayed and almost fell down again. 'Best to end her; there's no other way to stop her.'

'I came here to save lives, not take them. Come on.' Aviel took Lirriam's hand and dragged her out, for she was struggling to walk. Aviel pulled the cell door shut but it would not stay shut; the lock had been cut through.

'Space shearer.'

'What?' said Aviel.

'The knife. Give it here. Be careful with it.'

Aviel gave Lirriam the space shearer. In the cell, Maigraith was wiping blood out of her eyes and trying to sit up.

'Hurry!' said Lirriam, her limbs shaking. 'The cell won't hold her.'

Aviel hauled Lirriam around the corner and out of Maigraith's sight. They reached the hole in the wall and Aviel went down on hands and knees to go through.

'No! Get back!' said Lirriam.

Aviel jerked away, fell and landed on her back.

'Cut another one,' said Lirriam. 'White blade.'

As Aviel sat up, the hole closed over and reverted to wall.

'Had you been in it when it closed,' said Lirriam, 'neither you nor I nor this temple would exist.'

Aviel slumped, feeling as though she was going to faint. She had not known.

'Come on!' Lirriam said urgently.

'It's all ... too hard. I don't know what I'm doing.'

'You're doing brilliantly. Cut the hole.'

Aviel did so, and it was the most uncanny feeling, being arm-deep in rock yet barely able to feel it. Everything was wrong about this.

'Go through! She's coming.'

Aviel wriggled through, expecting the solid stone to close on her at any second. Would she feel it, or would her death be instantaneous? At least it'd solve the problem of Maigraith, Aviel thought. She's been the bane of Santhenar for two centuries. It'd almost be worth –

*You're peering down the dark path again. Stop it!*

Aviel scrambled out, turned and reached through. She could hear Maigraith's stumbling footsteps, her ragged breathing. And Lirriam was still shaking, struggling to move by herself.

'Give me your hands!' said Aviel.

She grabbed Lirriam's wrists and heaved her into the hole, but before her head emerged she stuck and Aviel could not budge her.

'She's got my legs,' said Lirriam.

This had to end *now*! Aviel picked up the space shearer, cut a hole at head height and leaned through. She was above Lirriam's legs now. Maigraith, whose face was all bloody, was on her knees, heaving Lirriam back by the ankles. Using the blue blade, Aviel cut a head-sized block of stone out of the wall and dropped it on Maigraith's right shoulder.

*Crack*. The shoulder collapsed and she fell sideways, crying out in pain. Her collarbone must be broken.

'You little bitch!' she choked. 'The minute I get out of here, *you're dead.*'

She caught one of Lirriam's ankles but had to let go; her injury was too painful. She put a hand on her shoulder and began to speak a healing spell, then stumbled away. Going for a sword, presumably.

If she succeeded, she would hack Lirriam in two. Aviel was about to withdraw when a faint red glow drew her eye, from the floor next to the block of stone. It was the black stone Maigraith had taken from the enemy's sus-magiz in Alcifer – the Waystone. Aviel pocketed it, heaved on Lirriam's arms once, twice, and again, and she was through.

'Touch the white blade to the holes in the wall,' said Lirriam.

Aviel did so and the dimensional holes filled in. She helped Lirriam to her feet.

The guard's bodies were still where they had lain before, though the rain was heavier and the path Maigraith had made through the rock-pile illusion had filled in. No one had come to investigate; the sounds of violence from inside the cubic temple would not have carried.

Aviel looked around.

'What's the matter?' said Lirriam.

'Llian was here, unconscious. Maigraith must have knocked him down after she killed the guards.'

Lirriam walked around the cubic temple. 'There's no sign of him. What's the plan?'

'Maelys was taking a controller crystal to Rulke,' Aviel said quietly. 'If you're safe in the construct, he'll take off at 2.30 a.m. and create as much chaos as possible while the power lasts, so Karan can get Sulien and Jassika, and anyone else she's rescued, out of Skyrock. Flydd's gone down to do something to the node.'

Lirriam gave her an enigmatic look. 'How long will the crystal last?'

'Not long.'

'And then?'

'I don't know.'

'We'd better get to the construct, then.'

'Do you think Maigraith can gate herself out?'

'With my Waystone, anything is possible.'

Aviel took it from her pocket and held it out.

Lirriam's eyes grew huge. She reached out and took it, pressed it to her forehead and her lips, and put it away. 'If you hadn't already earned my undying gratitude, you have it now.'

Aviel felt a little glow. 'What about Llian?'

'I'm in no state to go looking for him. We have to follow the plan.'

Aviel knew it, but it felt wrong to be abandoning him.

'One more thing,' said Lirriam.

'Yes?'

'Don't tell anyone where Maigraith is. *Anyone*, you understand?'

'Not even Rulke?'

'Especially not Rulke. Don't mention her at all, if you can help it.'

'All right,' said Aviel, wondering why not. Was Lirriam planning to get rid of *her* rival? And if she was, was it Aviel's duty to stop her?

Life was too complicated.

# 35

# THE PLAN WOULD HAVE FAILED

L *irriam is free!* Rulke's mind-speech was an explosion of joy.

How had Llian done it? Karan should have had more faith in him.

Flydd, Wilm and Ilisial had headed down an old tunnel that Flydd thought might lead beneath the node. Karan was creeping up a steep, rock-walled passage, hoping to emerge in the great arched tunnel at the base of Skyrock, and Klarm's knoblaggie was heavy in her pocket. Flydd had asked her to give it to Jassika and Karan wondered why. Did he think Jassika might do something useful with it, or did he want her to have a memento of her father ... at the bitter end?

She mind-called Rulke. *What about Llian?*

*After he freed Lirriam, someone knocked him out. Aviel found him lying outside the cubic temple.*

*What was* she *doing there?*

*She went through the gate, sometime after you did.*

*Why? She was never part of the attack team.*

How had Aviel got out of the chaos chasm, anyway? Karan's brief time there, and in the waste magic-filled mine tunnel that led away from the base of the pit, had been hideous. Nothing had seemed real there and she'd felt that the rock was alive, and that it hated her. And feared that, if her boots sank into the soft floor of the tunnel, it would turn back to hard rock around her ankles and trap her there.

And she had to go back that way to gate out. Assuming the gate stayed open that long.

*A misguided impulse to do good, apparently. Lucky she did; she got Lirriam out of the cubic temple. But by then Llian was gone.*

*Taken?*

*I don't know. Maelys went out to look for him and hasn't come back.*

Karan tried to mind-call Llian but could not sense him. If he had been captured, they would torture him to find out why he was there. The enemy would soon discover that an attack was planned, and not even Rulke's diversion with the construct would make any difference then.

But if Llian had been taken, it could not have been long ago, and he might hold out an hour or two. Karan prayed that he did because Rulke's diversion was more than an hour away. She had to put Llian out of mind, painful though that was, and focus on her own impossible part of the plan.

*I'll soon be going in,* she said to Rulke. Her head was already throbbing and the last thing she needed was aftersickness now, so she cut him off and mind-called Flydd. *It's on.*

*Good luck!*

It would take a hell of a lot more than luck. But she had to focus on getting into the tower and finding Sulien, Jassika, M'Lainte and Tiaan in time. If she could, she might just get them out.

1.30 a.m. The Merdrun's Day of All Days began at sunrise, four and a half hours away, though the sus-magizes and artisans who had to bring about the True Purpose would arrive to prepare for the great day long before that. Time was critical now. If it took too long to find the prisoners and free them there would be no chance of getting out of the tower.

The passage terminated at a stone stair, cut into the rock. As Karan followed the flights up, the howl of the wind became louder with every step, and the darkness gradually gave way to a blue, shimmering light that grew ever brighter. Then suddenly she could see out – and it was dazzling, unbelievable.

The walls and ceiling of the massive tunnel were crusted with uncounted millions of sapphires, and the light came from inside them, brightening and darkening in waves that passed from one end of the tunnel to the other, and back again, ever changing.

It was astonishingly beautiful. But what was it for?

She crept up. The paved floor was wet, though the rain had eased to showers. Lines of slender pillars, also crusted with sapphires, ran the length of the tunnel, supporting the arches.

A steep staircase on the far side, two hundred yards away, led up into the tower. Six guards, spread across the entrance, watched the fog-wreathed compound. There was no reason for any of them to turn and look back into the tunnel, but if one did while she was crossing it, she would be seen instantly. In the original plan, Maigraith was supposed to put a concealing illusion on Karan, but she had fled without casting it.

Karan's throat was itchy dry. It would be a miracle if this worked. She shook her head in an effort to clear it. She still felt dizzy and nauseous from the chaos chasm, and it would be worse on the way back.

She gathered her cloak around her and checked on the guards. They were all staring outwards. She flitted across the tunnel, breathing raggedly, her heart beating painfully fast, and reached the stairs. It was less likely that they would see her here, but she went up slowly, keeping low and stepping carefully. Any hard footfall would echo through the tunnel and betray her. The treads were uncomfortably high, and she was breathing heavily by the time she had ascended six flights and came to a wide landing.

She crouched against the side wall, caught her breath and continued. If someone came down there was nowhere to hide. Karan reached the top of the stairs, more than a hundred feet above the floor of the passage, and passed through an opening into the large room M'Lainte had called the control chamber. It was dimly lit by red wall lamps.

The chamber was about twenty-five yards across, with a high, fluted ceiling, and was shaped like an open flower with eight petals. A massive, off-centre column was semi-circular on one side and concave on the other. An oval slab of clear quartz set in the floor gave a view of the entrance and part of the sapphire tunnel.

High above it a menacing model of the jagged Merdrun glyph, cut from black iron plate and a good eight feet across, was suspended from two pairs of cables, one attached to a ring on one arm of the glyph, the others attached the same way on the other side. Karan shivered.

Steps curved up to a mezzanine level on the southern side, overlooking the control chamber. The main stairs continued up. Another staircase, very steep and narrow, was visible through an open door on the northern side.

Karan slipped up the main stairs, her bad hip throbbing with every step. The next level contained meeting rooms and storerooms, though most were empty of furnishings, as if the Merdrun had only carved them out to meet the requirements of the tower's design.

The prisoners were held on the level above that and a guard stood watch. Karan drew the baton Flydd had given her and crept towards him. From the back he was heavily built, with a bald, shaven head marked by a deep diagonal scar, and he was moving his feet up and down rhythmically, as if he had restless legs. She was raising the baton when he turned. She lunged and jammed the spiny end into his voice box. *Zzzzt!*

He convulsed, mouth spraying saliva, eyes wobbling in and out as if something was trying to force them from their sockets. He drew in several desperate breaths, shuddered wildly and collapsed, a bitten tongue protruding out between peg-like teeth. Rivers of snot oozed from his nose and down his chin.

Karan gagged him and tied his wrists behind his back with cord she had brought for the purpose, then, with a series of heaves, got him into an empty room and closed the door. If she was still here when the effects of the stunner wore off, the plan would have failed.

To the left were a series of circular cells. Each had a stone shelf for a bunk, a hole for bodily wastes and a door made of ironwork, wrought into repeating patterns of the Merdrun glyph. There was no privacy – subhuman slaves did not need it.

The prisoners, all adults, were asleep on their pallets but she could not free them; she had to stick to the plan. In the third cell she recognised M'Lainte, though she had lost a lot of weight.

Karan touched the lock with the device Flydd had given her, but the door did not open.

M'Lainte sat up painfully. There were bruises on her arms and face, though when she saw Tiaan her eyes gleamed. 'I never imagined you would get in. Underestimated you.'

'You don't look well.'

'I'm a lot better now you're here. What's happening?'

'I can't open the door.' Karan tried Flydd's opener again, with no result.

'Give it here.'

Karan passed it between the jagged bars. M'Lainte sat on her bunk and took the device apart. Karan summarised what Rulke, Flydd and she hoped to do.

'The girls are over the other side,' said M'Lainte, her fingers working rhythmically. After a brief glance at the innards, she had not looked down again. Whatever modifications she was making to the lock-cracker, she was doing them by feel. 'Sulien hasn't been harmed yet.'

'What about Jassika?'

'Beaten ... to force Sulien to work harder.'

'At what? I've tried to mind-speak her but got nothing.'

'Blocked,' said M'Lainte. She slumped against the wall and closed her eyes for a moment. 'They've been training her ability to far-see. Didn't want any distractions.'

'Far-see what?'

M'Lainte touched Flydd's device to the lock and the door opened. She handed it back. 'Get Tiaan out first – sixth cell. We need to talk.'

'Is she all right? We heard she was gravely ill.'

'Not as ill as the enemy believed. And Lirriam healed her as part of Rulke's bargain.'

Karan was torn. One part of her just wanted to free the girls and head back to the chaos chasm and the gate. But it was more than forty minutes until Rulke's diversion and the more she could learn in the next few minutes, the better.

She slipped across to the sixth cell and opened the door. The woman she had seen briefly in the construct, in Alcifer, sat up. She was around Karan's age, though taller and with short black hair, and she looked better fed than she had three weeks ago.

'I'm Karan,' she said. 'M'Lainte said to –'

'Not here,' Tiaan said quietly.

She followed Karan to M'Lainte's cell and they went in and sat on the bunk.

'Why are they training Sulien to far-see?' said Karan. 'Can you guess?'

M'Lainte and Tiaan exchanged glances.

'They think they've kept it secret,' said Tiaan with a superior smile.

'But ...?'

'They needed some mighty mech-magical devices but did not know how to design or build them. They had to use M'Lainte's skills, and mine, and we've worked out what they're up to. The great tunnel below is going to become the sapphire portal.'

'Why are they making a *portal*?'

'Santhenar is just a stop-off,' Tiaan said quietly. 'They're going home – to Tallallame.'

'What?' It took a while for it to sink in. Karan's voice rose. 'Are you saying that all the killing, and all the ruin they've wrought here, was just *incidental*?'

M'Lainte shushed her. 'After the Mariem were cast into the void, the Faellem created a block to prevent them, or their descendants, from ever returning. But a tiny flaw developed in the block and they can now reach Tallallame from Santhenar – though only rarely. Today is one such day, when the moon is full and the whole of its dark side is showing. The window to Tallallame opens at sunrise and closes again eight hours later.'

'Are you saying the Merdrun's goal has always been to conquer Tallallame and take revenge on the Faellem?' said Karan.

'Yes.'

'They'll have a fight. There are also hundreds of thousands of lyrinx on Tallallame.'

'But when the sapphire portal breaks through the barrier around Tallallame,' said M'Lainte, 'it's been designed to cause a psychic shock that will render every intelligent creature there senseless, possibly for days. The Merdrun plan to gate to every town and enclave, and put everyone to the sword. It'll be the biggest bloodbath of all time.'

Tiaan went pale. 'I didn't know that.'

'I only worked it out last night,' said M'Lainte. 'When I was thinking through some peculiarities in the design of the gate-opening device.'

'We have to warn them. We've contacted the lyrinx in the past. My old friend, Ryll –'

'It's not easy to make a far-speaker to call between worlds – even if we had all the components. But if Karan can get you out, Flydd might have what's required.'

'That'll be too late.' Tiaan lay back on the bunk and closed her eyes. 'It's probably too late now.'

We were right, Karan realised. They did want a world cleansed of humanity – but it wasn't our world. 'Then why do the enemy want to use the gift-burner on us?'

'They learned long ago,' said M'Lainte, 'that, if they identified a threat, it was best to eliminate it at once.'

'Why haven't they done so already?'

'The gift-burner takes a prodigious amount of power, and until the portal is open they don't have any to spare.'

'But with the magiz dead, how are they going to open such a gigantic portal?'

'The devices in the control chamber do most of the work. Any competent sus-magiz should be able open the portal at the appointed hour …'

'But?'

'Envisaging the destination clearly and precisely enough to target such a void-cleaving portal is immensely difficult. Skald claims to be highly skilled in far-seeing, but I think he's been training Sulien to do what he can't do himself – and lying about it.'

Karan choked. 'Isn't that dangerous? For her?'

'Very.' M'Lainte went to the porthole and looked up at the stars. 'Twenty minutes until Rulke's diversion. Get Sulien and Jassika out and go.'

Tiaan rose, rubbing her eyes.

Panic flared. Karan fought it down. She had to believe she could do this. 'Thank you, M'Lainte. Come on.'

M'Lainte shook her head. 'I'd only hold you back. I'll take my chances.'

'But there's time.'

'No, there isn't. Run, you've got a daughter to save.'

## 36

# LIKE A HUMAN BULLET

Wilm was amazed that Flydd could stand up, given the pain he was in. Even more surprising that he could find the way in this maze of old tin mine tunnels.

'Wilm, stop!'

Wilm, who was a couple of yards ahead, froze. 'What is it?'

Flydd went past, probing ahead with his glimmering staff, and looked down. 'An unmarked shaft. And I can't see bottom.'

Wilm swallowed. 'Are we far astray?'

'Quiet, let me think.'

This was taking too long. At this rate they would still be underground when Rulke took off in the construct. And Ilisial was more agitated than usual, head jerking, fingers tapping, eyes staring. Why had Flydd brought her? Wilm prayed she wasn't going to have another breakdown, but feared she would.

'We'll have to jump,' said Flydd.

'Where?' she whispered.

'Across the shaft and down six feet to the next tunnel.' Flydd pointed and Wilm made out a faint, darker circle. 'Go first, Wilm.'

The shaft was only five feet wide, an easy jump on solid ground. Far from easy here, since the tunnel entrance was small. If his jump was high, he might hit his head on the wall of the shaft and fall down it. A fraction low and he could break his knees on the hard lower edge of the tunnel. Same result.

Thinking about it only made it worse. Wilm judged the distance and sprang.

Too high! He ducked his head, his hair brushed the top of the tunnel and he was in, landing hard and swaying backwards and almost overbalancing. How close was he to the edge? He shifted his weight and toppled forwards, safe.

'Wilm?' Ilisial said hoarsely.

'I'm all right.'

'Move back.'

He got out of the way and she leapt across, bending forwards to clear the roof and landing neatly on all fours beside him.

'Your turn, Xervish,' said Wilm.

'Give me a minute.' Flydd was rubbing the shoulder Maigraith's blast had dislocated.

'I don't see how he can do it with one arm in a sling,' Wilm said quietly. 'Get ready to grab him if –'

'He won't like that.'

Flydd went to the edge but backed away. 'Nope.'

'Do you want us to go on without you?' said Wilm.

'Don't be ridiculous. I won't know how to do the job until I see the node.'

He raised his staff, crouched and made a spiralling shape behind him, like a coiled spring. *Boing!* Flydd was ejected from the tunnel like a human bullet, down and across and straight at Wilm. His good shoulder hit Wilm in the chest, knocking him down, and Flydd landed on top of him. His staff clattered away and its lighted tip went out.

He disentangled himself. 'Not my best shot.'

'How did you do that?'

'I just thought of it and did it.' He retrieved his staff, made light at the tip and gave Wilm a fierce look. 'Couldn't have you catching me like a baby.'

'No need to thank us,' Wilm said sarcastically.

'When you do something useful, I'll thank you.'

'Bloody old bastard's nearly as sour as Klarm,' Wilm muttered. Then he felt bad, given what a hero Klarm had proven to be.

'I hope to be,' said Flydd.

They followed the tunnel for a while, crunching on broken rock from a roof fall, then down into a long, ankle-deep pool of warm water, along a dry tunnel in hard grey rock and down again. It was hot now, and humid. Sweat trickled down Wilm's front and back.

'Xervish?' said Wilm.

'What now?'

'How can we attack the node if it's impossible to reach it from above, or from the sides.'

After a long pause Ilisial said, 'Xervish didn't say anything about from below.'

'Are you going to?' said Wilm.

'Not if you keep pestering me.' Flydd paced along. 'During the war, the Chief Scrutator wanted to know if this node could be dug out and taken to where power was needed most. I told him that was absurd, but he knew best.'

'I assume it didn't work,' said Wilm.

'We lost a lot of miners trying. The rock's rotten and the tunnels kept collapsing, and the closer they got to the node the hotter it was. Miners were collapsing from heat stroke, and some had inexplicable burns – sometimes on the *inside*.'

'So you went wide and deep, avoiding the rotten rock, and tunnelled up underneath the node,' said Ilisial.

'But even with yards of solid rock between my miners and the node above, their clothes and hair were starting to smoulder.'

'If it's so hard to reach the node, how did the Merdrun tap its power?' said Ilisial.

Flydd shrugged. 'They don't care if a thousand slave miners die, as long as each one gets an inch closer.'

As they descended, the air grew ever warmer, and so humid it was an effort to breathe. Wilm's clothes were sodden with sweat and he was starting to feel faint.

The steeply sloping tunnel levelled off and they splashed through puddles of green water, like thin jelly, that clung to their boots. Their tunnel ended at a ragged hole, through which he saw a steamy tunnel with smooth, curving walls.

'This is it,' said Flydd. 'I was worried it would have fallen in.'

They clambered into the curving tunnel, onto something soft and slippery that gave beneath Wilm's boots.

'I originally thought to use the field-blocker Aviel took in Thurkad,' said Flydd, taking it from his pack with a gloved hand. 'Yggur and I rebuilt it in his workshop at Fiz Gorgo, to make it stronger. But it isn't going to work.'

'Why not?' said Ilisial.

'Node's too powerful; the field blocker would burn out.'

'Have you got a plan, then?' said Wilm.

'Batter the node down with your head,' Flydd muttered.

He brightened his staff and headed around the curve. The tunnel was doughnut-shaped and about thirty feet in diameter, with the central 'hole' being a ten-foot-wide stalk of fractured rock. The air had a spicy odour, like nutmeg. The ceiling dripped thick green water from a myriad of cracks, and the walls and floor were sheeted in a growth like green mould.

He extinguished the light. 'Don't move; don't talk.'

As Wilm's eyes adjusted he made out a faint blueish glow issuing from cracks in the roof of the tunnel above them, and from the fractures in the stalk. 'Is that the node, above us?'

'Yes,' said Flydd, 'and if we're here too long we'll be crisped up like roast chickens.'

# 37

# YOU FESTERING LITTLE WORM!

And the plan is?' asked Wilm.

'Making it up as I go along,' said Flydd.

'What have you made up so far?' Wilm said irritably.

His head was aching, it was hard to think straight, and he did not want to be down here a moment longer than necessary. He avoided thinking about the probable fate awaiting them once they got out. He turned and Ilisial had gone into that blank-eyed stare again. Great!

Flydd put a hand on the rock stalk, then jerked it back, wincing and shaking his hand. The skin was smoking.

'If we can bring this down,' he said, 'the node and the rotten rock above it should fall in, burying it twenty feet deep in hot rubble.'

'The Merdrun will dig it out again,' said Wilm.

'Not in time for their True Purpose – or to use the gift-burner on us.'

'Are you planning to use a blasting spell?' said Ilisial.

'Something like that,' Flydd said.

'I heard you attacked a node once before,' said Wilm. 'Didn't it go badly wrong?'

Flydd hunched his narrow shoulders. 'We didn't exactly *attack* the Snizort node, Irisis and Ullii and I. The lyrinx had a node-drainer there and we – Irisis, she was the artisan – reversed the direction of it.'

'It did go badly, though?'

'It burned out the node, sending a column of fire half a mile in the air and melting a crater in the ground – and left two mighty armies – ours and the Aachim's – at the mercy of the lyrinx. To this day, they've never trusted us.'

'What makes you think this won't be just as bad?'

'I'm not trying to harm the node.'

'But if it collapses,' Wilm persisted, 'anything could happen.'

'If we do nothing, the enemy will use the power of the node to destroy everyone gifted, in the world.'

Ilisial let out a small, anguished cry.

The glow was flaring, turning a deeper and brighter blue, fading, then flaring again. And now Wilm made out a faint ticking sound, rising to a low *thrum* then fading back to a tick. With each *thrum*, water or steam gushed out of the cracks in the tunnel roof, and the fractured column of rock supporting the node. It felt as though something was beating, like a rocky heart, up in the node.

'What is a node, anyway?'

'A natural concentration of force,' said Flydd.

Wilm was none the wiser. 'And how –?'

'Wilm,' said Ilisial savagely, 'shut up!'

Wilm missed M'Lainte, who had patiently and cheerfully answered all his questions, even the impertinent ones. Why had Flydd brought him, anyway? There was nothing Wilm could do here.

Flydd began to walk around the rock stalk, shielding his face with his hands. 'This is taking too long. We'll still be down here when Rulke makes his diversion.'

And that might leave them with no way out. The Merdrun would take the sky galleon, but they wouldn't bother with a handicapped girl who could never do a slave's work. They would kill Aviel on the spot. Wilm clenched his fists helplessly.

Flydd went still, staring at the wall.

'Xervish?' said Ilisial.

His lips were moving. What was the matter?

He shook himself and looked around. 'It was Karan. Mind-calling. A few problems.'

'What?' said Wilm.

'Later. It ... might be all right.' He walked along the curving wall. 'I think ... here,' Flydd said to himself. 'Wilm, this is your moment. Draw your sword.'

Wilm drew the enchanted blade. Flydd indicated a point on the rock stalk where three sets of fractures converged.

'Thrust here. Right to the hilt.'

'What for?' said Wilm.

'Your blade cuts anything, even rock. Shove it in, cut around in a circle a foot across, and pull it out.'

*What?* said Akkidul. *How dare you? Don't listen to the ugly old fool. No, no!*

Wilm thrust the point of the blade into the rock. It did not feel like rock; more like a mould-threaded cheese. The whining voice cut off. He thrust harder until the blade went in all the way, then forced it through the rock in the beginning of a circle. The sword grew so hot that he could not hold it. He backed away, shielding his face.

*You festering little worm*, said the sword. *I'll get you for this.*

'You can't stop halfway!' cried Flydd. 'Finish the circle.'

Wilm tried but the hilt was so hot that it burned welts across his fingers.

'Ilisial, you've got gloves!' said Flydd. 'Finish it!'

Ilisial shuddered. 'It's an evil blade.' But she drew on her thick leather gloves.

*Touch me and I'll make you pay, girlie*, said Akkidul.

'Shut up, Akkidul,' snarled Flydd, 'or I'll bury you here and let the heat erase you.'

Ilisial's eyes grew huge and wild. She gasped, controlled herself with a visible effort and took hold of the hilt with both hands. Smoke rose from her gloves. She winced but forced the blade around through the rock until it had completed an eight-sided shape, then wrenched it out. One of her gloves burst into flame. She slapped it out on the wet wall.

The light pulsed a brighter blue; it was burning Wilm's skin. The thrumming became the beating of a great drum, far away, *booom, booom, booooom*. Jets of hot water squirted out of cracks.

'Prise out the plug of rock,' said Flydd. 'Quick!'

Ilisial thrust the sword in again, cut across the circle, then across once more. Pieces of fractured rock fell out. She dropped the sword, tore off her smouldering gloves and thrust them into the water on the floor. Steam hissed up.

Wilm ducked past her and began to pull the rotten stuff out of the hole.

'Not with your hands!' said Flydd.

Wilm's fingers were smoking. He wiped them on his sodden pants and prised with the sword, and Ilisial and Flydd with their knives, until a hole had been created there, an arm's length deep.

*You were warned, girlie*, said Akkidul.

'Sheathe the damned sword,' said Flydd.

Wilm did so and thrust it down hard.

'Back!' said Flydd. 'Don't look at the hole.'

It was now glowing blue-white, the light flaring and fading in faster cycles than before, and the booming became a *thump, thump, thump*.

Wilm and Ilisial backed away and turned their heads. From the corner of an eye Wilm saw Flydd's lips move. Was he counting under his breath, or gathering the courage to do something dangerous? He rubbed his bad shoulder and winced. In the garish light his face was blanched, the facial scars standing out like purple ridges.

He thrust the tip of his staff into the hole, and his lips moved in what Wilm assumed to be some mighty spell. There came a muffled *crack*, a tiny flash of yellow.

Flydd wrenched his staff out, gasping. The right side of his face was bright red, as if badly sunburned, and his eyes were streaming.

Boiling water squirted out of a crack to the left, and scalding steam from a fissure to the right. The light flared brilliantly blue-white, then purple, then dwindled to a dull red-orange.

*Boom, boooom, booooooooom.*

'Run!' said Flydd. 'Back the way we came.'

The doughnut-shaped tunnel was full of steam now and hot water was ankle-deep on the floor. The ground was shaking so violently that the water was surging back and forth.

Wilm ducked under the steam blasting from a shoulder-high crack and around a pulsing jet of boiling water coming from another crack. The slippery growth under-foot was churning, a myriad of many-legged creatures trying to escape the hot water. He kicked them off his boots.

Ilisial was shuddering and moaning and shaking her head violently. It looked as though she was going to have another of her attacks.

'Akkidul hates me,' she whispered. 'It wants to kill me.'

Wilm reached for her hand. She clubbed at him with her other hand, and the mad look in her eyes mirrored the time she had tried to brain him with a rock at the Sink of Despair.

'Ilisial!' snapped Flydd. 'Take Wilm's hand. The sword is sheathed; it can't harm you.'

'It's whispering, *hate, hate, hate.*'

'Wilm's saved your life twice, remember?'

She took Wilm's hand. Her grip was crushingly tight. They splashed through tunnel after tunnel, climbed ramp after ramp, and the booming sound was all around them now. Pieces of rock shivered away from the walls and fell from the roof.

*Boom, boooom, booooooooom.*

'It should have fallen by now,' said Flydd. His back was bent and he was in a lot of pain. 'This is not good.'

'How can you tell it hasn't?' panted Wilm.

'You'll know if it does,' he said direly.

They were climbing a steep adit, slipping on grey slimy muck on the perpetually wet floor, and Flydd was struggling. It had been dark when they came down, but now threads of pale light issued through cracks in the rock all around them. Was the node going to explode, as the one at Snizort had? But this was the greatest node in the world; if it went up it must obliterate Skyrock and everyone for miles around.

That would solve the problem of the Merdrun, at least. But would he, Flydd and Ilisial be obliterated in an instant? Or be trapped underground with no way to get out?

If he had to die, he much preferred it to be at the hands of an enemy with a sword. It might be quick or it might be slow and agonising – he had seen plenty such deaths on the battlefield when he'd fought the Merdrun before – but at least it was natural.

*Boom, boooom, boooooooom.*

Flydd stopped. 'Can't go on.'

'How far to go?' said Wilm.

'It's about four hundred yards to the base of the chaos chasm, where we left the gate.'

'How do you know it'll still be there?' said Ilisial, letting go of Wilm's hand. She seemed better now.

'I ... don't.' Flydd crouched down, wheezing.

'What is it, surr?'

'Aftersickness.'

'I hadn't realised you suffered from it.'

'We scrutators had ways of putting it off. Spells and protections ... but it always catches up to you. Hoped to delay it until after we finished ... but I used a mighty spell under the node.'

'I'll carry you the rest of the way,' said Wilm.

'Be damned!' said Flydd. 'Not a baby.'

'You're talking like one.' Wilm heaved Flydd over his shoulder. 'Lead the way, Ilisial.'

'Arrogant little pup!' muttered Flydd.

'Shut up or I'll drop you on your head.'

Flydd was heavier than he looked. Wilm stumbled after Ilisial.

*Boom, boooom, boooooooom.*

'It's getting louder,' said Ilisial.

The floor of the tunnel shook violently.

'Cross your fingers,' said Flydd. 'The stalk under the node might still collapse.'

They reached the end of the tunnel, where it fell away into that deep shaft. Wilm put Flydd down. He stood upright, supporting himself on his staff, and looked across and up to the tunnel entrance on the far side.

'Never jump up there,' he said.

'Can you bring the gate here from the bottom of the chaos chasm?' said Ilisial.

Flydd moved his staff in a wobbly circle, murmured the words of a spell. The gate did not appear. He repeated the spell, with the same result.

'What's the matter?' said Ilisial.

'Must've damaged my staff when I thrust it into the hole to cast that mighty spell.'

'Can you fix it?'

'Could take days. Besides, I'm not sensing the gate. It must have closed – and I don't have the power to make one from scratch.'

'Then ... we're going to die here,' said Wilm.

*Boom, boooom, booooooooom.*

# PART II

## RESOLUTION FROM DESPAIR

# 38

# WE CAN'T GET PAST THEM

Karan followed Tiaan to the cells on the other side and put an eye to the peephole of Sulien's and Jassika's cell. The girls were asleep on their stone shelf bunks. Her eyes misted.

'Before you free them, we'd better check down below,' said Tiaan.

'What for?' said Karan.

'In case the enemy come early.'

None of the little porthole windows here looked east. They scurried down the stairs, trying to make no sound, but on the next level the portholes looked west.

'Control chamber,' said Tiaan.

They ran down to the next level. Broad corridors extended from the walls of the control chamber to windows at the four points of the compass. A blue wall clock with jagged black hands said ten past two.

They went to the large, circular eastern window. The officers' compound had lights along the walls and many moving lights around a large tent at the entrance. The officers were up already, preparing for the great day, though the army camp was only sparsely lit.

'They won't wake the soldiers for hours,' said Karan. 'We can do this.'

Heading back to the stairs, they passed a broad bench seat built into the concave side of the column. A binnacle in front of it had a series of control levers and wheels and a pair of glassy plates, not unlike the controls of a thapter. The seat faced east and the rising sun would be visible through the window.

'This where the sapphire portal is controlled?' Karan asked.

Tiaan nodded absently. Her lips were moving as if she were thinking something through.

A number of tables were scattered around the chamber, each with a device or apparatus on it. Karan glanced down through the quartz plate in the floor and her heart gave a gigantic lurch. When she'd come up, the tunnel had been empty apart from the guards at the eastern entrance, but there must be a hundred people there now.

'Tiaan!' she hissed.

Skald was near the bottom of the stair, wearing red magiz's robes with the glyph in black across his chest, talking to an officer in the uniform of a High Commander. Durthix. Five sus-magizes waited behind Skald, and behind them twelve red-robed young men and women, acolytes, formed a curving tail. Durthix's personal guard, eight rows of ten soldiers, stood on full alert, their weapons drawn, halfway across the tunnel, next to a series of tables covered in maps and papers.

This was a disaster. 'I thought the final preparations were due to begin at 4 a.m.,' said Karan.

'The enemy sometimes give false dates and times,' said Tiaan.

She looked beaten. Karan knew that Tiaan had three children, far away, and their father had been killed when she was abducted. No wonder she was so anxious.

'What's up there?' Karan pointed to the mezzanine.

Tiaan shrugged.

If Karan had freed Sulien and Jassika as soon as she'd entered, she might have got them past the guards and back down to the chaos chasm and the gate. Too late now. The Day of All Days had begun and, with so many people in the sapphire tunnel, Rulke's diversion would be wasted. In a few hours the Merdrun would set off the gift-burner and go through the portal, leaving Santhenar in ruins.

Durthix, Skald and the generals gathered around a large map covering one of the tables. Karan could not make out any details.

'Doesn't look as though they're coming up yet,' said Tiaan.

'I'll try to contact Rulke via mind-speech.'

But Karan could not sense him. Nor Llian.

Tiaan was watching her hopefully. Karan shook her head. 'I'll try Flydd. If he can cut off their power, we might get the girls away in the chaos.'

'I'll take a look up there,' said Tiaan, and headed up the curving stair to the mezzanine.

*Xervish?* Karan called, fearing that he would not answer either.

*Karan,* he said faintly.

*How's it going down there?*

After a long pause he said, *Slowly, and I'm not confident it's going to work. How about you?*

Karan's head throbbed. *I found M'Lainte and Tiaan and the girls, but the High Commander is down in the tunnel, along with Skald and about a hundred others. We can't get past them.*

An even longer pause. *Nothing I can do,* Flydd said in a hopeless voice.

2.30 a.m. Dark red flared in the distance as the construct took off. The floor shook. Fiery orange streaks arced down, one striking the compound wall and blowing an enormous hole in it.

A second missile bounced off the wall further along, without exploding, rolled across the ground for a few hundred yards, fell into the chaos chasm and went off, hurling a rainbow-coloured fountain of waste magic up and out in all directions. The floor shook, and shook again, as if the whole of Skyrock was quaking.

The construct hurtled towards the entrance of the sapphire tunnel, turned sharply and raced over the wall in the direction of the officers' compound. Fire erupted there as well.

The Merdrun in the tunnel were staring after Rulke. In the distance, Karan could hear the snap of catapults and javelards. Tiaan ran down the steps from the mezzanine, putting something in her pocket.

'What's up there?' said Karan.

'Storerooms for devices and spares. Pantry, galley, library.' Tiaan looked out the eastern window at the waste magic fountaining out of the chaos chasm. 'Did Rulke do that?'

'Accidentally.'

'But the gate won't have survived the blast.' Her voice rose. 'We've got no way out.'

Karan could not speak. Her wits seemed to have deserted her.

'Back to M'Lainte,' said Tiaan. 'Quick!'

They raced up to her cell and told her the grim news.

'Is there anything we can do?' said Karan. 'Anything at all?'

M'Lainte did not speak for a while. 'To get yourselves and the girls out? No. But ...' She stared up at the carved rock ceiling, the index finger and thumb of her right hand gripping the fingers of her left hand one after another, as if ticking items off on a list. 'No, it can't work.'

'I'll try anything!' said Karan. 'I'm not tamely waiting here to die.'

M'Lainte's eyes seemed to be weighing her up. 'I suppose ... if anyone *could* do it ... it would be you.'

'Do what?'

'Take control of the portal away from Skald.'

Tiaan spun around, staring at her. '*What?*'

Karan choked. 'How?'

'It's directed and opened from the control chamber,' said M'Lainte, 'but the device that *creates* the portal, a gigantic twinned crystal, is mounted at the top of the iron tower.'

'Why is it up there?'

'This portal, the biggest ever to be created, requires mighty forces to form it; dangerous forces to anyone with the gift. The twinned crystal has already been aligned, in azimuth and elevation, to direct the portal to Tallallame. Once Sulien far-sees the destination, Skald will mind-link to her and use that image to target the portal to the precise destination. And open it.'

'Um ... what are you proposing?' said Karan.

'If someone could get to the top of the tower, and change the orientation of the crystal –'

'The portal would go wrong. But Skald would notice.'

'Not if the crystal is turned at the last minute, after he checks Sulien's far-seeing. His own talent is too feeble to detect the change. And it's not possible to see through such a mighty portal, so the Merdrun wouldn't know where they were going until they came out the other end.'

'Where would they be going? The void?'

'No, you'd have to choose a suitable place to send them. Somewhere real.'

'This ... seems far-fetched.' No, Karan thought, it was ludicrous.

'It *is* far-fetched. But it's your only chance.'

'How can the crystal be turned, anyway?'

'There's a worker's entrance and stairs at the northern end of Skyrock, to keep them away from the secret areas. But no one gifted can go anywhere near the twinned crystal – it's too dangerous.'

'The only ungifted people here are Wilm and Llian – assuming Llian hasn't been caught. But Wilm's underground with Flydd. And Llian is terrified of heights.'

'What you do, if you do anything, is up to you,' said M'Lainte unhelpfully.

'There must be guards outside the northern entrance.'

'Yes, but Maelys' taphloid – the little, egg-shaped device she wears around her neck – will conceal her from anything but direct contact with an enemy.'

'I didn't know that.' Karan had often seen Maelys touch it but had assumed it was just a good luck charm.

'And if Llian's with her it would help to conceal him.'

'I tried to call him earlier. Couldn't reach him.'

'It might be blocking you. Keep trying.'

Wilm was a better alternative. He was so reliable. Karan sat on the floor, cross-legged, and mind-called Flydd.

*Are you out yet? I need Wilm –*

*I don't even know if we're going to get out,* said Flydd.

It was Llian, or nothing. She tried him again.

*Karan?* he said in a wisp of a voice. *Is Sulien safe?*

*No. We're stuck in the tower; the enemy came too soon.* She told him what she needed, but nothing else, in case he was caught. *Can you get to the top of the iron tower and rotate the crystal? No one gifted can do it.*

There was a long pause. Karan imagined Llian looking up and up to the very top, more than a thousand feet above the ground. How could she ask him to do such a climb? He would be caught, or he would fall and be killed.

*No, it's a stupid idea*, she said. *Forget it.*

*If I succeeded, it would give you a chance.*

*I don't see how you can do it by yourself, and Maelys can't go near the crystal.*

Another pause, as if Llian was speaking to her. But Maelys had spent most of the past month staring into the Mirror of Aachan and Karan did not have much confidence in her.

*We'll have a go*, said Llian. *Maelys thinks she can get us in the northern entrance. When she can't go any higher, I'll climb the last bit, and move the damned crystal.*

*I'm sorry*, said Karan. *Sorry for everything!*

*We can talk about that afterwards*, he said stiffly. *If there is one.*

Her head was throbbing badly and, once aftersickness began, it would get worse for hours. Maigraith's gift was as painful as she had promised. But Karan had to speak to one more person, the most difficult of all to reach.

It took a long time to contact Malien, and her voice was barely audible. She listened in silence, then said, *It can't work.*

*The alternative is we die and the Merdrun burn out every gifted person on Santhenar before they go through the portal.*

*It can't work,* Malien repeated.

*Malien, one obsession has driven them for aeons – war, and winning. After they've taken Tallallame and killed everyone there, they'll come back to conquer Santhenar, and without any magical gift we'll be an easy target. And then they'll move on Aachan.*

*I expect you're right*, said Malien. *Why don't you direct the portal to the void?*

*M'Lainte said it has to go somewhere real.*

*I'll see what I can do.*

*If it takes longer than a couple of hours, it'll be too late.*

*Don't push me!* Malien snapped, and she was gone.

After Rulke took off in the construct, Durthix called Skald, the generals and the sus-magizes to an urgent meeting in the tunnel.

'How did he manage it?' said Durthix. 'Did he have outside aid?'

'Senior sus-magiz Lurzel says not,' said Skald. 'None of the wards have detected any kind of a gate, and they were crafted and set by Dagog. And no one has entered the compound without being stripped naked and searched.'

'Nonetheless, Rulke is gone.'

'Lurzel thinks he must have contrived to hoard a small amount of power over the past weeks – just enough to get away and make a few token strikes on us on the way. Showy, but he hasn't done any damage.'

'Except to our morale.'

'It matters not. In three hours we'll be opening the portal and going home.'

'I still don't like it,' said Durthix. 'Where did he go?'

'The construct was tracked for five or six miles, north-east. It went down there and our trackers don't show any power being used since.' Skald looked west at the setting moon, and smiled. To Merdrun, the dark face of the moon was a good omen. 'Lurzel believes Rulke has no power left and can't move again.'

'But why, after all this time aiding us in order to keep Lirriam safe, would he abandon her?'

'Perhaps he gave up hope of saving her and decided to save himself?'

'I'm uneasy. Can you send someone to check on her?'

'Now, High Commander?'

'Is there a problem?'

'Only an experienced sus-magiz can open a passage through the wall of the cubic temple, and they're all busy preparing for the portal. But after it's opened –'

'All right,' said Durthix. 'As you say, the compound hasn't been breached. I'm just over-anxious. Such a day. Such a great day!'

Karan's stomach heaved violently. She crawled across to the waste hole in the floor and threw up.

'Aftersickness?' said M'Lainte.

'Clearly, I wasn't meant to have the gift of mind-speech.'

'Pace yourself. You're going to need all your strength ...'

The headache was like having spikes hammered through the sides of her skull. 'Not sure I've got much left.'

'And there's still the gift-burner to deal with.'

'Ugh!' Karan pressed the heels of her hands to the sides of her head. She hadn't thought about that. 'Where?'

'It's mounted on a stone spine at the bottom of the pyramidal pit behind the cubic temple,' said Tiaan.

Karan's stomach heaved again but only bitter liquid came up. 'Can't – think.'

'Send Wilm. Tell him to use the black sword, he'll know how. But he'll need help.' M'Lainte looked out the porthole again. 'It's a quarter to four. Call Flydd!'

But he did not answer. 'Mustn't be out yet,' said Karan.

'Go and check on the enemy. Lock us back in our cells first.'

'I can't go back,' cried Tiaan. 'I can't be a helpless slave again.'

'If a guard comes up and you're not in your cell,' said M'Lainte, 'one of the sus-magizes will read the signs and they'll put a thousand guards on the search. They'll find you and Karan, and our allies out in the compound, and it'll be the end of us all. Go!'

From the look in Tiaan's eyes, Karan might have been personally sending her back to slavery, and after she was locked in her cell Tiaan clung to the jagged bars like a drowning woman.

'Don't fail my children,' she said in a cracked voice.

Wilm sat on the damp floor of the tunnel and rubbed sweat out of his eyes. It wasn't easy to accept the end, trapped down here and waiting to die. Nothing like facing death in battle, where everything was such a blur that there was rarely time to think at all.

'I've lived an interesting life, and a long one,' said Flydd. 'But even so …'

Wilm eyed Flydd's scarred face, which looked as if most of the muscle had been scraped off and the skin put back over the top, and the twisted fingers that had been broken by a torturer and not allowed to set properly. Wilm wasn't sure he wanted to live *that* interesting a life.

'If we can get across the shaft, and the gate has closed, we'll climb out through the chaos chasm,' said Flydd.

'We'll still be trapped in the compound.'

'Time to worry about that if we get there.' Flydd looked up across the shaft.

'I've got rope in my pack.'

'Nothing to tie it onto,' said Ilisial listlessly.

She was reverting to the apathetic state she'd been in at the Sink of Despair, after Klarm had flown up the mountain on the spellcaster, and she was dragging them down with her.

'I've got an idea,' said Wilm.

'Go for it,' said Flydd.

'What if I tie my rope around the hilt of my sword and hurl it up into the roof of the tunnel?'

'Tie the rope around the hilt before you draw the blade, just in case Akkidul doesn't like it.'

Wilm made a few climbing knots in the rope, tied it around the hilt and drew the sword. Flydd passed his hands over it and murmured a few words.

'A small sticking spell. Best I can do.'

There wasn't room here for Wilm to raise the sword above his head. Flydd and Ilisial went backwards to give him room, Flydd holding the loose coils of rope. Wilm swung the sword out to the side and back, and picked a solid-looking knot of rock in the roof of the upper tunnel.

'Not too hard,' Flydd said quietly.

Wilm aimed, swung and let the sword go. It flew up and true, embedding itself to the hilt in the rock. He tugged on it. It did not budge.

'Nice work,' said Flydd. 'I'll go first, in case it pulls free. I'm the lightest.'

'No, I'll go,' said Wilm. 'Since I'm the heaviest. If it holds me ...'

No one said the obvious. Flydd fashioned a rope harness around Wilm.

He gave the rope another tug, gripped the lowest of the climbing knots, went to the edge, took a deep breath and stepped out. And swung against the other side of the shaft, cracking his knuckles painfully.

He looked up. Had the sword slipped a little? He could not be sure. He reached up to the next knot, pulled himself up, and the sword slipped out an inch. Wilm's heart lurched painfully.

*Scared, Wilm?* said Akkidul. *You should be, the way you've treated me.*

Wilm was terrified but must not show it; the sword only appreciated strength. 'So should you, you crapulous length of third-grade metal. If I fall, I'll pull you out and you'll lie beside my bones at the bottom of the shaft until the end of time.'

His hands were so sweaty he could barely hold the knot. He clung on with one hand and his knees, wiped the other hand, and continued.

As he neared the top the sword slipped again, as if to terrorise him, but it held and he scrambled over the lip of the tunnel and in, to safety. He took off the harness and tossed it down.

'You next,' said Flydd to Ilisial.

Her eyes were staring; she was shuddering fitfully. 'Can't,' she said.

'Yes, you can,' Flydd said calmly, knotting the harness around her middle.

'Akkidul hates me.'

'Don't be ridiculous. Why would it?'

'Because I called it a killer. And it is, *it is, it is ...*'

'Wilm,' said Flydd, 'pull the blade out and embed it in the floor. And hold it in place.'

Wilm did so and Flydd said, 'It can't pull free now. Go!'

She did not move. He pushed her and she swung out and thumped into the wall of the shaft, but just hung from her harness, moaning.

'Pull her up, Wilm,' said Flydd.

The hilt was shuddering in his hands, trying to slide out of the stone. Maybe it did hate Ilisial. But Wilm did not need it now. He heaved her up, then Flydd, whose injured shoulder would not allow him to climb the rope.

Wilm unfastened it and sheathed the sword, which had said no more.

*Boom, boooom, booooooom.*

'To the chaos chasm!' said Flydd. 'Run!'

*Boooooooooooooooom.*

Wilm jumped. 'That sounded a lot louder.'

'It was,' said Flydd. 'The next one will be *the one*. Come on!'

They raced through the gloom back to where they had come out of the gate, Wilm supporting Flydd and, for the last fifty yards, carrying him. They reached the point where they had taken off their protective metal suits, put them on and continued the rest of the way, the woven metal rasping with every step, the lead booties thumping.

The chaos chasm was empty apart from a few slowly whirling tendrils of luminous waste magic. The stepped walls of the chasm glowed in luminous blues and greens and yellows. The toadstools and other growths that had been here before were charred down to bare rock. There was no sign of the gate.

'What happened here?' said Wilm.

'No idea,' said Flydd.

Ilisial sank to the glowing floor of the pit and covered her face with her arms.

'We can't stay here, Ilisial.' Flydd prodded the crumbling rock, which proved no harder than stale bread. 'We've got to go up.'

'If we go up,' said Ilisial, 'the enemy will kill us.'

'Waste magic will do the job quicker, even with our metal suits.' Ilisial did not move. 'Wilm, carry her.'

'What about you?'

'Have to manage, won't I?' said Flydd.

Ilisial did not protest when Wilm heaved her over his shoulder and headed up the spiral of the cart track. They reached the surface near the compound wall, which had been partly eaten away. It had stopped raining but the compound was wreathed in fog and coloured banners of waste magic, and it was bitterly cold after the humid heat of underground. Pools of water on the paving stones had frozen.

Blurry glows marked the positions of lamps on the top of the wall. A brighter blur, tall and blue and white, was the twisted spire of Skyrock half a mile away. Wilm wondered how Karan was getting on.

They took off their metal suits. Wilm's hands looked as though they had been scalded and his face felt the same. Flydd was worse; there were blisters all over his face, hands and arms. Ilisial's dark skin had protected her, though one side of her face was redder than the other.

*Booooooooooooooooom.*

The ground lifted a few inches under their feet and settled again. Loose stones bounced down the steps into the chaos chasm, making little sound on the soft rock. The blue and white glow of Skyrock went dull and something at the top of the iron tower emitted a bright orange flash. The blue light from the sapphire-lined tunnel went out.

'Have we done it?' whispered Wilm.

But the glow from the tower reappeared, and then from the tunnel as well, though not as brightly as before.

'The node might have been damaged,' Flydd said dully, 'but it's still giving them power. We failed.'

'What do we do now?'

'Hide, not that it'll do us any good.'

They slipped in between stacks of rock slabs. It was still as dark as ever, and the moon, whose dark side was completely showing now, was declining towards the west. 4 a.m., Wilm judged. Two hours until sunrise.

When it all ended.

'No sign of the construct,' he said.

'The crystal would only have powered it for a few minutes,' said Flydd.

Rulke had held so much promise. When he had been found alive, Karan and Llian had been overjoyed. *The only man the Merdrun ever feared.* She had been sure he would turn the tables on the enemy.

But Rulke had hidden in Alcifer for a month and, after being captured by Skald, had used his construct to help the enemy. As far as Wilm knew, Rulke had never lifted a finger to help his former allies.

'I reckon he used the crystal to fly away,' said Wilm. 'He never intended to help us.'

Flydd sighed. 'I don't want to agree with you, but ... his diversion has only made it worse.'

# 39

# SO THE ENEMY DON'T GET SUSPICIOUS

K aran dragged herself down to the control chamber and squinted through the quartz plate. Durthix, Skald and the generals were still at the tables, and the sus-magizes and acolytes were gathered near the stairs, studying instructions inscribed on tablets.

Beyond the eastern window the sky was still dark; it was about an hour until dawn. There were lights everywhere in the army camp now. The soldiers were preparing for the great day. Skald would soon come up and she wasn't mentally prepared. She had to make more time. Time for Rulke to return from where he'd set down the construct – *if* he was coming back. After nearly losing Lirriam he might not want to take any more risks.

M'Lainte's outrageous plan could go wrong in so many ways. Everything relied on Llian and Maelys, yet if the taphloid failed they might be caught before they could get into the northern entrance. Or Llian might freeze halfway up the iron tower, and fall.

Stop it! You're making things worse.

Karan headed back to the cells. Sulien had to know she was here, and that she had a plan, feeble though it was. She mind-called from outside.

*Come to the door, quietly.*

Sulien roused sleepily, sat up and a beautiful smile spread across her face. Karan put a finger to her lips and pointed at Jassika. Sulien came across. She looked thinner than before, tired, and very pale.

'I've got a plan,' Karan whispered, 'but Skald's coming and I can't do it yet. I'll mind-speak and tell you what to do.'

Sulien looked crushed, but nodded.

'Give this to Jass – Klarm wanted her to have it.'

Karan put the knoblaggie into Sulien's hands. She turned away, turned back and squeezed Karan's hands through the bars, then returned to her bed and lay there, staring at the ceiling and quivering.

The guard Karan had stunned was stirring. She stunned him again, checked his gag and bonds, and headed down. What if M'Lainte was wrong? The Merdrun might have fed her and Tiaan false information.

Agonising about things she could do nothing about would only undermine her when she needed to be strong. She crept up to the mezzanine and hid in one of the storerooms. Shelves held mech-magical devices large and small, none of which she recognised. By leaving the door open and climbing onto a bench, she could see the centre of the control chamber and part of the eastern window.

After Karan left, Sulien shook Jassika awake. She had to trust her now.

'Mummy came, and she brought this. Klarm wanted you to have it.' Sulien gave Jassika the little brass knoblaggie.

Jassika's eyes widened, and she took it in both hands and pressed them over her heart. 'Thank you,' she whispered.

'Do you know how to use it?'

'Not really. Klarm taught me a few tricks.'

'What kind of tricks?'

'You know.'

'No.'

'Make fog, burn through stuff with light, that sort of thing. He was going to show me more when I was older ... and he had the time.'

Sulien knew all about that. Karan and Llian were always saying, *when I have the time.*

'How did Karan get in?' said Jassika.

'She didn't say. She's got a plan to save us, but it's going to take a while. We have to act normal, so the enemy don't get suspicious.'

'I'll do my best.'

Sulien prayed that she could, because Jassika was absolutely glowing. She didn't look like a slave girl now. She looked as focused and determined as her father had.

After a couple of minutes, the door to the stairs was opened and Skald entered the control chamber, followed by his five sus-magizes and twelve acolytes, and ten guards. He ordered the guards to bring down the slaves.

More sus-magizes entered, then Sulien was led down, along with Jassika. One of the acolytes took Sulien to the bench seat. She was pale and trembling, and Karan felt stabbed to the heart. Did Sulien think she was going to be killed once the portal opened? Was there any hope of pulling this insane plan off?

Jassika was made to stand a few yards away and an acolyte waited beside her, holding a thin cane. Was she here as a whipping girl, to force Sulien to focus? There were long welts on her legs and arms, but she looked proud and defiant. Her left hand was in her pocket, probably holding the knoblaggie, and perhaps it gave her confidence. Had Klarm taught her any useful magic? Karan wished she had taken the trouble to find out.

Skald put a set of complicated goggles over Sulien's eyes, their red frames covering half her forehead and part of her cheeks. He made adjustments to little wheels on the sides and top, as if focusing a set of field glasses, and sat beside her.

He was a formidable man, though Karan did not sense the rage she had detected before he'd tried to assassinate Flydd. Had he been humbled by his defeat in Thurkad, or had the death of his enemy, the magiz, liberated him? He spoke quietly to Sulien, and occasionally she nodded or replied. She did not seem afraid of him.

The acolytes formed curving wings to either side of the bench. The sus-magizes were supervising dozens of artisan slaves standing behind a variety of devices, some controlled by levers, others by spoked wheels like the helm of a sailing ship. Karan had no idea what any of them were for.

Skald went to a round table and picked up a partly unrolled scroll. He raised his right hand and began moving it like a conductor, first pointing to each of his three senior sus-magizes in turn, then to the ten juniors. Was he directing them in the complex magics required to open the sapphire portal, break through the block around Tallallame and create the mind-shock that would lay everyone on that world low for days, so the Merdrun could run through the portal and slaughter them?

It must be so. And the sky was growing light in the east. Dawn was breaking.

*Thump. Thump. Thump. Thump.*

The floor of the control chamber was quivering ever so slightly. Through the eastern window Karan saw a vast column, the Merdrun army marching in perfect synchronisation, coming down the broad road towards the gates. They were still closed, but it would not be long now.

She had to speak to Malien. Everything depended on what she had to say.

It took a long time to contact her, and every minute's delay was marked out by the thump of the marching army, and the faint vibration as 150,000 pairs of heavy boots struck the ground in the same instant.

*Malien, I'm almost out of time. Have you got anything for me?*

*Azimuth 274 and a half degrees. Elevation 68 and three-quarter degrees.*

*Thank you. What do I do then?*

*I'll send an image of the destination to Sulien.*

*Can you do that?*

But Malien was gone and Karan's aftersickness was growing again; each time she mind-spoke was more painful than the time before. Her head was such a mass of pain that it was a struggle to think. And once the portal was open and the Merdrun were going through, Durthix and Skald would no longer need the gifted slaves. Skald would trigger the gift-burner.

Wilm's ears and fingers ached and he was miserably cold. As he pulled his sodden coat around himself, ice crackled and broke off. Dawn had broken, though it was still dark in the compound. Sunrise was the best part of an hour away and they were trapped.

Ilisial was staring into nowhere and her apathy seemed worse than before. There was an unnerving emptiness about her, as though she was just eking out the hours. What had Skald's partial life-drinking done to her? Wilm could not ask. Perhaps no one who had not been through it *could* know.

Was there any way out for them? Rulke was gone, no one knew where. Flydd had burned himself badly trying to destroy the node and had nothing left. And the others at the campsite – Yggur, Tulitine and Nish – had no way of aiding them. Maigraith, the one person who might have helped, was focused on destroying her rival and did not give a damn about anyone else.

There came a mighty thud from the other side of the compound. Wilm climbed up onto the rock stack so he could see above the mist, and looked east.

From cauldrons mounted on the compound wall to either side of the gates, beacons of blue fire blazed up fifty feet high. Drums thundered. The pair of gates furthest to the north were heaved open, creating an aperture forty feet across, and clamped back to back. The second pair of gates opened, then the third, and all the way to the tenth and southernmost gate. It was a majestic sight, as clearly it was meant to be. The drumbeats rose to a crescendo, then ceased.

'Today's the day the Merdrun have been working and fighting towards for the past ten thousand years,' said Flydd.

Ilisial roused a little. Her teeth were chattering. 'How long we got?'

'When the sun rises, it'll shine through the gates and through the sapphire tunnel – a great symbolic moment. That's when they'll do whatever they're planning to do.'

The ground quivered, quivered again, and Wilm heard a faint *thump, thump* that he recognised from the Isle of Gwine. An army of Merdrun, marching in perfect synchronisation.

Up the hill beyond the gates, columns of Merdrun appeared, marching in from the north and east and south. They were clad in their hardened leather armour. The crimson chest plates were marked with the Merdrun glyph in black and their helms had triple black spikes on top. They converged into one column on the broad road that led down between the officers' and slaves' compounds, and continued towards the gates. It would have been a magnificent sight, had they not been the enemy.

'For today, everything has to be perfect,' Flydd said in a fading voice.

# 40

# ONCE HEARD, REMEMBERED FOREVER

T ake my hand,' said Maelys, removing her gloves.

'What for?' said Llian thickly. His head still felt fuzzy from the blow, material or magical, that had knocked him out after he crawled out of the cubic temple.

She drew an egg-shaped metal object out from her cleavage and closed her fist around it. It was vibrating, ever so slightly.

'My taphloid helps to protect me. And if you're holding my hand, you too.'

He removed one of his gloves and took her free hand.

'You're freezing,' said Maelys.

'Can't seem to get warm.'

They crept across the paving towards the northern end of Skyrock. It had stopped raining, but the wind was stronger, churning the mist and the coloured banners of waste magic. Llian could hear soldiers marching but could not tell where.

'How does it protect you?' he said.

'It makes me hard to see ... among other things.'

'How does that work?'

'Don't you ever stop?'

'What?'

'Asking questions?'

'I'm a chronicler. I need to know everything.'

The northern end of the tower appeared out of the mist. The wind moaned between the blue and white spirals.

Llian stopped at the edge of a patch of mist. 'Guards!'

'Of course there's guards,' said Maelys. 'But I think I can get past them.'

Llian had no such confidence. Merdrun sentries never failed in their duty.

The northern entrance did not go through to the central core of the tower; it opened into one of the stone spirals that wrapped around the core like oval tubes. Two uniformed Merdrun patrolled the area, never following the same path twice, and occasionally intersecting and exchanging a few words. The area was lit by lamps mounted high on each of the spirals, though they only cast a diffuse bluish light through the mist.

'Hold my hand *really* tightly,' whispered Maelys.

Llian did so. She closed her other fist around the taphloid and headed for the door, staying within the thickest patch of mist. Llian's gut tensed. Their path would take them to within a few yards of one of the guards.

Maelys slowed to allow the man to pass in front of them. He was on alert, his gaze constantly sweeping the area. He was turning. He was looking right at them. He must see them! Maelys' small hand clamped around Llian's.

The guard did not react. He kept going, to intersect the other guard fifty yards away.

Maelys tugged and Llian followed, to the door. It was blue, like the rest of the spiral. She touched her taphloid to the lock, which made a soft whirring sound and the door came open a foot. They slipped through and he pushed it shut.

It was almost as dark as outside, though a glimmer from above revealed broad steps, cut from pale rock, following the curve of the spiral upwards.

'You can let go,' said Maelys. 'But if we see anyone, grab hold again.'

'Do you think we will?'

'You'd know better than I would.'

'Skyrock was finished two days ago and everything cleaned up.'

'Doesn't mean they don't use these stairs.'

Karan mind-called Flydd. *You out yet?* If he said *no*, there was nothing she could do.

*Yes.* He sounded exhausted.

*Is Wilm still there?*

*Where else would he be?* Flydd snapped.

*Touch him; I don't know how to reach him.*

Flydd must have gripped Wilm's arm because his presence slowly grew in her mind.

*Wilm? It's Karan. I need you to destroy the gift-burner before it burns everyone gifted, the way the magiz burned out Klarm. Can you do that?*

Wilm must have been afraid but he did not hesitate. *I'll try. Where is it?*

*M'Lainte said –*

*Is she all right?* cried Wilm. *I've been worrying about her.*

*She's not been treated well,* sent Karan. *But she's in good spirits.*

*Can you get her out?*

Karan suppressed her impatience. *Will you listen? We don't have much time.*

*Sorry.*

*M'Lainte said there's an amphitheatre cut into the ground behind the cubic temple – like an inverted pyramid with five sides.*

*We came past it. It's not far.*

*The gift-burner is at the bottom of the pyramidal pit, mounted on a stone spike. It can be destroyed with your black sword. M'Lainte said you'd know how ...*

Wilm was silent for a few seconds. *I think I know what she means. Is it dangerous?*

*I imagine so. And you'll need help to get up the spike to it.*

*Flydd can't help.*

*What about Ilisial?*

A long pause. Karan could hear Wilm speaking in a low voice, though not what was said.

*She'll come with me.*

But he sounded anxious now. Had her troubles come back? Should Karan send him off on a deadly mission with a mentally unstable woman who had once tried to kill him?

There was no choice. Try, or die.

*Make it quick. Once the army comes in, no one will be able to move inside the compound without being seen.*

*Going now.*

She had to make one last mind-call, the most difficult one. Pain sheared through her head and her belly and hip; it hurt a lot more to mind-call people who lacked the gift. She doubled up on the bench in the storeroom, fighting it. No one else could do this.

*Llian? Did you get in?*

*Yes.* He was panting, out of breath. *Long climb to iron tower, though.*

And a harder one up it to the crystal at the top. Karan had once been a skilled climber but even for her it would be difficult. Miserably cold, with no protection from the wind, and Llian's fear of heights was acute. Karan had seen him freeze in terror on several occasions, years ago, and the second time, near the top of the monumental tower of Katazza, it had almost killed them both. But if the twinned crystal could not be moved the whole ridiculous plan would fail.

*What's the matter?* said Llian.

*Sorry. Just ... thinking about things.*

*What's your plan?*

*I daren't tell you, in case they can pick up mind-speech.*

*If – when – I get to the top, what do I do to the twinned crystal?*

Karan recited the azimuth and elevation Malien had given her. There was a long silence.

*Do you need me to repeat –*

*I'm a chronicler! Once heard, remembered forever.*

*Don't move it until I call. Around sunrise. A little before, or a little after.*

It was like a miniature of their life together – Karan giving the orders and demanding the impossible of him, but unable to say why. She broke the mind-call.

Could M'Lainte's plan work? Skald was an enigmatic man – brilliant, creative, bold and determined. A brave man who had single-handedly turned defeat into victory a number of times. Could he do it again?

What drove him, apart from the cowardice of his father, and what did he fear, now that his enemy the magiz was dead? If she found out, she might be able to use it against him. He had appeared to be a selfless man, self-sacrificing for the good of his people and their True Purpose, yet Klarm said Skald had broken one of the Merdrun's greatest commandments and taken the slave architect, Uletta, for his lover.

Even from this distance, Karan's sensitive's gift was picking up his hidden emotions. At this critical moment, the culmination of the Merdrun's age-long dream that Skald was making possible, he was in torment. Why?

She dared not try to link to him to learn more; he might detect her intrusion. But he had been training Sulien in far-seeing for a couple of weeks, and she had accidentally linked to him long before that, when the Merdrun were searching Mistmurk Mountain for Flydd's cursed *Histories of the Lyrinx War*. Did Sulien know, or could she guess, what troubled him?

This, Karan realised, was a transformative moment in their relationship. In the past she had always tried to shield Sulien from her gift. Not to deny it, but not to push it either. She had seen too many over-driven children, and some had been broken by it.

Though Sulien's gift had been driven from the moment she had far-seen the Merdrun five months ago. It had been forced to develop rapidly because the first magiz had been trying to kill her to protect their secret weakness, and further heightened by her battles with the triplets magiz, who had wanted to take over Sulien's mind. And now Skald had driven Sulien's talent for far-seeing to heights she would never have reached on her own. There was no going back.

Karan leaned forwards and looked down into the control chamber. She could not see him, but the sus-magizes and acolytes were donning helmets made from finely woven wire.

*Sulien, what's going on?* she mind-spoke, softly.

*Skald's ordered everyone to put on silver-wire helms. And they're putting them on us as well.*

*What for?*

*I don't know.*

Before using a little gift-burner on Klarm, Dagog had ordered everyone in the room to put on silver-mesh helms. In the invasion the Merdrun had collected all the silver they could find, and taken all the silversmiths, to protect themselves from the gift-burner. Skald must be getting ready to use it, on humanity.

And Wilm might not have reached the pyramidal pit yet. It could take him and Ilisial another fifteen minutes, even more, to get to the gift-burner and destroy it. She had to delay Skald.

She crept out of the storeroom. The mezzanine level was empty. She went to the edge and peered down into the redly illuminated control chamber, looking for the mechanism that operated the gift-burner.

Most of the devices had an operator, either a sus-magiz or an artisan watched over by a sus-magiz. But one device, to the right of the bench where Skald had been seated next to Sulien, was unoccupied. It had a cluster of controls that she could not see clearly, and to the side a lever with a chalcedony handle rose from the top of a curving slot. Was that it? Surely it had to be.

Karan slipped into the galley, found a large pot which she filled with cooking oil from the pantry, and carried it into the library next door. She piled books and papers on the central stone table, poured oil over them and set it alight. It could not set fire to Skyrock itself, since it was carved out of solid rock, but it might gain Wilm enough time.

She scurried back to the storeroom and waited. Within minutes, smoke was belching out the galley door and spreading through the control chamber. Karan had hoped for chaos and panic, but the Merdrun's discipline prevailed.

Skald halted operations and snapped orders. A sus-magiz ran up the curving steps to the mezzanine, followed by a group of acolytes, and disappeared into the library. They would soon have the fire out, and then they would find her. There was nowhere to hide.

Her presence here would come as a massive shock. How had she got in undetected? Were there other intruders? What were they up to? With the gate due to be opened in about an hour, would Skald order a search of Skyrock, or just take sensible precautions?

The smoke had reduced visibility to a few yards, and most of the Merdrun had gathered outside the door to the main stairs, coughing and wiping their streaming eyes. Could she gain a few more minutes?

Karan covered her nose and mouth with her sleeve and darted down, then across to the central column. Her eyes were stinging, her nose running. She took hold of the long lever and heaved it sideways, forcing with all her strength, and the brittle cast metal snapped. She jammed it into the slot and was shoving it down when she was grabbed from behind.

Someone thumped her in the back, and someone else in the side of the head. Furious acolytes surrounded her. Karan fell to her knees, put her head down and tried to protect it with her arms. The aftersickness was so much worse now, and her head was ringing from the blows. They seemed determined to give her the beating of her life, and if they killed her, all would fail.

There was only one hope left, the tiniest, insignificant one. Karan had to send Sulien the plan – then leave it to her.

As the Merdrun army approached the gates the column split into ten, one column outside each open gate, then stopped, stamping their booted feet in unison. The sound echoed back and forth across the bowl-shaped valley.

'Twenty-five wide, each column,' said Wilm, who was used to estimating enemy numbers on the battlefield. 'The full column, when they come together after they enter the compound, will be two hundred and fifty troops wide.'

'Marching shoulder to shoulder, that's the width of the sapphire tunnel,' said Flydd. 'And I can barely stand up.' He swayed on his feet, his eyes went blank for a moment then he snapped, 'Where else would he be?'

'Surr?' said Wilm.

Flydd reached out and gripped Wilm by the right arm. 'It's Karan. In Skyrock. Wants to mind-speak to you.'

*Wilm? It's Karan. I need you to destroy the gift-burner before it burns everyone gifted, the way the magiz burned out Klarm. Can you do that?*

Karan was speaking directly into Wilm's mind and it was the most peculiar feeling. He did not know how to mind-speak back to her, so he just said it aloud. 'If you tell me what to do, I'll try. Where is it?' And it must have worked, because she replied.

She told him what she wanted him to do, and where to go.

'Karan says I'll need someone strong to help me destroy the gift-burner,' said Wilm.

There was a long silence. Flydd spread his burned hands, helplessly.

'Xervish can't do it,' said Ilisial.

There was a long pause. 'Then I'll have to go by myself,' said Wilm.

'I'll go. I owe you.'

'No, you don't.'

'I owe you more than I can ever repay,' she said in a harsh voice. 'And it'd be better than waiting here to have my gift burned away. I'd sooner be dead.'

'All right,' said Wilm. 'Karan, Ilisial will go with me.'

It was still relatively dark as they crept across the compound. The drifting mist was tinged in rainbow colours by vapours blasted out of the chaos chasm, and the paved ground was icy.

They reached the pit, which sloped down to a point like a five-sided inverted pyramid. The sides were benched like an amphitheatre, and high steps ran down the middle of each side, though Wilm could only see down a few yards. Below that the darkness was absolute.

Ilisial's dark eyes reflected the writhing banners of coloured light. She opened her mouth to speak, but no words came out. She grabbed Wilm's hand, her strong fingers crushing his, but pulled away.

Was she thinking that a much smaller gift-burner had erased Klarm's gift in an instant? If the enemy set this one off while they were down there, it might burn her whole mind out. Could he rely on her at all?

'Time's running out,' said Wilm.

They went down the steps to the point where the light ended. Ilisial stopped, a shadow in the gloom, and turned. 'I'm sorry, Wilm.'

'What for?'

'I'm broken ... and I can't be fixed. But I shouldn't have taken it out on you. I could have killed you, that day.'

When she'd gone crazy and tried to brain him with a rock. 'You'd seen awful things. Suffered more than anyone should.'

'You're a good man, Wilm.'

'I –' Wilm did not know what to say. 'Thanks for telling me.'

'This – today – is probably going to be the end.'

'Everything's different when you could die any minute. Things that used to matter, don't. Things that were never important become vital.'

'You know so much more about life than I do.'

'I wouldn't say that.'

'You've been in a dozen desperate situations and got out of all of them. You've fought and lived and loved and lost, and you're still grieving your friend ...'

'How do you know about Dajaes?' said Wilm.

'Klarm often talked about all you'd done, when you weren't there. He admired you.'

Wilm took a step backwards. 'I always thought he despised me.'

She shrugged. 'People are strange.'

Ilisial among them. What did she want from him? Forgiveness? *Things that were never important suddenly become vital.* But there was no time to find out. 'We'd better hurry.'

# 41

## YOUR SICKENING LIAISON

Four acolytes had Karan on her knees and she felt sure they were going to kill her.

Then Sulien was there. She caught an acolyte from behind by her long black hair and jerked it so furiously that the young woman landed hard on her back. The next acolyte swung a punch at Sulien but was caught by the scruff of his neck and lifted a foot in the air by Skald.

'Sulien – must – not – be – harmed!' He tossed the acolyte aside. 'Leave Karan to me.' He raised his voice. 'Back to your posts; time is critical. Acolytes, calm the artisans and get ready to resume.'

The door to the upper stairs was opened and a current of cold air began to disperse the smoke. Skald bent over Karan, and the look in his eyes was ferocious. *'How did you get in?'* he said in a low, ferocious voice.

She had a story prepared, but unless she was absolutely convincing he was liable to order a search of the tower and compound. Flydd, Wilm, Ilisial, Llian and Maelys would be discovered and the plan would fail.

'Maigraith,' Karan lied. 'She can make undetectable gates. She sent me here so I could rescue Sulien.'

'How were you to get out?'

'Maigraith sent Rulke a power crystal.'

'But?'

'I was about to free Sulien,' she said truthfully, looking into his eyes, 'when I saw you and Durthix, and all your people, down in the tunnel. I had no way out.'

Skald glanced at the clock on the wall – a disc of blue stone whose black hands formed halves of the jagged Merdrun glyph – then, anxiously, out the eastern window. The sky was much lighter now.

'Bind her to a chair,' he said to two acolytes.

He took Sulien under one arm, carried her, still struggling, back to the far-seeing bench and strapped her down. 'Leave your seat again,' he said quietly, 'and Jassika and your mother will be flogged. Got it?'

'Yes,' Sulien whispered.

Jassika was looking up at the massive, black-iron model of the Merdrun glyph, suspended high above. Sulien swallowed. It seemed like a very bad omen.

He put the red-framed goggles on her, then ran back to Karan. 'We have unfinished business.'

'If my aim had been better when you tried to assassinate Flydd –'

'This is wasting time. Gag Karan,' Skald said to a sus-magiz. 'Don't damage her, otherwise I'll never get the best out of Sulien.'

'And after the portal opens?' the sus-magiz said eagerly.

'Do whatever you wish with her.'

Chills spread through Karan. It probably meant drinking her life. Skald stood by while she was tied to the chair.

She mind-called Sulien, gave her the essence of the plan, and said, *This is the most important thing you have to do.*

*Yes, Mummy?*

*After Skald checks the destination and opens the portal, mind-call Llian immediately and tell him to move the crystal. Then change to the new destination Malien sends you. Can you do that?*

*Yes, Mummy.*

No child should ever be put under so much pressure, but what choice did Karan have?

*One last thing. If anyone can find the Merdrun's weakness, it's you. I think Skald is the key and you know him better than anyone. It may be the only way to save –*

'Just to be sure,' said Skald as Karan's gag was pulled tight, 'since I know you have a psychic gift ...' He pressed the point of his rue-har into her forehead and her mind-speech cut off. 'It's gone.'

Karan could sense Sulien's emotions – terror and dread – but could not mind-call her, or contact her in any way.

'Skald!' Durthix was bellowing up the stairs. 'It's nearly sunrise. Is everything going to time?'

Skald ran to the top of the stairs and yelled down. 'Yes, High Commander. Nearly ready.'

～

Skald raced back to Sulien and gave orders to a pair of acolytes, who carried across a large frame on a stand and set it in front of her. Five metal etching plates, mounted down the left side, showed different views of a large, dome-like hill, craggy on one end, with three clusters of standing stones on its sides and a fourth cluster at the top, rising out of a great forest. The plates looked ancient, and were, clearly, magical, though Sulien had not seen them before.

But she had seen some of the coloured paintings based on the plates. Skald had shown them to her recently and had kept at her training until she could clearly envisage the hill, the standing stones, the crag and the forest. Only now had she learned, from Karan, that they depicted the destination of the portal, on the world of Tallallame.

Skald sat beside Sulien and adjusted the knurled wheels on the goggles until the paintings came into clear focus. He began to draw power, immense amounts of it. She turned; his face was ruddy, and he was trembling. This gigantic inter-world portal, far bigger than anything ever attempted before, would take all the power the Merdrun had.

He turned her head back. 'Don't look at me. Look at the first painting – and begin the far-seeing.'

Her heart gave a great leap, and she felt panicky. *Mummy, help!*

Karan did not answer. If Skald had destroyed her mind-speech, Karan and Sulien would never speak that way again. She had to go on, alone.

She glanced across at Jassika, who was staring at her. *I can't do this by myself,* Sulien sent.

Jass's lips moved. What was she trying to say? It might have been, *I'm with you, Sools. I know you can do it.* Her left fist was clenched in her pocket. Clenched around the magical knoblaggie.

Sulien gave a tiny nod and turned back to the images. Had Jass guessed something of the plan? She was brave and resourceful, and gifted in ways Sulien knew nothing about. It stiffened her spine. She was not alone.

She memorised each of the magical etching plates and brought the images together in her mind the way Skald had taught her, so they converged into a three-dimensional image that she could move around in her mind's eye, and see the hilltop and the standing stones from any direction.

It was hard, but she had done this kind of thing many times in her training. Now she had to do it with the five coloured paintings, and it was going to be a lot harder. There was far more detail in them, and she had never trained with more than three paintings.

She converged the first two paintings into a three-dimensional image in her mind's eye and added the third. Then the fourth, but she lost the second image and had to start again.

'I don't think I can do it,' she said. Her hands were sweating. Everything depended on this working.

'You *will* do it,' said Skald.

Sulien tried again, and again lost the second image. Her head was throbbing; she had never done a far-seeing this difficult before.

'Shall I flog the whipping girl?' said the acolyte with the cane, eagerly.

'No!' cried Sulien.

Jassika stiffened. 'If it helps you, I can take it.'

Sulien had never been prouder of her. 'How could flogging my dearest friend help me to do better?' she said softly.

Jassika gazed at her for a long moment, then wiped her eyes on her arm and stood taller.

Skald started again. This time Sulien left the troublesome second painting until last, and the five all came together as one.

'I have it,' she said softly.

'Show me,' he said.

She mind-linked to him, as she had so many times now, and allowed him to see what she was seeing, moving the viewpoint in a full circle around the hilltop.

'It's the destination,' he whispered. 'It's Traitor's Crag, on *Tallallame*.'

She sensed joy and triumph, and no Merdrun had worked harder nor more cleverly than Skald to bring the Day of All Days about.

Yet she was also picking up guilt and shame, and a terrible sadness, almost like grief. The guilt she could understand, since she felt sure he had conspired to kill the magiz, and that had cost the lives of many other important Merdrun. And the shame from his forbidden liaison with the slave architect, Uletta. But why the grief?

Was this the key to their secret weakness?

Her head was aching, as it always did after an intense session of far-seeing, and it was taking all her strength to hold the three-dimensional destination in her mind. From below, Durthix shouted orders at Skald, who ran to the top of the stairs to reply.

A very different three-dimensional image flashed into Sulien's inner eye – a barren, stony landscape with mountains all around. *Got it?* Malien said across a faint link.

*Yes.*

*Hide it deep. Don't let anyone know you have it.*

Malien was gone. Sulien made sure the mental image was perfectly clear – a talent she thought came from Llian – and buried it deep.

Her headache grew worse. Skald came back and the next few minutes were a blur of softly spoken orders, and strange powers and magics being used by the sus-magizes and artisans elsewhere in the control chamber. She was vaguely aware that he was struggling to draw enough power from the node – opening the portal took far more power than keeping it open. And that he was losing faith in himself. A suffocating terror was rising in him, that he could not do it.

No, that he could not do it *this* way. There was another way to gain power, but he kept shying away from it, violently.

Skald was struggling to control his emotions, but it was more necessary than ever here. Expressing joy and triumph was permitted, no, *expected* after a great goal had been achieved, but never before.

It was almost time, and he was almost out of time. Only minutes until sunrise, when it would shine straight through the sapphire tunnel on the Day of All Days. If he could pull this off, it would be the greatest moment of his life, or any Merdrun's life.

He glanced at Sulien. She had far-seen Traitor's Crag with beautiful clarity. When he checked it, and saw their long-lost homeland, Skald had struggled to hold back tears.

The portal was almost fully powered. Another minute and it would be, and then only one thing would be left to do, at the moment when the full circle of the sun became visible above the eastern horizon.

But could he do it? His far-seeing gift was small. Could he take the destination from Sulien clearly enough to open the portal there? He had trained doing so with many images, and had made gates to some of those places, but a small local gate was very different to a monstrous, world-spanning portal.

Up on the mezzanine, the artisan slaves who had contributed most to the great day had been assembled to witness the triumph. M'Lainte was seated on the far left. She had not been treated well by Dagog, and Skald felt dishonoured. She was also the greatest mechanician Santhenar had ever seen, and this day would not have been possible without her.

Or Tiaan, who stood beside her, looking down as if, even on this momentous day, her thoughts were far away. On her children, Skald assumed. She looked up at him and her face hardened. He had almost killed her on that desperate flight from Alcifer, yet she had given her all and he felt a spasm of guilt. He had sworn to send her home to her children, but Dagog had refused to allow it, and in the frantic days since his death the promise had slipped from Skald's mind.

It could not be kept now; there was no power to spare for even the tiniest gate. The sapphire portal, and the gate he planned to make to escape with Uletta after the portal had been closed, would take all the power he could raise.

None of the other slaves mattered; he did not know their names and barely recognised their faces, except one. Standing tall at the back was his beautiful Uletta, and the sight of her made his heart sing. Soon, within the hour, they would be free, and safe, and together.

Blue lights caught Skald's eye and he glanced down through the quartz plate. Small sections of the sapphire-crusted tunnel were flashing bright blue, fading and flashing again. Everything was coming together to create the vast dimensional portal to another and far better world, their long-lost home world that every Merdrun ached for.

Giving up that dream had come at a heavy cost. Heavier than Uletta could imagine or understand. But she loved him, and Skald had never been loved before, or even cared for. For her love, he would give up everything.

～

Sulien no longer needed to look at the paintings – the image of Traitor's Crag was fixed in her inner eye. She turned her head and, through the magical goggles, the people in the control chamber swam dizzyingly before her eyes. Then Senior Sus-magiz Lurzel's face zoomed into focus beside the paintings, only a couple of yards away.

Sulien started and her heart began to thump. He gave her the shivers.

'More power, Skald!' Lurzel was a remarkably narrow man. His shoulders were no wider than hers and his long back had a lopsided hump. He slithered across to Skald, his flat, snake-like head held at an angle, and she wondered if his tongue was forked. 'It needs a lot more power to open.'

Sulien did not catch Skald's reply, but his face had gone a ruddy brown and was covered in droplets of oily sweat, and he had a tremor in his left arm. Something was wrong.

Sus-magiz Lurzel came closer, emanating righteous anger. Sulien looked away. He was a dangerous man and she did not want to attract his attention. They spoke in low voices for several minutes. Skald's face went from red to grey and she picked up guilt again, and a terrible fear.

Lurzel gestured at Sulien, who looked straight ahead. 'Why is she here?'

Sulien did not hear Skald's reply but it seemed as though Lurzel was threatening him. She had to help Skald, any way she could. She looked at the five paintings again and made sure the image was absolutely clear.

Skald drew power and continued to discharge it into the sapphires that lined the tunnel. His face went red, the sweat reappeared, and his knuckles were white on his controls as he took more, and more, and even more.

Sulien felt a stab of panic and the destination started to blur and separate. With an effort, she brought it back into focus. Her head was throbbing and she wasn't sure she could hold the three-dimensional image much longer. If he did not open the portal soon, Lurzel might take over, and if he did, she and Karan and Jassika would die.

The floor quivered. 'Enough?' Skald said to Lurzel.

The sus-magiz looked up from his own controls. 'Almost.'

Skald strained harder. Drops of sweat the size of peas fell from his face. Every time he drew more power, pain speared through Sulien's head and pulses of nausea surged through her. She would have thrown up, but her stomach was empty. They had not given her breakfast. Because she wasn't going to live long enough to need it?

Then Jassika was beside her, holding her up. 'You can do it, Sools.'

'I ... don't think I can.'

Jassika reached out and something small, round and cold touched Sulien in the crook of her left arm. The knoblaggie. 'There, you feel better now, don't you?'

The pain and nausea were gone, though whether it was the magic of the knoblaggie or just the knowledge that Jass was doing everything she could for her, Sulien could not tell.

A ray of orange light touched the eastern window. The uppermost curve of the sun had just tipped the horizon.

'Three and a half minutes until the sun's up, Skald!' bellowed Durthix from below.

Three and a half minutes for the plan to work, or fail. Three and a half minutes to live or die.

'Don't think I can draw much more power.' Skald's face was scalding and a tremor had developed in his left arm. The massive draw was burning him, as it had burned Tiaan on the long flight from Alcifer.

'In the trials yesterday and the day before there wasn't a problem,' said Lurzel. '*Why now?*'

'Quakes must have damaged the node. The flow keeps dying down and flaring up, and it's burning me on the inside.'

'Then fix it!'

'I – don't know how.'

'You wanted Dagog dead,' said Lurzel softly. 'And once he was, you engineered things to become acting magiz.'

Skald felt the blood drain from his face. 'What are you talking about?' he whispered.

Sus-magiz Lurzel edged closer, lowered his voice further. 'He had two people watching you, you treacherous swine. Before Yallav went to the meeting and was killed by the spellcaster, she shared her evidence with Sus-magiz Ghiar. And Ghiar told me.'

Skald choked. This could not be happening. Not *now*.

'About your sickening liaison with the slave architect,' Lurzel said relentlessly. 'And your criminal neglect of your duty in checking the spellcaster. If it *was* only neglect, and not a plan to murder our magiz at a time when he could not be replaced. I'm in two minds about that.'

Skald noticed that Sulien had gone still. Had she overheard? If she had, she might lose it, and that would be the end.

'Why is the child here, anyway?' said Lurzel.

'Dagog ordered me to train her far-seeing gift.'

'But why is she here *now*?'

'Her gift gives a little boost to my far-seeing. I can't explain it better than that.'

'Well, get on with it then.'

'What are you going to do about ... the other stuff?' Skald whispered, clutching the control levers with his big hands.

'On the Day of All Days?' Lurzel's flat head swayed from side to side and his glitter-eyed stare was mesmerising. 'If you *can* open the portal and send us home, you may be untouchable. Though I pray not. Get the power we need, Skald, no matter how much it hurts. If you can't, I'll blow you to bloody rags and attempt the far-seeing myself.'

Lurzel went back to his post. Skald removed the far-seeing goggles from Sulien's face and put them over his own eyes. If Lurzel saw them on her again, and checked, he would discover that she was far-seeing the destination, not Skald.

Focus! The nation is relying on you. The sun was a blazing semicircle now, and he hastily drew more power. Brilliant blue rippled from one end of the tunnel to the other, then expanded out in all directions. The sapphire-clad tunnel was fully powered.

The floor shook again. There had been quite a few quakes since Rulke's dramatic escape in the construct, though none had done any damage. The tower was designed to survive far greater forces.

A surge like a blue lightning bolt flashed from the central column, high above Skald's head, to the western side of the control chamber, where it stuck a sus-magiz, killing him instantly and setting the clothes of two acolytes alight. They were quickly extinguished but when Skald looked down through the quartz plate the tunnel no longer glowed blue.

He drew power. Nothing. He tried again. 'The node's failed!'

Sus-magiz Lurzel slithered across and examined the controls. 'It can't fail. Probably a rock fall has damaged the node tapper.'

Skald swore. It wasn't a disaster – the window to Tallallame was eight hours long

– but it would rob him of the symbolic triumph of opening the portal at full sunrise. 'We've got a spare. Get artisans and miners down there, now.'

Lurzel gave orders and an acolyte ran down the stairs.

Lurzel moved closer and lowered his voice. 'That's going to take all day, Acting Magiz – *if* they can get to the node at all. If it's a bad collapse, as I suspect, the miners will have to clear it away and you won't get any more power from the node for days.'

And the Source was gone with the construct. 'But the tunnel roofs were specially shored up, to prevent this kind of accident.'

'The rock's rotten down there. All the shoring in the world wouldn't be enough for a big quake.'

'Skald!' bellowed Durthix from halfway up the stairs. 'What the blazes is going on?'

Skald choked. What was he supposed to tell Durthix? 'Then ... it can't be done.'

Lurzel lowered his voice until it became a hiss. 'There's another way to get power,' he said meaningfully. 'It's why we kept the slaves here after their work was done.'

'But General Chaxee said the portal needed an *untainted* source of power. I can't –'

'Chaxee's dead, killed by the spellcaster you failed to check properly. Besides, this is magiz business and there's no other way, *Acting* Magiz. Either you drink enough lives to open the portal, or we fail. And if we fail, I'll tell Durthix all I know.'

The thin-lipped smile stretched from one side of Lurzel's flat face to the other. He desperately wanted Skald to fail, so why hadn't he denounced him? Because Lurzel wasn't confident of his own ability to far-see the destination and open the portal. And short of hacking Lurzel's head off in the middle of the control chamber, which was unthinkable, Skald was beaten.

'If – if it's the only way,' he said in a dead voice. This must destroy Uletta's love for him.

He ran to the stairs and bellowed down. 'A small problem with the node, High Commander. We need a few more minutes.'

He looked up and Uletta's eyes were on him. It was clear to everyone that something had gone wrong. He would never forget her disgust on discovering that he drank lives, or how proud she had been when he'd sworn to never do so again. Despite many temptations, Skald had not drunk a life since returning from Alcifer, but there was no choice now.

The sapphire tunnel had lost some power and was only nine-tenths charged. He would have to drink many lives to make up the loss, but he could not do so in the control chamber. It would be too distracting to those whose vital work still had to be done.

'Send the slaves we no longer need up to the mezzanine,' Skald said to his acolytes. 'Guard them well; they might panic and run.'

But he could not bear for Uletta to judge him as a liar and an oath-breaker, a man she could never love. What if he sent her through a gate to their prepared refuge and promised to come later? In time she would understand.

He was heading up the curving steps when Lurzel caught his arm. 'Where are you going?' he said, his voice thick with suspicion. 'You can't leave now.'

Every sus-magiz and acolyte in the control chamber was staring at him. There was no hope of getting Uletta away now.

Skald had meant it when he'd sworn to drink no more lives, but duty to his people came first. Besides, no oath sworn to an enemy, to a *slave*, could ever take precedence over the oath that every Merdrun swore when they learned to talk, and renewed every year afterwards. *One for All.*

He avoided looking Uletta's way as he signed to his acolytes to march the first victim forward, an artist with a shaven head and enormous, almost purple eyes. He had done the magnificent paintings Sulien had used to envisage the destination, but he was just a source of power now.

Skald felt a surge of anticipation. What he was about to do was terrible, but it was also glorious. He pressed the tip of his rue-har to his forehead until it pierced the skin, and cast the spell that would protect him from the emotions of his victims. Sad creatures all, in thrall to their emotions, but *he* was different. He was Merdrun!

He pointed towards the victim, spoke the spell and made the gestures, and tore the artist's life out of him. Euphoria swelled until Skald thought his heart was going to burst; scalding power sang through his veins.

The artist crumpled like a deflating balloon. Skald turned to the next store of power, a tiny old woman who had done the most important engravings in the tower. She cursed him and spat at him, her hatred battering him, the emotions getting to him despite his protective spell.

'Cover their heads!' he said harshly. Nothing could be allowed to hinder him now.

# 42

# DESTROY THE GIFT BURNER

Wilm and Ilisial felt their way down through the inky fog. It was cold and clammy, and condensed in droplets on their hair and eyebrows. There was no light here except for an occasional coloured glow from a swirling banner of waste magic, blasted out of the chaos chasm hours ago. Wilm kept well away from them.

They reached the base of the pit, a channel that ran around the sides. It felt about six feet wide. 'The spike's on our left,' said Ilisial, her voice oddly muffled by the fog.

The spike was smooth, though it felt like polished stone rather than metal. Wilm walked around, trailing his fingers across it; it was only a couple of feet through the middle.

'It's like a five-sided obelisk, and the gift-burner is at the top.'

'How are we supposed to get up there?' said Ilisial.

He continued, reaching as high as he could. 'I can't feel a ladder, or rungs or anything.'

She said nothing.

'I could try to cut the spike down with Akkidul,' he said doubtfully. 'Though ... when I was a kid our neighbour tried to cut down a tree and it fell on top of him. It was horrible. It took him hours –' Don't go there. It might set off another panic attack in Ilisial.

'Have you ever cut a tree down?'

'No.'

'It's too dangerous. Especially in the dark. What – what if I stand on your shoulders? There might be a ladder further up.'

'I could stand on *your* shoulders. Our reach would be the same – about twelve feet if I stretch right up.'

'Don't be ridiculous, you're heavier than I am. Stand against the spike.' Ilisial tied a glowstick to her forehead with a length of cord.

Wilm put his back to the spike, cupped his hands and she stepped up, then, with a grunt, onto his shoulders. He could hear her sliding her hands up the smooth sides of the spike but the light of the glowstick did not reach far enough for him to see.

'Nothing,' she said.

He did not know whether to be glad or sorry. How was he supposed to destroy the gift-burner, an incomprehensible device he had never seen before?

'Can you boost me a bit higher?' said Ilisial.

He went up on tiptoes, the arches of his feet aching under the strain. 'Any better?'

'No. Pass up the sword, in its scabbard. I'll feel around above me.'

Wilm took the scabbard off his belt, checked that Akkidul was pressed down all the way and passed it up. Ilisial swayed on his shoulders as she probed up higher, and he thought she was going to fall, then he heard a metallic click and a scraping sound.

'Think that's a rung,' she said.

'Pass the sword back.'

Ilisial buckled it around her hips. 'I need another eighteen inches. Hold your hands up above your head, like little platforms.'

'If you fall, and land on the edge of the channel –'

'Just do it!' she snapped.

Wilm did so. 'Step onto my head, first.'

'All right,' she said quietly.

She stepped up onto his head with her left foot, then the right, swayed and threw her arms around the spike. The strain on his neck and the balls of his feet was immense.

'Can't stay on tiptoes – much longer,' he said.

Ilisial stepped up onto the platform of his left hand. He locked his elbow, his muscles spasming under the weight. She stepped onto his right hand and he felt the pressure as she stretched up.

'Got it!'

Some of her weight went off him, then the rest, and her boots rang on metal rungs. Her glowstick shone more brightly, a diffuse round glow through the fog.

'I'm on a square platform at the top of the spike. Gift burner's in the middle. It's a complicated device. I don't know –'

'I'll toss my rope up.'

He did so and she caught it and tied it on. Wilm pulled himself up, using the knots he'd tied earlier, found the rungs and climbed to the platform.

The gift-burner was illuminated by Ilisial's small glowstick, though all Wilm could see was an oblong case, a few feet across and a foot thick.

'How are we supposed to destroy it?' she said.

'M'Lainte said I'd know how, from when I was at the Sink of Despair.'

'I don't understand.'

'Klarm told me to destroy the spellcaster by hacking through it with Akkidul, then across the first cut. But he told me exactly where to strike.'

Ilisial prised up the case with her knife and studied the mechanism. It meant nothing to Wilm.

After several minutes of consideration, she pointed to a small box marked with a circle in a square, on the left side. 'I think the heart of it will be in there. Cut it across, and across the other way.'

He drew the black sword, afraid that he was doing the wrong thing. 'What if I don't hit it squarely?'

'I don't know.'

To the right of the little box, a stubby crystal was pulsing from pale lemon-yellow to dark mustard yellow. 'Is that important, do you think?

'Um ... it might be what does the gift-burning.'

'Then wouldn't it be better to smash it?'

'Tell me, Wilm,' she said in a voice that so reminded him of Klarm, 'which one of us is the artisan, and which is –?'

'Sorry!' he snapped. He held the sword out, hilt first. 'You know where to strike. Why don't you do it?'

He regretted it the moment he spoke, but she grabbed the sword and raised it high.

*What?* said Akkidul. *No! How dare you give me away again – and to* her!

'Shut up, you evil lump of metal!' Ilisial choked and swung violently at the metal box.

But she had not used a sword before, and her blow went astray. Or maybe the sword swerved sideways – in the dim light, Wilm could not tell. The blade only clipped a corner off the metal box, slammed diagonally down on the crystal and, oddly, did not cut through, or break it, but glanced off in a shower of sparks.

Ilisial drew back, wincing. The blow had jarred her to the shoulders. She was raising the sword to strike again when the yellow crystal went orange, red, purple then blue-white, crazed all over and shattered into a thousand pieces like window glass, and the fragments exploded out in all directions.

Wilm ducked. Ilisial did not react in time and a cluster of blue-white fragments struck her in the middle of the forehead and stuck there, glowing balefully.

Her eyes crossed; she let out a faint cry and dashed the fragments away. They had made a series of bloody cuts on her brow in the shape of the Merdrun glyph. She dropped the sword, her knees gave and she slumped to the frosty platform.

'*It's – gone!*' she said in a faint little voice, and fell onto her side, knees drawn up.

'What's gone, Ilisial?'

*Her gift,* said the sword, and Wilm sensed its glee.

Had it provoked him, and Ilisial, deliberately? Perhaps, being trapped inside a dead length of metal, it could only truly live through others. Was that why Mendark had buried it in a box in the desert?

Why hadn't Wilm done the job himself? He would have struck true. And if the sword had managed to swerve in his strong grip, he had no gift to be burned out.

He jammed it into the copper sheath and bent over Ilisial. Her eyes were closed, and she was panting, and very cold. He had to get her away from here.

'I'll help you up,' he said.

'Can't get up.'

Wilm fashioned a rope harness around her middle, lowered her to the base of the spike, then tied the rest of the rope to the platform and climbed down. Ilisial's breathing was even slower and weaker now. She needed urgent treatment but he did not see where she was going to get it.

He carried her up out of the pit and back across the compound. The light was brighter now; it would soon be sunrise. The mist had thickened, though once the sun rose it would quickly disappear.

He carried Ilisial in between the stacks of cut stone and laid her down in front of Flydd. It felt as though history was repeating itself. He had failed her, as he had failed Dajaes.

He explained what had happened. 'Is there anything you can do?'

Flydd bent over her, probing her head with his fingertips. 'I don't think so. A better healer might ... if we had one.'

'Lirriam's a great healer, isn't she?'

'So I'm told.'

But she might not be coming back. Wilm leaned back against a stack of frigid stone and closed his eyes. He had done all Karan had asked of him and had given her the best chance he could. So why did he feel such a failure?

# 43

# A SICK, SELF-DISGUSTED ECSTASY

The acolytes tied rags over the faces of the slaves and, the moment the little old engraver's face was covered, Skald drank her life. It proved surprisingly strong; it gave him three times as much power as he had expected, and it was glorious!

His suppressed addiction woke like a ravening beast and he drank the lives of the slaves standing in the front row, one after another, then discharged the power they had given him into the sapphire-crusted tunnel. It began to flash blue, in sections. Not long now.

Three lives he took, four, five, then ten and twenty, and he could feel himself inflating a little more as each of his victims was drained. Everyone in the control chamber was staring at him, and Skald was sure he was a foot taller, his shoulders six inches wider. He was boiling, his skin had gone the colour of the Crimson Gate – the fatal gate – and every nerve in his body was a red-hot wire.

Even Lurzel was backing away now. The fool knew he was beaten.

Twenty-four victims, and the sapphire tunnel lit up a brilliant, glaring blue. Skald laughed and reached out towards the twenty-fifth, M'Lainte. Her face wasn't covered; the acolytes had run out of rags. What power she could give him!

'Skald!' Durthix bellowed.

Skald felt a surge of annoyance. How dare the high commander interrupt at so critical a moment!

Lurzel struck Skald across the side of the head. 'It's charged. Open the portal!'

Skald was about to drink Lurzel's life when he came to his senses. That would be madness. He shuddered, looked around and smiled. Finally, he had the power! Once the portal was open and the Merdrun nation had gone through, he would close the portal, make a gate to a far-off part of Santhenar, take Uletta by the hand and escape with her.

Only then did he truly appreciate what that meant. All his life it had been *One for All*. The self meant nothing; it was the nation that mattered, and all Skald had ever wanted was to escape his father's tainted name and be a respected part of the nation. Yet now, on the Day of All Days, he was planning to repudiate his people and go into exile. What would that do to him?

He could not bear to think about it, so he took refuge in the one drug that could ease all pain – more lives. Tiaan had pushed M'Lainte to the floor, and Skald was reaching out to Tiaan when she met his eyes. Shame burned him. He had sworn to send her home and he had broken his oath.

But no oath made to an enemy could ever be valid. He was about to drink her rich life when she dived out of sight. No matter, the life he wanted most of all was Karan's. But he could not have it either. Not in front of her daughter, when he still needed Sulien's far-seeing.

On the other side of the mezzanine a group of slaves had covered faces, and he drank the lives of the first, the second, the third. It was bliss. He reached out to the next and he was so powerful now that her life began to peel away easily, effortlessly. The pleasure was incomparable; erotic.

'Skald, no!' gasped Uletta.

She tore the rags away from her face and he realised, with a stab of horror, that he had begun to drink the one life he had been desperate to save.

Uletta lurched to the railing. 'You promised, Skald. If you love me, even a little, *drink no more lives.*'

She was a trifle withered, but still beautiful. She would always be beautiful to him. He did love her, and always would. But when he looked around, every Merdrun in the control chamber was eyeing him in disgust. He was not one of them anymore. In his liaison with a slave he had broken one of their greatest prohibitions – and now he had betrayed even her.

The tunnel was fully charged and he could open the portal in an instant. Little time had been lost. The sun was only two finger-widths above the horizon.

But now Skald was confused. How could he abandon the beliefs of a lifetime? How turn his back on his people at the moment they, and he, had always yearned for? If he did, would he end up a desperate, embittered outcast?

He looked from Uletta to the tunnel, to the rising sun, to the staring Merdrun, and back to Uletta. She was reaching out to him lovingly, despairingly – and all his life he had yearned to be loved.

'I can forgive you,' she said, and her voice was soft, gentle, and low. 'But no more lives, Skald. No more!'

Dagog had been right. Each life Skald drank was like a different wine. Some were thin and some were sour, some unripe, some sickly sweet, and a rare few were majestic, unforgettable, almost overwhelming. M'Lainte's life would have been like that, he felt sure. He could still taste the first sip of Uletta's life, and it was glorious.

He longed for more, even though that would be betraying her. Yet if he spared her and fled with her, he would be betraying his people and all they stood for. How could he decide?

He was trapped; whatever choice he made, he would be a monster. What was it to be?

Flee with Uletta and he would end up a despicable outcast, and so would she. Her own people would turn against her and she would probably end up hating him, in which case he would have betrayed himself and his people for nothing.

Or betray her? Skald would have the joy of fulfilling the True Purpose, doing his duty and taking his people home. And he might even survive it, especially if he could contrive Lurzel's death soon afterwards, then humble himself and take his punishment.

When he looked at it that way there was only one choice. It was the right decision, the brave decision, and before anything else the son of a coward must be brave.

In the instant that his choice was made, the intoxicated euphoria from drinking all those lives overwhelmed him. He could not stop now. He had to have all of her.

Skald reached out to Uletta, began the draw and turned away. He could not bear to look into her eyes and see her contempt. He continued, sucking the life out of her in a sick, self-disgusted ecstasy.

But she was not going to go tamely, not Uletta. Withered and blanched but still beautiful, she ran down the curving steps and hurled herself at him, her fingers hooked into claws. He could not move and she slammed into him, knocking him backwards. She staggered towards him.

'No,' he cried. 'Stay back!'

She looked around at the other Merdrun, and not even snake-faced Lurzel could meet her blazing eyes.

'Your acting magiz,' she said, biting her words off and spitting them in Skald's face, '*this monster, Skald*, is on the outside what every one of you are on the inside. You deserved to be sent through the Crimson Gate, all those aeons ago. Evil, Stermin named you, and evil you chose to be. With the remaining seconds of my life I curse you, Skald, and every Merdrun in existence.'

It was a mighty curse and the watchers drew back, shaken to the core at the most important hour of their lives. Skald reeled. What was happening to him?

'Drink her!' gasped Lurzel. 'Finish her now.'

'With my dying breath I lay this curse on the Merdrun nation,' she said in a voice that everyone in the chamber would remember to the end of their days. 'You will *never* go home. You will *forever* be exiles. The slave drivers will become *slaves*.'

'Kill her!' shrieked sus-magiz Ghiar. 'Take her life and break the curse.'

Though when Skald looked around the control chamber, every sus-magiz, acolyte and guard wore the same expression of unutterable horror. The Merdrun had an oath for every occasion and they knew an unbreakable curse when they heard it. They were damned.

Uletta swayed, recovered and focused on Skald again. 'You are the vilest traitor of all,' she said softly, wearily. 'Not only have you betrayed your people and your lover – yes,' she said in a ringing voice, 'I was his lover, fool that I am, and I believed his promises – but you've betrayed yourself. I wish you a long and agonising life, Skald.'

There was only one way to end the agony, and Skald took it, though he knew it made him irredeemable. He took all the life he could find in her.

Sulien had the goggles over her eyes again and was glad she could not see much. She did not witness any of the life drinking, though she knew what was going on. Her sensitive's gift picked up the agonies of Skald's victims, and his own exhilaration and ecstasy, horror and guilt and self-disgust. He was a tormented man.

Then Uletta cried in pain and betrayal. 'You promised, Skald. If you love me, drink no more lives.'

He had not realised that he was drinking *her* life, and now he was in agony. He loved her, wanted her, craved her love and longed to run away and be with her, yet he was disgusted that he had so broken the prohibition. And he wanted the approval of his people even more. He was desperate to open the portal so they could go home. He wanted to go home too, and Skald was terrified of what would happen if he turned away from them. Yet equally terrified that, once the Merdrun did go home, Lurzel would call him out as a traitor, a liar and a murderer.

A tormented man, indeed. He was shuddering with eagerness as he continued to drink his lover's life, yet churning with revulsion.

*Reveal your people's weakness*, Sulien thought. *Show me, now!*

Uletta sprang and crashed into Skald. She was pale and shrivelled, and a full six inches shorter than she had been only a few minutes ago, but she had a fierce dignity that Sulien could only admire.

She cursed Skald, and the Merdrun nation. 'You will never go home. You will forever be exiles. The slave drivers will become slaves.'

Waves of anguish boiled out of Skald and, in a blinding flash of insight, Sulien understood what Uigg the drum boy had hinted at before he died, but could not bring himself to say plainly.

And what she had seen when she'd sneaked into Skald's room and touched his rue-har to her forehead. The Merdrun's denial of all human emotions and feelings was their secret weakness, their fatal flaw, and it was stronger in Skald than any other Merdrun she knew.

*A child of a lesser race can defeat us if her mighty gift is allowed to develop* – But develop what?

The ability to flood the Merdrun with their long-suppressed feelings? To attack them by bringing all their hidden memories, painful emotions and unbearable traumas to the surface? Yes! And, Sulien realised, in pushing her far-seeing gift so fast and hard, Skald had also strengthened her other gifts. He had created the weapon that could defeat him, *if* she could use it.

She reached out blindly with her left hand and caught Jassika's hand. She was still holding the knoblaggie and, though it wasn't something Sulien could use, she drew strength from it and from her friend.

Uletta's unbearable pain was still echoing back and forth through Sulien's mind, and she took it and amplified it and mind-blasted it at Skald with all her strength. He reeled backwards, gasping. Then, one by one, Sulien deluged him with the over-whelming emotions of his other victims today, from the first, the purple-eyed artist, to the last.

Now she triggered Skald's own suppressed emotions and buried memories, starting with his mother flogging him and cursing him after his father's execution, when the distraught little boy had foolishly asked her if she loved him.

Next, the torment he had relived over and over from his first victim, Tataste, and the discovery of the bodies of her little girl and boy in that foul cellar.

Sulien took these emotions, amplified them and hurled them back at him, battering him down, until she saw the realisation in his eyes. He was a monster, and his people were monsters, and he was overcome. He crumpled to the floor next to Uletta, moaning.

But why stop at him? It was the Merdrun's secret weakness, after all. Sulien broadcast the agonising emotions to everyone in the chamber.

Skald began to scream, because he was now reliving all his victims' agonies as if they were happening to himself. His arms thrashed and he was so charged with power that it blasted out of him, overturning tables and the devices on them, bursting many of the lamps and killing several acolytes and a sus-magiz, and bringing down the front of the mezzanine, and a dozen withered bodies.

Sulien could see right through to the storerooms now, and M'Lainte and Tiaan were gone. Thankfully, he had not drank their lives.

Three sus-magiz were down, most of the acolytes and half the guards. It was the one attack they could not defend against, because ten thousand years of emotional denial had destroyed their resilience. They simply could not cope.

'What's the matter now?' Durthix bellowed from the stairs outside. 'The sun's up. Open the damned portal, *or we fail!*'

Skald pulled himself upright. He was drenched in sweat; his skin had gone the colour of grey mud and only the whites of his eyes could be seen. But it was an order and he had to obey. He wrenched the goggles off Sulien and put them on himself.

Durthix burst in, his nailed boots skidding on the floor. He stopped dead, taking in the chaos: Uletta lying withered on the floor, one arm pointing accusingly at Skald; Skald, gasping and trembling; many of the Merdrun dead or driven out of their wits, or hunched in foetal positions. Durthix was a perceptive man. He would read the scene like a book.

'Is the deputy architect dead?' he said.

'Almost,' said Lurzel from the other side of the chamber.

'What's the matter with Skald?'

'The acting magiz has given way to his emotions,' said Lurzel, who was clearly keeping the tightest possible rein on his own, though his shrill voice told that he was also struggling to cope with the emotional deluge.

'So I see,' said Durthix, who did not appear to be in any difficulty. 'Why is the girl here?'

He was looking at Sulien. She quaked.

'She's gifted in far-seeing,' said Lurzel. 'Apparently her presence boosts Skald's own ability.'

'Then do your duty, Acting Magiz Skald,' Durthix said coldly. 'It's all you have left, after your abominable crime.'

Skald jerked around like an automaton and, face frozen in horror, staggered to the control bench and fell onto it beside Sulien. His aura was foul now and his smell was worse, as if the lives he had consumed were decaying inside him. He had something of the stink of the former magiz, Dagog, though not as bad. Not yet.

She shuddered and leaned as far away as the straps would let her. She was very cold and very afraid. Her teeth were chattering.

'Do you still have the destination?' he said out of the corner of his mouth.

Sulien closed her eyes and, to her surprise, the three-dimensional image was still there. 'I-I can see it as c-clearly as looking through a window.'

'Show me again.'

He mind-linked to her the way they had practiced, and she showed him the dome-shaped hill with the clusters of standing stones, the crag, and the untouched forest all around it.

'Tallallame!' he sighed. 'And now it's ours.'

Skald sent the image to the controls and drew on the levers. A cool, humid wind wafted up the stairs and grew until it was sighing through the tunnel – the portal was open at last.

'The Day of All Days!' cried Durthix, sinking to his knees and allowing his forehead to touch the quartz plate in the floor. Down below, the tunnel had filled with churning, sapphire blue mist. 'We're going home.'

He sprang to his feet and thundered down the stairs.

Karan felt a brief psychic shock when the portal was opened, and a flaring pain in her head and heart. She tried to mind-call Rulke but failed. Flydd did not answer either, and when she attempted to reach Wilm she felt only an awful, incomprehensible pain.

Did she have any mind-speech left at all? She did not think so.

The aftersickness was really bad now but she had to keep trying. Through the eastern window she could see the long shadows of the Merdrun army, 250 soldiers across and 600 deep, coming through the tenfold gates at a fast march. They would reach the entrance to the portal in minutes, and if they managed one row per second it would take ten minutes for the army to pass through.

She bit down on the emotions before they crippled her. The critical part of the plan lay ahead – assuming Llian was still alive.

*Llian?* She feared for him most of all. She had forced him to face his worst fear. Was he already dead, broken from the fall?

*Llian? If you can hear me, move the crystal.*

She felt nothing. She sent him the same message via a mind-link, an older but far less reliable skill, then a sending. Again, she sensed nothing. Fear was crippling her. The leading ranks of the army were out of sight below the window frame now.

*Sulien, tell Llian to move the crystal. And you have to far-see the new destination, right now.*

Karan was looking right at Sulien, but Sulien did not react in any way that might indicate she had heard.

With the power failing, Rulke had been forced to land the construct on a windswept prominence, and he and Lirriam had set out to walk back to Skyrock, many miles away across a series of rugged ridges and ravines. She had not dared use the Waystone; the Merdrun had drawn so much power into the gate-opening mechanism that it had warped space dangerously.

Aviel watched them go. Unable to sleep, she had spent the last of the night on the construct's lookout platform, wrapped in one of Rulke's heavy coats, watching the changing patterns of light around the distant tower and agonising about what was going on there.

Chances were that everyone would be killed or captured, and the Merdrun would come and take the construct back. They would have no use for her. But if she left, how long would she survive in this hostile wilderness?

If only she'd made it up with Wilm before he'd gone through with Flydd and Ilisial.

## 44

# YOU'VE ONLY GOT ONE MINUTE

Maelys and Llian went out a roof door onto the flat top of Skyrock, which was lit by light filtering down from blue cladding on the iron tower. The wind was much stronger here, howling around and between the iron beams, and the bluish light made it seem even colder, more eerie and threatening. Frost glittered on the rooftop and on every surface. The eclipsed full moon, all of its dark side showing, would set in the west at sunrise.

Llian looked up, and up. And up. His fingernails dug into his palms and he wanted to run all the way down again. 'I – I don't think I can do it.'

'This is the ultimate test,' said Maelys. 'For all of us. Pass it and we may survive. But if we fail, it's the end of Santhenar. That's what's at stake here, Llian.'

Llian knew. Rulke and Karan had also said it. It made it no easier to do the impossible.

The five-sided iron tower was fixed to the top of Skyrock with iron bolts as thick through as his thigh, and ran up, narrowing steadily. Another four hundred feet, he recalled. He had been in the construct when Rulke lifted the sections of tower into place, and the shrouded, portal-directing mechanism last of all. It was no longer shrouded.

'How do we get up there?' he said.

'There's bound to be a ladder.' She looked around. 'There.'

It was just a series of rungs bolted to one of the upright members of the tower, and they ran up without any landing or resting place, or rail or caging to prevent unwary climbers from falling all the way down.

'I'll go first, shall I?' said Maelys.

'Good idea. That way, if I fall –'

'You're not doing our morale any good,' she said waspishly.

'You don't have to go. You can't go close to the twinned crystal anyway.'

'My job is to get *you* up there. Move!' She started climbing the icy rungs, but winced and dropped down again, and went through her pack. 'Sharp ice.'

He got his gloves out and put them on. It would be slippery, too. Terrific!

At first the climb wasn't so bad. Since the rungs were inside the frame of the tower, there was some protection from the wind, and the blue cladding gave the illusion that they were safe. But the moment Llian looked down, from around eighty feet up, the illusion vanished and a spasm of terror surged through him.

'Just look up.' Maelys hooked an arm through the rungs and scrubbed the accumulated frost and ice from her gloves. 'I'm not enjoying it either.'

'What if there's someone up top?' he said. 'They could just push us off ...'

'Let's face the dangers as they arise, eh?'

'Tell me about the taphloid,' said Llian. Talking would help to take his mind off the drop, the fall, the smashing impact ...

'Well,' began Maelys, 'it's ancient. Made by Kandor the Charon for his son, Yggur, to –'

'Yggur is *Kandor's* son?' This was big news, an important detail of the *Histories* that would have to be updated.

'Yes, though his mother was an old human woman.'

'That explains a lot about Yggur. You'll have to tell me all about it, after all this is over.'

She allowed him to think about that for a minute or two, then said, 'Kandor put lessons in it, to teach Yggur magic and protect him when he was a boy, but after Kandor was killed Yggur's mother fell on hard times and sold the taphloid.'

'That would be more than 1,200 years ago,' Llian mused. Talking was good; he'd climbed thirty feet without once thinking about falling to his death.

'It ended up in the Great Library but was stolen in a lyrinx raid and eventually came to my father. When I was a kid, he put in his own lessons to teach me my gift but ... things went wrong and I never learned much magic. Though it's always protected me.' She looked down at Llian. 'What's wrong between you and Karan?'

He did not want to talk about it. 'What's wrong between you and Nish?'

She told him about her son being stillborn, two years ago, and that she believed Nish just wanted her to get over it.

'I've never met him, so I can't have an opinion. But ... are you sure the Mirror isn't driving you apart?' Llian had often seen her gazing into it, in the hours they had been trapped in the compound.

'Yalkara erased all its memories before she gave it to me,' said Maelys curtly. 'It was a gift for my son. Her grandson.'

It was hard to argue against such a powerful Charon but Llian had to try. 'The Mirror was always a lying, cheating, malicious device, never to be trusted. It deceived the greatest people I ever met. Including Tensor, who it was made for – *and* Faelamor, perhaps the greatest adept in the history of the Three Worlds.'

'What's your point?' she said irritably.

'I'm sure Yalkara did erase its memories. But I'll bet she didn't change its nature.'

'What do you mean?'

'It was made for Tensor by his teacher when he was a young man, as a magical outgift – a graduation gift. But magical devices are usually changed when they're taken between the worlds, and it was corrupted. It lies to everyone, Maelys. Or it shows people what they want to see, but always twisted in some subtle way. What's it showing you that you can't keep away from it? What lies is it comforting you with?'

She gave him an icy glare.

Up they went, and up. A hundred feet, two hundred, three. The wind grew ever stronger, and colder, and howled more piercingly the further they climbed, and every rung up here was coated with little needles and blades of ice. They were three-quarters of the way up now. Llian's knees were shaking and his legs and back were aching. His gloves, cut in many places by sharp ice, provided little protection from the cold and his fingers were so stiff he could scarcely bend them.

He checked below. No sign of the enemy. And the light was growing rapidly. Sunrise was not far away.

'Not far now,' said Maelys.

And he had to be ready the moment he got there.

At one stage during its installation with the construct, wind had torn open one side of the canvas shroud and Llian had seen the platform and mechanism clearly. The huge twinned crystal was mounted on an eight-sided frame fixed to the top of the tower, and the azimuth and elevation adjusted by toothed wheels a couple of yards in diameter. The platform itself had no safety rails, nor would there be any protection from the wildly gusting wind, and he had to change the orientation of the crystal by himself.

They climbed ever up. Only forty feet to go. Only thirty. Through gaps in the cladding he could see the Merdrun army now, a broad column of red armour beginning outside the open compound gates and stretching half a mile up the road. It reminded him of the Isle of Gwine and the terrible battle fought there. Not being a fighter, Llian had played little part in it, but he had been close by and the blood and violence and horror and death would forever be with him.

He was so immersed in those memories that he had climbed twenty feet without realising it. Only ten to go. There was no cladding up here and he was fully exposed to the wind. Only five feet.

Maelys gasped. She was hanging by her hands ten feet below him, swinging back and forth. Her feet must have slipped off the ice-sheathed rung. Pain stabbed him; she was going to fall!

He was backing down, wondering how he could help her, when she cried, 'Go on! There's no time.' One of her scrabbling feet found the rung, then the other.

'You sure?'

'Twinned crystal has overwhelmed my taphloid,' she said limply. 'It's burning my nerves. Can't go any higher.'

'You got any rope?'

'Some cord. You want it?'

'No, tie yourself on. When I rotate the crystal, the pain may get worse. And when Skald opens the portal –'

'I know. Go!'

He went up as fast as his shaky limbs would allow. The ladder ended at the platform and he had some bowel-churning moments clambering onto it in the gusting wind. He clung on to the side of the mount and studied the device. The twinned crystal was V-shaped, made of two huge, pale green crystals each more than six feet long, arising from a single crystal at the base. The crystals were almost transparent and had silvery, thread-like markings inside them, like six-sided spiderwebs.

And though Llian had no gift for the Secret Art, this close to the crystal its power was scorching him. His eyes stung and he could smell burning hair. If he spent too long here, he would be cooked.

The lower graduated wheel was mounted horizontally and set the azimuth, or direction. The upper wheel, mounted inside it at an angle, adjusted the elevation angle. He tried to move the azimuth wheel but it would not budge. Was it jammed? No, a little latch locked it in place. He freed it, and the elevation wheel, and recalled the numbers Karan had given him.

*Azimuth 274 and a half degrees. Elevation 68 and three-quarter degrees.*

What connected it to the control chamber, way down in the tower, and to the sapphire-crusted tunnel where the portal would form? Ah! A thick copper braid, wound around with lacquered cloth, ran from the base in which the twinned crystal was set, looping around and then under the mount, and into a hole in a wooden block embedded in the platform.

Underneath, a long length of wooden dowel ran down beside the ladder as far as he could see, and he felt sure it was hollow inside, as if the copper braid ran down the centre. To the control chamber? Was that how the crystal's orientation was used to direct the portal that would open in the sapphire tunnel? What else could it be?

With a knuckle, Llian touched the copper braid where it emerged from the winding of lacquered cloth.

*Crack!*

He was hurled onto his back, gasping. His hair was standing on end, his knuckle was burned and blistered, and his right arm was numb.

'What was that?' called Maelys.

'A nasty shock. I'm all right. It's almost sunrise. What if –?'

'Don't – say – it! That's doing the enemy's work for them.'

How could he not, when he did not know Karan's plan and could not contact her? Clearly, Flydd's plan to collapse the node had failed, and where the hell was Rulke? How had Karan ended up being trapped in Skyrock anyway? Everything rested on her now, and it would only take one little failure, one unexpected attack that could not be fought off, one accident of fate ...

The upper curve of the sun rose above the horizon. A minute passed, then another.

'Where are you, Karan? What's going on?'

No answer.

# 45

# THE ACTING MAGIZ HAS BETRAYED US

Sulien was watching Karan and longing for guidance, but Karan could not move or speak, or mind-speak. She might be signalling with her eyes but Sulien was too far away to see, in the dim light. It was all up to her.

What had Karan said? *After Skald checks the destination and opens the portal, mind-call Llian immediately and tell him to move the crystal. Then change to the new destination Malien sends you. Can you do that?*

But the portal was open already! Skald had opened it a minute ago. What if it was too late now?

*Daddy? Daddy?* Sulien mind-called.

Nothing. Had the enemy got him?

*Daddy? Daddy?*

Still nothing.

*Daddy? Daddy?*

Then she heard Llian reply, though he was very faint, and there was a peculiar buzzing in the background that put her nerves on edge.

*Daddy, move the crystal, right now!*

*Mechanism's heavy. It'll take a couple of minutes.*

*Quick, Daddy!*

Two minutes could be too late. Sulien looked desperately at Karan but found no comfort there. The new destination! Sulien looked for the picture Malien had sent her but could not find it. Her head was throbbing mercilessly, and she had buried the picture too deep. Where was it? Why could she never remember things when she really needed to?

She turned to Jassika, signalling with her eyes. Help! Jass surreptitiously touched her arm with the knoblaggie. There it was! Sulien brought the image to the surface and examined it from all sides. A barren, stony landscape with mountains all around. No, cliffs! She sent it to the controls the way Skald had done with the Tallallame destination, and felt a sharp pain at the base of her skull.

Had she done it? She had no idea. Maybe it was something only Skald could do, though if so, why would M'Lainte have suggested the plan?

Sulien could just make out Durthix through the clear plate in the floor. He was pacing at the eastern entrance to the portal tunnel, along with three of his generals. It was the greatest day of their lives and they had no reason to suspect anything was wrong.

Had it worked? Had Llian turned the twinned crystal in time?

Karan had told Llian not to move the crystal until she said to. But she'd also said it would be around sunrise – a little before or a little after. The sun was fully up now.

There came a bright blue flash from the ends of the tunnel, more than a thousand feet below. The tower shuddered and Llian felt a piercing pain behind his eyes. He cried out and caught frantically at the azimuth wheel, the sharp teeth cutting into his fingers, to stop himself from being thrown off. A small shaking of the ground at the base of the tower was magnified into a huge one here. The tip of the tower was swaying fifteen feet across the sky and back again.

'Maelys?' he yelled.

'Lucky I tied on,' she said shakily. 'You all right?'

The tower slowly stilled. He was watching the rising sun, now several fingers' width above the horizon, when he realised that Sulien was calling him, very faintly.

*Daddy? Daddy?*

'What's the matter? Why are you calling me? Has something happened to Karan?'

*Daddy, move the crystal, right now!*

'Mechanism's heavy; it'll take a couple of minutes.'

*Quick, Daddy!*

Had she heard him? He had no idea. Llian heaved the azimuth wheel. It barely moved; the twinned crystal must weigh the best part of a ton. He heaved again and it slowly began to turn. 240 degrees. 250. 260. 270. 280. Too far! And it was as hard to stop as it had been to start. He got it back to 274 and a half degrees and dropped the latch into place.

He heaved the elevation wheel. It did not budge. Heaved again. Not a shiver.

The mental clock in his head was counting down the seconds. Two minutes gone already, and Sulien had said, *right now*. What if he couldn't reset the crystal in time? Would the whole plan fail?

He heaved again and again. Why wouldn't it move?

Ah! There was an additional lock – a pin pushed through a small hole to fix the elevation wheel in place. He yanked it out, tugged on the wheel and it started to rotate. Where were the numbers. There, on the other side. He set the elevation to 68 and three-quarter degrees and shoved the pin home.

'It's done!' he cried. 'Maelys, it's done.'

Now all they had to do was get down again – and pray that they did not encounter anyone on the way.

The front of the column of soldiers was only yards away from the entrance. Why weren't they going through? Could Durthix see through the portal to the destination? No, the sapphire tunnel must be a quarter of a mile long and it was full of mist. Perhaps, Sulien thought, he was giving final instructions to the officers who would lead the troops through and into battle.

The tower shuddered, flashed red then went blue again. The gentle breeze coming through the portal died and became a strong wind rushing into it. Durthix stepped back and waved the advance guard through, six officers leading an immaculate column 250 soldiers wide. He stood at attention as they passed by. The soldiers moved quickly, eager to get to the other end and do the job they'd been training for. The wind caught them in their backs, pushing them until they were forced to jog, as if even nature wanted this invasion to happen.

*It's open*, Sulien mind-called to Flydd, Rulke and Llian, though she had no idea if they could hear. *They're going through. But we're still trapped in the control chamber.*

It was the great flaw in M'Lainte's plan. Even if everything else went perfectly, there was no way to get out of the tower, and the last of the Merdrun were bound to kill everyone here before they entered the portal.

In only eleven minutes, by the clock on the wall, the army had gone through, and dozens of laden wagons and other gear. Only Durthix's personal guard remained. Now the civilians were entering the portal, joyously. The wind had picked up and Sulien saw one or two old people blown off their feet.

Durthix watched them for another quarter of an hour, then headed up to the control chamber, accompanied by a dozen guards. His normally hard face was glowing; he was almost overcome with joy. An allowable emotion, in the circumstances.

The sapphire portal flashed red then returned to deep, glowing blue. Skald was too overloaded by those unbearable emotions to take it in. He paced back and forwards, one part of his mind on the most glorious sight of his life, the army jogging through the portal, the other part tortured and guilty.

The ecstasy that came from life-drinking had worn off quickly this time. How could he have repudiated his oath to Uletta? How could he have drunk the life of the woman he loved and had sworn to save – the only person who had ever loved him? She was still twitching on the floor, but she could not be saved, and the agony was so awful that he considered drinking his own life to end it. No other sacrifice could measure up.

But Skald could not do that either. Not after living the torments of his victims, from the very first and most poignant, Tataste. Not after the agony he had gone through after partially drinking his own life five or six weeks ago. He did not have the courage to do that again. Perhaps he was more like his father than he had thought.

He barely noticed the last of the army running through the portal, or the civilians hurrying after them. He could imagine their joy. They were going home at last. But there was no joy left in the world for him.

When had he turned from a selflessly brave soldier, thinking only of the good of his people, to a man who had betrayed every oath he had ever sworn? How had he come to this? And was there any way out?

Skald hoped not. He just wanted the nightmare over.

Sulien saw Durthix enter the control chamber, smiling. But when he saw her on the far-seeing bench with the goggles over her eyes, he froze.

'Acting Magiz, what's going on?'

Skald looked around dazedly. 'High Commander?'

'Why is that child wearing *your* far-seeing goggles?'

'I – I don't know.'

He went a sickly green. Had the awful truth just occurred to him? Skald sat beside Sulien, checked his instruments, tore off the goggles and squinted through them, then crammed them over her eyes again.

In a panicky whisper, he said, 'Show me the destination.'

'Why are you asking her?' said Durthix. 'Lurzel, get over here.'

Lurzel slithered across.

'Why is the child wearing the far-seeing goggles?' said Durthix. 'Has she worn them before?'

'Several times. But I thought ... I assumed ... Skald said she was boosting his own far-seeing.'

Durthix swept his fist at Skald's ear, knocking him aside, and bent over Sulien. 'Did Skald far-see the destination, or did you?'

'I did,' she whispered.

'Show me.'

This was a deadly moment. If Durthix discovered the truth he might kill them all. 'I can't. Can't see Tallallame anymore.' Sulien slumped sideways and deliberately cracked her head on the hard frame of the bench. It really hurt. She lay still, watching through almost closed eyelids.

Durthix went so purple with fury that the heavy bristles of his beard stood out like quills. He heaved Skald to his feet and shook him.

'You became acting magiz under false pretences,' he thundered. 'You can't see worth a damn. *What – have-you–done?*'

'I – c-c-c – I c-c –' Skald could not get the words out.

Durthix struck him a blow that sent him flying fifteen feet across the control chamber, crashing into the chair Karan was tied to and breaking it. He rolled off her and struggled to his knees, shaking and shuddering.

Durthix tore away the straps binding Sulien to the bench and tossed her aside. 'Lurzel? You can far-see, can't you?'

'Tolerably well.'

'Check the destination!'

Lurzel sat on the bench and put the goggles over his eyes.

Durthix ran to the stairs and bellowed down at the people racing through the portal, 'Stop! Stop!'

But with the howling wind, and the thunder of tens of thousands of boots on the floor of the tunnel, they could not have heard him. He ran down further and bellowed again, but Sulien felt sure it was too late. Almost everyone had gone through.

Lurzel had the goggles over his eyes and the frame on his head, and was moving his head gently from side to side. Sulien held her breath.

Durthix ran in, panting. 'Well?'

Lurzel choked and wrenched the goggles off. 'High Commander ... I fear that the acting magiz, driven by his foul and treacherous lust for the slave architect ... has betrayed us. I can't see Tallallame at all. Admittedly, my skill at far-seeing is modest, but with so great a portal open our home world should blaze in my far-sight like the sun at midday.'

'You and you!' said Durthix, pointing to two acolytes. 'Run through to the end of the tunnel, then come back and tell me what you see.'

'I don't think they can come back, High Commander. Not into the teeth of that gale.'

'Rope together and tie your rope to the bottom of the stairs. After you've looked out, haul yourselves back.'

The acolytes ran. The last of the Merdrun were passing through, save for Durthix's personal guard. Durthix waited at the top of the stairs. Sulien lay where she had been thrown, afraid to move in case she attracted his attention.

After ten minutes neither of the acolytes had returned.

'They're taking too long,' Durthix said to Lurzel. 'How can I know if the portal opened at the correct destination?'

'Check the twinned crystal. If the azimuth and elevation are unchanged –'

'How long to get an air-floater up there?'

'Fifteen minutes, at least ... but in this wind we'd never get anyone onto the platform.'

'What about a gate?'

'No gate can be made within miles of the sapphire portal, High Commander. The small gate would be destroyed by the portal. Or worse.'

'Who's the fastest climber?' Durthix rapped to the acolytes.

'Not them. They're gifted,' said Lurzel.

'Guards?' said Durthix.

A pair of young men stepped forward. Identical twins, light and lean and sinewy.

'Run up and climb the tower. Lurzel, tell them the original azimuth and elevation, and give them a farspeaker.'

Lurzel did so.

'If the twinned crystal has been moved,' Durthix continued, 'move it back to the original position. If you find any intruders, kill them.'

The twins ran. Sulien looked across to Karan and saw her own agony reflected in Karan's eyes. Llian would still be high up the iron tower. He would not have a chance against two highly trained Merdrun.

*Help!* Sulien mind-called to Rulke and to Flydd. *We're trapped in the control chamber – and Durthix* knows.

There was no response.

# 46

## ON THE TABLET OF INFAMY

The few red lamps that still lit the chamber faded; the sapphire portal was taking a lot of power. A heavy mass of cloud covered the rising sun, plunging the room into gloom.

Already the sound of running feet was dwindling to nothing. All the Merdrun had gone through except Durthix's guards and a couple of small forces, engaged on special duties at the farthest reaches of Lauralin, who had not responded to the order to come to Skyrock and must remain in exile. A cruel fate, but not as cruel as Skald's would be.

The unbearable emotions that he, like every good Merdrun, had spent a lifetime suppressing flooded him again. Skald realised that his eyes were leaking tears and squeezed his eyelids shut, but it did not help. His mother had been right to curse and condemn him. For as long as the Merdrun lasted his name would be an infamous one, up there with Stermin himself. No, Skald's name would be more reviled. Stermin had not betrayed his people; he had just been a fanatical fool.

On the Tablet of Infamy, Skald's name would be supreme.

Karan had freed herself from the broken chair but her hands were still bound. She watched Durthix stalk back and forth, almost giving way to his own emotions – rage and fear. The mass of cloud had spread out to cover the eastern half of the sky and it was even gloomier in the control chamber now.

He sat on the far-seeing bench and put the goggles on. He had been a skilled battle mancer. Would he be able to see the true destination? If he did, their lives would be measured in seconds.

Durthix cast the goggles aside. Evidently not. He looked down through the quartz panel, ran down to the portal tunnel and out, peering up at the tower, then slowly came up the stairs, his fists clenched.

He walked across to Skald and kicked him in the head, then roared, 'Get the mess cleaned up.' The acolytes went up to the mezzanine and dragged the pitiful corpses out of sight, then began on the bodies in the control chamber.

Durthix looked down at Uletta, who lay on the floor where she had fallen. 'Leave her.'

She was barely alive, yet still she projected hatred and contempt at Skald. He could not bear to look at her.

A farspeaker buzzed. Durthix ran across and spoke into it. 'Yes?'

'There are two enemy further up,' said one of the twins. 'We're only thirty feet below them.'

'Can you identify them?'

'Llian and Maelys. And the twinned crystal is pointed the wrong way; they've changed it.'

Durthix staggered, looked around wildly. 'Where does the portal lead?'

'We don't know, High Commander.'

'Kill the intruders. Be quick!' He turned to Lurzel. 'Can you work out where our people have gone?'

'No, High Commander. Magiz Dagog did the original calculations to direct the portal to our home world, but he told no one how it was done.'

'Can it be redirected to Tallallame?'

'We don't know, High Commander. We'll have to discuss that. It'll take a little time.'

'Well, can we bring our people back here?'

'Against that wind? It won't be easy.'

'Find a way!'

'At once, High Commander.'

Durthix turned, surveying the chamber. 'Only one person could have organised all this, and it wasn't the child.'

He was looking at Karan, who saw her doom in his eyes and could do nothing about it. The guards climbing the tower would soon kill Maelys and Llian. Then Lurzel or one of the other sus-magizes would either far-see the destination in Tallallame or, if they could not redirect the portal, they would find a way to bring the Merdrun back to here.

He wrenched her gag off. 'Speak!'

'I did it,' she said, struggling to her knees. The pain in her head was almost as bad as it had been hours ago. 'I mind-called Llian and Maelys. Sent them up the tower. Told Llian to turn the crystal ... moment portal was opened.'

'Would you have me end her, High Commander?' said Lurzel.

'Drink her life, you mean?'

'It would punish her –'

'You're far too like your former master, Sus-magiz,' said Durthix. 'It's why I didn't elevate you to acting magiz. No, you will *not* end her life. Karan is bold, tenacious and brave, and I honour her for it. When it's time to put her to death I will do it, in a manner befitting an enemy hero. Besides, we may need her.'

'What for?'

'The child may have to far-see Tallallame again, and far-seeing requires absolute focus. We'll hardly get the best out of her if you've just slaughtered her mother.'

Llian was struggling down towards Maelys when she hissed, 'Someone's coming!'

A pair of guards burst out through the top door of Skyrock, ran to the rungs and began to scramble up them.

'They've been sent to kill us,' said Llian. 'And turn the crystal back.'

'Doesn't bode well for Karan and Sulien,' Maelys said soberly.

Llian could not bear to think about them. There was nothing he could do, for her or himself.

The guards were climbing fast. They would be well armed, superbly trained and aching for glory. Llian was desperately cold, his fingers so stiff and sore he could barely bend them.

'They'll reach us in ... about three minutes,' he said.

'I've got a knife,' she said, almost absently. 'And I know how to use it.'

But she was a small woman. 'They've got long arms and long knives. They'll outreach you. You'll have to come up.'

Maelys was about fifteen feet below. She took off her gloves and untied the cords binding her to the rungs. Her fingers were bloody from sharp ice. She went to put the cord in a pocket but missed and it fell. She clung to the rungs, looking down as though she had just lost a vital part of herself.

Maelys closed her bloody fingers around her taphloid for a moment, then pushed it down inside her shirt and came slowly up, one rung, two, three. She stopped and drew it again and held it in her other hand. Her teeth were bared; she must be in great pain.

The wind was gusting wildly now. Llian clawed his way up onto the platform and lay there, looking down. The sun was well up now but provided little warmth, and a thick grey cloud mass, creeping up from the south, would soon cover it.

Maelys was now stopping after every rung to clutch her taphloid. Six rungs to go. And their hunters were nearly halfway up.

She stopped, her forehead pressed against the next rung. 'I can't do it, Llian.'

'Yes, you can.'

'It's ... excruciating. Just want to let go. Just want pain to go away.'

Was she talking about the present pain, or her life and the people she'd lost? An icy gust curled around and struck at the back of Llian's neck. What if she let go?

There had to be a way to get her up, but he had no rope, and there wasn't room on the rungs for two. If he went down and tried to help her with one hand while he held on with the other, he knew what the result would be.

But he had to find a way, and it came to him. Telling the end of one of the greatest climbs in the Histories, to encourage and distract her.

'"*I can't go up*," he quoted in his most resonant Teller's voice. "*I'll fall.*"

'"*You're too close to the wall*," Karan screamed at him. "*Lean out!*"'

'Llian?' said Maelys.

'It's from the *Tale of the Mirror*,' he said in his own voice. 'Karan climbed the outside of the great tower of Katazza to try and rescue me from Tensor. But she got stuck, and like a fool I went out the window to help her – and froze in terror.'

'Go on,' she whispered.

'*But Llian couldn't; he was terrified of heights. Karan's heart was thumping so hard that she thought it would split open. In her mind's eye she saw him fall, a plunge that seemed to take hours, and the knowledge that he could do nothing to save himself roused her.*

'*Suddenly the way opened up and she found a trickle of strength she didn't know she had. She unclipped her rope, tapped out her lowest spike and forced herself up onto the highest. Reaching up, she banged the spike into a tiny gap between the slabs of lapis lazuli. Chips of blue gemstone showered down on her flaming red hair. She tried to attach her rope but the clip would not go through the eye of the spike. It was squashed flat.*'

Llian reached down towards Maelys. Her mouth was open and she was gazing up at him, mesmerised. 'One rung,' he said.

She managed a rung but stopped again.

'*Karan fastened onto the spike she was standing on and tried to hammer out the lowest one but it snapped off, a flaw in the metal. She unclipped, climbed onto the top spike but could not reach the previous one to knock it out. She'd have to go up the last bit, the hardest and most dangerous of all, free-climbing. I can't do it, she thought, but one look at Llian swaying on the platform, his white face and desperate stare, and she knew she must.*

'One rung, Maelys.'

It was much harder this time. Maelys' face was twisted in agony and twice Llian thought she was going to fall, but she got both feet onto the rung and clung to the one above her, gasping.

'*Up Karan went. She crabbed sideways to take advantage of another crack, then stretched sideways again to a crevice she could press her toe into, if she could get it there. Desperation strengthened her screaming arms, her trembling fingers for just long enough, and she did it. She got a toe to the cleft, her fingers onto the sloping ledge, and forced herself up until her face was level with Llian's feet. Her sweaty fingers slipped on the edge.*

'You can do it, Maelys. Only four to go.'

Maelys' eyes, screwed shut, were leaking tears that the wind streaked across her cheeks, but she made the next rung. Below her, the two guards were climbing rapidly. Llian had to get her to move quicker.

*'Karan jammed the point of her hammer in, then tried to pull herself up ... but her muscles refused to budge. Llian moaned. She tried again, and with a convulsive movement she was beside him on the ledge, gripping his shirt. She reached up but the rope was beyond her fingertips.*

*"Get the rope!" she said.*

*'But Llian was swaying dangerously, too afraid to open his eyes. Karan felt a burning pain in her chest. She pushed him back against the wall, slammed her pick into a beautiful crack and looped her rope around it, not that it would hold if they fell. Her knees almost folded with relief. No, don't relax! Quick, before your strength fails. Holding Llian with one hand, she struck him in the face with the back of the other.*

*"Open your eyes, you bloody idiot! Get the rope!"*

*'Llian snatched at the loop and clung to it like a lifeline.*

*"Hold it tightly and stand firm while I climb you. Ready?"*

*"Yes," he whispered.*

'Another rung, Maelys,' said Llian. 'Just one more rung.'

She managed another rung, and another after that. Only two to go. But her teeth were chattering and she still had not opened her eyes. She hooked an arm around the rung, reached into her shirt and squeezed her taphloid desperately.

'Do you think,' she said softly, 'it would help if I looked in the Mirror?'

'No!' he shrieked. 'I'll get you up, Maelys.'

*'Karan weighed Llian up, frowned, then sawed a length off her safety rope and tied it tightly around his chest. The other end she took in her teeth. Slipping beside him into a crack, and using handholds he could not even see, she climbed above him. She reached out with one foot, rested it on his shoulder, holding the makeshift rope made from his spare clothes in one hand, just a moment, even those few seconds of relaxation a marvellous relief, but knowing she dare rest no longer. The other end of Llian's rope she clipped to the loop, the fabric of her trousers caressed his face then she went up the cloth rope like a sailor, onto the glorious window ledge, up the smooth walls below the window ... and in to safety.'*

Maelys shuddered, opened her eyes for an instant, screwed them shut and went up another rung.

'You're doing brilliantly,' said Llian. 'One to go.'

Maelys did not move.

'You can do it. One rung and I'll be able to help you.'

Maelys struggled up the last rung and stopped again.

'"*Come on, Llian!*" *Karan yelled.*

'*And he tried, but climbing ropes wasn't one of his skills. She heaved and he half-climbed and was half-hauled up and over the wall, and she dumped him onto the floor. Karan lay there, gasping, unable to move. Her muscles were locked in cramp.*'

Maelys was never going to make it up over the edge of the platform by herself. Time for Llian to pay his dues. 'Give me your hand,' he said, standing up and bracing himself against the wind.

'I'm heavier than I look,' said Maelys. 'You'll never lift me.'

'I'm stronger than I look. Keep going.'

But she was moaning and shuddering, the tears now freezing on her cheeks. She reached up to catch the edge of the platform, but her arm fell. She could not do it.

Llian went down on hands and knees and crawled to the edge, keeping low where the pressure of the wind was less. He went into a crouch, held on with one hand and reached down with the other. 'Take my hand.'

Her bloody hand groped up, clutched his, but let go again.

'Don't you trust me to hold you?' he said.

'I – trust – you. Can't hold on.'

'Yes, you can.' He stretched down a little further.

This was madness. One wild gust from behind would hurl him over. But what did he have to lose? If this failed, they were both dead.

Maelys reached up again, though it was clear that she had given up. She had lost everyone that mattered to her except Nish, and she and he had been estranged for months. She just wanted to slip away.

'*Take hold of my wrist!*' he said in his most commanding Teller's voice.

Maelys obeyed, and her small hands were stronger than Llian expected. He closed his hand on her wrist with all his strength, squeezing as if he were trying to crush it. Anything less and he would not be able to hold her.

He pushed up with his thighs and leaned back into the wind. This was a deadly moment; any gust could overbalance him and tip them over. Her feet left the rungs and he was holding all her weight. She was right; she *was* heavier than she looked. She was pulling him off balance.

He leaned back further, heaved, and she was swinging through the air over an eleven-hundred-foot drop, her eyes as round as saucers. He squeezed her wrist crushingly, swung her up and around, and onto the platform. Safe! If they could ever be safe with their hunters only a hundred feet below and climbing as fast as ever.

She lay on her side, doubled up, and began to rub the silvery metal surface of the taphloid around her face. The pain seemed to ease a little.

'I'm – all – right!' said Maelys, as if she could not believe it. 'Finish the tale.'

*'Karan rolled over, pushed herself to her knees and crawled unsteadily over to Llian. Her face was white and she was trembling all over, but the miracle had happened. She was alive and he was, and they were together at last. She stood on her knees and opened her arms to him.'*

But before Llian could speak the last line, Maelys said it for him. *'"That was the stupidest thing you've ever done. And the bravest."'*

'You know the *Tale of the Mirror*?' said Llian.

'By heart. I read it over and again when I was young, and we were hiding from the God-Emperor.'

'Then why –?'

'It's one thing to know an inspiring story,' said Maelys. 'It's entirely different to have the greatest Teller in the world, the very man who was the subject of it, Tell it in a desperate attempt to save your life.'

For a moment, he glowed. But just for a moment, because she had doubled up, clenching her fists. She rubbed the taphloid across her forehead.

'Crystal's burning my mind,' she whispered. 'Know what Tiaan went through on the flight from Alcifer.'

'Does the taphloid help?'

'I'd be dead without it.'

'Just – hold on. I can't do this by myself?'

'Do what? Have you got a plan?'

'Not yet.'

## 47

## KILL THEM AND TURN IT BACK

A red-faced sus-magiz came staggering up the stairs, panting. 'Node-tapper, High Commander.'

'What about it?' said Durthix.

'New one's in place. We've got all the power we need.'

'If only you'd waited, Skald,' said Lurzel vindictively, 'you needn't have drunk your lover's life after all.'

Skald reeled and his face went red, then white, then a sickly green. 'You said there was no other way,' he whispered. 'You said it would take ages.'

'It's not a lie if you tell it to a traitor.'

'You made me attack my own true love, out of *malice*?'

'I didn't *make* you do anything, Acting Magiz. You chose your own path. And everything I *did* do, I did for the good of my people. *One for All*, Skald, not *All for One*.'

Lurzel, who clearly had been loyally serving his despicable former magiz all this time, had destroyed him. No, Dagog had. He'd had the last laugh after all.

No, be honest. Skald had destroyed himself.

He forced himself up on trembling legs. Nothing left now but to confess. Even if they succeeded in directing the portal back to Tallallame, there could be no going home for him. No forgiveness either. Nothing good would ever come his way again, but at least he would face his cruel end with courage.

'High Commander.' Forbidden tears ran down Skald's cheeks but he did not wipe them away. He was nothing! He raised his voice. 'High Commander, sus-magizes, acolytes and guards. I must confess my crimes.'

Durthix was looking at him in utter contempt. The sus-magizes' rigidly controlled faces showed nothing, but he had been one of them and knew what they were thinking. He had committed the worst betrayal of all and must be publicly executed, with savage and prolonged cruelty, in front of the entire Merdrun nation.

'Though I knew it was forbidden, I took Uletta as my lover. I conspired with her to save her fellow slaves and escape to a distant land, to abandon my own people and break my most solemn oath. I lied to the former magiz about my gift for far-seeing, and lied again to Durthix. I passed Sulien's far-seeing gift off as my own – and I killed the magiz –'

'*What?*' cried Durthix.

Skald had to get it all out. 'Dagog ordered me to check the spellcaster and make it safe for him. I checked it and felt sure the dwarf had subtly restored it to its former deadly state, but I did not make it safe.'

'Why – *not?*' Durthix was almost apoplectic with fury.

'Dagog always hated me, because of my father's ... c-cowardice. From the moment I was made sus-magiz he longed to drink my life, and soon he would have. And also –'

'What?' said Durthix.

Skald could not have said it while the magiz was alive, but he could now. Not that it would save him. 'The magiz had me train Sulien to far-see because he planned to drink her life, *and* her great gift, and use it to overthrow you and restore the supremacy of the magizes, and the old ways.'

Durthix went very still. He was thinking it through.

'I've dishonoured myself in every way, High Commander, but I speak truly. I overheard Dagog talking to Yallav about it. There was only one thing to do, to save the True Purpose and myself. I let him take the spellcaster, hoping it would kill him ... though I – I did not know he planned to demonstrate it to a roomful of generals and senior sus-magiz. I –'

'Enough!' said Durthix, very softly now.

'I haven't finished confessing.'

'You could not betray your magiz's treasonous plot against me, yet you could *conspire to have him killed*?' Durthix said incredulously.

He punched Skald in the mouth, knocking him down. It was a tremendous blow and Skald could feel broken teeth and a mouth full of blood. He tried to rise but Durthix put a huge boot in the middle of his chest, pressing him down, then tore Skald's rue-har from around his neck and, with its sharpest point, scored through the Merdrun glyph on his forehead until it was an unreadable mess.

He slashed Skald's face, again and again, ritually mutilating him. The pain was awful but Skald endured it in silence. The message – utter rejection and exile from his people – was not so easy to bear. But he deserved it.

'Sus-magizes, acolytes,' Durthix said, beckoning them, 'you will bear witness.'

They gathered around Skald, who did not move. He had to take his punishment.

Durthix bent, still holding the shard between thumb and fingers, and slowly lowered it towards Skald's right eye.

And it broke him. 'No!' he cried. '*Not that.*'

'So you *are* a coward,' said Durthix contemptuously. 'Dagog was right about that as well.'

Durthix thrust the shard into Skald's eye and twisted. Skald felt a blinding flash of pain then all sight in that eye was gone.

Durthix thrust the shard in until it penetrated bone at the back of Skald's eye socket. 'You are acting magiz no longer. You are nothing.' He wrenched the shard out and tossed it onto the floor.

Uletta made a choking sound that might have been bitter laughter, then the light drained out of her eyes. Such agony tore through Skald that he arched up from the floor until only his boot heels and the back of his head touched anything solid. Durthix forced him down again.

'Take the coward down to the portal,' he said to the acolytes. 'Keep him safe. His torment has just begun.'

Four acolytes hauled Skald down the stairs. He did not struggle. He was incapable of doing anything but suffering.

The wind was howling into the sapphire portal now. Ahead he could see nothing but mist; no way to tell where he was going. The acolytes, forming a human chain from the bottom of the stairs so they would not be carried through as well, pushed him out into the gale.

It carried him forwards and he had to run, or rather stumble, to prevent himself from falling over and sliding along the tunnel floor on his bloody face.

Despite the wind, the passage seemed interminable. Had this mighty portal, surely the largest ever created, stretched out even time itself?

The wind died, the shimmering blue light was gone, and he was falling out the exit for ten or fifteen feet, then tumbling down a steep slope with loose rocks and gravel rattling down with him. Wrecked wagons lay here and there, their contents spilled. But Skald did not smell the cool, humid, forest-spiced air he would have smelled on Tallallame, the lushest and most beautiful of the Three Worlds. It was hot here and smelled of baked rock and pungent, burning brimstone. It was also dry. Very dry.

The mist cleared and with his one eye he saw the awful truth. The portal had discharged all three hundred thousand Merdrun into a steep-sided crater, a scorching landscape of bare black rock and red, scalded earth that no one could ever have confused with Tallallame. Steam and white fumes issued up from cracks here and there.

A small red sun beat down on his head. There was not a tree or a bush. No shade of any kind, and the floor of the crater sloped up on all sides to sheer, unclimbable walls of shiny black rock. It was a sweltering, waterless prison, and the irony was a bitter one. For all their existence the Merdrun had sought to escape the void into which they had been exiled long ago, only to be imprisoned in a barren wilderness.

Skald's catastrophic folly had sent the entire Merdrun nation here, condemned them. His betrayal was a thousand times worse than he had imagined up in the control chamber. He turned and looked back towards the portal's exit, a huge, misty circle high above. Durthix might well call his people back, but it would not be easy to reach the exit and go back against that howling gale.

Several groups of Merdrun came towards him, but stopped and backed away. Everyone seeing him would know what his ritual defacement meant. He was the foulest traitor of all, the sus-magiz who had robbed them of their aeons-long dream, and the agent of their ruin.

They wanted to tear his limbs from his body, but everyone knew better than to lay a finger on someone who had been so savagely marked. The prescribed punishment would be exacted in due course, to the last splinter of fingernail and the last shred of bone.

'What have you done to us?' said Halia, the most senior of the surviving generals. 'Where is this place?'

'Aachan,' Skald said dully. 'The red-headed bitch sent us here to enslave us. We've been in thrall ever since the day Merdrax cut his leader's cube from the Crimson Gate and cast its corrupt enchantment on every one of us. And now we're slaves in truth.'

For the Merdrun, who had always prided themselves on being superior to all and answerable to no other, it was their worst nightmare.

# 48

# TIRING OF THE GAME

While Durthix was ritually mutilating Skald and taking him down to the tunnel, Sulien lay on the floor of the wrecked control chamber, where she had been thrown, watching through one slitted eye.

Karan was on her side in the wreckage of the chair, surreptitiously trying to free her hands and feet. There was no sign of Jassika. Was she dead? Had her body been dragged away and dumped with the others? The thought was unbearable. Not brave, bold, reckless Jass.

*Help!* Sulien called again. *We're trapped in the control chamber and it's really bad. Help, help!*

No response. No sign that anyone had heard her call.

Then, as Skald was being dragged down to the portal, she felt a little *tap-tap* in the middle of her head.

*We're coming,* said Rulke. *Can you hold out?*

*Where are you?*

He was gone without saying whether he was two minutes away, or twenty. Even two minutes was likely to be too late.

Durthix came back and went into a huddle with Lurzel and Ghiar, the other surviving sus-magiz. Sulien could not hear what they were saying.

They separated and Durthix said, 'This time, you will show me the destination first.'

'We can't far-see well enough, High Commander,' said Lurzel. 'But you could try your leader's cube on the girl.'

Durthix took the small red cube from around his neck, bent and touched one face to Sulien's forehead. The arid, cliff-bound crater flashed into her mind.

'Where is that?' said Durthix. Clearly, he and the sus-magiz had seen it too.

'I don't know,' said the sus-magiz.

Durthix heaved Karan onto her back with the toe of his boot, cut off the gag and held his sword vertically above her throat. 'Well?'

Sulien's heart almost stopped. If he let the hilt slide through his fingers, the weight of the sword would pin Karan to the floor.

'Aachan,' she croaked.

'Why did you send my people there?'

'To save *my* people.'

He struck the side of her head with the flat of his sword and Karan doubled up. Sulien felt the ringing in her mother's head and saw the bright spots before Karan's eyes. Durthix strode to the farspeaker and called the guards climbing the tower.

*They'll be dead within minutes,* said the twin with the farspeaker. *Do you want us to turn the crystal back?*

'Not yet!' said Lurzel. 'We have to think it through – see if it's possible.'

'Why wouldn't it be?' said Durthix.

'Interworld portals are enigmatic, High Commander. Much trickier than local gates; far more dangerous, and less predictable. We have to be sure.'

'Don't move the crystal until I give the order,' said Durthix through the farspeaker.

The leading guard was only eighty feet below. Maelys was doubled up near the edge of the platform, as far as she could get from the crystal. Llian went down on his hands and knees and prowled around the great mechanism, looking for something to use as a weapon. He could feel the immense power of the twinned crystal blazing on his face, frizzing his hair and drying him out like a corpse in the desert, but there was nothing he could use to defend them.

Wait, what about the copper braid that had given him that nasty shock? He put on his gloves and touched it with a fingertip, but felt nothing. He went to the other end, where the braid, covered in windings of lacquered cloth, passed down into the wooden dowel, and heaved. It did not budge. Llian got out his knife, made sure he was holding it where there were no holes in his glove, and hacked at the braid.

Sparks fountained into the air, a shock leapt up his arm and he was hurled onto his back again. The braid had melted into a clot where the knife had touched it.

He worked the braid back and forth at the clot until it snapped, and unreeled it from around the mechanism, holding the cloth-covered section with the exposed copper sticking out.

'It's not much of a weapon,' said Maelys.

'All I've got.'

The two guards were only twenty feet below now, and climbing fast. They looked like identical twins. How relentless their training must be, to have come so far, so quickly. He felt a shiver of fear. The leading guard drew his knife and held it between his teeth.

Llian's best chance was to attack the guard as he climbed onto the platform. If he got up here, he would kill Llian and Maelys in seconds. Llian took off his coat, the icy wind searing into him, threaded the wrapped braid down through his right sleeve and put the coat on again.

The guards stopped six feet below and leaned out, the better to see. Using his gloves, Llian wrapped the bare braid around his knife, just below the hilt. A few red sparks fell to the platform. He held the knife out, knowing any competent fighter would penetrate his defences in seconds.

So quickly that Llian barely saw him move, the first guard reached the edge of the platform and pulled himself up. He was on the platform, rising to his feet, snatching the long knife from between his teeth and reaching out.

I'm a dead man, Llian thought.

He slashed with his blade. The guard laughed, easily evaded the blow and lunged. Llian threw himself backwards, fell hard against the elevation wheel and had nowhere to go. The guard reached down to thrust his knife into Llian's belly. Llian swung wildly, trying to protect himself. A foot of unwrapped braid slipped from his coat sleeve and the blade of the guard's knife struck it.

*Crack-crack!*

An almighty shock slammed Llian against the elevation wheel again. Red sparks fountained up and the guard was hurled backwards. He landed on the edge of the platform, his arms wheeling, a look of disbelief on his handsome face, and toppled out of sight.

The second guard, who was about to climb onto the platform, cried, 'Timli, no!'

Llian rose, his back aching and his hand partly numb, took hold of the hilt in his smoking glove and held it out. He had survived through good fortune, not skill, and he could not do it twice.

'Don't let him get onto the platform,' said Maelys.

'Don't touch any metal with your skin.'

As the guard came up in a rush, Llian jammed his blade against the iron edge. Again the shock, the cracking and a great fountain of sparks. The guard stiffened, his short hair stood on end and his clothes burst into flame. His fingers lost grip and he fell after his brother.

'That,' said Maelys after a long silence, 'was legendary.'

Llian could not speak. He had just killed two people and it was hard to take in, hard to cope. He felt very cold now.

'What now?' she said.

He looked down and saw a red-clad acolyte at the tower door. She appeared to be talking into a farspeaker. 'They're bound to send more attackers.'

'And they won't be defeated so easily.'

Llian moved as close to the twinned crystal as he dared, for it was warmer there, leaned back and closed his eyes. Was Karan all right? Was Sulien? He had no way of knowing ... but it was hard to think so. The odds had always been too great.

It had probably all been for nothing.

The shard-like rue-har, which Durthix had used to put out Skald's right eye, was a few yards away from Sulien. It was a perilous magical thing, but it was also a weapon of sorts. She edged towards it.

'What? He killed *both* guards?' said Durthix into the farspeaker.

Sulien's eyes flooded. Daddy had beaten them! But he wasn't safe yet. No one was.

'Keep watch!' said Durthix. 'I'm sending up four this time.'

Durthix picked them from his personal guard – not young and lithe ones, as before, but big, scarred veterans. 'Climb to the top of the iron tower with all possible speed. Hack Llian and Maelys into gobbets and hurl them down. Stay there and be ready to turn the crystal when I give the order.'

The four guards, who wore swords, helms and leather armour, ran out.

Llian could not survive again. *Rulke, Flydd*, she sent. *Four guards are going up to the iron tower. Stop them or they'll undo everything.*

There was no way of telling if her mind-calls were getting through.

Durthix beckoned to Lurzel and the other sus-magizes. 'Who among you can far-see clearly enough to find the destination on Tallallame?'

Sulien took the rue-har and surreptitiously rubbed it on the leg of her pants, to make sure none of Skald's tainted blood remained.

After a long silence, Lurzel said, 'None of us, High Commander. Far-seeing is a rare ability. And seeing clearly enough to open a dimensional portal to another world is vanishingly rare.'

'Lucky I didn't kill the child, then.'

They all turned towards Sulien. She trembled. If there was no way to find the destination in Tallallame again, maybe they wouldn't bother with Llian. She held up the rue-har, so they could all see it, then pressed it to the centre of her forehead and thrust. Pain speared through her skull.

'It's gone,' she said, dropping the rue-har.

'What's gone?' said Durthix.

'My far-seeing gift.'

'She's lying,' said Lurzel. 'There's little power in a rue-har when wielded by someone ungifted.'

'But she *is* gifted,' Durthix said dully. 'If it's gone, our people are condemned.'

'Will you follow them to Aachan, High Commander?'

'While a single Merdrun remains free, we'll keep searching for a way to liberate them – and take them home.'

He did not sound confident. 'Put a blade to her mother's throat,' said Lurzel, 'and take the child to the far-seeing bench. We'll soon see if she's lying.'

'What if she's not?'

'Use the knife – on both of them.'

Lurzel heaved Karan into an unbroken chair, tied her again and pressed a serrated blade to her throat. Two acolytes carried Sulien to the far-seeing bench and put the goggles over her eyes.

As she moved her head, she caught a glimpse of Karan's throat, and the knife, magnified by the goggles. Little drops of bright red blood welled out from the points of the serrations. Sulien felt a scream building. Past traumas were rising in her subconscious and she could not hold them back much longer. If they flooded her, she would lose it as badly as Skald had when she had flooded him.

Sulien fought them down. Everything depended on her now. *Hurry,* she mind-called, *or they'll bring the Merdrun back from Aachan. Go to the iron tower first, or they'll kill Daddy and turn the crystal back.*

But even if Rulke did come, what could he do when Durthix still had eleven guards here, and probably more below? Besides, Rulke could not be in two places at once.

The five paintings were replaced in front of Sulien and one of the acolytes turned the knurled knobs of the goggles until the images came into sharp focus. Her head throbbed. She did not know what to hope for – success or failure.

She glanced at the first image, and instantly the destination on Tallallame sprang into her mind, just as it had before. She did not need to look at the other four paintings but she did anyway, studying each of them in turn in a desperate attempt to gain time. She grimaced and held her head.

But she could only gain time for Karan. There was no more she could do for Llian or Maelys.

'Report!' said Durthix from some distance away.

The acolyte's voice came from the farspeaker. 'I can hear the guards running up the stairs towards me. In five minutes the job will be done.'

*The job* meant killing Daddy. Oh, to have that rotten acolyte in her power!

'Well, Lurzel?' said Durthix.

'Do you have the destination on Tallallame?' hissed Lurzel, his snake eyes glittering.

'Almost,' lied Sulien. 'Far-seeing gives me really bad aftersickness. Can't think.'

'You don't need to think, just far-see,' said Durthix. 'Encourage her, Lurzel.'

'Pressing the blade against your mother's throat,' said Lurzel. 'If I cough or twitch, or my hand shakes –'

Sulien could see the blood, a lot more than before. She was beaten. 'I – I have the destination.'

Durthix let out a small, choked-off cry of joy. 'Is the portal still powered, Susmagiz?'

'Yes,' said Lurzel.

'Can you redirect it from Aachan to Tallallame?'

'I don't think so.'

Durthix went very still. 'Why not?'

'Tallallame can only be reached via Santhenar. It's why we came here in the first place. But does it count if the Tallallame portal was re-directed to Aachan the moment it opened?'

'Well, does it?' said Durthix.

'We don't think so, High Commander. But … Dagog kept that kind of knowledge to himself.'

'Dagog kept far too much to himself, curse his treasonous heart and shattered bones. If the portal goes wrong, will everyone in it be annihilated?'

'We believe so,' said Lurzel. 'And we won't be able to reopen it.'

Durthix cursed. Sulien turned so she could see Karan, and wished she hadn't. Ribbons of blood were running down her neck.

'It's still open to Aachan. We'll fix lines of ropes to the floor of the tunnel and throw the ends out the exit so our people can haul themselves back – as many as can come through in the next six hours. Then Sulien will reopen the portal to Tallallame and they'll go through as planned. We can do it. There's still time. You,' Durthix said to one of his guards, 'run down and tell my troops to get the ropes out of the main storeroom, and get it done.'

The guard ran out and down the stairs. Sulien was crushed. Everything they had done, so painfully, was about to be undone. A minute passed. Then another.

A tiny reflection, in the gloom high above, caught her eye. Jassika was up there, reaching out with a bare foot towards one of the cables that held the massive iron Merdrun glyph suspended. Surely she wasn't planning to walk across it?

She stepped out onto the cable. Sulien had seen her rope-walk before, in Thurkad, but she'd had a pole to keep her balance then. Jassika had nothing here. If she fell, she would break her ankles and someone would cut her throat.

Jassika swayed, recovered, swayed, recovered again and went forwards. But what on earth did she plan to do? She wasn't carrying a weapon, or anything she could drop on an enemy's head.

*Guards will reach the top of the tower in the next minute,* said the acolyte through the farspeaker.

'Keep talking,' replied Durthix. 'Tell me everything.'

Sulien caught Karan's eye, magnified through the goggles. Her face was the white of an egg and her eyes were swollen and staring. It brought back that ghastly scene in the cave, after the triplets magiz stabbed her in the belly so she would slowly die.

But Sulien hadn't been totally helpless, then. She did not think she could take any more. Again she felt a scream building up and fought to contain it. It was all up to her and she couldn't do it. She had nothing left.

She glanced up again. Jassika was halfway across to the suspended glyph now but there was a tremor in her left knee. She was going to fall!

*Llian's at the edge, holding a puny little knife.* The acolyte laughed derisively. *The guards are going up on all four sides. Whatever he did last time, it won't work again.*

The door on the northern side of the control chamber edged open and Sulien saw shadows moving behind it. Her heart gave a little jump. The surviving guards, acolytes and sus-magiz were watching Durthix. But even if Rulke was behind the door, what could he do?

*The guards are just below the platform. Llian has nowhere to go.*

*Boom!* The door slammed open and Rulke exploded in, followed by a host of gaunt, long-faced Whelm, their faces lit by a savage joy. The perfect master they had sworn to serve an aeon ago was back and their greatest desire was to fight alongside him.

They hurled themselves at the enemy, taking them by surprise, and most of the acolytes were cut down in seconds. The guards were fighting furiously but they were greatly outnumbered, and Sulien saw the moment when Durthix knew they were beaten.

'It's over,' he panted. 'Kill Karan and the child!'

Sus-magiz Ghiar was creeping towards the chair Karan was tied to. Sulien heaved at her straps but could not loosen them. She could not help her.

Jassika ran the last ten yards along the cable and sprang onto one jagged arm of the Merdrun glyph, which tilted. She threw her weight the other way, steadied it, pulled out the knoblaggie and reached down to the ring where the two cables on the far side attached to the arm. A searing white flash severed the ring and the glyph swung down on the other pair of cables like a pendulum.

Jassika rode it down in an arc, threw her weight to one side, the glyph swung sideways and the sharp end of one of its arms struck Ghiar in the back and went straight through her.

Jassika fell off, rolled over and threw up.

Sulien freed one hand, then the other. Lurzel, serrated blade in hand, was edging towards Karan, trying not to be noticed. Sulien pulled one of the framed paintings off the stand and scurried after him. As he reached Karan, Sulien raised the painting high and slammed it down on his head. The wooden panel split and Lurzel's head came through, leaving the painting around his serpentine neck like a huge rectangular necklace. She spun it and the splintered wood tore into his throat.

He was reeling around, trying to free himself, when one of the Whelm hacked him down. Sulien took the serrated knife, cut Karan free and dragged her out of the way.

'Look away, darling,' said Karan. 'You don't need to see this.'

And Sulien could not hold it back any longer. 'I keep seeing the triplets magiz stabbing you,' she said in a panicky voice. 'And Dagog coming for us at Stibbnibb. He stank like a dead dog. And Skald drinking Uletta's life. Mummy, I can't breathe – I can't –'

Karan put her arms around her. 'Hold it down, just until we get away.'

'What about Daddy?' Sulien wailed.

Karan hugged her desperately.

The chamber was littered with dead and dying, Durthix taking on two or three Whelm at a time and fighting like a berserker – as if it was the one thing left that he could control. Most of the Whelm were down now.

He had dropped the farspeaker when the attack began. Someone spoke through it, though Sulien could not make out the words. She did not want to know; it could only be the worst news. But she had to know.

She pulled free and crawled across to it. 'What did you say?' she said in the deepest voice she could manage, though no one could have mistaken it for a Merdrun.

*He's fallen!* the acolyte said shrilly. *He's –*

Sulien choked, then her eyes burned and tears ran down her face. The second last of the Whelm kicked it aside and she heard no more.

Durthix cut down the last of the Whelm. He was the only Merdrun standing, but he was so superior that he wasn't even out of breath. He sprang at Rulke and they fought hand to hand, and Karan could see that they were well-matched. Rulke was bigger and had a longer reach, but whenever he made a stroke that pulled on the long scar in his side, he winced. He kept looking towards the doorway, as if expecting reinforcements, but no one came.

Durthix was taking advantage, constantly attacking that side, his blows getting ever closer. He had drawn blood three times, and his next strike cut a gash between two of Rulke's lower ribs.

It was not a bad wound, but it slowed him, and Durthix drove him backwards towards the door through which Rulke had entered. His rear foot slipped on blood and the movement drew a gasp from him. Rulke tried desperately to recover but fell to his knees, exposing his neck.

Karan cried out as Durthix moved into position, his big, square teeth bared, the sword drawn back as he prepared for a beheading blow. Rulke knew he was going to die, and Karan could not bear to watch. The moment he fell, Durthix would butcher her, Sulien and Jassika.

Durthix was about to swing the blade down when Jassika ran towards him.

'Jass, no!' cried Sulien.

Jassika hurled a small, brassy object at Durthix. And all her stone-throwing in the forests at Stibbnibb paid off, because it struck him a glancing blow on the right temple and his stroke went astray. Rulke scrambled backwards.

Durthix stood there for a moment, rubbing his temple and swaying, then went after Rulke, determined to finish him off. But a curvy woman with shining opaline hair raced through the doorway, carrying a blue-bladed sword, and put herself between Durthix and Rulke.

'Where did *you* get to?' said Rulke.

'Rulke's mine,' she said to Durthix. 'You won't touch him.'

Durthix laughed derisively. He was much taller and his sword was a foot longer. 'You won't last a stroke.'

But she sprang to one side, so quickly that she was a blur, and lunged, penetrating his defences and gliding the point of her sword upwards to draw blood from his thick upper lip. She leapt backwards.

'I could have cut you anywhere,' she said, with a provocative little bow. 'I'll take your blade ... *if* you care to surrender.'

Durthix looked disconcerted and Karan was amazed, because Lirriam did not look like a fighter. How could anyone move so fast?

Durthix lunged and directed a flurry of blows at her. She casually parried each cut and thrust and slash as if she had twice as much time as he did.

'Surrender?' she said.

'Merdrun do not surrender!' he thundered.

'Right shoulder, then.' Lirriam cut him there.

He attacked even more furiously and she retreated a couple of steps, then said, 'Left eyebrow.'

Her surgical stroke went through it from left to right, flooding blood into Durthix's eye. He dashed it away and came at her again, swinging wildly now, trying to batter her down with sheer power.

'Left knee,' said Lirriam. 'Right thigh. Left forearm.'

Neat cuts appeared across his left knee and right thigh, the latter nicking the artery and spurting blood. The third blow took his left arm off at the elbow, creating another bloody fountain.

Durthix was weakening and Lirriam, clearly tiring of the game, slammed the flat of her blade across the side of his head, knocking him to his knees. She scored across the black Merdrun glyph on his forehead as if cancelling it, kicked the sword from his hand and, while it was spinning through the air, cut it in two with her blue-bladed weapon.

'Who are you?' he whispered, trying to staunch his bleeding arm and thigh at the same time. 'Where did you come by such power?'

'I'm the last of the Five Heroes who came out of the void and founded the land of Hightspall, on another world,' she said. 'Before that, I was what the Merdrun would have been if you hadn't corrupted yourselves – with this!'

Lirriam drew a foot-long crystal from the small pack on her back and held it up. *The greater good requires the doing of evil to evil*, she said softly, reading the script etched down each of the long sides.

'How dare you take our Founder's Stone? You defile it by touching it.'

She tossed it aside like a piece of rubbish. Durthix pressed his lips to his leader's cube, whispered something, then dived for the Founder's Stone. But as he soared past, Lirriam ripped the cube from his neck and he fell sprawling onto the quartz plate in the floor, his arm and thigh pulsing blood, and the stone skidded away.

She thrust the blue sword into the quartz plate, and it shattered. Durthix fell through and plummeted a hundred feet, landing on four of his guard and flattening them. A blast of wind caught the dead, and the broken but still living, and tumbled them through the portal to Aachan.

Rulke nodded his thanks and Lirriam bowed and stepped back. He came across to Karan and lifted her to her feet. She looked deathly and Sulien felt no better.

Rulke picked up the farspeaker. 'Let's have it.'

*We're coming down*, croaked Llian. *We're safe. Are Karan and Sulien –?*

'Llian?' Karan shrieked, snatching the farspeaker and pressing it to her forehead, her eyes, her lips. 'You're alive?'

*What about Sulien?*

'I'm good, Daddy,' she whispered. 'I'm really good now. How did you do it this time?'

*I didn't do anything. You did.*

'But – what?'

*You called Rulke and he sent a dozen Whelm up. The enemy were climbing up over the sides of the platform when the Whelm got them with crossbow bolts.*

'But the guards were wearing armour,' said Karan.

'From below,' said Rulke, smiling grimly, 'there are certain places that armour doesn't cover.'

Karan swayed, looking as though she were going to faint. Rulke caught her.

Sulien took the farspeaker. 'Come down, Daddy.'

*Don't worry*, said Llian. *I'm not climbing anything higher than a bar stool, ever again.*

Rulke drew Karan aside. 'When this is all wrapped up,' he said quietly, 'go and sort things out with him.'

Karan's shaky smile vanished. 'What are you talking about?'

'Lies and secrets! They've festered too long.'

'Mind your own damned business!'

'It is my business, because Llian saved me, and more importantly, he saved Lirriam.'

'So?'

'If you don't want him, I've got a job for him, one that will take him away for years.'

Karan had to sit down. 'What job?'

'Just sort things out.'

# 49

# TO BECOME SLAVES, OR DIE

S kald slumped in the middle of the crater, his once handsome face grotesquely mutilated and his blind eye weeping. He was isolated, despised, condemned, and full of self-loathing and despair. And doomed to relive Uletta's agonies, and his betrayal of her and his people, for as long as he lived.

His people were lost and desperate. They had food in their packs and supply wagons but not water, since Tallallame was a rainy world and water could be had everywhere. There was none here, and it was sweltering in the sun-baked crater. Before the day was done the children, the old and the frail would begin to die of thirst. A few days later even the strongest and hardiest would be gone.

But that was not the worst. Skald's betrayal, and the failure of their high commander and magiz to realise that they had been duped, had robbed them of faith in their leaders. And the loss of the Founder's Stone, their Sacred Text for all the aeons of their existence, had crushed them.

Their deputed leaders, none of them a former general or sus-magiz, had no option but to bargain with the Aachim who watched from the rim of the crater. Skald, kneeling among the hot stones, knew it was going to be a hard bargain, though not hard enough for him. In a thousand lifetimes he could never atone for the ruin he had brought on his people.

'We're a deliberative and isolationist folk,' said Malien, hovering above them on a flying platform, out of arrow range. 'It wasn't easy for us to come together and take such a momentous gamble, in such haste. But we're the better for it. We have to grow, or fail.'

'Make your point,' said the Merdrun's leader, a grey-haired old woman called Yix.

'For your crimes, the Merdrun nation is sentenced to thirty years of hard labour, to help make parts of Aachan habitable again. If you serve your sentence faithfully, and submit to moral instruction to recover the humanity that you cast away long ago, *and learn the lesson*,' Malien did not sound hopeful, 'at the end of that time you may negotiate the terms of your freedom.'

'But ... that's enslavement,' said Yix.

It was the one punishment the Merdrun, who had always believed themselves free, and superior, could not bear.

'It's nothing compared to the savagery you inflicted on your victims, or the bloody trail of terror your people carved across the void for thousands of years.'

'It was necessary.'

'Liar! Your armies did not fight and conquer a hundred other races living in the terrible void for any noble purpose. You slew and conquered, then abandoned all you had won – taking nothing to improve the lives of the Merdrun you claimed to be fighting for, because your leaders wanted your people to remain hungry and desperate. You killed and destroyed for one purpose only – to train yourselves for the final battle, thousands of years in the future. The battle you will never fight.'

'We – will – fight,' said Yix. 'One day.'

'What about this day?' said Malien. 'Will you give up your weapons and accept the offer – or should I come back in a week?'

Skald knew Yix would accept. The Merdrun had no choice but to become slaves, or die. And accept Yix did.

The Aachim lowered tanks of water, then left them in the crater to bury their dead, among them Durthix and the four soldiers he had crushed in his fall.

Skald staggered across to Yix. 'I deserve death too,' he said brokenly. 'Will you give it to me?'

Yix magically raised her voice, so every one of the three hundred thousand Merdrun could hear. 'The former acting-magiz and self-admitted traitor begs for death. Will you give it to him?'

The few who cried 'Yes!' were drowned out by the majority's roar, 'Never!'

'Your people have spoken,' said Yix. 'We're going to work very hard to keep you alive, Coward and Traitor Skald, and prolong your agony for the full term of our enslavement. You will be the lowest of the low, a slave to the slaves – and every day will begin, and end, with a recital of your treacheries and betrayals – including your betrayal of the woman you claimed to love.'

Skald screamed until he tore the lining of his throat and began to cough up blood. The emotions, that he had never learned to deal with, overwhelmed him.

∾

'The Merdrun have accepted Malien's terms,' said Karan after Malien broke the link. Skald's tormented face was seared into her memory and his agony still rang in her ears. 'What do we do now?'

She knew what she needed to do. Have it out with Llian, before it was too late. But that was not something they could do in public, nor when they were exhausted and traumatised.

'The portal is closed but the war isn't over,' said Flydd, who had recovered a little in the night. 'Whilever Skyrock exists, it will be a temptation and a threat.'

'The Merdrun are clever,' said Rulke, 'and relentless. They might secretly raise another magiz and find a way to reopen the sapphire portal. It all has to be brought down, and Skyrock, the iron tower and the sapphire-lined tunnel destroyed.

'Right now,' said Flydd, 'I'd have trouble knocking down a sandcastle.'

# 50

# NOTHING COULD COMFORT HIM NOW

Aviel was on the lookout platform when the construct set down next to the sky galleon in a corner of the compound at 9 a.m. An eight-sided stone pavilion stood nearby, its ceiling studded with glowing sapphires, and next to it was a well lined with neatly cut stone, with a rim of surplus blue stone. It was the most tranquil spot in Skyrock.

With the portal closed and the wards broken, gates could be made to Skyrock, and Flydd had brought the sky galleon and Nish back, and the contents of Aviel's scent potion tent, though not Yggur or Tulitine. The exhausted survivors lay on stretchers wherever they could find protection from the chilly wind.

All but the only one Aviel had eyes for. Wilm was kneeling on a folded canvas in the shadow cast by the wall, twenty yards from everyone else, holding Ilisial's hand.

Aviel limped across. Ilisial's lips were blue and she was barely breathing. Was she dying?

'Wilm,' Aviel said softly. 'I'm so sorry. I was so afraid. I –'

He glanced at her, and his eyes lit up momentarily, but he nodded and said, 'Thank you,' as if she were no more than a distant acquaintance. He turned back to Ilisial.

It was crushing, but she tried to make allowances. Wilm and Ilisial had worked together for ages and it must be unbearable to see her like this. Yet Wilm was Aviel's oldest and dearest friend, and she sat quietly in the background in case he needed her.

Lirriam came. She was a great healer and a master of Arts no one on Santhenar had ever heard of. She studied the jagged scabs on Ilisial's high forehead, looked into her eyes, and pressed her head to Ilisial's head for a minute or two, her head cocked as if listening to what was going on inside.

Wilm explained what had happened down at the gift-burner.

'And before that?' said Lirriam

'She saw her whole family brutalised and murdered in the war. When she was a little girl. But that's not for me to talk about.'

'What about at the Sink of Despair?'

'Skald started to drink her life. I stopped him, but Ilisial hasn't been the same since. And when her gift was burned out ... I – I felt her agony, though I'm not the least bit gifted.'

'So did I,' Lirriam said quietly. 'From miles away. I'm sorry, Wilm. Some troubles can't be healed.'

He grabbed her hands. 'You've got to try.'

Lirriam gently disengaged him. 'That would be cruel. The only good thing left in Ilisial's life was her work ... and the gift-burner robbed her of it. She just doesn't want to go on.'

'But ... why can't you heal her?'

'No one can heal a burned-out gift. The only thing you can do is be with her until the end. That will comfort her.'

But not Wilm. She was wasting away before his eyes, and he was shrivelling with her. It tore at Aviel's heart.

People came up to shake his hand and congratulate him for all he'd done under the node and at the gift-burner, but he could not acknowledge them. Wilm could only see his own failure, and not even the astounding victory over the Merdrun moved him.

'I let her down, just as I failed Dajaes,' he said brokenly. 'She's dying because of me.'

Aviel kept her silence. Nothing could comfort him now. She reached out to him but he shrugged her off. He just wanted to be alone with Ilisial.

Aviel went away, hurting desperately.

A hundred yards away, M'Lainte was sitting with her back to the well, also dying. Tiaan, Nish, Maelys, Karan, and the others were gathered around. Karan wiped her eyes. She was going to miss the wonderful, cheerful and immensely competent old woman, without whose brilliance and generosity none of them would be here now.

'Pour me another glass, Xervish,' said M'Lainte. 'This one's got a hole in it.' She laughed, choked and laughed some more.

'I don't know what you're so damned cheerful about,' he muttered, as he uncorked another of the good bottles from the sky galleon.

'This is the best day of my life for dying. The sun's come out, the enemy have been vanquished and delivered to an ironically appropriate punishment, there's good wine and cheese, and I'm surrounded by old friends and new.' M'Lainte gazed in Wilm's direction and her smile faded for a moment. 'Most of them.'

'What happened?' said Karan. 'Last night you looked well enough, considering.'

'After all Skald's life drinking, and Sulien's emotional deluge, Tiaan and I took advantage of the chaos.' M'Lainte stopped to catch her breath. 'Shouldn't have run up all those flights of stairs, though.' She stopped again, panting. 'Burst something inside.'

'Why were you running up the stairs?' said Llian.

'Something we had to do,' M'Lainte said vaguely. 'Doesn't matter now.' She quaffed her glass and held it out for a refill.

'Might be an idea to take it easy,' muttered Flydd.

'Says the world champion pisspot. If you don't lighten up, Xervish, I'll spill the beans on the night you took advantage of an innocent young artisan who'd had one too many ales –'

'*I* took advantage?' he cried. 'You weren't exactly young, and you certainly weren't innocent. I was a junior scrutator, yet you threw me over your shoulder like a sack of turnips and carried me back to your room. The indignity! And then you had your way with me – *three times*.'

'Why, so I did,' she said, chuckling. 'I'd forgotten that bit. But I was referring to you stealing my construct sketches, afterwards.'

'I didn't steal them. I just –'

'Borrowed them without permission for the next three years.' She raised her glass. 'And together we changed the course of the war.'

Flydd clinked glasses. 'Good days among the bad.'

'Thank you, friends,' said M'Lainte. She drained the glass, smacked her lips, and slid sideways, dead.

He slowly put down his glass. 'Ah, M'Lainte, there'll never be anyone like you again.' He kissed her on the brow, laid her down and closed her eyes, and turned and trudged away.

But at least she had a good death, Karan thought. M'Lainte went on her own terms, in her own time.

Rulke had been catching Karan's eye all morning. She stalked up to him and took him by the arm.

'Something the matter?' he said.

'It won't be today, or tomorrow,' she snapped.

'What are you talking about?'

'Having it out with him.' She glanced across to Llian, who was asleep on a canvas stretcher, one arm extended towards Sulien on the next stretcher. Karan's eyes stung. She did not deserve him. 'I'm exhausted, and aftersickness is still killing me eight hours later, and I haven't slept. And I can do without your bloody nagging.'

'Guilty conscience, Karan? I didn't mean today. I said, *When it's all wrapped up.*'

He wandered away. She found an empty stretcher in the shade, lay on her back and closed her eyes. She couldn't think straight for lack of sleep, but her mind was churning. How could she tell Llian the truth about her mother's death, after all this time? To say nothing of her worse secret.

And what had Rulke meant by, *If you don't want him, I've got a job for him, one that will take him away for years*?

She got up, restlessly. In the distance, teams of Whelm were removing the bodies of the dead artisans from Skyrock and bringing them across. The enemy dead had been left in an empty storeroom.

By 10 a.m. the old human dead had been laid out respectfully on the paving stones, in a cool, shaded place, and covered with canvas from abandoned tents. It was the best they could do. At the head of the line lay M'Lainte, not yet covered, and smiling even in death.

'Without her there would have been no victory,' said Karan. 'She gave me the whole plan, but in a way that made it seem my own.'

'She was the greatest mechanician I ever met,' said Flydd, wiping his old eyes. 'She could work magic with those thick fingers.'

'I once saw her turn a mad idea into a working device in under an hour,' said Tiaan. 'She was a miracle worker.'

'M'Lainte was good to me,' said Wilm, who had left Ilisial's side to stand beside the old woman one last time. 'She trusted me and supported me, and never took offence at my ill-mannered questions.'

'She was always generous, always kind,' said Flydd. 'And surprisingly good at all kinds of things. I remember another night, long ago –' He looked around, and to Karan's astonishment there was a faint flush on his weathered cheeks. 'Never mind.'

He knelt beside her and kissed her on the forehead, his tears spotting her doughy cheeks and sagging jowls.

'Mummy?' said Sulien, tugging at Karan's sleeve. 'Jassika wants to see her father's body and I – I don't know what to do.'

'I'll come.'

They went down the lines of the dead. There were a lot of them, including Klarm and others killed during the past couple of days, their bodies brought from a chilly basement, and the twenty-eight whose lives Skald had drunk. Uletta's face was set in an expression of such desolation that Karan had to cover it up. She had died alone and unnoticed, and Skald's betrayal of the woman he had claimed to love was going to give Karan nightmares for years to come.

Jassika was pacing back and forth, arms stiff, fists clenched, face blanched. She had lost weight over the past six weeks and she was all knees and elbows now. And bruises.

'I hate you,' she hissed as she passed the small mound between all the normal-length ones. She whirled and stalked back. 'I hate you, I hate you, I hate you!'

She threw herself on the ground and burst into tears.

In her exhaustion, Karan could not think of a thing to say, apart from, *I'm really sorry*, which seemed meaningless.

Flydd forestalled her by sitting down beside Jassika. 'You do know that Klarm was a hero,' he said quietly. 'I think he was the bravest man I ever met.'

'Stupidest man *I* ever met,' Jassika muttered. 'And a disgusting old lecher.'

'That's not true,' said Flydd. 'He liked talking to women, and listening to women talk, and being with them. And they liked him too. Even after their ... um, liaisons were over, his lovers all remained friends with him. You can't say that of many people.'

'The old bastard drank too much.'

'He'd seen terrible things, Jassika. Sometimes he just needed all the voices to stop. But drink didn't change Klarm for the worse; he was just as generous and just as kind as he was when sober.'

'He was never around; he spent more time with his trollops than with me.'

'I never said he was perfect. But he never stopped loving you. He sacrificed his life to give us the chance to rescue you.'

'I still hate the short-arsed little bastard,' she muttered.

'And if he heard you say that?' Flydd said mildly.

Jassika's eyes watered again. 'He'd grin and give me a hug and say, "Well, I *am* a short-arsed little bastard."' She managed a feeble smile.

'Come on. It's time to say goodbye.'

He lifted the canvas and stood to one side, looking down at his old friend. Klarm's face was blistered, parts of his beard and leonine head of hair had been burned away, and his clothes were charred in places, but the lines of his face had smoothed out and he looked younger and less troubled. He was still a handsome man.

'I was afraid to look,' Jassika said softly. 'Afraid of what the spellcaster had done to him.' She knelt beside Klarm and took his hand in hers. 'But he looks –'

'Like a man who did his best,' said Flydd. 'And knew at the end that it was enough.'

She tidied his clothes and brushed his hair back over his noble brow. 'Goodbye, Daddy,' she whispered, and squeezed his hand and got up.

Flydd covered him.

'What's to become of them?' said Jassika.

'We'll take our friends with us when we go, and find a nice, peaceful place to bury them, far from anything the Merdrun ever touched.'

'And me?' Jassika was trembling. Doubtless, Karan thought, realising that she was now alone in the world.

'We'll talk about that later,' said Flydd. 'Don't worry.'

'I do worry,' Jassika said softly, and walked away.

It was after eleven and the sun was warm. They sat in the shade under the pavilion for an early lunch. Nish and Llian had plundered the high commander's abandoned pantry and returned with baskets of delicacies and bottles of wine. They already seemed like old mates. Llian had always found it easy to make friends. Karan felt more alone than ever.

How was she going to tell him? And what would he do? The thought was terrifying.

'For such an austere race, they quickly learned how to indulge themselves,' said Nish, paring the green wax from the top of an ancient, triangular bottle.

Llian held out a glass. He loved good wine and had not had it in a long time. The rubbish they'd had at Gothryme in recent years had barely been good enough for making vinegar. Karan ate a bit of bread and cheese but could not taste it. Lingering aftersickness took all the pleasure out of eating.

She lay on the cool floor in a corner of the pavilion and tipped her hat over her face. Just fifteen minutes of sleep. Even ten would be better than nothing ...

*Boom!*

It shook the floor of the pavilion like distant thunder, wrenching her out of her doze. She yawned, rolled over and tried to get comfortable again. Her hip was aching.

'That was a gate, a big one,' said Flydd. 'Do you reckon it's Maigraith, turning up after all the work is done?'

'Maigraith is always subtle,' said Maelys.

As Karan sat up, a large gate flowered a few hundred yards away, and a big, robed sus-magiz burst from it, followed by a company of crimson-armoured Merdrun and two junior sus-magiz, both women.

'How can they have come back from Aachan?' said Nish, heaving himself to his feet, one-handed.

'That's not an inter-world portal,' said Flydd. 'It's a *local* gate.'

'Then where have they come from?' said Llian. 'What do they want?'

'I should think that's obvious.'

'Lirriam!' bellowed Rulke. 'Come back!'

Lirriam, who had been strolling not far from the gate when it opened, was blasted off her feet by the sus-magiz, and two soldiers ran and took her captive. The sus-magiz rapped out orders. 'You know what to do. Go!'

A couple of hundred troops raced towards Skyrock. The remainder, about thirty, charged towards the allies, led by the sus-magiz, and surrounded them.

'Surrender,' he said. 'Or you will die.'

# 51

# HE NEVER STOPPED LOVING YOU

No one was armed; they had lain their weapons aside hours ago. Lirriam's captors led her across and the sus-magiz relieved her of the Waystone, his eyes gleaming as he inspected it.

He was a big, square-faced man with a long scar across his chin. He looked as though he had lost weight recently, and a grey pallor underlying his dark skin suggested he had not seen the sun for some time.

'Where is the Founder's Stone?' he said.

'Back in the cubic temple,' said Lirriam. There was a large bruise on her left cheek from the blast he had used to knock her down, and her left eye was swelling.

'Who are you?' said Flydd.

'Widderlin. Senior sus-magiz. Dagog exiled me to the far south, and I couldn't come back while he lived.'

'Why not?' said Flydd.

'A good hater was Dagog,' Widderlin said candidly. 'And fearful of rivals – as well he might be, since I was his equal in some ways and his superior in others.'

Karan wasn't sure she liked the sound of that.

'But when he was killed, the ban broke,' Widderlin added.

'That was three days ago.'

'We had a long march across the frozen wastes to find a suitable field. I was preparing to gate back when Durthix called, urgently, with his leader's cube.'

Widderlin looked along the line of prisoners. 'A girl of nine years, small for her age, green eyes and long red hair. Take her.'

As two soldiers took hold of Sulien, it felt as though Karan's belly had been torn open again.

Widderlin addressed them. 'I'm of a different mind to most of my people, and I don't want any unnecessary killing. If we're to make a new start in our home world, we must begin now.' He gave a wry smile. 'I put this argument to Dagog and was exiled. But if anyone resists, I won't hesitate to put them down. I *will* bring my people back from slavery.'

He paced down the line. 'Karan Fyrn. What does our Most Wanted list say about you?' He thought for a moment. 'A sensitive with a gift of linking and sending. Fiercely loyal, brave and daring. You orchestrated our defeat, yes?'

'With M'Lainte's help,' said Karan. She could not allow him to think Sulien had anything to do with it. 'But she's dead.'

'A pity,' said Widderlin. 'I had need of her.'

He was fiddling with his rue-har as he spoke, and now pressed a flat side of it to her temples, left then right. Karan's eyes fluttered and she crumpled and fell.

Llian gasped; for a second he had felt the pain jagging through Karan's head.

'Bind Karan and bring her,' said Widderlin. 'We have two and a half hours to reopen the portal, bring our people back from Aachan and send them to Tallallame.'

Widderlin extended his hand to Sulien. 'Your mother's tricks won't work with me. Do you want to know why?'

'Yes,' she whispered, shrinking back from him.

'I can far-see as well as our old magiz. *Take my hand!*'

Sulien took it and he ran with her to Skyrock. Another guard carried Karan after him, and inside. The remaining guards bound the prisoners' wrists and ordered them to follow, but halfway across the compound they forced everyone to the ground. Llian, Flydd, Wilm, Nish and Maelys, Rulke and Lirriam and Jassika, and Tiaan by herself. So few.

Their ankles were tied and one of the sus-magizes cast an enchantment which caused Llian's bonds to tighten around his wrists and ankles like cold iron. Another enchantment fixed their ankle ropes to rings that rose out of the paving stones.

From here, he could see into the tunnel. The soldiers were hammering parallel lines of spikes into the floor and tying ropes to them, stretching them lengthwise down the tunnel and out the other end.

'Can they do it?' said Llian.

'It'll take at least twenty minutes to get someone to the top of the tower,' said Llian, 'and fix the cable –'

A gate opened at the top of the iron tower, on the platform.

'No problem making a gate there now, with the portal closed,' said Tiaan.

A robed sus-magiz came out and bent down. There came a brief flash and sparks fountained up. The figure worked there for a few minutes, presumably rejoining the braided cable Llian had severed, and went back through the gate.

~

It was like last night, but worse, because Karan lay on the floor of the control chamber, bound hand and foot and as still as death, and Sulien could not reach her by mind-calling.

Rulke's Whelm had taken away the dead and mopped up the blood, but the stains remained, and the smell of death, the jagged edges of the quartz plate through which Durthix had fallen to his death, and the gory iron glyph that had impaled Sus-magiz Ghiar.

Everywhere Sulien looked, it triggered the horrors of a few hours ago: Karan and Jassika being beaten; all those lives being drunk; Uletta's hideous betrayal and the way she had cursed Skald; his breakdown and maiming; the bloody battle after Rulke and the Whelm burst in – and the awful fear that Karan and Llian were about to be killed.

It had not gone away.

'Stand there.' Widderlin indicated the column next to the far-seeing bench.

Sulien waited there while he prowled the chamber, inspecting everything and issuing orders to his two sus-magiz, who were operating various devices as if they understood exactly what to do. Occasionally they called him and he gave further instructions. The stand with the etching plates and wooden panel paintings of the destination was placed to the right of the far-seeing bench, and the painting Sulien had broken over Lurzel's head put back, though its centre was gone.

The glyph-handed clock on the wall said just after midday. In two hours, the window that allowed the Merdrun into Tallallame would close for 287 years, but was that good or bad? Good for Tallallame, bad for Santhenar. If Widderlin could reopen the portal to Aachan the Merdrun would come back, determined to avenge their humiliation, and they would be a lot worse this time.

He returned to the far-seeing bench, sat and worked the controls. Unlike Skald, he was quick and confident. He knew exactly what he needed to do, and if he could far-see as well as the old magiz, why had he brought her and Karan here?

The tunnel sprang to light, a shimmering sapphire blue, and the wind whistled into it. The portal to Aachan had been reopened.

Widderlin called his sus-magizes across. 'It's 12.25,' he said. 'Can we do it, Palahaz?'

The older of the sus-magiz, who was almost as thin as Lurzel had been, though not at all snake-like, glanced down through the hole in the floor and shook her head. 'This portal is much smaller than the original. It only occupies the central third of the tunnel, and even with the ropes we'll be lucky to bring ten thousand through in the next hour, against that wind.'

'We don't have an hour. Once they come through, we've got to close the Aachan portal before we can open one to Tallallame, and that will take time.'

The younger sus-magiz was a big, muscular young woman with a shaven head and bushy black eyebrows; she would have been a beauty to Merdrun eyes. 'Then ... we can't rescue our people,' she said, her voice quivering. 'Or save them from the crushing burden of defeat and enslavement.'

Widderlin's big hands clenched and unclenched, but he said brusquely, 'Save the emotions for the end, Vahayla.' He handed her a farspeaker. 'Take a squad. Run to the far end of the portal and call the strongest of our fighters through.'

'What about the wagons?' said Palahaz.

'We'd never get them through against the wind. Just the best three thousand troops, and the air-scooters.'

She stiffened. 'So few?'

'With three thousand soldiers, and the thousand spellcasters, we can carve out a beachhead in Tallallame and decimate our enemies. We can still achieve part of the True Purpose.'

'We don't know how to use the spellcasters.'

'Skald does. Order him back. Most of his crimes will be forgiven if he can command them ... and succeed.'

'Are you sure?' said Palahaz. 'His failures and betrayals –'

'He previously showed great courage and brilliance,' said Widderlin, 'and we can't hope to succeed without the spellcasters. Even a small win will give hope to our people and make their enslavement bearable. And one day ...' His voice shook. 'One day, those of us who have thrived and grown on Tallallame will be strong enough to break the prohibition. We will make a portal directly to Aachan to free the rest of the Merdrun nation, *and deal death to our enemies.* Run, Vahayla! There's not a second to spare. Report when you get there.'

She raced out. Widderlin and Palahaz returned to their devices. Sulien's hands weren't tied but there was nothing she could do this time.

After a couple of minutes Vahayla's voice issued from the farspeaker. 'The first and strongest are coming through, Sus-magiz. But it's slow progress against such a wind.'

'And Skald?' said Widderlin.

'I've called for him.'

Aviel could not bear to see Wilm in such pain and be unable to help him. Nor, at this great moment, could she take much joy from their victory when her dearest friend was so low. She had to get away.

She trudged off and was out of sight on the far side of the sky galleon when a gate opened, disgorging a company of Merdrun. Most of them raced to Skyrock; the rest took the allies prisoner. Aviel scurried across to the stone-lined well and crouched behind the low coping, praying that the enemy did not realise she was missing. Though why would they even know she was here?

She was close enough for her acute hearing to pick up the gist of what was said. The sus-magiz only had hours to reverse the portal to Aachan, bring the Merdrun back, then recreate the original portal and send them through to invade Tallallame.

The moment he headed for Skyrock with Karan and Sulien, Aviel crept towards the open gates of the compound, and outside. She knew the layout of the camps, having seen them from the granite bluff with Flydd's spyglass.

To her right had been the officer's camp, which had comprised thousands of tents, though the invaders had taken most with them. There was also a stone meeting hall and an armoury whose doors stood open. There were still some weapons and pieces of armour inside. On the left, only a hundred yards away, was the gate to the palisaded slaves' camp, with a small guardhouse to the right. The gate was closed. The soldiers' and civilians' camps had been further up the hill.

A good mile and a half away, up near the rim of the valley, was the shadowy mass of the Whelm's camp. They had sworn to serve the Merdrun during the brief invasion two centuries ago, and thousands had since renewed their oaths, but Rulke had cast them into confusion by coming back from the dead and reminding them that their ancient oath to him, their greatest and most beloved master, still held.

A few dozen had helped him capture Skyrock and save Llian and Maelys, though most had been killed. What must the remainder be thinking, now that their Merdrun masters had abandoned him? But the Whelm scared Aviel and she had no idea how to appeal to them. Besides, it was too far for her to walk.

She would have to try to rouse the slaves.

# 52

# AND DECIMATE OUR ENEMIES

A few minutes later a flight of six air-scooters went by, and shortly the leading foot soldiers appeared, pulling themselves along the ropes. One of the surviving generals came up, Halia. Widderlin outlined the plan. She nodded and went down to brief her officers. Vahayla came back, flushed and panting.

'Is all in order?' said Widderlin.

'Skald has been found and is on his way. Though ...'

'What?'

'The army would not stop at 3,000. Every Merdrun soldier wanted to come through. What do we do when it's time to close the portal?'

Widderlin went still. 'Leave that to me,' he said after a painful pause.

No one was looking at Sulien. She went over to Karan, who was deeply asleep, or unconscious, or under a spell. Sulien could not tell.

She knelt beside Karan, holding her cold hand, but that was disheartening, so she wandered towards the eastern window and no one tried to stop her. The Merdrun troops were forming ranks outside the opening of the tunnel, fifty across and twenty deep already. A thousand, and more were hauling themselves out every second.

Skald was escorted up to the control chamber. He was a gruesome sight, battered and bloody, the glyph scratched out on his brow, blind right eye oozing, torn mouth gaping to reveal broken teeth.

'Spellcasters?' said Widderlin.

'In the storeroom to the left of the entrance.' Skald shot a hate-filled glare at Sulien. There was nothing left of the strong but sometimes kindly man who had trained her in far-seeing. He was a monstrosity now.

'You know how to activate them?'

'They'll obey my voice commands. I set them up ...'

'After you betrayed Dagog,' Widderlin said coldly.

'Yes.'

'This is your one chance, Skald. This can pay for most of your past crimes. Can you do it?'

'Durthix destroyed my sus-magiz abilities when he put out my eye.'

'And you need to be a sus-magiz to command the spellcasters.'

Widderlin moved his hand in the air and, across the room, the discarded rue-har glowed acid-green. He retrieved it and thrust it into Skald's temple where the Merdrun glyph had been.

'Your abilities are temporarily restored. Get it done.' He handed Skald his rue-har.

Skald went down. Widderlin paced. Vahayla and Palahaz were back at their devices.

'How long to close the Aachan portal and reopen the one to Tallallame?' he said.

'We have the power,' said Palahaz. 'Will it take long to far-see the destination?'

Widderlin's eyes flicked to the stand with the plates and the paintings. 'I already have it.'

Sulien was looking down at the gathering soldiers when a spellcaster flitted around the side of the tower, then another and another, then swarms of them. She choked. The whole slave camp had been abuzz with the slaughter they had done to Dagog and the others in that meeting room. And to Klarm.

Widderlin stood beside her, looked down and smiled grimly. 'Not how I would have chosen to go home,' he said. 'But needs must.'

The glyph-handed clock said 1.15. Three thousand soldiers had assembled outside now and hundreds more were coming through. To their left, at least eight hundred spellcasters hovered. They could be heard over the wind, like a swarm of angry hornets.

Skald was out in front, ready to give their personas their orders. If he chose revenge he could annihilate Llian, Rulke and the other allies in seconds, and not even Widderlin would be able to stop him.

Widderlin took a deep breath, and again his big fists closed and opened. 'Close the Aachan portal.'

'But there must be a thousand troops in it,' said Vahayla, dismayed. She was very emotional, for a Merdrun.

'I only called for three thousand.'

'They were hungry for victory.'

'They disobeyed orders, and if I wait for them to come through there can be no victory, because more will come behind them, and everything we have striven for these past aeons will be as nought. *Close the portal!*'

Palahaz reached for a lever with an orange, cross-shaped knob on the end, and thrust it forwards. The glow from the portal went out.

And just like that, a thousand men and women had died, perhaps obliterated in an instant, perhaps cast into nothingness. Sulien could not take it in.

'What's happened to them?' she whispered.

'No one has ever been able to find out,' said Widderlin in a harsh voice. 'Go and move the twinned crystal to the Tallallame setting.'

Palahaz gated to the top of the tower. Widderlin strode towards the far-seeing bench and Sulien followed. She could not bear to think what was going to happen once they took all those spellcasters to Tallallame.

'Will you lead our troops through?' said Vahayla.

'I'll stay here until last,' said Widderlin, 'in case there are problems with the portal. Accompany the advance guard. Report back everything that happens.'

Vahayla's face was glowing. She wasn't afraid; this was the greatest moment of her life. 'Will the far-speaker work from Tallallame?'

'Only as long as the portal stays open. Good luck, Sus-magiz. Though you shouldn't need it – the mind-shock when the portal opens in Tallallame will render most of our enemies helpless for hours. Perhaps days.'

And the Merdrun would walk up and slaughter them. If only there was a way to warn them. But she could not mind-speak to aliens from another world.

Widderlin sat on the far-seeing bench, pushed the goggles aside and looked down at her. Even seated, he was taller. 'I don't need you,' he said as if he had read her mind. 'Or anything to far-see the destination. I've been dreaming it since I was a boy.'

'Then why did you bring me here?'

'So I could keep an eye on you.'

Palahaz came back. Widderlin used his levers again, the tunnel went blue, fog formed in it and a gentle breeze came whirling up through the broken plate in the floor. A scented breeze, flowers and herbs and a cool, moist forest.

'Traitor's Crag, Tallallame,' sighed Widderlin. 'Home!'

A flight of spellcasters whistled through the portal, barely visible through the thickening fog, and below them moved a dark mass, the advance guard of the invasion force. It would not take long. This breeze would not hinder them.

Vahayla's voice came from the farspeaker, deeper than before and rather stretched out. *Nearing the end of the portal. The fog is thinning.*

'It'll disappear at the exit,' Widderlin said, as though to himself.

*I can see Tallallame!* Vahayla cried. *A bare hill with standing stones, surrounded by forest, just like the paintings. I'm out! I'm in our home world. It's* beautiful!

'And deadly!' snapped Widderlin. 'Keep watch.'

Within minutes the Merdrun army was through and racing up to occupy the top of the hill.

*The spellcasters are swarming everywhere, looking for enemy to attack,* said Vahayla. *None seen so far. General Halia has established a defensive position. All is to plan.*

Aviel crept to the gates of the slaves' compound. They were made of split logs, mounted vertically and a good sixteen feet high, held closed with an iron chain secured to a lock the size of a pumpkin. Did the slaves even know their masters were gone? They could see little from inside the palisade wall.

They would have heard the soldiers on the march, and must have seen the blue radiance of the portal in the night, but how, through the prism of terrorisation and brutality, could they assess such things? Wilm had once been held prisoner by the Merdrun in a similar slave camp, and he had told Aviel how apathetic most of the brutalised slaves had been. How despairing. When merely looking a guard in the eyes could mean death, how could they be otherwise?

But not all of them. Wilm had never given up, and when Llian had freed him – a small miracle in itself – and given him back the black sword, Wilm had led the rebellion that resulted in the defeat of the Merdrun army. There must be people in this vast camp who had not given up.

Inside the open guardhouse, a spike had been hammered into the wall, but where were the keys to the gate? She searched the guardhouse three times but could not find them anywhere, and she was painfully aware how quickly time was passing.

Aviel went back to the compound gates and peered through, and her heart gave an almighty thump. The portal was open and thousands of Merdrun troops had assembled outside the tunnel entrance, along with a swarm of hovering spellcasters. But what were they doing?

Soon they began to move through. They were invading Tallallame, of course, but what then? It was well after 1 p.m. The Tallallame portal would close in an hour and could not be opened again, but if Widderlin stayed behind he could reopen the Aachan portal at any time, and hold it open until all the Merdrun escaped back to Santhenar. She had to prevent that, and only an army of slaves could do so.

Aviel went back to the guardhouse. Where could the keys be? The guards would hardly have taken them. She was walking back and forth when she saw something shining in the dirt, twenty yards away. As they left, a guard must have hurled them away.

She took them and hurried to the gate. Both keys looked the same, so she thrust the first one into the padlock. It went in for a good eight inches but would not turn.

She moved it in and out several times, found the right place, turned it with both hands and the lock came open. Aviel disengaged the chain and heaved one side of the gate. It did not budge; it must have weighed tons.

'Hoy!' she yelled. 'Nearly all the Merdrun are gone! Push on the gate!'

It took several minutes to gain the slaves' attention, and another minute before anyone found the courage to believe her, then the gate creaked open and she was facing hundreds of thin, grimy prisoners, and tens of thousands more behind them. What was she supposed to say? How could she – a small girl who had no idea how to inspire a crowd – possibly move them?

By naming people every one of them would have heard about. People they could respect and be inspired by.

'My name is Aviel,' she said, 'and I came with Flydd. The Merdrun are gone, all but a handful, but I need your help.'

They just stared at her.

'Xervish –' Aviel's voice went shrill; she lowered it a fraction and tried again. 'Xervish Flydd, who saved Santhenar in the Lyrinx War and helped to topple the God-Emperor. And Nish, and Maelys Nifferlin. And Karan Fyrn, and Llian, who wrote the Great Tale, the *Tale of the Mirror*. And Rulke! You know who Rulke is. He's here and he needs your aid.'

The slaves began to whisper among themselves.

'They need your help, urgently,' Aviel said.

Nothing.

'The Merdrun were going through the sapphire portal. We tricked them and sent the portal to Aachan, to a place from which there is only one way of escape – if the portal is reopened.'

She reached out to them. 'They only number a couple of hundred, but they've captured my friends and they'll beat us unless you stop them. You can do it! How can two hundred Merdrun stand against tens of thousands?'

A lean, weather-beaten man stepped forwards with a glint in his eye, and several other people followed, men and women.

'We can't fight them with our bare hands,' he said.

'The enemy's armoury is just over there,' said Aviel, gesturing with her thumb. 'They've left surplus weapons behind. If you creep across, so the enemy in the compound don't see you –'

'You and you,' said the weather-beaten man to a pair of slaves, 'race up to the Whelm's camp and tell them that their former master, Rulke, requires their service.'

They ran out the gate.

'What are you waiting for?' he said to the slaves behind him. 'All of you who have fought before, follow me around the back to the enemy's armoury, making no sound. Then arm yourselves and prepare for battle.'

## 53

# GET OUT OF THE WAY!

Llian and the other ten prisoners were still bound to rings in the centre of the compound. The guards waited nearby, swords drawn. Widderlin was taking no chances.

The minutes ground into an hour. Llian stared at the tunnel and the eastern window of the control chamber. Figures moved inside it though he could not identify them. Despite Widderlin's words, Llian felt sure everyone would be killed once the portal was reopened. It would only take a minute to cut down the prisoners. Why wouldn't he eliminate the risk?

The tunnel brightened to a brilliant sapphire blue. Wind rushed into it, the note rising to an eerie whistle and then to a howl, and the middle misted out. The portal was open.

'Can he divert it directly to Tallallame?' said Flydd.

'Merdrun can't reach Tallallame from Aachan,' said Rulke. 'They'll have to come here, close the portal and reopen the original portal to Tallallame.'

Shortly the first of the armoured troops appeared, ready for battle, and assembled outside the entrance.

'If they want to do us in,' Llian muttered, 'it'll only take –'

'Morale!' snapped Flydd.

Shortly Skald appeared, and even from this distance he was a horror of a man. He stopped to stare at them and Llian imagined he could feel waves of hate directed their way. A uniformed general took Skald's arm and pointed towards the base of the tower.

'What's Skald back for?' said Maelys.

Flydd, who carried a small spy scope, reported the details. Skald went into a storeroom in the side of Skyrock. Shortly, a spellcaster flew out, then swarms of them. They settled in ranks next to the troops, all but one that came whirring across. It circled low above the prisoners, its funnel-tipped arms slowly rotating to point at Rulke, then Flydd, then Llian.

Wilm moaned, and every hair stood up on Llian's head. Wilm had seen them operating. He had seen them kill.

The general bellowed at Skald, who shouted an order. The spellcaster made another slow circle, as if giving him the finger, and flew back to the others.

'Morale just took a beating,' Rulke said wryly.

'They're not for us,' said Tiaan. 'They're for our old friends, the lyrinx.'

'If only there were a way to warn them,' said Flydd.

'As soon as Widderlin opens the portal to Tallallame,' said Rulke, 'mind-shock will render them all unconscious.'

'Now who's ruining morale?' Llian muttered.

The Aachan portal was closed, the Tallallame portal reopened, and fog gushed out and billowed across the compound, though it was not thick enough to blot out the spellcasters swarming into the portal and three thousand soldiers storming after them.

'I can't bear to think about it,' said Nish.

He had fought the lyrinx for years, Llian knew, but Nish had later become friends with some of them. Tiaan was staring into nowhere; she had also known them well. The lyrinx could stand against any warlike race, though not when mind-shocked into unconsciousness. The Merdrun and their spellcasters would kill them by the tens of thousands.

Fog continued to issue from the portal and drift across the compound. The soldiers had all gone through, though Widderlin's two hundred remained.

The control chamber clock said 1.30. The Tallallame portal would soon close. Would Widderlin kill Karan and Sulien and the allies then? Karan was still unconscious, though why would that bother a man who had just erased all those soldiers in the portal? A man who, despite what he had said about wanting no unnecessary killing, was prepared to murder the mind-shocked inhabitants of Tallallame by the thousands.

*I can hear fighting*, said Vahayla through the farspeaker. *Just a skirmish.*

There came a roar the like of which Sulien had only heard once before, after she had been carried away by a lyrinx from the Whelm's long abandoned city of Hessular. It seemed to strike some primal fear in the Merdrun because the sus-magiz spun around, her mouth open, and even Widderlin looked uneasy.

Another roar, louder.

*We're under attack!* said Vahayla. *Lyrinx, thousands of them. They were hidden around the base of the hill. Camouflaged like chameleons and concealed by mighty illusions. They're – so – big!*

'The spellcasters will take them down,' said Widderlin. 'We knew some lyrinx would be unaffected by the mind-shock.'

*They're more than eight feet tall, males and females! And armoured, and their claws are like knife blades. They were waiting to ambush us. Sus-magiz, they* knew *we were coming!*

Widderlin reached Sulien in a few strides and lifted her to eye level. 'How did they know?' he grated.

'It wasn't me,' she squeaked. 'I can only mind-speak to people I know.'

'What about Karan?'

'Skald burned out her mind-speaking gift.'

Widderlin stared at her so intently that he might have been reading her smallest thoughts. He tossed her down and picked up the farspeaker again.

*Lyrinx are storming up the hill from all sides, cutting straight through our ranks. Not even our strongest soldiers can stand against them.*

'Halia and Skald will soon sort them out,' said Widderlin.

Vahayla did not speak for some time, though roars and shrieks and sounds of battle continued to come through the farspeaker.

'Vahayla, report!' said Widderlin.

Another couple of minutes passed, then she said shrilly, *They're coming from all sides. Half our officers are down, and ... we've lost a thousand troops in five minutes. Widderlin, Halia's dead – and one of the lyrinx is* eating *her!*

Liquid explosions sounded as though Vahayla was vomiting.

'What's happening with the spellcasters?' Widderlin rapped out.

*Skald is shouting orders – and they're flying wherever he orders – but they're not attacking.*

Widderlin paled. 'Why not? He got the original spellcaster to kill Dagog. And these ones are identical.'

*I don't know, Sus-magiz. And ... I don't think Skald knows, either.*

Widderlin stared into space for a minute. 'That damned dwarf!' he said to sus-magiz Palahaz. 'Flydd's *Histories* said Klarm was the most cunning of all the scrutators.'

'I don't understand,' she said.

'He *wanted* Skald to capture the spellcaster at the Sink of Despair, because Klarm had already neutralised it. And our thousand copies were built the same way – neutralised.'

'But the original one killed Dagog, five generals and four sus-magizes.'

'When Klarm took it apart in Skyrock and put it back together again, he must have made a tiny change to restore it to its original condition, but it was never done to our thousand spellcasters. They're useless – and Skald never realised!'

'Maybe he did,' said Palahaz. 'But the possibility of freedom on Tallallame was better than eternal slavery on Aachan.'

'No, I think he failed to realise the full extent of Klarm's cunning.'

'Are you going to call our troops back?'

'Merdrun never retreat,' said Widderlin unconvincingly.

*They've cut our formations into pieces and surrounded them. Widderlin, in another ten minutes we'll all be dead.*

'How many left?' he snapped.

*A thousand*, said Vahayla. *At most.*

'Can you get back to the portal?'

*Some of us.*

'Turn back! We have a new target.' Widderlin called Palahaz across. 'The True Purpose has failed and our home world is lost. But we can still bring the Merdrun nation back from enslavement. We can still have Santhenar.'

Her thin face twisted in agony. She nodded stiffly.

'Retreat through the portal, Vahayla. Order the rear-guard to defend it to the death. The lyrinx must not come through to Santhenar.'

Sulien heard Vahayla relating the orders, then running, gasping.

*I'm in the portal.*

'How many troops are coming through?'

*Maybe – three hundred. Plus – a hundred in the rear-guard.*

Sulien shivered and hugged herself. So many dead, so quickly. And when the Merdrun came back, after such a crushing defeat they would be savage in revenge.

The fog in the portal was thinner now. A handful of soldiers ran past and out into the compound. Then a company of more than a hundred, several smaller squads and finally a few isolated individuals.

'Vahayla?' said Widderlin.

*Rear-guard's fighting desperately. They're holding. They're not –*

'Report, Vahayla!'

Silence.

'Vahayla is dead,' said Widderlin.

Heavy footsteps shook the tower and a mass of lyrinx stormed by, pursuing the last of the soldiers.

'How many lyrinx came through?' said Widderlin, who did not have a clear view from where he stood.

'A couple of hundred?' said Sulien, though she knew it had been less than one hundred.

'Widderlin?' cried the sus-magiz. 'Should I close the portal?'

'The dream is over,' he said in a dead voice. 'We're not going home.'

He drew his sword and walked across to Karan.

'Don't kill Mummy!' screamed Sulien.

Widderlin turned, and the look in his eyes was awful. He had lost everything.

'What would be the point?' he said with a small bow. 'We'll all be dead soon enough.' He bypassed Karan and headed down the stairs.

Palahaz followed and Sulien crept after them. Were they planning to kill Llian and the other prisoners?

She stood in the entrance, the weirdness of the portal streaming all around her. She went out of its range, just in case, keeping to the patches of fog that covered part of the compound. A hundred yards away, battle was raging, two hundred Merdrun fighting about sixty lyrinx. It could go either way.

It was hard to think of the lyrinx as being allies, but she had her fingers crossed for them. Then Widderlin's two hundred guards charged out from behind one of the spiralling blue columns and attacked from the rear, and Sulien knew they were going to win. She looked away. She did not want to see any more killing, ever.

Skald staggered out of the Tallallame portal, unscathed but emotionally scarred by the most horrific battle he had ever been through. The lyrinx had not been mind-shocked, and fighting them had been terrifying, since they could kill a Merdrun with a single, savage blow. He had not run, though. He was not a coward; he would *never* run from the battlefield.

But he had been ordered to make a shameful retreat.

Widderlin stepped out in front of him. 'Your spellcasters failed, Skald, and it's cost us our home world.'

Merdrun did not make excuses. 'Yes, Sus-magiz.'

'Because the dwarf duped you from the beginning. Klarm wanted you to take the spellcaster because he'd already modified it so it could not attack.'

'Yes, Sus-magiz. I understand that now.'

'You thought you were so clever, but he fooled you at every step. You never realised that our thousand spellcasters were useless.'

'Klarm fooled everyone, Sus-magiz. Even Dagog.'

'Whom you betrayed to his death.'

'Yes, Sus-magiz.'

'Even Sulien duped you. She took advantage of your weakness to change the portal's destination, and you never realised. You're a gullible man, Skald.'

'Yes, Sus-magiz. Are you going to execute me?'

'You want me to, don't you?'

Skald said nothing. Of course he wanted to die, but only a coward begged for death.

'You're going to live a very long life, Skald. Though even if you had ten lives to live, it would not be enough to punish you for your treachery and incompetence.'

'No, Sus-magiz,' Skald whispered.

'Wait there.' Widderlin pointed to Skald's left. 'You will be dealt with once we've taken Santhenar back.'

'Yes, Sus-magiz.'

Skald stood there, watching the fighting between Merdrun and lyrinx, and burning with rage. Though not against Widderlin. Skald accepted the need for his punishment, as a lesson to all. But he ached to avenge himself on the small band of allies who had brought about his ruin.

Rulke and Flydd were a few hundred yards away, along with others Skald could not identify from here, and they were bound and helpless. Why hadn't Widderlin killed them at once? Because he was soft; Dagog had been right to exile him.

Skald crept across. What a joy it would be to open their throats and see the terror in their eyes as life bled out of them.

Or better, drink their lives! Skald had lost that gift when his eye was put out, but Widderlin had restored all Skald's sus-magiz abilities with his rue-har. Who to start with, the easiest or the hardest? If Skald took Rulke's life first, it would give him such power that he might even take on Widderlin, if he chose to.

Perhaps he would. Widderlin lacked the ruthlessness to crush Santhenar utterly. There had been a time when Skald had lacked ruthlessness, but not anymore. He was going to destroy every one of his enemies.

He emerged from the fog and the bound victims were only yards away. Tiaan, Llian and Lirriam were there too, and several others he did not know, though not the ones he wanted most, Karan and Sulien. They must be in the control chamber. Well, he could deal with them later.

A big man appeared out of the fog, creeping their way. Blood was crusted on his swollen face and his right eye was an oozing socket. He carried a sword in one hand and a staff in the other, and he was shuddering and shaking and muttering to himself.

It took Llian a while to recognise the man, though the moment he did he knew what Skald wanted. Revenge. The horror Llian had been trying to suppress for weeks – of having his life drunk – overwhelmed him. And the blind, helpless terror, the revulsion, the sickening ecstasy, Skald's ecstasy, that Llian had felt second-hand.

It was enough to crack anyone's sanity.

~

Skald was having second thoughts. He had never regained his former strength, and Durthix's beatings, the loss of his right eye and the desperate battle on Tallallame had weakened him. Skald might not have the strength to drink Rulke's life straight off. He would take Llian's first.

And how Skald craved it! The last eight ruinous hours had reduced him to a shadow of his former self and nothing else could restore him. Such joy he had felt when drinking the slaves' lives, such incomparable power. Even with Uletta –

He dared not follow that thought, for fear of the forbidden emotions flooding him again. The emotions that had ruined him and undermined so many others in the control chamber at sunrise. He suppressed them ruthlessly. Sulien had discovered the Merdrun's secret weakness and used it to attack him, and she and her mother had to be killed before they revealed it to anyone else.

Probably, they already had. All the more reason for every one of the allies to die. Skald reached out to Llian, who was shuddering with horror but could not move. His life had been surprisingly strong, Skald remembered. And rich, unusual in one who lacked the gift. Dagog had been right. Lives were like wine and Llian's was one of the better vintages, well-aged and at the peak of its drinking.

Skald cast the spell and began the draw, and Llian screamed. His life-heat began to pump through Skald's veins and his nerves were tingling. Bliss!

But then a shadow moved in the fog to his left. A big shadow. Bigger than any of the Merdrun, and with a very different shape. A massive head, a mouth that could have enveloped the whole of Skald's skull. And the teeth!

He choked, the life-drinking broke and the warmth in his veins was replaced by biting cold. His outstretched arm shook. He was afraid. No, terrified. On Santhenar he had seen what the lyrinx did to fallen Merdrun, when they had the time. They had *eaten* them, and no more horrible fate could be imagined.

The shadow moved forwards and became a wingless lyrinx, smaller than most of them but a foot and a half taller than Skald and twice his weight. Its extended claws, a good six inches long, were gory, and there was blood on its arms and down its armoured chest and belly.

'Ryll!' cried Tiaan, as if they were old friends. 'You got my message?'

The lyrinx's smile was terrifying. 'About the portal's destination, and the mind-shock?' Ryll said in a voice so deep that Skald's broken teeth vibrated in his gums.

'Eight hours ago. We had just enough time to protect ourselves and prepare the ambush.'

Skald felt a sickening lurch in his belly. Duped *again*? 'How did you know?' he choked.

'Dagog forced M'Lainte and me to design and craft the portal opener and the twinned crystal mechanism,' said Tiaan. 'No one else had the mech-magical skills to do it, and last night M'Lainte worked out the destination.'

'But you were imprisoned ... how did you warn him?'

'In the chaos after you drank all those lives, Skald, M'Lainte and I ran up to the device storeroom and built an inter-world farspeaker. Didn't take long; we'd done it before, years ago.'

'What – you going to do?' said Skald.

'I'm going to deal you the punishment for oath-breakers,' rumbled Ryll.

Skald could barely speak. 'What – that?' he said hoarsely.

'I'm going to eat you,' said Ryll. 'Given how many good lives you've drunk, *little man*, I'm sure you'll appreciate the irony.'

He took a step towards Skald, flexing his claws and opening his bucket-sized mouth. Skald drew the borrowed sword he had taken to Tallallame. His heart was pounding so furiously that he could hear it, and the ice was crystallising in his veins.

He could kill Ryll. The Merdrun had slain hundreds of lyrinx today. They weren't invincible. But Skald no longer had confidence in himself. Ryll would disarm him with a single blow, disembowel him with another, then feed on his entrails while he was still alive. And Skald could not appreciate the irony.

Face him down! he told himself. Die in combat. And if he eats you afterwards, how can that matter to a dead man?

But it did matter, and he could not face it. He dropped his sword and his rue-har, and turned and stumbled away from the battlefield. Behind him, he heard laughter, but to his surprise the lyrinx did not come after him.

Ryll had returned to the surviving lyrinx, called off the attack and led them back to Tallallame. Shortly the blue glow went out. Widderlin ran back, his robes flapping, and scrambled up the stairs to the control chamber.

'He's reopening the portal to Aachan,' said Nish. 'They're taking Santhenar back.'

Within minutes the tunnel was flashing and fading blue.

'Five minutes,' said Flydd, 'and they'll be hauling themselves through. And the first thing they'll do –'

'Saying it doesn't help,' said Lirriam.

The Merdrun troops, who still numbered a couple of hundred, waited outside to welcome the rest of their army.

'It's over,' said Flydd. 'Nothing we can do now.'

There came the thunder of many drums, beaten randomly, a battle cry as if from a thousand throats, and an untidy horde burst out of the fog. The leaders were clad in blood-red armour and wore white helms, but the rest were dressed in slaves' rags.

'Where the blazes did they come from?' said Nish.

'Keep low!' hissed Flydd.

They crouched down in the fog. The horde, armed with swords, axes, knives and clubs, stormed towards the Merdrun. Attackers and defenders closed, and a furious battle began, far too close for comfort.

'Slaves must've broken into the armoury,' said Nish. 'Can they do it?'

'An untrained, poorly armed rabble against the finest fighters in the void?' said Flydd.

The slave horde outnumbered the Merdrun by at least three to one and they were fighting bravely but were steadily cut down. They were led by a tall, lean officer who matched the best of the enemy blow for blow.

'The way he fights seems ... familiar,' said Flydd.

'This is a dangerous place to be trapped,' said Flydd to Rulke. 'Anything you can do?'

Rulke shook his head. 'The enchantment Widderlin put on our bonds is beyond my skill to break.'

'Or mine. He's a master.'

Llian could not move his feet more than a few inches, and his brief surge of hope was fading. Two-thirds of the slave army had fallen, while the best part of a hundred Merdrun remained on their feet. Widderlin came running from Skyrock, bellowing orders and pointing to the tunnel.

Whatever he had said, it gave the enemy heart, for they formed a tight formation and drove the attackers back. Only a few hundred were left and they weren't a match for such disciplined fighters. At the edges, the slaves began to bleed away into the fog.

'That's it,' said Maelys. 'We're done.'

Skald passed Widderlin and Palahaz, who, after the Aachan portal was reopened, had come down to fight with their troops. He could not meet their eyes. He was too ashamed.

He ran into the portal and the wind almost lifted him off his feet – it wanted to carry him back to Aachan, and perpetual enslavement. As he reached the far end, which led down to the barren crater in Aachan, hundreds of soldiers were pulling themselves up the dangling ropes and into the portal.

He staggered past them, moaning in terror. His entire brave and brilliant life had been undone. As Skald's mother had predicted, when pushed to the limits he had revealed his true nature.

He was a coward, like his father.

The wind howling into the Aachan portal had carried the fog with it. The whole compound was visible now, though Llian could not take anything in. Those few seconds of life-drinking had redoubled the horror and he did not think he would ever be whole again.

'We can't stay here,' said Nish. 'They'll soon be coming through in their thousands.'

Flydd picked up Skald's rue-har and touched it to his bonds. They fell away and he began to free the others.

'Can we get to the sky galleon?' said Rulke. 'It's closer than my construct.'

But it was three-quarters of a mile away, they would have to pass Skyrock to get to it, and they wouldn't make it because a formation of Merdrun blocked the way. Besides, that ghastly moment had left Llian's knees like rubber and his nerves so dead that he could barely stand up. Lirriam had not fully recovered from Widderlin's blast either, and neither Flydd nor Nish looked up to running.

'Not a chance,' said Flydd. 'The chaos chasm is our only hope of getting away.'

'But Karan and Sulien are in Skyrock,' said Llian.

'And we can't get them out.'

Before Flydd could move, there came a distant whine and the sky galleon shot into the air.

'Who the hell is flying it?' said Flydd.

'The Merdrun abducted quite a few pilots, early on,' said Maelys, squeezing her taphloid as if to conceal herself.

'It's going to crash!' Nish said hoarsely. 'Get out of the way!'

The sky galleon was hurtling towards them, only ten feet above the ground. It turned at the last second, zoomed upwards, looped the loop and plunged down at the Merdrun formation. The soldiers held firm until the last second, then hurled themselves flat and the sky galleon passed only a foot above their heads, the gale created by its passing dragging some of them for yards.

It soared up again, did a double loop and plummeted down, levelling out so close to the ground that the soldiers who had risen were battered aside. It turned sharply, carved a tight ascending spiral around Skyrock, and then around the iron tower. It slowed, inched forwards and nudged the top of the tower with its bow.

The iron tower quivered. The sky galleon nudged it again, and again.

'There was only one pilot in the world who could fly like that,' said Flydd.

'And she died in the thapter crash near Ashmode,' said Nish.

There were goose pimples all down Llian's arms, and the scorched hair on top of his head was standing up, and for the moment he could forget about what Skald had done to him.

The sky galleon nudged the top of the tower a fourth time and the great bolts at the base, that fixed it to the top of Skyrock, began to tear out of the stone. The tower tilted. The sky galleon drove into the platform and the twinned crystal came out of its mounting and fell, and the azimuth and elevation wheels with it.

They bounced off the top edge of Skyrock, the metal singing. The glowing twinned crystal fell free, grazed one of the blue-clad spirals that encircled the central core with a shower of bright sparks, fell for a number of seconds then hit the paving stones eleven hundred feet below and smashed into a thousand fragments.

One toothed wheel slammed into the paving beside it. The other went rolling down one of the spirals and shot off the bottom like a hoop from a slippery dip, bouncing across the compound before falling on its side and spinning there for a minute or two.

The bright blue portal went dead and became the sapphire-lined tunnel again. Nothing could reopen it now. Llian lurched that way. The tunnel was empty, and the far side of the compound was visible through it.

What had happened to the Merdrun who had been coming through from Aachan? Had they ceased to exist or ended up *between*? Or nowhere? He wasn't sure he wanted to know.

Flydd ran to the surviving Merdrun. 'You're beaten!' he bellowed. 'The portal can't be remade, and thousands of freed slaves are coming.'

'And Whelm!' said Rulke, who was looking the other way. 'Put down your weapons.'

'Merdrun aren't allowed to surrender,' Llian said to himself.

It looked as though they were going to fight to the death and try to kill Flydd and the allies. But when a host of Whelm burst through the gates of the compound, Widderlin, who had lost his left hand, shouted an order. The soldiers dropped their weapons and put their hands in the air, and the Whelm surrounded them.

The sky galleon looped the loop again, disappeared behind Skyrock and emerged from the eastern end of the portal tunnel. It turned sharply over the compound gates, raced back, set down at high speed and skidded dangerously for a good fifty feet in a deluge of sparks before sliding to a stop only twenty feet away.

The weather-beaten captain who had led the white-helmed attackers so ably came running and reached up to the sky galleon. A small, sturdily built woman leapt into his arms, almost downing him, then yanked his helm off and kissed him on the mouth. She slipped to the ground and, holding hands and grinning, they bowed to their dumbfounded allies.

'Flangers and Chissmoul,' whispered Flydd, and Llian was amazed to see a tear winding its way down one scarred cheek. 'But ... we saw the thapter crash and burn. We felt sure the enemy had booby-trapped it.'

'They had, when they realised that *they* could never make it fly,' said Flangers.

'When it lost the field,' said Chissmoul, 'we knew we were going to die.' She shuddered.

'But the booby-trap triggered a gate. You would have seen the flash when it opened and pulled us through – to Skyrock.'

'Because the enemy wanted every pilot they could get.'

'One second the thapter was falling, the next we were here, and enslaved,' Flangers said soberly. 'I never understood why they didn't kill me.'

'Well, you're my first lieutenant,' said Flydd.

'What about me?' cried Nish.

'Never thought of you as a man who needed titles, Nish,' said Flangers, grinning.

Flydd laughed. 'What a beautiful day. Victory snatched from defeat, and joy from despair.'

'Not for all of us,' said Llian, looking back towards the line of canvas-covered bodies.

Wilm had bolted back to Ilisial the moment he had been freed and had not looked up.

'How did you know what was going on, anyway?' said Flydd. 'If you were ... excuse the term ... ignorant slaves? And how did you get out of the compound?'

Flangers took ten steps back to the sky galleon and called up. 'Would you come out?'

A silver-haired head raised itself above the gunwale. 'Aviel?' said Llian.

Flydd looked astounded. 'I never realised you weren't among us.'

'I like it when I'm not noticed,' she said softly. Then she raised her lovely face. 'Well, you idiots had gotten yourselves caught. Someone had to do something.'

To everyone's astonishment, Flydd pulled her into his arms and hugged her like a long-lost sister. 'I'm glad you like not being noticed. We owe you the world, every one of us.'

## 54

# I HAVE NO FURTHER NEED OF YOU

Let's get to work,' said Flydd. 'The Merdrun took all the food with them and if we don't do something a hundred thousand slaves will starve. And then there's the perennial problem of the Whelm.'

'They're coming now,' said Sulien, with a small shiver. A deputation of the gaunt, long-legged, grey-skinned Whelm was approaching. 'Um, Mister Rulke?'

'Yes, Sulien?' he said.

'I once spent time with the Whelm, in their ancient homeland of Salliban. They weren't all good to me, but Idlis was.'

'I remember him,' said Rulke, looking back down the years. 'He wasn't clever, but he was a dogged and loyal servant, one of my best.'

'He was the best of them I ever met. He went against his own people to save my life, because he had sworn to Mummy to protect me. I want to honour him.'

'He helped to heal me when half my bones were broken,' said Karan. 'And came to help deliver our beautiful daughter. Without Idlis, we both would have died.'

'Then stand beside me when I speak to them,' said Rulke. 'For Idlis's sake.'

'Master,' said the Whelm leader, bowing to the waist. 'My name is Gisli, and I speak for my people.'

'Then speak, Gisli,' he said politely.

'We have come, Perfect Master,' she said, 'to ask what you require of us, today and forever.'

'Remove the bodies outside the tower to burning piles outside the compound,' said Rulke. 'All except a few we will take with us.'

'Yes, Master. And after that?'

'Nothing, Gisli,' he said in a carrying voice. 'Forever.'

She went very still, then turned and looked back at her people. Every Whelm in the great gathering was staring at Rulke in disbelief. 'But ... Master? We do not understand.'

'An aeon ago, your ancestors swore to serve me for as long as I lived, or had need of you – *and to take no other master*. Some of you cleaved to that oath, but most did not. When I was imprisoned in the Nightland many Whelm took another master.'

'You were imprisoned for a thousand years.'

'Nonetheless, you swore a sacred oath, and broke it. Then the Whelm swore to Yggur, only to abandon him when I was freed.'

'Because you called on our ancestors to obey their prior oath to you.'

'And many Whelm came and served me faithfully. Many others did not. Then, subsequently, you took other masters.'

'We believed you dead, Master.'

'But I wasn't dead. *For as long as I lived*, your ancestors swore. Finally, in the most grievous betrayal of all, many Whelm swore to my eternal enemies, the Merdrun. Until their leader of two centuries ago, Gergrig, was defeated and killed.'

'And our oath made null.'

'Yet when Durthix led the new invasion of Santhenar, you renewed your oath to him, without him asking for it, and aided him in his atrocities.'

'We must have a master, Master,' said Gisli. 'You know this of us. Without a master to serve, and obey without question, we are nothing.'

'I am not happy with your blind obedience,' said Rulke, 'nor your endlessly seeking a new master, like shuttlecocks in the wind. More often than not you have allowed evil people to commit dreadful crimes, absolving yourself of blame and responsibility by claiming that you were just obeying orders. No more, Whelm!'

'What are you saying, Master?'

'You swore to serve me as long as I lived, *or had need of you*. I have no further need of you. Whelm, I thank you for past service and hereby cancel the oath. You are free. Go in peace.'

'But Master, how will you get by without servants?'

'The old Rulke was erased in Fiz Gorgo. The Rulke who came back two centuries later has no need of servants or empire or conquest. Besides,' he said quietly, 'I will soon quit this world, and go where no Whelm can follow.'

The Whelm wailed, an awful sound that shook the teetering iron tower and shivered Sulien to her bones. She remembered it from her time in their custody, just before they swore to the Merdrun and betrayed her.

'Gather outside Skyrock after the bodies have been removed,' said Rulke, 'and a gate will be made to send you home to Salliban.'

'Yes, Master.'

'One final duty I lay on you, to take the surviving Merdrun with you. Guard them for thirty years and treat them no worse than you do yourselves.'

'And then, Master?'

'If they have worked hard and learned their lesson, you may decide to set them free. I leave that to you.'

He bowed. Gisli, her old face tortured into lines deep as ravines, bowed until her stringy hair swept the paving stones. The other Whelm bowed equally low.

'Yes, Master,' she whispered. 'We are very sorry, Master.'

'Never call me Master again, nor anyone else. You are a free people now and you have your homeland back.'

They turned and trudged away, looking beaten down.

'Was that true?' said Karan.

'What?' he said absently.

'That you will quit this world and go where none can follow.'

He pressed a hand to the wound in his side, which had leaked a small amount of blood.

'I'd prefer you kept it to yourselves. No one else need know, for now.' He smiled and shook Karan's hand, then Sulien's. 'Thank you for standing with me. I'd better get back. The slaves have no food and must be sent home, and that will require many different gates. Go, get some sleep.'

Karan was half asleep on one of the bunks in the sky galleon when it occurred to her that Maigraith had not been seen in ages. Not since Aviel had revealed her treachery, in fact. What was she up to now?

# 55

# GO IN AND CONFRONT YOUR ENEMY

Aviel dreamed that she was back in her perfumery workshop, down the back yard of Shand's house in Casyme. The shelves and benches held her well-used glassware and equipment, everything was sparklingly clean, and the garden was full of flowers and herbs whose scents she was looking forward to extracting over the next few months. And best of all, there was no one around to pester her.

'Wake, it's coming dawn.' Someone was shaking her shoulder. 'It has to be done now.'

'Go away!' Aviel was desperate to get back to her dream. 'Not getting up until next year.'

'Now!' the woman said quietly.

It was Lirriam, and perhaps there was magic in her voice, or perhaps it was just the tone of someone used to being obeyed. Aviel, inured to people ordering her about, was suddenly wide awake. She heaved the covers back.

'*What* has to be done now?' she said.

'You'll see when we get there. Quick, I don't want anyone else to know.'

'Why not?'

'Not here!' Lirriam hissed.

Aviel put her boots on and followed. What was Lirriam planning to do, and why did she want Aviel's help?

Outside, the compound was peaceful, almost beautiful, apart from the scatter of moon-touched shards of the twinned crystal, and the wreckage of its mechanism. Beyond the wall of the compound, four pyres were still burning, one for the Merdrun, one for the slaves, including the twenty-seven whose lives Skald had drunk before Uletta's, one for the lyrinx and one for the fallen Whelm. Fortunately, the wind carried the smoke away.

Up the hill, all was dark. Gating the slaves back to their home cities, and the Whelm to Salliban, had occupied Rulke, Lirriam and Flydd all the previous afternoon and most of the night, even with the power of the node and the use of the Waystone.

Lamps fixed around the base of Skyrock still glowed here and there, and some of the blue cladding on the tilted iron tower, though a number of lengths had fallen off in the night, smashing and scattering fragments for a hundred yards around. They would look beautiful when the sun struck them later in the morning.

Lirriam headed through tendrils of mist to the cubic temple. 'Why are we here?' said Aviel.

'We've come for Maigraith. You've earned the right.'

'But what do you want?'

'I owe you my life, so I will answer – but not now.' She handed Aviel the space shearer.

'Do you want me to let her out?'

'If you think that's best.'

'What if I don't?'

'We could both walk away. No one else knows she's inside – and without the space shearer, not even Rulke can get in.'

'This is a test, isn't it? You know how I'm drawn to the dark path. Are you testing me to see if I have what it takes? To be your servant?'

Lirriam burst out laughing. 'Dear child –'

'I'm not a child!' Aviel snapped.

'You're sixteen! You won't come of age for years. Besides, I may be far gone in wickedness – I am! – but I'm not so debased as to corrupt children.'

'Why me?'

'You saved the day today –'

'All I did was –'

'If I say you saved the day, Aviel, *you saved it!*' Lirriam snapped. 'And the night before last you saved my life. Enough talk. Go in and confront your enemy.'

Aviel cut a hole through the wall as she had done before, and scrambled in. It was just as unpleasant as last time, and she felt the possibility of annihilation just as keenly.

She stood up and looked around warily. All was as it had been before – dimly lit, cold and still, the air stale. No, there was a hint of death now. Not decay, it was too cold for that, but the scent of blood and flesh.

Aviel was about to head down to her left, towards the cells, when something rose on the other side of the main chamber.

Like a wraith, Maigraith was, pale and moving like smoke. So pale that she might have spent years in here, rather than a day and a quarter. Aviel screwed her courage to its most desperate peak, gripped the space shearer and turned to face her.

'It was the summon stone,' Maigraith said in a voice slow and drear.

'What was?'

'I realised it the moment I destroyed it with the nivol you made. Because finally, in that instant, I was freed from its malign influence. It started long ago, when Karan put *hrux* in my dinner and it almost drove me out of my mind, and I hid up in Carcharon. Perhaps I was led there, because while I was there the summon stone linked to me, infected me and fed my obsession for the next two centuries. It drove me to become the Numinator. I could have done so much, but my life has been wasted ...'

'You're blaming the *summon stone*?' said Aviel. 'You're unbelievable!'

'I'm blaming *Karan*,' she ground out.

'Anyway, it's over, no thanks to you. The enemy are gone. Defeated.'

'I sensed it.' Maigraith showed no pleasure or curiosity. 'What do you want?'

What *did* Aviel want? She had thought she wanted Maigraith punished, not least for turning Aviel toward the dark path from which she feared she would never escape.

No! she thought. Take responsibility. Whatever you did, it was your choice.

'You used us badly,' said Aviel. 'I want reparation.'

Maigraith came closer. 'I can make your bad ankle the mirror image of your left ankle. It'll never trouble you again.'

It was tempting. But the look of her ankle, and the way it restricted what she could do, were part of who she was, and she did not care to change it. The pain was another matter.

Though if Aviel were to climb back up the slippery path, she had to make sacrifices.

'I want nothing for myself. Right your wrongs – those that can be righted. But don't do it for what you'll get out of it. Do it for –'

Colour flooded Maigraith's drawn face. 'How dare you lecture me!'

She ran past Aviel, dived through the hole in the wall, and vanished.

Jassika had risen early and left the tent. Sulien was wandering aimlessly around the camp. For the past half year she had lived on the edge, constantly needing to be alert to dangers great and small. She had longed for peace and often daydreamed about going back to their humdrum life at Gothryme, where one day, even one month, was much the same as the next. But everything had changed so rapidly yesterday that she could not adjust.

The sky galleon had gone out early but Flydd was still around, so Sulien assumed the brilliant but reckless Chissmoul had taken it. If only she had asked Sulien to go with her. Everyone else was so earnest and grim as they went about a thousand important jobs. No one needed her help, though.

Yesterday, and for days and weeks and months, she had been in the fight of her life, and the things she did had really mattered. But everyone was too busy to talk to her now. Karan and Llian just wanted her to go away and play, like any normal child her age.

Sulien did not think she could ever be a child again.

'Something the matter?' said Flydd, who had just emerged from Skyrock, tucking something into his bag.

Sulien kicked a sapphire across the paving stones. 'They just want me to keep out of the way.'

'Come with me. I've got a little job that'll be just right for you.'

Her heart soared. 'What is it, surr?'

'Don't *surr* me, child. Call me Xervish.'

'Only if you stop calling me *child*.'

He stopped, looking down at her thoughtfully.

'When adults say it, it's to put me in my place. "Go away and play, child. We asked great and dangerous things of you before, but now we want you to be a child again."'

'They have your best interests –'

'I *know*!' Sulien stamped her foot. 'I'm not stupid.'

'But you *need* to be involved. I was the same when I was a boy, caught in great dangers in the endless war.'

She studied him thoughtfully. It was almost impossible to believe that this scarred, grizzled old man could ever have been a fresh-faced boy.

'I was,' he said quietly, as if he had read her thoughts. He gave a great sigh. 'Come on.'

'Where are we going?'

'To witness the meeting of two old enemies. And I don't want it to take place here, where everyone is watching.'

'Just you and me?'

'Just you and me.'

They went out the tenfold gates, around to the left and along beside one of the volcanic dykes that radiated out from the pinnacle. Inside the compound they had been cut down to ground level but here the dyke, a ridge of pale rock, projected fifteen feet from the ground. Only the blue and white spirals of Skyrock, with the leaning iron tower on top, could be seen above it.

'Xervish?' she said.

'Mnn?'

'The old woman and the old man at Stibbnibb ...'

'They were killed by Dagog's blast. I don't think they suffered. Did they treat you badly?'

'No. The old man hardly knew I was there.'

'He was dreadfully shy. And the old woman?'

'She wasn't kind. But she wasn't cruel either. She made me stronger.'

'Well, there you go, then,' said Flydd, smiling to himself.

Rulke rose from a shelf of rock he had been sitting on. 'Xervish?' he said, frowning. 'Why have you brought her?'

Sulien stopped, thinking she would be sent away.

'She needed to be here,' said Flydd.

Rulke studied her for a moment, then sat again. 'If you say so.'

'How are you feeling?' said Flydd.

'A trifle anxious, since you ask.'

But you're a great man, Sulien thought. What can you possibly be anxious about?

'I expect I would be too,' said Flydd.

No one spoke for a few minutes. Rulke must be meeting Maigraith. She had believed him dead for more than two centuries, and since discovering that he was still alive she had been obsessed with getting him back. But surely their reunion was a private matter. Why had Flydd brought her here to witness it?

Sulien's keen ears picked up the distant whine of the sky galleon, and shortly it appeared in the east, but flown so carefully that it was hard to believe Chissmoul was at the controls.

It set down fifty yards away and silence fell, apart from the creaking and groaning of its frame as it adjusted to being on the ground. A ladder was lowered on the far side; Sulien heard metal ring against stone. But why would Maigraith come by sky galleon? And why wasn't Lirriam here?

A wheeled chair was pushed around the bow of the sky galleon by a tall, willowy old woman. Not Maigraith, and neither was she in the chair. A big man sat there, his hands gripping its arms.

Yggur was greatly changed from the strong, vigorous man who had helped them escape to the future from the top of Shazmak less than two months of Sulien's life ago. He was an old man now, and looked it.

The wheels of the chair rattled as it approached, and Sulien sensed the tension in Rulke. His face was drawn, and he was standing so rigidly erect that it must be pulling on his scar.

The wheeled chair stopped ten feet away. Yggur pushed himself to his feet. He might once have been as tall as Rulke, though his back was bent and he was a head shorter now. His hair was grey and thin, but his eyebrows were dark brown, and his eyes were the same frosty blue-grey that they had always been.

'Rulke!' he said coldly.

'Yggur,' Rulke said as quietly as a sigh.

Having been schooled by Llian in the Histories, and having read several of the Great Tales including the *Tale of the Mirror*, Sulien knew that they had been mortal enemies.

'I owe you,' Rulke said.

Yggur acknowledged it with a tilt of his long head. 'But I'm past my time, and not long for the world. I – I –' He seemed to be going through a great internal struggle, then said, in a rush, 'I forgive you.'

Rulke took a step backwards. 'You *forgive* me?' He sounded uncomprehending, shocked. 'I would not have thought *forgive* was in your vocabulary. It's never been in mine.'

'It wasn't. But time heals.'

'For some. Well,' Rulke seemed to be struggling to find any useful words, 'thank you.'

He stared at the ground for some time, and Sulien wondered if he were looking deep inside himself, for courage.

'I am truly and deeply sorry,' he said at last, 'for what I did to you. Though ... I possessed your mind in self-defence.'

'Not solely in self-defence. There was pride and anger and bitterness too.'

'With reason. The Council was exerting all its power to trap me. It used the woman I loved, and was betrothed to, as bait – then sent her to a cruel and needless death. And that bastard, that unutterable swine, Mendark, contrived it.'

'He did. Though he loved Santhenar with all his heart and was always acting to protect it.'

'Which I acknowledge. But that's beside the point. When did an excuse ever help? I make none, Yggur. I did what I did ...'

Again he paused for a long time. 'And it caused you torment then and ever after, and troubles you to this day.'

Yggur shuddered. 'To have one's mind possessed by another, even briefly, and to have the ghost of that presence squatting there, observing every action, judging every thought, robbing one of all control – it's been my bane, Rulke.'

'I know,' Rulke said softly. 'I know.'

He came forwards, extending his hand. After a long hesitation Yggur took a single step forwards and shook Rulke's hand.

'I can lift the presence from you,' said Rulke.

Yggur pulled free and staggered backwards, shuddering, his face twisted in terror. 'Do you think I'd ever put you in my power again?' he choked.

'I too will soon quit this world, Yggur. Before I go, I must set right what wrongs I can.'

Flydd's head jerked up. What was Rulke saying? Sulien wondered. That he was dying too?

The woman behind Yggur's wheeled chair laid her fingers on his arm and whispered in his ear. After what appeared to be a long inner struggle, he nodded stiffly.

'I accept your offer,' he said to Rulke. 'I would give anything to be free, before I die.'

Rulke came closer and spread his huge hands to enclose Yggur's head on the left side and the right. Yggur's face twisted. Clearly, it was taking all his self-control to not jerk away.

Rulke whispered what Sulien took to be words of power. Yggur went rigid, as if he had been turned to stone. Had Rulke betrayed him after all, in one final revenge?

Of course not. Rulke stepped backwards, hands hanging by his sides, and he was shaking. Whatever he had done, it had taken a lot out of him.

Yggur slowly stood upright, his formerly bent back straight, and the strain faded from his long face.

'It's gone,' he said in wonderment. 'The demon in my mind, the anguish, the torment – after 1,200 years it's finally gone.'

'I owed you,' Rulke said simply. 'I had to repay.'

They faced each other for a minute or two, not speaking, then Yggur said, 'I have a gift for you. It's not repayment for what you've done ... We'd already planned it ... but anyway ...'

'A gift – for *me*?' Rulke seemed bemused.

The woman came forwards, moving slowly and stiffly. Hints of a former beauty remained in her aged face. Shivers ran up Sulien's back.

'My name is Tulitine,' the old woman said, a trifle anxiously. 'I was a seer and a healer.'

'Yes?' said Rulke.

'I am the only child of Illiel, your second son who was raised by the Faellem, and fathered me in his old age. I am your granddaughter.'

'Oh!' said Rulke, astounded and overcome. 'Tu-li-tine,' he said in wonderment. 'My *granddaughter*.'

He opened his arms and she went to him. 'You're the only relative I have left,' he said.

'I also have a grandmother ... but we've long been estranged.'

Sulien was watching them, tears in her eyes, when she realised that Flydd was tugging at her sleeve.

'Leave them to their moment,' he said. 'Yggur also has business with you.'

'*With me?*'

'Go with him. He has something to say to you.'

Wondering, she took Yggur's arm, and they walked away along the great dyke. He was slow, though not as slow as he'd been when he rose from his wheeled chair a quarter of an hour ago.

When the others were out of sight behind the sky galleon, Yggur found a flat bench in the dyke and sat down, sighing.

He patted the rock beside him. 'Sit with me, Sulien. You look a trifle shocked.'

'It's only been two months.' He looked so old.

'Not for me, though that doesn't matter. I wanted to thank you. You've done more than anyone could have asked of you.' He paused. 'But I can see you don't want to talk about that.'

'I just want to go home and live a normal, boring life again. But we have no home. Gothryme was probably ruined in the war, and it doesn't belong to us anyway.'

'Home is where you make it,' said Yggur. 'I'm sure you and Karan and Llian will find a way.'

'We're broke. We've got nothing but what we brought in our packs.'

'Then you're no worse off than half the people in the world.'

'But Mummy and Daddy have been fighting a lot lately. Mummy's ... um ... a bit controlling. And Daddy never stands up for himself. And I'm scared he's had enough.'

Yggur's frosty eyes seemed to lose focus, as if he was staring through the solid stone back to the camp at Skyrock.

'Sometimes good people just can't get on. It's no one's fault; it's just the way things are. But they'll never stop loving you.'

I know, she thought. But I want us to be together, like we used to be.

He put a hand in a pocket and drew something out, concealed in his fist. 'This was yours, back in the past, and I've kept it all this time. And used it once or twice. Flydd said it was dead, and I'm sure it was to him, but I think you'll be able to do something with it. Something that will make the place you end up at a little more like home.'

Sulien held out her hand and Yggur dropped an old, battered piece of carved wood into it, like three intergrown balls. It was the mimemule, a treasure that Faelamor had left to Karan in partial reparation, and it could be used to recreate things by magical mimicry.

'No need to tell your parents about it,' he said slyly. 'Karan didn't approve, I recall. Let's keep it between ourselves, eh!'

To his great astonishment, and her own, Sulien threw her arms around the grim old man and hugged him until his bones creaked.

# 56

# I DID ALL THOSE THINGS OUT OF LOVE!

W here have you been?' said Karan when Sulien appeared at their camp, in the corner of the compound near the stone-lined spring, with Flydd. 'I've been looking everywhere for you.'

'Nowhere,' said Sulien.

There was a smug look in her eye, as if she knew something Karan did not. Karan scowled at Flydd, who made a *What have I done?* gesture and jerked his head towards the well. Benches and tables had been installed there and Rulke was sitting with Nish and Tiaan, Llian, Aviel, Lilis and Maelys, and Yggur and Tulitine. There was no sign of Lirriam. Karan had not seen her all day. Nor Wilm, for that matter.

Karan's stomach knotted. With the Merdrun seen off, all their insoluble problems had come back to the fore. Where were they going to live, how would they make their living, did Llian still want her ...?

'What's going on?' she said, falling in beside Flydd.

'You can't put the responsibility of saving the world on Sulien's shoulders one minute, then treat her like a nine-year-old the next.'

'What would you know about child raising?' she snapped, nettled, though she knew he was right.

'More than you realise. Half the adults I've had to deal with over the past fifty years have acted like children some of the time,' he said pointedly. 'And some of them most of the time.' He looked the other way and his eyes narrowed. 'And here comes one of them now.'

It was Maigraith, though not as Karan had ever seen her. She must have used the rejuvenation potion again because she looked even younger than last time, certainly less than thirty. She wore a powder-blue gown that clung, albeit modestly, to her slender figure. Her chestnut hair had been cut short, she wore a silver fillet around her throat and a large, heavy gold ring on her left hand. Her cheeks were becomingly flushed and the flecks in her indigo eyes glowed carmine. She looked almost beautiful.

Aviel had crafted a mighty rejuvenation potion, and Karan wondered if she should ask her for some. No! No good could come from such things. And yet, how could it hurt – how could it ever hurt – to look and feel and be a little younger? Would it make a difference with her and Llian? Karan lifted the lock of hair with the grey hairs, eight of them now, and sighed.

Maigraith came up to them. 'Would you give us some privacy?' she said politely. It must have cost her; she was used to giving orders and being obeyed.

'Whatever you have to say,' said Rulke, 'you can say it in front of my friends.'

Llian looked startled at being described as Rulke's friend.

'Very well,' said Maigraith, twisting the gold ring. 'Rulke, you and I swore to one another. *Forever*, we said.'

'That was before I died. Death cancels all obligations, Maigraith.'

'No one comes back from the dead. You were under a stasis spell. We loved and we swore; how can you not honour your word?'

It would never work on Rulke; it would only turn him away. But it was not Karan's place to say it.

'We did love,' he said in a low, soft voice that quivered with emotion. 'I acknowledge it. But that was 224 years ago.'

'Forever!' she said, and the iron was back in her voice. 'We exchanged rings. What happened to yours?'

Rulke raised his left hand. 'I'd forgotten I had it.'

Maigraith winced.

'It wasn't there when I was freed from stasis,' he said. 'Yalkara might have taken it off before she put me in the statue. Or maybe it fell off – I lost a lot of weight.'

'Be true to your word, Rulke!'

'You speak of honour, Maigraith, but I see no honour in your life since we parted. And I did look; I talked to people who knew you, and read everything said about you in Flydd's *Histories*, trying to find a trace of the woman I had loved, and sworn to.'

Maigraith swayed on her feet, breathing fast and shallow.

'You allowed our son, Rulken, the twin who physically resembled me, unfettered reign until he became a monster and was slain by the fathers of the many girls he had outraged. Yet you sent Illiel away as if he were worthless.'

'He took after my Faellem ancestors,' she said, 'who so abused me.'

'He was our son! You should have treated them and loved them equally. And then, Maigraith, the abused became the abuser. You treated Karan abominably, and harassed Sulien and Llian mercilessly. Not to mention all the sickening things you did in your time as the Numinator.'

'I did it all out of love!' Maigraith cried, looking desperate now. 'To bring your people back from extinction, so your greatness would not be lost.'

'How dare you claim it was in some warped homage to me?' Rulke said quietly. 'You didn't want to recreate the Charon, you wanted to build something *better*.'

'That's not true.'

'Llian,' said Rulke, 'would you quote Maigraith's words to Karan again?'

'*Who else can a triune's son mate with but a triune's daughter?*' said Llian. '*From our loins spring a new people, a new species, perhaps with more of the strengths and fewer of the weaknesses than those that engendered us. Let us agree to pair them, now.*'

'You wanted to play God with the remnants of Charon blood in triunes and blendings, Maigraith, and that was unforgiveable. That's why you're nothing to me now.'

'I wish I'd killed your fat little trollop!' Maigraith said savagely.

'And now we come to it,' said Rulke. 'I held back from mentioning Lirriam, the most beautiful and brilliant woman I've ever met, and I asked her to stay away. This is between you and me. But I know what you tried to do to her. If you'd done nothing else, your offences against an innocent woman would have caused me to break my oath.'

'And,' he added, 'would you like to know the cruellest irony of all?'

'No, I wouldn't!' she snapped.

'Do you recall the tale Llian made up, about my mythical twin brother, Kalke?'

Maigraith ground her teeth.

'Incidentally, in Charon the word *kalke* means *gullible fool*. Though, to be fair to Llian, he didn't know it at the time.'

'Llian the Liar!' cried Maigraith, fixing him with a skin-scorching glare. 'You're dead!'

'Llian is under my protection,' Rulke said evenly. 'Getting back to the beautiful irony, it was your magical search of the void for Kalke that created the trace ...'

'What trace?'

'The one that led Lirriam to discover Santhenar, and me.'

Maigraith swung around and pointed at Llian, preparing to blast him down. 'I should have killed you when I had the chance.'

Karan sprang up, knowing there was nothing she could do to save Llian, but Rulke clamped his fist around Maigraith's hand and forced it down to her side.

'It's over, Maigraith. Even *you* must see it now.'

She slumped onto a dust-covered bench, staining her beautiful gown, and put her head in her hands.

Karan, still shaking, could not but take a small, vindictive pleasure in her downfall. But Karan knew she was flawed too; she had harmed many other people, not least of them Llian.

'And yet,' said Rulke to Maigraith, 'at least you acted out of love, warped and obsessive though it was. Love, no matter how twisted, is surely better than the hatred and bitterness that drove Stermin to send the Merdrun through the Crimson Gate in the first place, and which the Merdrun leaders inflicted on their people ever after.

'I did love you once, Maigraith, and I offer you the chance to redeem yourself, once you've made restitution to your victims.'

Maigraith looked up, and in those few minutes she had aged twenty years.

'The scent potion's failing,' said Aviel. 'I wondered how long it would last.'

'The scent potion is perfect,' said Maigraith, handing her the little green, cut glass bottle, which was still half-full. 'It would have kept me young for another twenty years, enough to have had a child and raise it to adulthood. But I used my Art to cancel it. Youth is just a burden now.'

Already she looked a little shrunken. Age lines were reappearing on her face, the skin of her neck sagged like crepe, and her hands were age-spotted. She flinched as Karan approached.

Karan reached out to her and said the hardest words she had ever had to say. She could not condone what Maigraith had done, and they would never be friends, but it was time to let the rage go.

'Let's put the past behind us,' she said, and embraced her.

Karan could not remember ever having seen tears in Maigraith's eyes, but they were flooding now. She was overcome.

She rose, raising her head and stiffening her back. 'I can't repair any of the things I've broken, but I will do all I can to make amends.'

'All I want is a grandmother's embrace,' said Tulitine.

Maigraith held her close, and long, then went to Yggur.

'We were lovers, briefly,' said Yggur, extending his hand, 'and then we were enemies. But because of you I found Tulitine and she's all I need.'

Maigraith shook his hand and passed on, to Rulke.

'Just your best wishes,' he said, 'for me and Lirriam.'

Maigraith choked them out, unconvincingly.

To Llian she said, 'I can't do anything to help you with your great problem, but –'

'What problem are you talking about?' he grinned. 'I have dozens.'

'The trauma of having your life partly drunk – twice. But I will make over my diaries to you.'

'What for?'

'They set down plainly, and with absolute truth, everything I've done in the past 224 years. And how, as the Numinator, I did all I could to ruin your good name and cast you as Llian the Liar.'

'Thank you,' said Llian. He wasn't a vengeful man, and to a chronicler the Numinator's diaries were beyond price.

Maigraith went to Karan. 'I cost you Gothryme and your every possession, and could have cost you your family as well. I can't do anything about the suffering I put you through. All I can do is say I'm sorry, and offer you every possession *I* have, to do with as you will.'

'I don't want anything of yours,' Karan said coolly. Clearly, *she* was feeling vengeful, after all.

'Forgiveness cuts both ways, Karan,' said Flydd. 'You need somewhere safe to live. Take her offer, if not for yourself, then for your family, otherwise worthless scavengers will. And you can do great good with the fortune that's left over.'

'All right,' said Karan. It might resolve several problems at the same time. Or at least, make them more bearable.

'And finally –' Maigraith reached out and touched Karan on the forehead. Very gently, but pain flared behind her temples.

'What have you done to me?' Karan whispered.

Maigraith gave her a sad little smile. 'The enemy took your mind-calling gift away. I – I thought you might like it back.'

Aviel was next. 'I don't want anything for myself,' she said to Maigraith. 'Can you help Ilisial? Not even Lirriam can heal her, and poor Wilm is in agony.'

But Maigraith could not do anything either, and Ilisial died an hour later without opening her eyes, or giving any sign that she knew Wilm had waited so faithfully by her side.

# 57

# IT'S AS DECEITFUL AND MALICIOUS AS EVER

I t's not enough,' said Maigraith late that afternoon. 'There's only one way to make up for the ruin I've caused, and make my failed life meaningful. My mentor and cruel oppressor showed me the way long ago ... but do I have the strength for it?'

Karan felt a sudden chill, and it was not due to the cold southerly wind blowing, or the coming night. They had taken over the stone meeting hall at the back of the officer's compound, and everyone but Rulke and Lirriam were seated around a roaring fire. They had repaired to the construct when the day's work was done and pulled up the ladder.

Maigraith walked down the hall to the fireplace at the other end, sat in the solitary chair and stared into the flames, her thin shoulders heaving.

What could she mean? It took Karan some time to work it out. Maigraith's *mentor and cruel oppressor* had been Faelamor and, remembering her fate, shivers ran down Karan's back. But Maigraith looked settled for the moment, and Karan turned back to the others.

'Whilever Skyrock exists,' Flydd was saying, goblet in hand, 'the Merdrun might be able to reopen the portal from Aachan and come back for their sacred Founder's Stone – and if they do, they'll exact a vengeance so terrible that –'

'No need to spell it out, said Tulitine, glancing at Sulien and Jassika, who were playing a game nearby, using a six-sided board and a selection of sapphires in different hues of blue. They were also, clearly, taking in every word.

'The only way to prevent it is to tear Skyrock down to the foundations.'

'Skyrock is so cursed,' said Yggur, 'and so imbued with their dark sorcery, that it'll be even more difficult to destroy than the summon stone.'

'But there is a way,' said Maigraith.

'How?' said Flydd.

'The portal hasn't completely closed. It's … *dormant*.'

'I didn't know a portal could be dormant.'

'It's still there but we can't see it because it doesn't have an exit. And there's only one way to erase such a portal – by opening a second portal inside it.'

'Don't ask me to volunteer,' said Flydd.

'It has to be done,' said Yggur. 'The next war rises out of the ashes of the last, and it's been going on since Shuthdar stole the golden flute and brought it to Santhenar 4,000 years ago. We need a clean break with the past.'

'How can another portal be opened inside the dormant portal?' said Nish. 'Wouldn't it destroy everything around it? *And* whoever opened the new portal?'

'I will do it,' said Maigraith. She had almost reverted to her old appearance now, though she no longer looked haggard, but quietly serene. 'Don't try to talk me out of it.'

'It'd take a mighty gift to far-see the destination from inside so great a portal,' said Yggur.

'There's a way.' Maigraith extended her hand to Maelys. 'May I have it?'

'What?' said Maelys.

'The Mirror of Aachan. No more powerful seeing device has ever existed.'

'But it's my unborn baby's birthright. It's all I have of him.'

'May I see it?'

With great reluctance, Maelys gave it to her. Maigraith pressed the face of the mirror against her forehead for a minute or two, let out a small cry, then passed it to Yggur.

'You held it for a long time. What do you see?'

He spread his left hand and fingers across the face of the mirror, but jerked them away, staring at it.

'I don't doubt that Yalkara erased its memories,' Yggur said slowly, 'but its true nature is unchanged. It will always lie to you, Maelys, because it thrives on causing pain and creating discord. You'll never find peace while you keep it.'

'I don't want to *get over* my baby's death,' Maelys said furiously.

'Which is why I said *find peace*. But there must be happier memories of him – and his father.'

Maelys closed her eyes for a minute or two. 'There are,' she said dreamily. 'Take it, then. When will you go, Maigraith?'

'While my resolve still holds,' said Maigraith.

She took the Mirror from Yggur, went out the western door and headed down towards Skyrock. It was windy out, cold and clear. The sun had recently set and the dark moon, with just a paring of the bright side showing, was rising over the range to the east, its rays slanting down towards the sapphire tunnel.

'Sulien,' said Karan, 'would you run to the construct and tell Rulke to come?'

Sulien ran, and Jassika with her.

Everyone else followed Maigraith, twenty or thirty yards behind. 'She's struggling,' Tulitine said to Yggur.

Maigraith's back was bent and her head bowed, as if she were carrying a heavy load that grew heavier with every step towards the dormant portal.

'It'll fight her all the way,' said Yggur. 'It knows it's an existential moment for them both. But I hope Maigraith will prove the stronger.'

Rulke came running, holding his side and panting, and seemed to understand at once. 'Come ahead,' he said to Karan.

They passed Maigraith by and went towards the entrance of the sapphire-lined tunnel. Karan felt hideously uncomfortable – somewhere between here and the other entrance was the dormant portal, presently leading nowhere but possibly ready to explode open between Aachan and here, and bring the Merdrun back.

'The mirror is heavy,' said Maigraith, her face an eerie blue in the reflected light from the sapphires. 'So very, very heavy.'

'Not for much longer,' said Rulke.

'My entire life has been struggle,' she said, 'against one enemy or another. I lost many of those battles, but I can win this one.'

Rulke touched her cheek as she went by. 'You've been one of the greats,' he said softly.

'Seldom in a good way.'

'You might have been,' said Karan, 'had you not been so cruelly damaged by Faelamor, over so many years.'

'But after she was gone, under the summon stone's influence I made the wrong choices all by myself. And now I'm paying down the debt. Stand well back.'

'How far?'

'I think ... at least two hundred yards.'

Everyone but Yggur moved back. Maigraith went on, but as she reached the entrance she stumbled and fell.

'The portal knows,' said Yggur. 'And the Mirror, too. I've got to go to her.'

'Yggur, please,' said Tulitine, clutching at his hand.

'We once were friends and I've never stopped caring for her. I have to support her on her final journey.'

'Then go,' she sighed, half irritated and half exasperated. 'And come back.'

Yggur went to Maigraith and lifted her to her feet. And together, dwarfed by that vast opening, they passed within.

Karan clutched Llian's hand, squeezing hard. Maigraith and Yggur could scarcely be seen now, for the tunnel was flashing bright blue and black, and the ground was vibrating, as if the dormant portal was trying to open by itself and carry them away. Again, Maigraith fell to her knees. Again, Yggur picked her up and they struggled forwards.

'How can they do it?' said Llian, 'against such forces?'

'No one ever understood Yggur's full powers,' said Rulke, 'or where he came by them.'

'He came by them from his father, Kandor,' said Llian.

Rulke stopped as though he had run into a stone wall. 'Kandor! How did you learn that?'

'Maelys told me. Kandor originally made her taphloid for Yggur, when he was a boy.'

'Astounding! We must talk later.'

Maigraith and Yggur reached the midpoint of the tunnel, then Yggur bent and kissed her brow, steadied her on her feet and headed out again.

'She sent me back,' he said when he emerged and came slowly across to where everyone had gathered at a safe distance. Tears were running down his cheeks. 'She just needed a little help, but ... she's found her strength now.'

Maigraith was holding the Mirror as high as she could reach, the rays of the rising, dark-faced moon reflecting back off it. Blue-streaked mist was streaming around her now, tugging at her gown and her grey hair, but she stood against it.

'The portal is partly open,' said Yggur quietly. He paused. 'She's fighting its impulse to open fully and hurl her to Aachan.' Another pause. 'She's shaking the Mirror, trying to wrench it to do her will.'

'But can she?' said Karan, who had her own bitter memories from carrying it so long and so far.

'Maigraith is using it to visualise a destination no one else can ever see,' said Yggur, almost inaudibly. 'She's opening her own portal ... it can't stop her now –'

Pain pierced Karan all over, and all around her people were gasping, crying out, and clutching their heads.

A dazzling white hole appeared where Maigraith had been standing. It fountained scintillating streams of white and quicksilver straight up through the stone of Skyrock as if it inhabited an entirely different dimension, then out the top and high in the air, and sprinkled down all around. And went out.

The blue glow from the tunnel had gone out as well, and with a roar like a breaking wave a billion sapphires fell from the walls and ceiling.

Maigraith is gone, Karan thought. Such a towering figure in the Histories, for so long. It was hard to take in.

'Her gate and the sapphire portal have annihilated one another,' said Yggur, one hand pressed to his chest, over his heart. 'The threat is no more.'

'I once loved, and was loved,' said Rulke, and turned and walked slowly away.

'A great and terrible power has just been used here,' said Flydd. 'And it must never be used again, or even reported. The truth must be hidden, and the Histories must play their part.'

He was looking at Llian, and Karan felt for him. Llian, who had long railed against falsehood in the Histories and the Great Tales, was being told to create an untrue ending for his Tale of the Gates of Good and Evil.

'Llian the Liar,' said Llian wryly.

'There are good lies and bad lies,' said Flydd.

Yggur, now clutching at his chest, staggered back to Tulitine, took her hands in his, sagged against her and fell down, dead. And Tulitine lay beside him and wept.

'No!' cried Sulien. 'Not old Yggur.' She ran to him and knelt beside him.

Everyone gathered around, as shocked as Karan. It did not seem right. The gap he left was too big to ever be filled.

Tulitine rose and wiped her face. 'I think he knew it would kill him ... but he only had weeks left ... and he wanted to die on his feet, not in bed. He ...'

'Was a good man,' said Karan.

'Would you give me a few minutes with him?' said Tulitine.

They rose and moved away.

'There's something I still don't understand about the Mirror,' said Karan.

'Oh?' said Flydd.

'After the assassination attempt at the thapter site, I ran around under the bow of the sky galleon, chasing Skald. He crashed into Maelys and she dropped the Mirror of Aachan, and he stared at it for a few seconds.'

'So?'

'I saw the face of a woman there. I'd never seen her before, but I recognised her the moment I saw her in the control chamber. It was Uletta.'

'I didn't see any woman,' said Maelys. 'I was looking at the image of my little sister, Fyllis.'

'Which means the Mirror deliberately showed Uletta's face to Skald,' said Flydd.

'Why would it do that?'

'To make mischief. It picked his weakness – his need for love – and showed him the one slave woman he'd be attracted to who would also be attracted to him. And it caused his downfall. Had he not had that forbidden relationship with Uletta he would never have conspired to kill Dagog, and Klarm's plan would have failed. From such little things a world can be lost – or won. The Mirror has done us good for the first *and last* time.' Flydd shivered. 'It's damn cold. I'm going back to the hall.'

The others followed. Karan stood there silently, thinking about all the ways she had known Maigraith and Yggur, until a movement in the gloom to her left roused her.

'It's gone,' said Maelys, reaching out to Nish. 'I'm free!'

'Free to remember our son,' he said quietly.

'As he really was. It was lying the whole time. Would you ... like to find somewhere private?'

Maelys took his hand and they walked off into the darkness.

# 58

# THERE CAN BE NO WITNESSES

B ut the Merdrun's most toxic legacy remains,' said Flydd late that night, after Sulien and Jassika had gone to bed in the sky galleon, and Tulitine had retired to the tent she had shared with Yggur. 'What are we going to do about it?'

No one spoke. Aviel was sitting quietly in the shadows to the left of the huge stone fireplace, half afraid that if anyone noticed her, she would be sent to bed like one of the children. There was no sign of Wilm. After Ilisial's death, and her laying out, he had walked away and had not come back. Maelys and Nish had not returned either, and Rulke had gone back to the construct after the two portals annihilated.

Karan and Llian had barely said a word. Karan had known Maigraith best and longest, Aviel thought, and doubtless she had mixed feelings about her. Llian's lips were moving, as if he were reciting part of a tale to himself, or perhaps an elegy. Tiaan was dozing in her chair.

Aviel could not have said that she had ever liked Maigraith. She had gone out of her way to belittle Aviel and make her feel small and powerless, and there had been times when Aviel had felt sure Maigraith was going to kill her. Yet they had worked together for more than six weeks, and Aviel had more than once been moved by Maigraith's desperate yearning to have Rulke back.

She had been a bad person, but not wholly bad, and she had gone to her death willingly, even serenely, in partial atonement for the terrible life she had lived. Was it enough? Aviel had no way of judging the moral balance ... but it was enough for her to understand, and to forgive, and as she did a great weight left her small shoulders.

Rulke and Lirriam came in and sat beside Flydd, by the fire. Lirriam took a glass of wine. Rulke did not. It was the first time they had been seen together all day.

'The Founder's Stone,' said Flydd.

'What about it?' said Rulke.

'Stermin's Stone was the force behind the original Azure and Crimson Gates from which all the corruption came. It's the Merdrun's most sacred object, and the only way to erase the taint is to destroy it.'

'It's far more resistant than the summon stone. Won't be easy to destroy.'

'If the Founder's Stone can be unmade, it would, after the Merdrun have served their sentence, allow the possibility of their rehabilitation. But it's a deadly device that will do everything possible to protect itself. How can it be unmade?'

'It's protected by an ancient curse so mighty that not even Rulke can get near it,' said Lirriam. 'A curse far greater than the one that rendered the summon stone impervious to all but nivol.'

'But you took it to the control chamber,' said Karan. 'You held it in your hand.'

'I was one of the Five Heroes, and we were turned to stone for a very long time. There's an ... affinity.'

'I'd love to hear that story,' said Llian, his eyes glowing. He was incorrigible.

'It's not one I tell ... though ... since you risked your life to save me, you may have it. But not tonight.' Lirriam paused as if gazing back down the well of time. 'Petrifaction is how I ended up with this.' She stroked her shining opaline hair. 'And its residues allow me to touch the Founder's Stone and not be harmed. But I've no idea how to destroy it.'

Flydd emptied his goblet and reached for the bottle, but thought better of it and leaned back in his chair and closed his eyes.

'I do,' said Aviel.

Everyone gaped at her.

'You astound me,' said Flydd, sitting up smartly.

'Not me,' said Lirriam.

Rulke picked up the bottle and filled a clean goblet, sipped from it and leaned back in his chair, smiling. 'I look forward to hearing this.'

'Um ... we just saw that two gates can't be opened in the same space,' said Aviel. 'Well, two solid objects can't occupy the same place either. I learned that going into the cubic temple.'

'There's an eyewitness report from the Lyrinx War,' mused Flydd, 'of someone accidentally opening a gate into a solid object and sending something small –'

'What objects?' said Rulke.

'A needle – into a block of granite.'

'And?'

'No trace of the needle, or the block of granite, was ever found. Or the mancer who did it.'

'Any witnesses?'

'No, but I visited the scene a couple of days later. The ground had been melted to glass a foot deep and for a hundred yards around. Trees half a mile away had been blown over, and the ones still standing were charred on the side that had faced the granite block.'

Rulke shivered. 'I know of no power that could create such ruin. Nor want to know.'

'Nor had I, until then,' said Flydd. 'And I wouldn't suggest it if there was any alternative. In any case ...'

'What?'

'I don't know how to open a gate within a solid object – the resistance would be overwhelming.'

'I've got an idea,' said Rulke, glancing at Aviel.

He lowered his voice, and he, Flydd and Lirriam huddled together and talked for a while. Aviel did not catch what they were saying and wasn't particularly curious. Such things were for great mancers and adepts, people who knew the Secret Art backwards. All she wanted was for everything to be over so she could go back to making perfumes, and bring a little pleasure, and a little joy, to her battered world.

'If it could be done,' said Rulke several minutes later, 'what would you put inside?'

Flydd held up the little red leader's cube, cut long ago from the keystone of the Crimson Gate. 'Lirriam tore it from Durthix's neck before hurling him into the portal. It's also a corrupt artefact.'

'Two birds with one stone,' said Rulke. 'But there can be no other witnesses.'

'Tomorrow, then.'

The sky galleon had been loaded with the bodies of Klarm, Yggur, M'Lainte, Ilisial and Uletta, all decently prepared and shrouded. Wilm had come back in the night, though he had not said more than a few words to anyone, including Aviel.

Early in the morning, Flydd gave Chissmoul directions and everyone but he, Rulke, Lirriam and Llian went aboard.

'Not you,' said Lirriam to Aviel.

'What do you want *me* for?' said Aviel.

'Come.'

She climbed down the ladder, resentfully. She was so sick of people ordering her about.

'Aviel?' cried Wilm. His big hands were clenched on the rail and he looked distraught. 'Where are you going? Why aren't you coming with us?'

'She's choosing her path, Wilm,' said Lirriam.

'She's already on the right path. Wait – I'm coming.'

'Go back, Wilm!' Lirriam said sharply. 'You are not required here.'

The sky galleon lifted quietly, as befitted a craft containing the bodies of their friends, and flew north, Wilm still staring desperately at Aviel. She turned towards the cubic temple, wondering what Lirriam was up to.

'Not yet,' said Flydd. 'Wait until they're out of sight.'

'Seems a bit extreme,' muttered Llian.

'Doesn't one of the commandments forbid chroniclers from trying to influence an historical outcome?' Rulke said pointedly. 'And weren't you banned for breaking that commandment and causing my 'death'?'

'Sorry.' Llian looked away, though he did not appear sorry.

'It's gone,' said Flydd, and headed towards the cubic temple. 'Let's get this done.'

Aviel was thinking about her life and her path as they walked across, and when they reached the cubic temple she said, 'Um, Lirriam, Rulke ... can I do it?'

'This is adept's work,' said Flydd. 'You've done enough.'

'But I *need* to do it,' she said quietly. 'I've done terrible things, with Maigraith and *to* her. I'm terribly attracted to the dark path of mancery, and –'

'Oh, poo! I've never met anyone so thoroughly good and decent as you.'

She glared up at him. 'It doesn't matter what you think, Xervish. It matters what *I* think.'

'She's right,' said Lirriam. 'In Aviel's mind, she's done dark deeds and thought dark thoughts, and only by putting her life on the line can she turn her back on the path she fears.'

'What if she fails?' said Flydd.

No one spoke. Clearly, Flydd, Rulke and Lirriam were considering that possibility. Llian's lips were moving again and his eyes had a faraway gleam.

'I *will* have faith,' said Lirriam, and handed Aviel the space shearer and a pair of silky gloves. 'Put these on. You can't touch the stone with your bare hands. We'll wait by the construct. After you've done it, come out *immediately* and we'll fly to a safe distance.'

'We don't know precisely what will happen,' said Flydd. 'Or how quickly.'

'It took more than ten minutes for the space shearer hole to fill in,' said Aviel, drawing on the gloves.

'That was just a wall. The Founder's Stone will be more resistant, harder to cut a dimensional hole in, and it may not last as long.'

'Maybe not *nearly* as long,' said Lirriam.

Aviel cut a rectangular hole in the wall of the cubic temple and climbed through, and stood there, shivering. It was bitterly cold here. The Founder's Stone was back on the pedestal where it had been the first time. And even from this distance she could feel its pull, much as the summon stone had tried to draw her to it at Carcharon.

Why, though? It was a Merdrun thing, and she was of inferior human stock. What did it want?

'You never give up, do you?' she said aloud.

*Why are you here, girl?*

'I don't know,' she said slowly, but thinking fast.

*You're a worthless little cripple. But you can be rich, beautiful, honoured.*

'The scullery maid doesn't really turn into the princess. That story's just designed to keep the lowly content with their lot.'

*What do you want, girl?*

'Just a place of my own, so I can make my perfumes, unbeholden to anyone else.'

*You can have it. What else?*

'That's all. I'm not greedy.' Aviel moved a few steps closer to the Founder's Stone.

*You should be. I can fix your ankle in an instant.*

'No, thanks.'

*Then I'll ease Wilm's torment. It hurts you to see him suffer so.*

Now she was tempted, but she'd been there before. She went closer, and this time it was hard to stop. The soles of her boots were slipping on the floor as if there was a strong wind at her back.

*I can turn Wilm back to you.*

This gave Aviel pause. 'He'll always be my friend,' she said stoutly, praying it was true. 'He'll come back when he's ready.' But would he? She had a bad feeling that, after laying Ilisial to rest, Wilm would walk away, never to return.

*You're afraid of the dark path*, said the Founder's Stone. *That's why you're here – to risk your life doing what you think is good, in the hope that it will be a huge step away.*

'Yes,' she said.

*There can be no greater sacrifice than to give back, to the man you love, the woman he loves.*

The ever-present cold here was spreading through her bones. 'What are you talking about?'

*I could bring Ilisial back for Wilm.*

Had he really loved her? Aviel had tried to think of them as just friends, but love was an entirely different matter.

*If you truly love him, you'll give her back to him. So noble a sacrifice will turn you away from the dark path for good.*

Again, she was tempted. But Aviel had heard fairy stories about people – usually a child or a lover – being brought back from the dead, and it never went right. The ones brought back longed to return to death, while the people who had raised them gained only misery and despair, and sometimes, their own death.

'They're just cautionary tales, intended to dissuade people from yearning for the impossible.'

*This offer is real. Wilm can be happy again.*

Could he? Maybe it *was* possible.

'What do you want me to do?' she said.

*Touch the lowest face of the leader's cube to the apex of the Founder's Stone, and the air above it will glow red in a small circle. Use your space shearer blade to cut a dimensional hole around the red circle, then put the leader's cube through the hole. And you will have your wish.*

Aviel was considering it when she sensed the eagerness of the stone and drew back. Bringing people back from the dead was necromancy, and it was definitely one of the dark Arts. Besides, she felt sure it was a lie. What did the stone really want?

The leader's cube was a mighty magical artefact, one of the oldest in existence, but why did the Founder's Stone want her to cut a dimensional hole and put it through? Where would the hole lead?

To the Merdrun, on Aachan! The Founder's Stone wanted her to send the cube through so they could use its link to the Founder's Stone to turn the dimensional hole into a portal, and escape.

'No!' she cried, her high voice echoing in the still chamber.

She could feel its will battering at her own, trying to break down her defiance. And it would. It was age-old and used to domination.

She moved closer, until she could have reached out and touched the Founder's Stone. Around her neck, the leader's cube grew hot and heavy.

*Touch the cube to the apex, then cut out the circle and pass the cube through. Quickly!*

Aviel wanted to, just to escape the pressure of its will. The persona, or whatever it was gave voice to the Founder's Stone, must have realised that she was wavering, because the cajoling voice became harsh and commanding.

*You stupid little girl, you can't defy me. Do it!*

It was a mistake. All Aviel's life people had beaten and abused her, ordered her about and tried to dominate and control her, and it always put her back up.

She was close to the Founder's Stone now, and she thrust the two-pronged tip of the space shearer through the words etched down the side – *For the greater good, evil must be done to evil* – and into the crystal.

It was hard. Far harder than the thick stone wall of the cubic temple, which the space shearer had cut as easily as if it had been butter. The Founder's Stone resisted her all the way. The point of the blade had only gone in half an inch and it was taking all her strength to force it further. But she had to reach the centre of the crystal.

*I command you, stop!*

'Or what?' said Aviel. She had to maintain her defiance or it would quickly overwhelm her. 'I'm not Merdrun. You've got no authority over me.'

*I have the authority of pain.*

Agony shot through her bad ankle. Excruciating agony, as if the bones were being chiselled apart. Agony so bad that it was a struggle to stay on her feet at all. But the pain was a good sign, if she could endure it. It meant that she was on the right track; that the Founder's Stone was afraid.

Her arm was shaking now, cold sweat running off her brow. She pushed harder. Harder. Harder. The pain grew even worse; she could not think for it. Her existence was made of just two points: the agony in her ankle and the mindless pressure of her arm forcing the space shearer further into the crystal. This dimensional hole wasn't a neat circle; its edges were ragged and broken.

The resistance ceased. The crude circle was complete and a dimensional hole appeared there, blacker than black. But the agony was worse than ever, as if the stone knew pain was its best defence.

Aviel had to act quickly now. The hole might not last long in such a resistant crystal, and if she was still here when it closed again, she would be annihilated. She dragged the hot, heavy leader's cube from around her neck, and dropped it.

She tried to pick it up, but it grew so heavy that she could not lift it. She sheathed the space shearer, bent her knees and took the cube in both hands.

It was like lifting a large block of stone, but by heaving and straightening her legs she got it up onto the top of the pedestal, next to the Founder's Stone. Her heart was pounding, and her bad ankle was battered with new dimensions of pain.

The stone was even heavier here; there wasn't enough strength in her arms to lift it the six inches she needed. She tried again, and failed.

What if she took hold of the cube, bent her legs and straightened her arms until she was holding it above her head? Then she could use the greater strength of her legs to get it in position. She tried it, then slowly straightened her legs, using her thigh muscles to lift the weight.

Her knees wobbled and her arms were giving way. She was going to drop it on her head and the weight would crush her to the floor. Aviel slammed the cube down onto the pedestal beside the Founder's Stone. Though she only had to lift it three inches to slip it into the dimensional hole, it was three inches too far.

And time was racing by.

Fool! she thought. There's a hard way and an easy way.

She lifted the Founder's Stone from its mount. Her fingers stung even though she wore gloves. Its weight did not change. She turned it sideways and pushed the dimensional hole down over the cube.

I'm *doing evil to evil*, she thought. Is that going to save me from the dark path, or doom me?

*It's going to doom you*, said the stone. *Take – it – out.*

She turned the Founder's Stone upright, holding the cube in place inside it. The massive weight was gone. Aviel sat the stone back on its pedestal and ran.

At least, she tried to, but she only managed a couple of steps.

*Back! Now! Take it out!*

Pain sheared through her ankle, unlike anything she had ever felt before. Ten times worse. A hundred times. She could not bear to touch her angled foot to the floor.

*This is just a hint of what you'll feel if the cube and the stone annihilate. And it won't just last an instant, as it appears for people seeing it from the outside. Your agony will go on for eternity.*

'I don't believe you,' she gasped.

Aviel fell to her knees and tried to crawl, but that was excruciating. Any stress on her bad ankle sent such pain through her that she wept.

She crawled a foot. Screamed. Another foot. The pain grew worse again. She could not think, could not see. She was screaming so loudly that something tore in her throat and she tasted blood.

Mindlessly, she crawled on, having no idea if she was heading in the right direction.

'You can't go in there!' Flydd yelled. 'We've got to go *now*; she can't be saved.'

'I never abandon my friends!' Lirriam said coldly.

Aviel collapsed. She had nothing left.

She was lifted and held against someone's chest. No, a bosom; Lirriam's. She was gasping; she was in pain too.

'Leave me,' Aviel whispered. 'Save yourself.'

Lirriam staggered towards the hole and heaved Aviel out. She landed badly and the pain almost obliterated her. Lirriam was dragged out as well, bleeding from the nose.

'Run!' said Flydd.

He picked Aviel up and ran with her. Llian was supporting Lirriam, her arm around his shoulder. They staggered towards the construct, twenty yards away.

'Faster!' bellowed Rulke from the lookout platform.

Aviel's eyes felt sticky, as if she were weeping bloody tears. She could not see and could barely hear. Her torn throat burned.

Flydd heaved her over his shoulder and put one foot on the long ladder that led up into the cabin of the construct. He was struggling too.

'Here,' bellowed Rulke.

Aviel felt Flydd knotting a rope around her. Rulke lifted her in a series of jerks and lowered her through the hatch onto the floor of the cabin. Llian and Lirriam fell in beside her, then Flydd.

The construct's mechanisms roared. It shook and shuddered but did not move.

'Go!' bellowed Rulke.

She had no idea what he did, but the construct took off like a rocket. The pain eased. Aviel rubbed sticky muck out of her eyes and looked around. Lirriam lay beside her, panting, blood around her nose and mouth. Flydd was beside her, eyes closed and teeth gritted. Llian was sitting up, holding his head in his hands.

The construct curved up into the sky at such a steep angle that Aviel could see Skyrock, and the cubic temple beside it, through the side portholes. It looked tiny now, insignificant.

'Turn away!' snapped Rulke. 'Close your eyes.'

She did so, and put her palms over her eyes. The seconds passed. Had she succeeded or had she failed?

The burst of light was so blinding that it showed red through the palms of her hands. Another burst, even brighter. But there was no sound, apart from Rulke slowly counting, as if timing how far away lightning was from the delay before the thunder. 'Twelve, thirteen, fourteen, fifteen, sixteen –'

The construct was buffeted by a mighty wind blast, shaking it violently, and Aviel thought it was going to fall out of the sky. Rulke managed to control it and kept going for another couple of minutes, then turned the construct back.

'You can look now.'

An ominous black cloud, like a fist on the end of a stalk, rose up from the point where the cubic temple had been. But it was utterly gone and so was the tower of Skyrock. Not a trace of either remained, and when Flydd handed Aviel a spy scope she saw that the ground for a quarter of a mile around was boiling. The palisades and camps were gone, burned to ash. Even the stone had been melted.

'I wouldn't go too close,' said Flydd.

Rulke raised an eyebrow.

'There's bound to be waste, magical or material, and who knows what it would do to us.'

'Is the Founder's Stone gone then?' Aviel croaked.

'Annihilated, and the leader's cube,' said Rulke. 'The curse on the Merdrun is ended.'

'Go,' said Flydd. 'I never want to see this place again. And,' he was looking at Llian this time, 'what Aviel did can't be reported either. No one can ever know how Skyrock was destroyed – this force is too deadly.'

'By the time you've finished forbidding me,' muttered Llian, 'there won't be any tales left to tell.'

Flydd snorted. Rulke rolled his eyes. Lirriam managed a smile.

Aviel opened her eyes and closed them again. She had done the right thing, this time.

And her ankle was barely aching now. At least, no more than normal. Life was good.

In a grim slave camp on Aachan the lowest slave of all, the cowardly scum formerly known as Skald, started. As he looked around with his one good eye, a shard broken off his rue-har and embedded at the back of the empty socket glowed faintly green – with power. He pulled his eye patch down to cover it.

Would it ever be possible to restore a name so tainted as his own? There was only one way – by breaking his tormented people out of slavery and exacting revenge on their oppressors.

The lowest slave of all bared his broken teeth and went back to his work.

# 59

# WE HAVE TO HONOUR OUR DEAD

'Tullymool,' said Flydd as the construct settled beside the sky galleon and a large, extravagantly ornamented air-floater, on a wildflower meadow that ran down to a tree-lined stream. 'We'll stay here a week or two.'

An alpine plateau, mostly forested, with a river meandering across it. A pretty place. Llian climbed down, drawing in the fresh mountain air, so different from the tainted air of Skyrock. Skyrock was gone and the war was over. It was hard to take in. The Merdrun were never coming back. He would never see or hear or smell Skald again. That last, ghastly moment quivered in the depths –

*Don't go there! Rulke and Lirriam have talked through the life-drinking with you, again and again. You can beat it.*

He took deep breaths and looked around. A stone's throw away, a group of people were taking breakfast on one of the verandas of a large timber homestead. It had a vegetable garden on one side, a pair of tethered goats, and beyond them a number of ancient fruit trees were dotted with small, unripe fruit.

From the air Llian had seen a small town a few miles away, and scattered areas of farmland, the soil rich and dark red. Further east, a series of peaks ramped up to the western end of the mighty Great Mountains.

Nish and Lilis rose from the table and came across to meet them. 'How did it go?' Nish said casually.

'How did *what* go?' said Flydd, smiling.

'Excellent. Come and have something to eat.'

'At the end of the Lyrinx War I'd planned to retire here,' said Flydd. 'To that very cottage, as it happens.' He indicated a stone house half a mile away and on the other side of the stream. 'But events got in the way, and by the time the God-Emperor was overthrown and peace was restored, I'd lost the urge for it.'

'You'd found love, you old dog,' said Nish. 'Or was it lust?'

Flydd stopped abruptly, and for a moment Llian thought his craggy face was going to crack apart, but he shuddered and regained control.

'You sorted out your differences with Maelys since the Mirror was destroyed?' Flydd said coldly.

Nish smirked. 'Pretty much.'

'Well, finish the job!'

'Don't worry, we intend to.' Nish went back to the table.

'Had you found love, Xervish?' Llian wondered. Being both insatiably curious and thick-skinned, he had no difficulty asking personal questions.

'Mind your own damn business, Chronicler. Sort out your own affairs.'

'I plan to,' said Llian. 'I'm not the man I was ...' He shuddered and suppressed another dark moment. 'I'm making a new start, here and now.' He added softly, 'I hope Karan's ready.'

He embraced Lilis, whom he had first known as a twelve-year-old street urchin in Thurkad. It was still hard to come to terms with her being an old woman. 'Someone said you were working here, spying for Flydd.'

'Not spying. Just talking to his spies and informers, all over the world, and pulling everything together into a picture for him.'

'That would have been interesting.'

'Depressing, most of the time, constantly hearing terrible news and being able to do nothing about it. But ... let's look to the future.'

The long table on the twelve-foot-wide veranda was set for eighteen people. Karan was at the left end, with Sulien and a bald man whose back was to Llian. Then Wilm, Jassika, Tiaan and Tulitine, Maelys and Nish, and Flangers and Chissmoul. At the right-hand end sat an obese old woman who looked as though she had lost a lot of weight lately, and a small, dark, energetic looking young man.

Nish introduced the old woman as Yulla Zaeff, the former governor of the great city of Roros, which had been burned by the enemy, and her nephew Renly, the current governor.

Llian took the empty place between Sulien and Wilm. Sulien threw her arms around Llian and hugged him tightly. Wilm nodded to Llian and managed a smile for Aviel as she sat beside him.

'I was so afraid.' He grabbed her hand and squeezed it, but abruptly let go and stared stiffly ahead.

Karan was avoiding Llian's eye. He looked up at the bald man, who was short and square, weather-beaten and wrinkled – and oddly familiar.

'Shand? Is it really you?'

The old man scowled. 'Who the hell else would it be?'

'I thought – well, assumed ...'

'That I'd been fertilising the daffodils for the past couple of hundred years?'

'Sorry.'

Llian stood up and reached across the table, and Shand rose as well, and they clasped hands.

'You look ... um ...'

'Shorter?' Shand growled. 'Well, people shrink in old age, don't they? You've got that to look forward to, in the unlikely event your friends let you live that long.'

He grinned and he was the Shand of old. Not the cranky old man he had been before they came to the future, but the kindly fellow of long ago. He must have found peace since they parted.

'When we said goodbye, I ever expected to see any of you again.' Shand indicated a platter piled with quarter inch-thick slabs of bacon. 'Get started, we can talk later. And if you're nice to me, I might even crack open a bottle of gellon liqueur tonight, in honour of the occasion.'

Llian piled bacon on one side of his plate and added fried tomatoes, onions and potatoes. 'You can get gellon here, in the middle of nowhere?'

'For a Teller, you have an unfortunate way with words.'

'So Rulke keeps saying,' Llian said cheerfully. Shand was, after all, his oldest living friend – though their friendship had been rather chequered, over the years.

'I grow it,' said Shand.

The twisted old trees down the side. Llian had thought they looked familiar. 'Why here?'

'This is Shand's place,' said Lilis. 'He kindly let me stay, to do Flydd's work.'

'How long have you lived here?' said Llian.

'Couple of hundred years,' said Shand. 'Ifoli, known as Nunar these days, and I spent many years here, while she worked out the Laws of Power and I helped in my own small way. But ... she only had a normal human lifespan. Enough talking. Eat!'

After breakfast they carried the bodies down to a lens-shaped area of grass by the stream, where the soil was deep and soft, and five graves had been dug. They buried their friends one by one with all due ceremony and more than a few tears: Yggur, M'Lainte, Ilisial and Klarm.

Finally they laid to rest, separately, the utterly betrayed Uletta. Her face had not smoothed out in death.

When her grave had been patted down with shovels and marked, Llian looked for Wilm, but he had taken himself off again. It was late in the afternoon and it had been a long, tiring day. They repaired to the shade of Shand's ancient gellon trees.

'Yggur asked that there be no tears or long faces for him,' said Tulitine. 'He lived an extraordinarily long life and died a contented man, free of pain at last. He knew his end was close, these past months, and before we left Fiz Gorgo he packed crates of preserved delicacies and special bottles. He wanted us to send him off with a feast.'

'What an excellent idea –' Llian broke off. Jassika's eyes were red and puffy; Klarm could not have died a contented man, since he had been robbed of his gift, and he had been taken well before his time. 'I'm sorry, Jassika. I didn't think –'

She managed a smile. 'Klarm – Daddy – loved a party. That's how I'd like to remember him.'

~

'In another week or two we'll all be going our separate ways,' said Flydd.

It was a warm summer's night and everyone was sitting around lazily, well-fed and bone weary. They had given their dead the best send-off they could.

'Much of Santhenar is in ruins,' said Yulla, 'and millions of hungry, homeless people are crying out for help.'

'And we who have been leaders have to take charge,' said Flydd, 'before villains and plunderers steal what's left.'

'Nothing for me to do, then,' said Llian. 'Karan wouldn't put me in charge of an empty outhouse.'

Karan's eyes glinted and it looked as though she was going to say something cutting, but she bit down on it. Flydd scowled, and Llian wished he'd kept his mouth shut.

'We're leaving soon, Yulla, Renly, Lilis and I,' said Flydd, 'and there's a good chance we won't see some of you, perhaps most of you, again. But first, arrangements have to be made.'

He beckoned Jassika. 'Way back in Thurkad, Klarm asked me to look after you, if anything happened to him, and I swore I would. But I'm a cranky old bastard, and I have no home, and I'm sure you wouldn't want me to look after you *personally*.'

Jassika scowled. 'It's all right. I'm used to being dumped on strangers.'

'It's unkind to draw it out, Xervish,' said Karan. 'Jassika, Sulien insisted that her dearest friend live with us, and I think so too ... though we don't know where we'll be living. Probably in a tent.'

You might have consulted me, Llian thought, feeling the familiar tension rising. He would have agreed, of course, but clearly Karan had no intention of changing.

'I slept in a tree for a month at Stibbnibb,' said Jassika. 'And then in a stinking cell. A tent would be luxury.'

'Come here,' said Karan, and opened her arms, and after a short hesitation Jassika went to her.

'That's settled, then,' said Flydd, and frowned. 'Now to deal with Llian.'

'What have I done now?' cried Llian. He could not think of anything. Or was

Flydd planning to force his and Karan's troubles out into the open, in front of everyone? His face burned.

'Llian the Liar, I mean.'

Llian swallowed. 'Yes?' he croaked.

'Maigraith left you her diaries, but we wanted to make it official, so we've signed an affidavit that clears you of the ancient charge of murdering Wistan, the Master of the College of the Histories, and states that the name Llian the Liar was ordered by the Numinator, for revenge. Your good name is restored.'

'And there's plenty for you to do,' said Nish, 'since the scrutators corrupted the Histories, and even rewrote some of the Great Tales, for propaganda purposes.'

'Wasn't the College of the Histories destroyed in the Lyrinx War?'

'Long ago. But with the world in ruins, the Histories and the Great Tales matter more than ever. The Histories provide perspective, and lessons. And the Great Tales, comfort.'

'Though it'll take someone of high stature to restore the people's confidence in them,' said Yulla.

'*Me?*' said Llian, dazedly. 'Are you talking about rebuilding the college?'

'Chanthed is a ghost town and Meldorin an empty land. We're going to establish a new College of the Histories at Blatherie, fifteen miles from here. Yulla and Rulke, and Maigraith and I, have endowed it. And the mastership is yours if you want it.'

Llian looked helplessly at Karan, but her face was unreadable. 'I'm hopelessly impractical ... and not an administrator's bootlace. You'll have to find someone else.'

'Thought you'd say that,' said Flydd. 'Be Master Teller, then. It comes with a handsome stipend.'

'Excessively handsome, some might say,' said Yulla, 'since most of it comes out of my pocket.'

Flydd frowned at her. 'Oh, even after the ruination of Roros, I think your pocket is deep enough.' He turned back to Llian. 'You could spend a month or two a year at the college, teaching the Histories and telling one or two of the Great Tales, and the rest of your time at home, wherever home is, writing your tales and healing the Histories. What do you say?'

'That ... could work,' said Llian.

It was difficult to take in. An honoured position – and an *excessively handsome* stipend. At last he would be able to pay his way, whether he and Karan sorted out their differences ... or, more likely, could not.

'But before you decide,' said Rulke, 'I have an alternative proposition.'

'Must you?' snapped Flydd.

'Yes, I must. I won't put it to you today, Llian, but it's something you've long wanted from me. I mention it now because you can't have both – the one precludes the other.'

Llian found it hard to breathe. Could Rulke really be offering him his tale, to tell properly? What else could it be?

But why did it preclude a post at the new college?

'Wilm?'

It took Wilm a long time to realise that Flydd was talking to him. 'Yes?' he said dully.

He and Ilisial had given everything to fight the enemy, and this was their reward? Death for her, endless agony for him. He wasn't interested in anything anyone had to say. Words didn't change anything.

'You blame yourself for Ilisial's death,' said Flydd, 'but it had nothing to do with you.'

'What are you talking about?'

'Did you ever wonder why Mendark buried Akkidul, one of the greatest blades in the Histories, in a rusty old box in the desert?'

'Of course. But there was no way of finding out.'

'I can force it to tell the truth,' said Lirriam. 'If you still want to know.'

Would it make any difference? His failure would still be the same – losing his temper with Ilisial and handing her the sword in the first place. 'I suppose so,' said Wilm.

'Put it on the table.'

Wilm drew the black sword from its copper sheath and laid it on the boards.

*What are you doing?* it said querulously. *Sheathe me, this instant!*

'Speak true, Akkidul,' said Lirriam, touching it with the tip of her blue-bladed sword. 'Answer Wilm's questions.'

*Damned if I will!*

Lirriam touched her blade to one edge of the black sword and it cut a small notch there.

*Curse you!* Akkidul shrilled, though it sounded afraid now. *All right!*

'Why did Mendark dump you in the desert?' said Wilm.

*I betrayed him. But he deserved it; he never treated me right.*

'A sword that betrays its master is worthless metal, good only for the furnace,' said Lirriam. 'How did you become so corrupt, Akkidul?'

It shook on the table but did not speak. She cut a notch in the other edge.

*The summon stone,* said Akkidul. *Mendark was trying to be rid of it, many hundreds of years ago. But he went too close and it got to me.*

'It corrupted you. And from that day forth you could not be trusted.'

After a long pause, *I fought it ... but it was too strong.*

'Tell Wilm what you did at the gift-burner.'

*He handed me over to Ilisial!* the sword said in outrage.

'And?' said Lirriam.

*She hated me and feared me. She always called me evil.*

'But you *are* evil.'

*She had no respect. And Wilm insulted me,* again, *by giving me to her.*

'So you made Ilisial's strike on the gift-burner go astray, knowing it would kill her.'

*I didn't know. I'd never seen it before.*

'But you have sensed out a thousand other magical devices in your time, Akkidul. You knew what the gift-burner was for – and how to safely destroy it.'

*What if I did? She wanted to die, anyway.*

'What are you talking about?' cried Wilm.

*I was in your hand when Skald partly drank her life outside the cave. After that she was an empty shell.*

'That's not true! She was cheerful in the weeks we were working together to dig out the crashed air-dreadnought and build an air-floater.'

At least, most of the time. At other times, Ilisial had often sat by herself, staring into nowhere and shuddering.

*Outwardly. But in her heart she lived in terror that Skald would try to drink her life again.*

'Maybe she was in despair,' said Wilm. 'And maybe she could have been healed. But you killed her, out of malice.'

*I gave her what she truly wanted.*

Wilm wanted to smash the black sword against the wall, but it was ancient and heavily enchanted, and could not be damaged that way. He looked up and Lirriam was watching him. She was angry too. Silently, she reversed the blue sword and passed it across the table to him.

He wanted to hack Akkidul to pieces but restrained himself. 'No point ruining a good table.' He tossed the black sword on the grass.

*What are you doing? No! I know secrets, hundreds of them. I'll tell you everything. Or if you want money – you do, don't you, poor boy that you are – I know where every one of Mendark's lost hoards was hidden.*

'There's nothing I want that you can give me,' said Wilm. He drew the tip of the blue weapon across the black blade where it joined the hilt.

The black blade screamed, but it was cut off as the sword was severed. He cut the blade into small pieces, and the hilt and the copper scabbard too, and felt an overwhelming sense of relief. Akkidul was gone.

'I'll take care of them,' said Shand, gathering the pieces. 'I've got a furnace out the back.'

'Thank you,' Wilm said to Lirriam, handing her weapon back. 'That – helped.'

'What will you do now?' said Flydd. 'You're good with your hands. I can find you a master, if you'd like an apprenticeship. Or Yulla can, should you want to go further afield.'

'No, thanks. I'm going back to Meldorin.'

Aviel pressed a hand to her heart. 'Why, Wilm? I know you loved Ilisial, but –'

He stared at her. 'Are you trying to insult Dajaes' memory?'

'Of course not. I'm sorry.'

'I didn't love Ilisial, not for a minute. Do you think me so fickle that I would lose the girl I loved, then love another only months later?'

'I'm sorry,' she repeated.

'We went through a lot together, Ilisial and I, and she'd had a terrible life. I just ... cared about her.'

Aviel tried again. 'It's not your fault she died.'

'If I hadn't handed her the sword, she'd still be alive.'

'Maybe,' said Lirriam. 'And maybe her fate was already fixed. We can't know.' She walked away.

Wilm looked into Aviel's eyes. 'It's only been half a year of our lives since Dajaes died, and I think of her every day. But in the real world, 214 years have passed. I'm going back to the place where I laid her to rest, to pay homage to her sacrifice and try to find out why she, and Ilisial, were doomed to die.'

'And after that?' she said softly.

'I'll go looking for whatever it is that's missing in my life.' Wilm did not have much confidence that he would find it, though. He was empty.

～

'I hope you find it,' said Flydd, and turned to Aviel.

'I don't want anything either,' she snapped. 'I don't need my life arranged, thank you very much!'

'I wouldn't think of it. But neither can you make your perfumes under a tree. Lirriam can make gates anywhere with her Waystone, and she'll take you wherever you want to go. Even back to Thurkad, if –'

'Why would I want to go there?' said Aviel. 'I like it in Tullymool. The weather isn't too hot, and there's plenty of herbs and spices and flowers I've never seen before. If you could ... um ...lend me a small amount of money, though ... just enough to get a little hut built ...'

'I'm not a moneylender,' said Flydd.

That shocked her, but she told herself not to expect too much. 'No, of course not.'

'Why are you tormenting her, you miserable old bastard?' said Shand. 'Aviel, I'd be only too happy –'

'Do you think me that ungrateful?' said Flydd.

'Well, you were a scrutator.'

Flydd pulled a coiled document, on thick paper, out of his pocket and passed it to Aviel. 'I've signed over my cottage to you, plus the furniture, the gardens and the three acres of land around it. It's all witnessed and sealed.'

Aviel could not speak. She wanted to laugh; it was so ridiculous. Wanted to cry. 'I couldn't possibly accept such a gift.'

'It's not a gift, you little idiot,' he growled. 'Have you been recompensed for any of the great things you've done since you came to the future?'

'Like what?'

'Making us that huge batch of nivol, for instance.'

'No.' Though Aviel still had the diamond phial, and it had to be worth quite a bit. On second thoughts, maybe she'd keep quiet about that.

'If I'd found an alchymist capable of making nivol, it would have cost more than my cottage is worth.'

'I don't believe you,' said Aviel. 'It can't be –'

'It's true, Aviel,' said Maelys, who was snuggled up to Nish. 'The Lyrinx War cost a million lives, and the God Emperor's rule many more, and at least a hundred thousand died in the Merdrun's invasion. There's far more land than there are people to occupy it, and it's the same with empty cottages – you can buy one for a bucket of wormy apples.'

Flydd scowled. 'Not mine, you can't. But skills like yours, Aviel, are vanishingly rare and attract the highest price. Your cottage has a long, sunny room at the back, just right for a perfumery workshop. You'll have to clear out the spiders and cobwebs, then you can put your gear in right away. And I can send you anything else you require.'

'But –'

'Just thank me prettily and take it.'

Aviel was tempted to refuse, because she was fed up with people ordering her about, but she also wanted it desperately. And after all, she'd been so virtuous lately she could afford to compromise her principles, just this once.

'Thank you,' she said, giving him her loveliest smile. 'But where will you live?'

'I'll be too busy to need a home.' Flydd nodded to Rulke. 'I think Rulke and Lirriam have something to say.'

'Privately,' said Rulke. 'If you don't mind.'

Aviel walked down to the stream with them in the moonlight, wondering what they wanted.

'I owe you more than you can possibly imagine,' said Rulke.

'And so do I,' said Lirriam. 'And we can't let you go unrewarded.'

'I didn't do it for a reward.'

'It's a debt of honour. Would you see us quit this world with our debts unrequited?'

'I have my house and my workshop. There's nothing else I want.'

'What about your ankle?'

'I'm used to it.'

'You're limping badly. Is the pain worse than it used to be?'

'Well, yes.'

'How much worse?'

It had been a lot worse since Aviel had destroyed the Founder's Stone, but she did not want to say so. 'I – I can put up with it.'

'Let me see.'

Aviel wanted to refuse, though was it out of a genuine reluctance to get something she wasn't entitled to, or was it pride? A bit of both, she thought.

'When I made the rejuvenation potion for Maigraith,' she said, 'I knew I was doing wrong. We should stay as we're made. It's wrong to change that.'

'Even to avoid pain?' Lirriam knelt and removed Aviel's boots and socks, then enclosed her right ankle in one hand. She frowned.

'What's the matter?'

'The joint is badly damaged, the bone grinding away. One day, perhaps soon, you won't be able to walk without crutches, and how will you do your work then? Or wander far through forest and meadow seeking out ingredients for your scents?'

'I – I'll still have my garden.'

'Let Lirriam heal the pain, at least,' said Rulke. 'She's a fine healer. The best.'

'I *would* like to be in less pain,' said Aviel. At times she still felt the agony that had torn through her as the Founder's Stone attacked.

Lirriam touched each side of Aviel's ankle with a lumpy black stone, rather like the Waystone but smaller. The ankle joint and the bones around it went hot, then slowly cooled.

'You won't feel much difference for a few days,' said Lirriam. 'Good healings take time.'

'Thank you. What is that?'

'It's a healing stone.'

'It doesn't come from Santhenar, does it?'

'No.'

'When you said you were quitting this world, you didn't mean you were dying, did you?'

They exchanged glances. 'When I came back from the 'dead,' said Rulke. 'I believed I was the last of my Charon kind, and I didn't want to go on. That's why I didn't help Flydd and his allies; I didn't see the point of anything. But a few days later, when I was looking into the void and thinking about hurling myself into it, I saw the trace of the Waystone. I made a beacon and sensed Lirriam – and recognised the other half of myself.'

'The last of a lost branch of Charon,' said Lirriam, running her fingers through her shining opaline hair, 'from aeons ago. I too was lost; I too was incomplete. I too had spent a long time in stasis, surrounded by stone.'

'We can bring the Charon back from extinction, if we so choose – or eventually go to it together, content.'

'Is that what you meant by quitting this world?'

'No, we're going home. Just as Tallallame is the Merdrun's lost home world, so it is ours.'

'But you can't go there for another 287 years.'

'The Merdrun can't, but the Waystone can open the way between any two places or any two worlds, hence the name. We can go anytime we want, and we're going soon. Thus completing the great cycle that began when the Faellem betrayed our Mariem ancestors, long aeons ago, and cast them into the void to die.'

# 60

# I'LL NEVER SEE YOU AGAIN!

A fortnight had passed. Wilm watched Yulla Zaeff's magnificently baroque air-floater lift off. She and Lilis, the two surviving 'reckless old ladies,' were heading north-east to Roros to begin the disheartening job of restoring order, finding food and shelter for the best part of a million hungry people, and rebuilding.

'And now you're going as well,' said Llian. 'Do you really want to, though?'

Wilm did not want to discuss it. Not even with Llian, the friend he owed most to, and whom he most admired.

'Talk to me,' said Llian, sitting down on the wide steps up to Shand's veranda.

Wilm could not refuse him. He took off his pack and set it on the boards. 'There's nothing for me here.'

'Why not?'

'Aviel doesn't need me. She's got everything she wants in life.'

'Except a friend who understands her.'

'She's got Shand, again.'

'He's a good man, and a kind one, when he's not being a cranky old sod. But he's also an old, old man and he's had a life full of pain and loss.'

'Well, Aviel has Karan, and Sulien, and you ... Doesn't she?'

'Karan wants to go back to Gothryme,' said Llian in an unusually flat voice.

'And you don't?'

'I've never wanted it less. Meldorin is empty, apart from bandits and ne'er-do-wells. What's there for me now? Especially with the new college being set up near here. I can't live in Gothryme and also be the Master Teller at the college.'

'And then there's Rulke's offer,' said Wilm. 'Do you know what it is?'

'I can guess part of it.'

'And …?'

'It's even more incompatible with Gothryme … and Karan.'

'Then you've got some hard thinking to do.'

'I've been doing it for quite a while. Haven't reached any conclusion I can live with.' Llian shook himself. 'Stop changing the subject. We were talking about you and Aviel.'

'Here she comes now,' said Wilm, getting up.

'She's a wonderful girl.'

Wilm scowled, as if Llian had been offensively faint in his praise. 'Aviel's the most beautiful girl I ever met. And she's warm and generous and kind and true-hearted and brave.'

'Begs the question, then, doesn't it?'

She came up to him and stopped. Wilm felt the colour rising in his face. Why did he always react to her this way? He had rehearsed his departure a dozen times but now he could not think of a thing to say.

If only she wanted him to stay. If only she needed him.

'I wish you didn't have to go, Wilm,' she said, turning her lovely face up to him.

Then ask me to stay, he thought. Tell me how you feel – if you feel anything!

He kissed her on the cheek, and tried to embrace her, but after a couple of seconds she drew away, and gave the same embrace to Llian. She doesn't really care, he thought. She wants me to go!

'Bye,' he said, and heaved his pack onto his back and walked away, without looking back.

Aviel watched him go, tears streaming down her face.

'Something the matter?' said Llian.

She choked. 'Wilm's my dearest friend … and I'll never see him again.'

'Then why didn't you ask him to stay?'

'He's desperate to get away.'

'Actually, he's desperate for you to tell him you care, and that you actually need him.'

'Of course I need him …'

'But?'

'He needs to find his place in the world, and I don't think it's here. Not yet, at any rate.'

'That's not your problem, it's his. Tell him, before it's too late.'

Aviel gasped a breath, rose shakily and went after him. 'Wilm?' she said.

But his strides were three times the length of hers and he was walking fast, the distance between them widening by the second. She faltered. 'Wilm?' she said in a small voice.

He did not hear her.

'*Wilm!*' roared Llian in his most carrying Teller's voice.

Wilm turned. Llian pointed to Aviel.

She was afraid Wilm would keep going but of course he did not. To add to his other qualities, he was very well-mannered.

She ran after him, trying not to limp. She did not want his sympathy. Her ankle was less twisted and lumpy now, but it still hurt to run.

He met her halfway and she flung herself at him. He put his arms around her and it burst out of her.

'Wilm, I really need you.'

'You do?'

'Of course I do. You're the one solid thing in my life. The one person I've always been able to rely on, and trust. My dearest friend.'

His eyes were wet. 'Thank you, that means everything to me.'

'I thought you knew it.'

'You'd be amazed what I don't know and can't see, until it's pointed out to me.'

She looked back. Llian had disappeared. 'Are you still going –?'

'On a pilgrimage to Dajaes' grave. I can't forget her, even if everyone else has.'

'But that's past Chanthed! It must be a thousand miles away.'

'More.'

'You're going to *walk* all the way to Meldorin?'

'It's how I started out from Casyme with Llian, five or six months ago. I'm fit and strong and I've got a few coins in my pocket. Enough for a bed and a meal when I need one. Not enough to attract robbers.'

'A few coins won't get you far.'

'I'm a good worker. Everyone needs workers now, with half of Lauralin to be rebuilt.'

'It'll take a year, there and back, if you have to work your way.'

'At least.'

His eyes searched her face as if he were looking for a sign, and it was as if a great dam burst in her. She wasn't going to fail him this time.

'Of course you must go,' said Aviel. 'You loved Dajaes. But ...'

'Yes?'

'Promise you'll come back for my 18th birthday. That gives you a year and a half.'

Wilm studied her face for a long time, then took her hand. 'I promise.'

'I made you this a while ago.' She handed him a tiny bottle of perfume. The blend included the infinitely precious hoopis scent Klarm had given her when they first reached Thurkad. 'It's to remind you of here, and me. I only made two bottles, one for you and one for Jassika.'

'You gave me one of your perfumes once before,' he said. 'As I was going off with Llian to sit the college scholarship test.' He laughed.

'What?' she said.

'The idea of me being a chronicler.'

It was absurd, but she said stoutly, 'You were trying to find your way.'

'And I'm still trying. Thank you.' He put the bottle away safely. 'It's the most precious thing I own.'

He kissed her and hugged her, and she hugged him back, then he pulled his hat down and turned and headed west. She watched him until he was out of sight, started to go into Shand's house, but instead she went down through the grass to Flydd's stone-built cottage.

No, her cottage. She had the deeds to prove it. And her workshop. She had cleaned out the back room and set up her equipment, and today she was going to begin extracting the scents of herbs and barks and wildflowers for an entirely new perfume.

Aviel sang softly to herself as she worked. It was a hard road Wilm had set himself upon, and a dangerous road too. She wished she had made a scent potion to give him strength, and luck, and bring him safely home. But maybe that was the real magic in hoopis.

'What are we going to do now, Nish?' said Maelys that afternoon.

They were lying on the soft grass in the shade by the stream, their clothes scattered about, with rays of golden afternoon sunlight slanting down on them through the trees. It was a perfect summer's day, warm but not too warm.

'Should we have another go at rebuilding Nifferlin ... or would it be better to start again, somewhere else, if the memories are too bad ...?'

'What do *you* want?' she said. 'I want you to say it.'

'Why do you think I wouldn't say it?'

'I don't know. It's just – well, we've seen Karan and Llian tearing themselves apart because neither of them can give up what they want, and the other one doesn't.'

'You're not Karan, and I'm not Llian.'

'Don't you ever think about home – your childhood home, I mean?'

'My father was a monster,' said Nish, 'my brothers were miniature versions of him, and my mother couldn't stand up to any of them. And I was a rotten little shit. Believe me when I say that I never want to revisit that part of my life again. Home is wherever we live and are happy together.'

She smiled and laid a hand on his scarred arm. His strong, stocky body was a mass of scars. 'I can't believe I spent so long in thrall to that wretched Mirror. Or that I never suspected it was the cause of our pain.'

'Well, Yalkara said she'd cleansed it,' said Nish. 'And it wasn't the cause of *all* our pain. In its malice, it seized on divisions that were already there and used them to wedge us apart. I'm sorry. I should have been much more understanding.'

'You should have been.' She gazed up at the green-gold leaves. 'And I should have realised how dependent I'd become on it, and what it was up to. It wasn't as if there weren't enough warnings.'

She snuggled up to him again. 'Nifferlin has a lot of bad memories for me,' she added. 'The manor destroyed, *twice*. Our huge clan scattered. Father taken and dying in the God-Emperor's prison. Mother and my aunts dying or being killed, one by one. Beautiful Fyllis. My son with Emberr ...'

She wiped her eyes. 'But there were good memories too, before that. Lots of them. And all my family is buried there. I don't think I could bear to leave.'

'Then we'll go back and rebuild Nifferlin Manor. Flydd can take us in the sky-galleon, when he gets the time. And in the meantime, old Shand is good company when he chooses to be.' He gazed at her curvy figure. 'And you're better company. But how are you, inside?'

'The grief will always be there, but it's a normal grief now, not something warped and twisted by the Mirror for its own malicious purposes. And it would be wonderful to hear children laughing in the halls of Nifferlin Manor again, one day. What do you think, Nish?'

'I'm told they can be very healing,' said Nish. 'You are pregnant, aren't you?'

She thumped him on the shoulder. 'How did you know?'

He just smiled.

# 61

# THAT WAS A MIGHTY OATH

K aran rose late after another troubled night, knowing the old house would be empty. Their friends had probably arranged it so she and Llian could finally talk things through. Her stomach throbbed at the thought.

Flydd, Flangers and Chissmoul had set out in the sky galleon yesterday, taking Maelys and Nish home to Nifferlin, and Tiaan to Fadd and her children, only an hour's flight from there. Fadd was a rainy place and the Merdrun had not burned the city when they abandoned it, though the destruction was extensive. Tiaan's home had been destroyed but her children, and her father, Merryl, who lived with them, were safe.

Rulke, Lirriam and Tulitine had promised Sulien and Jassika a picnic at Five Waterfalls, a magical place twenty miles away that could only be reached from the air. Shand had left for a long forest walk. And Aviel, who finally had her workshop set up, was extracting her first scents and did not want to be disturbed.

Karan did not bother to dress, since no one but Llian was around and it was another warm, sunny day. She gave her hair a few perfunctory brushes, scowling at the grey hairs, seventeen of them now. She made tea and took a loaf of bread and a pot of marmalade out to the veranda. It reminded her of breakfast under the vines on the rear terrace at Gothryme.

She stopped, her eyes pricking. Rulke had pointed out, perhaps provocatively, that there was no obstacle to her going home now, and he had offered to take her there in the construct. She now had the means to restore Gothryme to the condition it had been in centuries ago, before a succession of wastrels had drained its coffers and unending drought had eaten what remained.

Karan turned the corner, and started. Llian was at the other end of the table, his journal open at two blank pages, staring into nowhere. He looked tired and rumpled, more so than usual.

They had not spent a night together in months. He had slept in a separate tent at Skyrock, and in another part of Shand's rambling old house since they'd come to Tullymool. She stood there, staring at him. Wanting him. More afraid than ever.

He looked up, and she realised that the slanting sunlight was shining straight through her thin nightgown, but he turned away as though nothing about her could interest him. Was it just her, or was it the ghastly experience of having his life partly drunk by Skald? Was he, as Ilisial had been, dying inside? And what if he dragged Sulien down with him?

'Skald,' she said, and it came out as a croak.

'What about him?'

'He tried to drink your life. Twice.'

'I don't want to talk about it.'

'But are you all right?'

'I've talked it through with Rulke a few times. Skald did it to him, too, and Lirriam helped him get past it. And they've both helped me.'

'Are you sure? You've been so quiet ...'

'I'm – all – right!' he snapped.

But was he? She sat, staring at the steam rising from her cup, then cut a thick slice of bread and slathered it in kumquat marmalade. Shand made it with molasses and it was almost black, strong and tangy.

Should she tell him? Then throw herself on his mercy?

She tried three times, but the words would not come out. She was too afraid.

'What are we going to do, Llian?'

'About your secrets?'

She jumped. 'W-what secrets?'

'Oh, come on! Even Rulke knew.'

'Knew what?' she whispered.

'After he dragged me through that gate to Alcifer,' Llian rubbed the stump of his little finger, 'it was one of the first things he brought up. He'd read Thandiwe's dreadful *Tale of Rulke* and blamed me, and he raised the topic of your secret, to hurt me. And it did!' He banged his forehead on his clenched fists. 'Rulke, of all people, knew more about our intimate life than I did.'

'I never told him anything about us.'

'Then he put two and two together and guessed the rest.'

'W-what did he say?'

'I'm not playing the secrets game any longer, Karan, because you always win. What happens next is up to you.'

'I don't know what to do.'

'Haven't I proven myself yet? What more do you require of me?'

She did not reply.

'Well,' he said coldly, 'since we had Sulien you've made all the decisions, so why don't you decide this as well?'

He rose abruptly, gathered his pencil and his journal, and walked away.

Karan sat there until her tea grew cold, nibbling the bread and marmalade but not tasting a thing. It was over. It was absolutely and utterly over. And there was no one she could talk to. At least, no one who would take her side. Or was there?

She climbed the narrow stairs to Shand's observatory, which stood a couple of floors above the centre of the house. It was a plain, square room, the walls and ceiling lined with boards lacquered to the colour of honey. Three sides had windows; in the fourth wall, a door led out onto a circular platform where Shand set up his telescope and used his orrery and armillary.

Karan opened the door and a window, for a cross-breeze, and closed the door on the stairs so no one could overhear. She sat on the floor, cross-legged, closed her eyes and reached out to Aachan with the mind-calling gift Maigraith had restored before she died.

*What is it now, Karan?* Malien said tersely.

'Um, how are you doing with the Merdrun?'

*They agreed to our final terms a fortnight ago, since they had no choice. But that's not why you've contacted me.*

'You're the only person I can talk to.'

*About Llian? That's for you and him to sort out.*

'No, about Mum killing herself.' Karan told Malien what she had told Flydd on that drunken night in the sky galleon.

Malien did not speak for some time, then she said, *I didn't know that, but it explains a lot. Almost everything.*

'I don't understand.'

*You've got to forgive yourself. You'll never be able to fix your life until you do.*

'Forgive myself for what?'

You *didn't fail your mother*, said Malien. *You were only 12 and it wasn't your job. Galliad failed her because he was a weak man who left the burden to you.*

'I should have answered her cries for help.'

*Vuula had a long history of false accusations, emotional blackmail, and threats of self-harm. And she'd spoken to you very cruelly – you were entitled to hide and nurse your wounds.*

'But I might have saved her.'

*She would have tried again.*

'How do you know?'

*Your father brought her to Shazmak a year before you were born. Even then she was unstable, and it was clear they were unsuited, but Vuula was beautiful and he wouldn't listen. After you were born and her screaming fits began, I went to Gothryme to help, but she was beyond help. And when your father rejected her it made everything worse.*

'Even so –' said Karan.

*If there was any fault in you the day she killed herself, you've paid for it a thousand times. It's time to forgive yourself and let your mother go ... and you know what that means?*

'Letting Gothryme go,' Karan said dully.

*It's just a burden now. Dig into your memories and find the good in Vuula – it was there when you were little – and say goodbye.*

'Flydd said that. But I didn't tell him what I'd promised Mum, long before she died.'

*Promised her what?* Malien said sharply.

'That I'd pass Gothryme on to my daughter. And as she lay dying, Mum scrawled on the floor, with her own blood, *Keep your promise.*'

*That's a monstrous thing to do to a child.*

Karan swallowed. 'Well ... as I stood beside her body, I ... I swore that I would.'

There was a long silence.

*A mighty oath*, said Malien.

A cruel pang of aftersickness struck. It was always bad when Karan mind-called Malien. 'But should I keep it, or break it?'

*I can't advise you.*

'How can I break an oath to my dead mother? But if I keep it, I've lost my family. Llian won't go to Gothryme and it's not right to ask him... but if he doesn't, I'm not sure Sulien will go, either.'

# 62

# IT'S THE INTENTION THAT MATTERS

From the moment Karan arrived in the future she had longed to go home, yet she spent the eight-hour trip in the construct agonising about it.

Though she loved barren Gothryme with all her heart, Llian had felt useless there, because he was banned from being a Teller, and she had selfishly refused to share any part of Gothryme's management with him.

But Bannador had been abandoned decades ago, and no other settlers would want her former estate, since there were far better properties for the taking. She could have it back. But should she?

The construct passed down through a fluffy little cloud and a grey-brown land opened out below them, though at first she did not recognise it. The River Ryme had changed its course and its almost dry bed was a couple of miles further away than it had been when she left. Two extra miles to carry water when it didn't rain.

Sulien, who had been unusually quiet lately, went up to the lookout platform and linked arms with Jassika. Karan stood at the front porthole windows, looking down. Should she let it go? Part of her wanted to, but how could she break so binding a promise?

'There it is!' Sulien yelled down through the open hatch. 'There's the keep. See it, Jassika? It's built of pink granite and it's *two thousand* years old ...' Her voice faded. 'Mummy?'

'What is it?' said Karan.

'Everything else is gone.'

It was after 1 p.m., a scorching day with not a breath of wind, when the construct set down next to a grey depression. It had been the swan pond for as long as Karan could remember, but it must have dried up years ago.

She climbed down the long ladder and stood there, staring at the desolate landscape, the thin, bare soil, so dry that even the weeds were wilted. The old keep still had its roof but the rest of the manor, and the stables and outbuildings, had crumbled away.

Llian stepped down and looked around, shaking his head. Sulien and Jassika had disappeared, exploring, no doubt.

'It's only been a couple of months in our lives since we left,' said Karan. 'I can't take it in.'

Llian took her hand and she was grateful for the contact. 'By the look of it, Gothryme's had 214 bad years. Karan, I'm sorry; I know you loved it.'

'The orchard's gone. And I can't even tell where the vegetable garden was.'

'Where I nearly cut my foot off with a spade,' he said wryly.

Her mind refused to accept what her eyes were telling her. Two months! It's *only* been two months. She burst into tears.

Llian put an arm around her, yet the distance between them did not lessen. He was being thoughtful, but his mind had not changed.

'You can rebuild,' said Shand, who had known Gothryme well. 'It'd only take a fraction of what Maigraith left you.'

'Meldorin is still an empty land,' said Rulke.

'Not for long. Refugees from the burned cities are heading west. And there's talk of Thurkad being rebuilt downriver, where there's a good harbour. Though I have to say –'

'What?' Karan wiped her eyes on her arm.

'Gothryme will never be as good as it was when you left,' said Shand.

'Why not?'

'When the Dry Sea filled, the climate changed. Places like Tullymool have greened but Bannador's drying out. I don't think you could farm it now, except along the river. And then only in the good years.'

'But with enough spent on it,' Karan said stubbornly, 'with a dam here and there, and ditches to catch runoff –'

'Almost anywhere can be made to bloom, with unlimited money. But is it worth it?'

'I swore I'd pass it down to Sulien,' said Karan through her teeth. The sun was beating down on her head and it was already throbbing. She had forgotten to bring a hat.

'Whether she wants it or not?'

The only happy spot Karan could find was the rear terrace, where they had taken breakfast on warm mornings, under the vines. The timbers had rotted away but the grape vines remained, their trunks as thick and cracked and twisted as ancient trees, their laterals intergrown to form a shady canopy from which occasional bunches of unripe grapes hung.

'Old vines made the best wines,' said Llian. 'This is going to be a great vintage.'

'Thank you,' she said, appreciating the effort he was making to find something positive here.

She sat on the paved ground, her back to a trunk. Rulke, Shand and Llian also sat. The stones were pleasantly cool, and it was a relief to get out of the blistering sun.

'So, Karan?' said Rulke.

'I want it back.' She did not look at Llian.

'What about you, Llian?' said Rulke.

'How can I decide my future,' said Llian, 'when you haven't told me your offer?'

'I would have thought you'd guessed – you're such a master at unravelling secrets.'

Rulke glanced at Karan. Was he hinting something to her? Probably, though she could not decipher it.

'I'd sooner you spelled it out,' said Llian.

'You did me a great service a while ago,' said Rulke. 'Enough to outweigh your manifest failures, flaws and foibles and follies and –'

'Don't hold back,' Llian said sourly. 'Itemise them for everyone's amusement, why don't you?'

'The sun would go down before I reached the end,' said Rulke, and Shand snorted. 'Very well, my offer is this.' Rulke paused for dramatic effect. 'And it's no less than the entire Histories of the Charon.'

Llian went still. Clearly, this was more than he had anticipated. 'You mean –?'

'Yes, Llian, I do. Our Histories from the moment when my people, who were then called Mariem, and shared Tallallame with the Faellem, were betrayed by them and cast into the void to die.'

'You have all your people's Histories in the construct?'

'Sufficient for the purpose, though I'm not letting them out of my sight this time. If you want to read our papers, and get the chance to craft a Great Tale from them, you'll come to Tallallame with us when we leave. In a day or two.'

So soon? Dread overwhelmed Karan. What Teller could resist such an offer? 'How long would it take?'

'Three years, at the very least,' said Rulke. 'Maybe four or five.'

'That's a long time,' said Llian. 'How about if I –?'

'If you're not prepared to make the commitment, the offer is null. It's all or nothing, Llian.'

'How can you expect me to decide so quickly?' said Llian.

'It's the greatest tale of all. You either want it or you don't.'

'How do you know it's the greatest? Everyone thinks –'

'I've read all Santhenar's so-called Great Tales,' snapped Rulke, 'and less than half of them are great. Many are mediocre and a few are outright lies. You may think you know a lot about the Charon, Chronicler, but you haven't heard a hundredth part of our greatness, or our adventures, since we were cast into the void.'

'The Greatest Tale of All,' Llian said dreamily. 'And I'd be the only Teller and Chronicler ever to see Tallallame, and hear its tales firsthand. It'd be worth almost any sacrifice.'

He looked around, caught Karan's eye, flushed and looked away. He was desperately tempted; she could see it in his eyes.

'Including your family?' she said coldly.

'You could come too. Karan and Sulien and Jassika could come to Tallallame, couldn't they, Rulke?'

'If they wanted to.'

Karan laid her forehead on the fissured trunk beside her. This was home.

'I can't go to Tallallame,' she said.

'Why not?' said Rulke.

'I promised my mother I'd pass Gothryme to my daughter.'

'How did that come about, exactly?'

'I don't want to talk about it.' It had been a sweltering day, much like today, and it was raising dreadful memory echoes.

'Always secrets!' Llian cried. 'That's the *real* problem.'

'I've had enough of this,' said Rulke. 'You *will* talk about it, Karan. Willingly – or I'll use my Arts to drag it out of you. Your choice.'

Karan choked. She had no doubt that he could make her tell, but he might extract more than she could bear to reveal. She told them about her mother's suicide, what had led up to it, and her discovery of her mother's body.

'As she lay dying, Mum scrawled on the floor, with her own blood, *Keep your promise*. And as I stood beside her body, believing that if I'd only answered her calls I could have saved her, I … I laid my hand over her heart … and I swore I would keep my promise.'

Llian looked as bad as Karan felt. Enlightened, yet horrified. He dropped his head into his hands and rocked back and forth.

Rulke's face hardened. He exchanged a significant glance with Shand, who nodded.

'Where did she die?' said Shand.

'An attic room, up under the roof of the old keep. She used to sew there, and paint and draw. And … scream.'

'Take us up,' said Rulke.

'I can't!' Karan felt so shaky it was an effort to sit upright.

'Why not?'

'After her body was taken away, and the room cleaned up, I locked the door and it hasn't been opened since.'

'Time it was – since it's the key to the whole problem.'

'If Karan doesn't want to go, we –' began Llian.

'Stop being a soggy biscuit, Llian,' said Rulke. 'If there was ever a time to stand up for yourself, it's now.'

'Come on,' said Shand. 'Before the girls come back. This has to be sorted.'

Rulke lifted Karan to her feet and they tramped in through the broken front door of the keep, and up the stairs. Her bad leg and hip were aching now, and so was the healed wound in her belly where the mad triplets had tried to kill her. Had it not been for Llian, she would have died that day. She owed him so much.

It did not help. Her oath was unbreakable.

As she hobbled up, every step brought old memories to the surface. Past the room she had shared with Llian, and the vast box bed where Sulien had been conceived, and born. Karan looked across to the small, wedge-shaped room on the other side, where she had slept as a little girl. Later it had been Sulien's room, and it was there that she had far-seen the Merdrun in a nightmare.

Up the narrow steps to the landing outside the attic door. The fatal door. It was sweltering up here under the roof, as hot as it had been that day. It might have been yesterday. Her heart was thundering, sweat running down her face and sides, terror making her hair stand on end.

'I – I can smell the blood,' she gasped. She turned to run.

Rulke blocked her way. 'There's no blood.'

'There would be if you were a sensitive.'

'Right now, that's the last thing any of us need. Open the door.'

'It's locked.'

'And you don't have the key,' said Shand.

'I do.' Rulke pressed a finger to the lock, something broke and the door came open.

The attic was gloomy, the two small windows thick with dust and cobwebs, and the smell of blood was overwhelming. Blood everywhere, on the floor, all over the floor and the walls and her mother's mad, twisted sketches.

'I have the key to that, too,' said Rulke, and touched the same finger to the top of Karan's head.

The smell memories vanished. The stains too. She had scrubbed the floor for hours after Vuula's body was taken away, insisting on doing it by herself as if she could scrub her own wickedness away. Then Karan had sanded the boards down to fresh timber. It had taken a day and a half, and the moment it was done she had locked the door, left a note for Rachis and left on that dangerous trek through the mountains to Shazmak, all alone.

'Where did your mother write it?' said Rulke.

She pointed. He held his hand out over the spot, palm downwards, and the words appeared as if freshly written, in shaky letters made by a finger dipped repeatedly in blood.

*Keep your promise.*

'I swore, on my mother's heart, that I would,' said Karan. 'How can I break that oath?'

'You can't,' said Llian quietly. 'And I would never ask you to.' He was pale and sweating, and looked as though he was going to fall down.

'What are you reading here, Shand?' said Rulke. 'This is more your area of the Art than mine.'

'Life had become unbearable for Vuula. If Karan *had* answered her calls, she would have tried again. And again.'

'But what was her state of mind? Were these words written in love, or grief? Or were they the product of a broken mind?'

'They were written to make Karan feel guilty,' Shand said in a harsh voice. 'And coerce her into keeping her promise.'

'Why would Mum think I had to be coerced?' whispered Karan. 'Until we fled to the future, I'd always planned to pass Gothryme to Sulien.'

'And now?'

She did not reply.

'I know more than a little about oaths, Karan,' said Rulke. 'About keeping them, and breaking them. Especially oaths between unequals. It's the intention that matters, and Vuula intended to strike back at you for not coming in time. To hurt you.'

'As if she hadn't hurt me enough already,' Karan said numbly.

'She was a most unhappy woman. But the dead can't bind the living, Karan, no matter how hard they try. And an oath coerced from a child by an adult is no oath at all. It is null.'

# 63

# NO, WE'LL ALL DECIDE

Rulke headed down the stairs, followed by Shand. Llian reached out and touched Karan's hand, very tentatively, then followed. What a kind man he was.

It's over, she thought. *My oath is null!* Morally and legally, at least – but that did not mean she was free emotionally. She still felt the pull of Gothryme. And if Llian did go to Tallallame with Rulke, what else would she have left?

When they went out again, Sulien and Jassika were waiting under the vines. Sulien was hopping from one foot to another, trembling with some suppressed emotion.

Karan suppressed her own agonies. 'Is something the matter, darling?'

'Um,' said Sulien.

Jassika nudged her in the ribs. 'You've got to fix this. No one else can.'

'Can't you say it? You're not scared of anyone.'

'You fooled the Merdrun and sent them to Aachan. Don't tell me you can't get through to these idiots.'

'Sulien, Gothryme's your heritage,' said Karan. 'I'm doing this for you.'

'But there's nothing left! I can't even find where we buried Piffle.' Sulien took a deep breath. 'Do you *really* want it more than Daddy? Or me?'

'It was passed it down to me so I could pass it to you. It's always been that way.'

'But you gave it up 214 years ago.'

'And now we can have it back,' Karan said desperately.

'Mummy,' Sulien said carefully, 'Gothryme's not home any more. I don't want it.'

'Aaarrrgh!' Karan slumped to the ground, shaking her head wildly. Even in the shade, the paving stones were heating up. 'I can't do this.'

'What about you, Daddy? Are you going to Tallallame with Rulke?'

He sat beside Sulien. 'We were poor when I was a kid, but Mum and Dad loved their work and taught us their crafts of scribing and illumination. And we were happy. Then Mendark came, when I was twelve, and offered me a scholarship to the College of the Histories in Chanthed. It was a great opportunity – one that would not come to thousands of other bright kids – but I was going to refuse.'

'Why, Daddy?'

'Would you leave your family at the age of twelve, and travel halfway across the world with a cold, demanding stranger?'

Sulien took his hand, shivering despite the heat. Karan had sent her away with the Whelm for her own safety when she was only nine, and look how that had turned out. Maybe she would be better off with Llian.

'Mum and Dad didn't want me to go with this strange Magister,' said Llian, 'about whom the tales were legion, and many of them dark. But my next memory is of signing the papers, and Mum and Dad signing as well, though they seemed as bemused as I was.'

'Mendark cast a spell on you,' said Sulien in a whisper.

'Some sort of compulsion, to agree and sign, then forget. But my sisters' reactions told the truth; he hadn't bothered to compel them. They refused to believe it and tried to talk us out of it, but the papers had been signed and I was Mendark's protegee for the next eight years, and if he chose, which he did, another eight years after that.

'He was a hard man, demanding and unforgiving of the slightest failing. I worked at my studies day and night, but it was never enough for him. I hated the college for the first five or six years, and everyone hated me because I was a cursed Zain, but I couldn't leave.

'The one thing that kept me going,' said Llian, 'was my promise to my family that I'd make them proud, and one day I'd come home and tell them the Great Tales. But by the time I had the money to go home, Mum and Dad were dead and my sisters were gone.'

'That must have been terrible,' said Sulien. 'If I lost you and Mummy, I think my heart would burst.'

'Mine too.' Llian took both of Sulien's hands in his. 'Mine too.'

'I love my calling,' he went on, 'and for the past ten years I haven't been able to practice it. Now Rulke has offered me the chance to write the Greatest Tale of All, and I need to do it, to honour my promise to my family.'

'By breaking your promise to your current family?' Karan snapped.

'You've had your say,' Shand said in a frosty voice. 'Allow Llian to finish his.'

'But Daddy,' said Sulien, 'you've already done a Great Tale. And when you've finished the *Tale of the Gates of Good and Evil* it'll be a Great Tale too, you know it will. You'll be the only Teller in the history of the world to write two Great Tales. Why can't that be enough? Do you really want to go to Tallallame for *years*? More than you want Mummy ... and me?'

'I don't know what I want,' he said. 'I ... don't know anything, anymore.'

'I do,' said Rulke. 'For the past six months you two have been fighting to save your daughter from the deadliest foe ever to come out of the void. You would have laid down your lives to protect her. And just the other day, it was Sulien's brilliance and utter determination that saved us.'

'And Jassika's,' Sulien said quietly.

'I'm not sure where you're going with this,' said Karan to Rulke.

'If you shut up for once, I'll tell you! You listened to Sulien and trusted her, and she saved us all. We all owe her – you, Llian, and me – and I'm not listening to this damned nonsense a minute longer.'

'Have your say, then!'

'The moment the war was won – the very instant – you both started treating Sulien like a child again.'

'She – is – a – child,' Karan said through her teeth.

'Rulke's right, though,' Shand said mildly, though with steel underneath. 'Don't be so bloody selfish. Since you came to Tullymool, all I've heard is what *you* want, Karan, and what *you* want, Llian. You haven't listened to a thing Sulien has said. It's time you asked her what she wants.'

Karan knuckled her forehead. They were right, but being ordered about always put her back up. 'I'm sorry, Sulien. Why don't you talk, and we'll listen?'

Sulien opened her mouth, closed it again. 'I, um, want you and Daddy to stay together.'

Karan glanced at Llian, who again looked as though he was going to faint. 'I'm not sure that's going to happen,' she said.

Jassika elbowed Sulien. 'Remember how we talked about playing the emotional card?' she said in a stage whisper. 'I used to be really good at it. Klarm felt so guilty he'd give me whatever I wanted.'

'Mummy, Daddy,' said Sulien, her lower lip quivering and her eyes huge and wet, 'I – I can't take any more. I'm having nightmares every night now, and sometimes in daytime a noise or a smell, or something someone says, sets me off and I'm back in that horrible time in the cave with the triplets, or in the control room when Skald was d-drinking all those lives. I can't bear it! I – just – can't – bear it any longer.'

There was a long silence, then Jassika said, in a grownup voice eerily reminiscent of Klarm's, 'Sulien's trying to tell you that she's been severely traumatised, *and she's only nine*. She can't possibly get better unless she has a calm, stable and united family.

Otherwise, she's liable to end up as miserable as you two. That's what you wanted to say, isn't it, Sools?'

'Yes, Jass,' said Sulien gratefully. She wiped her nose in a great smear along her sleeve. 'It's exactly what I wanted to say.'

Karan looked at Llian and this time he met her eyes. His jaw was set. Her belly throbbed. Was this it?

'I'll go first,' he said. 'Rulke, thank you for your generous offer, but I can't go to Tallallame with you, or tell the Charon's tale.'

'What?' cried Karan.

Rulke inclined his head to Llian. Karan could not tell whether he was relieved or disappointed.

'What are your conditions, Llian?' she said, unable to get all the acid out of her voice.

'I have no conditions.'

Karan could not comprehend it. 'Even if I insist on living here?'

He hesitated, then said firmly, 'Even then.'

An awful fear surfaced. 'Are you giving up on Telling? Is it the life-drinking? Do you just want everything to end, like Ilisial?'

'I told you, *I'm not Ilisial.*'

'But –'

'She never recovered from losing her family, and when she lost her gift she had nothing left but an aching void. I have plenty left.' He looked at Sulien, meaningfully.

'But to give up your dream – the Greatest Tale of All –'

'I have other tales to tell, and other dreams, Karan,' he said quietly. 'It would have been nice, had the time been right, but it wasn't, and I've let it go.'

And finally, she believed him. Irritating man! How could he discard his long-standing anger and resentment so easily? Or his dream? But he'd always had the ability to adjust quickly to changed circumstances, ones that might take her years to come to terms with. He was the better person. But had she won – or had she lost?

Vuula had been cremated and her ashes scattered, but Karan knew what her faithful steward, Rachis, would have said, had she been able to ask him.

*The past is done, Karan. You have to look to the future.*

Her decision was made. She rose painfully and got out the ancient front door key, which had been in her bag for months, and limped across to the long bump where Rachis had been buried. Karan laid the key over the point where his heart had been, long ago, and thanked him.

'Farewell, old friend,' she said, wiping her eyes.

'You're giving Gothryme away?' said Llian.

'I gave it away long ago. I – I just refused to admit it.' She went back to the shade under the vines. 'Where does everyone want to go?'

Jassika shrugged. 'I've been carried from one place to another since I was two. Anywhere we plan to live will feel like home to me.'

'You decide,' said Llian to Sulien and Karan.

'Stop being so bloody self-effacing!' said Karan. 'We'll decide together.'

'I vote we go back to Tullymool,' said Sulien. 'It was nice and green there, and Aviel's close by, and Shand. And Flydd and Lilis and Maelys and Nish said they'll come back from time to time. And we can look after poor old Shand when he's past it,' she added with a cheeky grin.

'Enough of the *poor old Shand* and the *past it*,' said Shand. 'I was old before you were even thought of, and I don't need looking after, thank you.'

'Tullymool isn't far from Blatherie, where they're going to build the new college,' said Llian. 'I'm looking forward to that *excessively handsome* stipend.'

'Maybe we could use part of what Maigraith left us,' Karan said tentatively, 'to buy some good farmland there. With a river that flows all the time, and a bit of forest. You can see the mountains from Tullymool. It'll remind us where we came from.'

She bit her lip. She knew what Llian thought about farming.

'Sounds perfect,' said Sulien. 'But where are we going to live now?'

'There's an empty stone cottage only a mile from Shand's place,' said Llian. 'Just three rooms downstairs and two up, with a rickety old staircase. But it had a homely air.'

'Maybe we could buy it,' said Karan, 'if the owner's willing to sell.'

'Wouldn't bet on it,' said Shand. 'He's a cranky old bastard.'

'Maybe Sulien can quiver her lower lip at him,' said Llian, smiling, 'and get those tears to well up in her big green eyes. She could talk a stone gargoyle around.'

A day later, back in Tullymool, they gathered by the construct. Rulke, Lirriam and Tulitine had said their farewells and shook hands with everyone.

'Thank you,' Karan said quietly to Rulke.

'What for?'

'For making the choice so stark.'

He smiled. 'I have no idea what you're talking about.' He turned away to Llian. 'Well, Chronicler, this is farewell. Unless you should come to Tallallame one day.'

It was tempting. The Greatest Tale of All.

'Don't even think about it,' said Karan.

'I'll be far too busy with the new college,' said Llian hastily. 'And my *Tale of the Gates of Good and Evil*.'

'And your family!' she said coolly, then forced a smile. It was harder to adjust to the new reality than she had thought.

'Good for you,' said Rulke to Llian. 'What will you do about Thandiwe's abominable *Tale of Rulke*?'

'I'll be arguing for it be struck off the list of the Great Tales and transferred to a new list, the False Histories,' said Llian, 'along with the tales and Histories that the scrutators turned into propaganda.'

'And the Great Tale that's a wicked lie, *Downfall of the Beasts*,' said Sulien.

'Who told you that?'

'Idlis did, when we were in Salliban. That wicked Skunder Krespin had the tale written to ruin the good name of the Whelm, so he could steal their homeland from them.'

'And without Idlis we wouldn't be here,' said Llian. 'Once it's done you can write to the Whelm and tell them.'

Rulke shook hands with him last of all. 'Goodbye, Chronicler. It's been ... interesting.'

'Good luck.'

Rulke turned away then, seeing that everyone's eyes were on Lirriam, who was holding up the Waystone, turned back and clasped Llian's hand again. 'This might be useful one day. Keep it out of sight.'

Llian palmed the small package and slipped it into a pocket.

Rulke climbed aboard and went to the controls. The Waystone glowed deep red in Lirriam's upraised hand, purple light flared out in all directions, and when Llian could see again they were gone to another world.

Shand had owned the stone cottage for more than a hundred years and seemed reluctant to give it up. Or maybe he doesn't want us as such close neighbours, Karan thought, given all the trouble we've been in over the years.

But he finally agreed, and Sulien wasn't required to quiver her bottom lip, though she did so during the negotiations, just for practice. It only took them five minutes to move in, since all they had was a pack each.

They were all sweeping and cleaning away the accumulated dust of years, and Karan was sighing at the rusty old stove and the work to be done to make the place habitable, when Shand put his head around the back door.

'Can't get rid of you,' she muttered. 'What do you want now?'

'Housewarming present.'

'It'd better be wine,' said Llian, who was carrying in wood for the fire. Sulien had chopped it, since she was far more experienced and could be trusted with an axe. 'There's not a drop in the house.'

'Buy your own damn wine,' said Shand, who was carrying a leather bag. 'You've had enough of mine over the years.' He looked across to Sulien. 'Come here. Got something for you.'

She went across, looking up at the old man. 'What is it?'

He handed her the bag. 'No damn use to me,' he said gruffly. 'Just makes a nuisance of itself.'

She reached in, then let out a cry of sheer joy. 'It's a *puppy!*'

She lifted out the little bundle of fur. It had big floppy ears and huge brown eyes, and it snuggled up to her and licked her hand. 'Idlis,' she said. "I'm going to call you Idlis.'

She looked around to thank Shand, tears of joy running down her face, but he was gone.

Shand came back that evening with a bottle or two, and he and Aviel helped them to warm the house that night. As they left, Karan noticed that Aviel wasn't limping at all, and smiled to herself.

Karan sprinkled lime blossom perfume, Aviel's housewarming present, on her fingers, then ran them through her hair. It took her back. Way back. She wiped her eyes.

Jassika went up to bed. Karan and Llian sat at the rough wooden table with Sulien, who had the puppy beside her in its bag, and looked at one another.

'I've got a present for you, Daddy,' said Sulien.

'There's no need,' Llian began.

'You'll change your mind when you see it,' she said smugly, and laid the battered old mimemule on the table.

'Where did you get that?' cried Karan.

'Yggur gave it back to me. He said it was nearly dead, but I might get one or two goes out of it.'

She clasped her hands around it, closed her eyes and strained, and an ancient, dusty bottle appeared in the middle of the table, rather like the one she had made the first time, back in Gothryme.

'I'm not sure I agree with you using it to make drink,' said Karan. She reached for the bottle but Llian got to it first.

'Oh dear,' said Sulien. 'That's the wrong one. It was supposed to be the Uncibular 81, wasn't it? That's only the 87. Should I –?'

'The 87 was an even better year, and it'll do very nicely to start our cellar,' Llian said hastily. 'Thank you, Sulien. And now it's time for bed.'

'You didn't mind me staying up late when I was helping you save the world,' she muttered.

'Well, it's saved, isn't it, and we're going back to the old rules. Off, *now!*'

Sulien picked up the puppy bag and skipped up the stairs.

Karan smiled a genuine smile, possibly the first since they had come to the future, and took Llian's hands. 'Welcome home.'

'Welcome home. You smell nice.'

But he was looking at her oddly. Uh-oh! Karan thought. Here it comes. I knew this was all too good to be true. 'What – what's the matter?'

'I'm sure it's my imagination ... or maybe Shand's housewarming grog ...'

'But?'

'Is your hair redder than it used it to be? I'd swear it's the same colour as it was the day we met.'

'Nonsense,' said Karan, fingering the little cut-glass bottle in her pocket that she had borrowed from Aviel. Vanity? Partly. 'It's just the lamplight.'

'Of course,' said Llian. 'Which reminds me – Rulke gave me this.' He put a small package, wrapped in dark blue waxed paper, in the middle of the table.

'What is it?' said Karan.

'Open it and find out.'

She opened it and found a small box inside. She lifted the lid and tipped the contents, a black pill, onto the table. She knew what it was and so did Llian. Rulke had given her one just like it long ago, to cure her triune infertility, and it had allowed her to have Sulien.

Karan gulped. The last secret was about to come out and she wasn't sure how well Llian would take it. What if it undid all the progress they'd made? 'I don't need it, Llian.'

'I know.'

'But ... what are you talking about?'

'Rulke told me in Alcifer that his black pill had *permanently* cured your infertility. He took great pleasure in saying that the reason we didn't have any more children – no, the flaw – was in me.'

Ulp! 'It's not in you,' said Karan.

'I know. Did you really think you could keep the secret from me?'

'I'm really sorry. I always wanted another child, and I knew you did too. But I was terrified –'

'That you'd die in childbirth next time?'

'It was a consideration, but not the important one. It was you.'

Llian rocked back on his rickety chair. 'You didn't want another child *with me?*'

'Don't put it like that.'

'How would *you* put it?'

'You were so unhappy at Gothryme. You weren't writing or telling or keeping the promise you'd made as a kid to your family. And I was bound by the oath I'd sworn on my mother's body. We were the immoveable object and the irresistible force, and it was tearing us apart. I just ... couldn't see that we had a future together.'

'And you weren't going to bring another child into such an unhappy family,' said Llian. He laid his head on the table and sighed.

'That's why I started pushing you away eight years ago.'

'You didn't have to. You know the precautions as well as I do.'

'But accidents happen,' she said, 'and willpower fails. And sometimes a little too much drink intervenes. I couldn't have another child when we were liable to fly apart.'

'And now?'

Karan put a hand in her pocket. 'Rulke gave me something, too.' She opened the little box and showed him the contents, a little blue pill.

'Rulke gave you that for *me*?' cried Llian. 'I don't need it; I'm not dead yet.'

'I never said you were.'

'The bastard's having a joke at my expense – casting doubts on my manhood from the safety of Tallallame.'

'At both our expenses,' said Karan. 'Well, let him have his fun; he did force us back together, after all.' She tipped the blue pill into his hand. 'Will you take it anyway, do you think?'

'Of course. When you take yours.'

Karan closed her eyes. It could give her the second child she'd always wanted. It hadn't been easy for her either, keeping Llian at a distance all this time.

'Mummy and Daddy, you've got to take your medicine!' cried Sulien from the top of the stairs. 'I want a little brother.'

'You're supposed to be in bed. Go!'

Sulien went into her room, though she left the door ajar.

Llian raised an eyebrow to Karan, questioningly.

'We'll see,' she said with an enigmatic smile.


THE END
of
THE GATES OF GOOD & EVIL


and the Three Worlds sequence that began with
THE VIEW FROM THE MIRROR
and continued through
THE WELL OF ECHOES

and
THE SONG OF THE TEARS


You can read more about Lirriam and the other Five Heroes in
THE TAINTED REALM trilogy.


There are more Three Worlds stories to come.
Subscribe to my newsletter for free books and special offers, preview chapters, news
and other great stuff.
https://www.ian-irvine.com/join-my-newsletter/

# OTHER BOOKS BY IAN IRVINE

THE TAINTED REALM TRILOGY

*Vengeance*

*Rebellion*

*Justice*

*ECO-THRILLERS*

THE HUMAN RITES TRILOGY

*The Last Albatross*

*Terminator Gene*

*The Life Lottery*

*FOR YOUNGER READERS*

THE RUNCIBLE JONES QUARTET

*Runcible Jones, The Gate to Nowhere*

*Runcible Jones and The Buried City*

*Runcible Jones and the Frozen Compass*

*Runcible Jones and the Backwards Hourglass*

THE GRIM AND GRIMMER QUARTET

*The Headless Highwayman*

*The Grasping Goblin*

*The Desperate Dwarf*

*The Calamitous Queen*

THE SORCERER'S TOWER QUARTET

*Thorn Castle*

*Giant's Lair*

*Black Crypt*

*Wizardry Crag*

# ABOUT THE AUTHOR

Ian Irvine, an Australian marine scientist, has also written 34 novels and an anthology of shorter stories. His novels include the Three Worlds fantasy sequence (**The View from the Mirror, The Well of Echoes, The Song of the Tears and The Gates of Good & Evil**), which has been published in many countries and translations and has sold over sold over a million copies, a trilogy of eco-thrillers in a world of catastrophic climate change, **Human Rites**, now in its third edition, and 12 novels for younger readers.

BUY EBOOKS

BUY AUDIOBOOKS

Printed in Great Britain
by Amazon